B.A. RICHARDS

A HAPPY BEGINNING

CITY OWL
PRESS

A HAPPY BEGINNING

CITY OWL PRESS
www.cityowlpress.com

Cover Design by MiblArt. All stock photos licensed appropriately.

Page Edges by Painted Wings Publishing Services.

Edited by Jessica Shearer.

For information on subsidiary rights, please contact the publisher at info@cityowlpress.com.

Paperback Edition ISBN: 978-1-64898-507-2

Hardback Edition ISBN: 978-1-64898-508-9

Digital Edition ISBN: 978-1-64898-509-6

Printed in the United States of America

For Mom & Dad
I did it. I wish you were here to see it.

CHAPTER ONE

"Are you one of the grooms?"

Alard Fairchild looked up from his phone, the world coming back into focus around him. Men and women swarmed about the hotel's lobby; a buzzing presence of optimism and nerves energizing the space. Multiple accents and languages reverberated off the mahogany wall panels; a noisy overture overwhelming his senses.

The woman in front of him came closer, pushing her ebony bangs from her ocher-colored eyes. "Do you speak English?" she asked, bending forward toward his face. Alard smelled the rose oil drifting from her skin, luring him closer to her lips.

His brain caught up a moment later, and he abruptly sat back, shaking his head to clear it. "No...yes." The confusion on her face made him laugh at his own awkwardness. "Sorry, I mean, yes, I speak English, and no, I'm not part of the wedding."

"Oh." A flash of disappointment in her eyes. "I had hoped you were my fiancé."

"You don't know your own fiancé?"

"It's an arranged marriage." She sat on the plush bench next to Alard, draping a garment bag over her lap. "My parents made the match through our church. I'm supposed to meet him today for the first time." She sighed and plastered on a smile and faced him. "Hi, I'm Shelia."

"Alard." He held out his hand, and she shook it, trying not to let the bag slip off her lap. He looked back at the lobby, focusing on the men in the crowd. "Maybe I can help? Does he look like me?"

"All my mother told me was that he had dark hair and hazel eyes. You have both of those."

It wasn't a lot to work with, but Alard pushed himself up. He scanned the crowd, examining all the dark-haired young men wandering about. It didn't take long before he found another man pacing with a picture in his hand. "Why don't you see if that's him?"

He helped her stand, holding the garment bag as Shelia straightened her dress. "Do I look good?" She bit her lower lip as she snuck a glance over Alard's shoulder.

"You look every inch a princess."

Shelia blushed, then shifted onto her toes to kiss Alard's cheek. "If that is so, you're a prince for saving me. Thank you." She took the garment bag and made her way across the room. Alard watched as they connected and hugged.

A minute later, Alard's phone buzzed from his pocket. He quickly pulled it out and asked, "Hello?" while his free hand covered his other ear to block out the conversations.

"Sorry, Al. I'm almost there. You won't believe the traffic out here." His law partner, James Wilson, shouted above the background noise.

"I think I can." Alard reached for his briefcase. "Listen, James, the lobby is insane. I'll meet you at the corner of Canal and Chartres and we can talk over a drink."

"Sounds like a plan."

Alard wove through the condensing mass of humanity toward the Canal Street exit. Ahead of him, two men entered the lobby through the hotel's spinning glass door. The taller one wore a well-tailored suit with an alluring blue tie. A black lanyard with a nametag hung around his neck, and he carried a leather briefcase. The second man was dressed in khakis with an untucked dress shirt and sunglasses perched on top of his head. They were talking to each other, not noticing as Alard popped out from between two brides and right into their path.

The men avoided colliding with Alard by mere inches, the only casualty being Alard's phone knocked to the floor.

"It's okay," Alard said automatically, leaning down to grab his phone. James continued complaining about the afternoon traffic from the tiny speaker.

As he picked up the phone, his knuckles brushed up against the fingers of one of the men—the one with the sunglasses. For the barest of seconds, Alard held his breath, feeling warm as his vision brightened.

"I'm okay," he continued, flustered. "You okay?" Alard asked the other men.

"Yeah, I'm good. Sorry about that." Sunglasses spoke, and Alard felt his dark brown eyes roam over his body.

Alard straightened and returned the appreciative glance. The man's coloring reminded Alard of a bow of dark walnuts waiting to be devoured. His soft, plump lips lifted into a smirk, as if asking, *do you like what you see?*

Alard attempted not to blush. "No, it's fine, really. The lobby is crowded."

"Al, are you even listening?" James's whine from the phone broke the moment, and Alard put it back to his ear. "Yeah, sorry. I'll be there in a minute."

Sunglasses's friend cleared his throat, looking at his watch. "Raz, we don't have much time before dinner."

Alard nodded to both men. "I should go anyway. Again, sorry." He moved toward the rotating door, taking one quick look back at the good-looking man. His eyes shifted, and he allowed himself to see the magic flowing through the room. A warm white glow emanated from where the couples gathered. Alas, where Sunglasses stood, the magic swirled away, not touching him.

Of course, Alard thought as he blinked his eyes back to normal and exited the hotel. *He's just human.*

The haze of cigarette smoke outside, right past the door, had Alard coughing while he turned to walk to the end of the block. At the streetcar station in the middle of the road, James jumped out the back door. He straightened his Hawaiian shirt and adjusted the strap of his laptop case on his shoulder. His blond hair was a mess that he tried to fix with his fingers as he crossed the street. "You'd think it was Mardi Gras with the amount of people on the street today. Did I miss something on the..." he stopped, looking around at people entering the hotel just behind Alard. "What's with all the wedding dresses?"

Alard chuckled as he slung his arm over his confused colleague's shoulder. "Mass wedding at the conference center tomorrow from what I've been able to make out." He led James down the side street behind the hotel.

"Think I can pick someone up on the way home?" James asked.

"Not unless you plan to marry them in the morning."

James shook his head. "Nope, no way. Me and marriages don't work. Ask my ex-wife."

"Don't need to. I was there when she burned the effigy in your courtyard."

"That's right." As they entered the next block, James turned them down Bourbon Street. "You got a place in mind for that drink?"

"Of course."

James groaned, raking his fingers through his hair again. "Al, we live in New Orleans—the city known for its music and nightlife. There is more than one fucking jazz bar in the city."

"I'm aware, but Fritzel's is the *best* fucking jazz bar in the city."

"Says you."

Alard laughed. "Plus, I was thinking about visiting the second floor."

The doors to Fritzel's sat wide open, waiting for night to fall and the crowds to appear. The stone walls of the English jazz bar were hidden behind a plethora of pictures, signs, and memorabilia. No lights hung overhead; the ambiance provided by an odd assortment of table lamps on shelves and an unused fireplace. Doorways and mirrors were framed with string lights, giving the bar a softer glow in its unique atmosphere.

Alard walked to the bartender, placing a fifty on the table. The woman smiled, tilting her head towards the back door in the second room. "Welcome back, handsome. Heading upstairs?"

"Of course, but do me a favor, Constance? Give James a double so he'll stop complaining."

"I'm not complaining!" James flopped onto a bar stool, his head falling back. "I'm just saying we can go to other places now and then."

"You're always complaining. I think you would die if you didn't have anything to complain about." Alard nodded when Constance dropped the half-filled whiskey glass in front of James. "You don't have to come up, you know."

"*You're* the one who wanted to talk." James rolled his eyes, sipping his whiskey.

"Catherine hasn't shown up yet," Constance told James. James gave her an appreciative nod, and she walked away to serve a new group of customers.

"Now what was so important that you needed to talk?" James was scrutinizing Alard's posture. James was a master at reading body language, which made him excel at cross-examining witnesses on the rare instance when divorce cases went to trial. Other times, like now, it made Alard self-conscious.

"It's something that would be better talked about upstairs." Alard snuck a look at his friend.

James narrowed his eyes, then sighed. "Fine, Mr. Drama Queen, but you owe me another drink." He stood up and walked to the back door.

Alard got up and followed. "I already bought you a drink!"

"Yeah, but you're making me go upstairs. That's a two-drink minimum request."

"Who's the drama queen now?" Alard laughed as they arrived at the closed door. He knocked three times. The door opened and a large gentleman stood in the doorway. He was tall, skin as dark as midnight, and his eyes were silver. His gaze flickered between the two, glaring at James a moment before resting back on Alard. "Yes?"

"The vampire sent us," Alard whispered, not wanting the passphrase to be overheard by the band ten feet away.

The gatekeeper stared at Alard a moment longer, then stepped back and let them through. Alard led James up a flight of stairs. The left side of the staircase was covered in mismatched windows woven together into a wall. The view out the windows was of a central, currently empty courtyard surrounded by four walls of glass and railings. Twinkle lights lit the way up the stairs, and at the landing was a bureau filled with knickknacks behind the display doors. To the right was a set of French doors with pink light casting through them. To the left was a balcony open to the courtyard. A cat bed, bowl of water, and an empty paper plate with the remains of food sat on the landing by the railing.

A mangy tawny cat crawled out from under the bureau and stretched as they reached the top stair. Alard crouched down and rubbed behind her ears. "Hello, pretty girl. Are you behaving yourself?"

The cat purred, pressing her head up into Alard's hand before walking towards James. James bent down and ran a hand along the cat's spine. "Hey, Misty girl."

Misty left the men and walked back to her cat bed, sat down, and started to clean herself. Alard stood back up, moved past James, and opened the French doors.

The room beyond the doors was dim, the main light emanating from red light bulbs in the ceiling fan, circulating the scent of rose and licorice. The two-room establishment contained a mini kitchenette and lounge in the back, a sitting room in the front, and a wall with a passthrough and doorway between them.

A crushed velvet couch and matching chair sat in front of the sitting room's fireplace with a round glass table between them. A miniature planetarium rested on top of a pile of leather-bound books. The Lepus constellation shone on the wall above the fireplace, a red dot among the white stars highlighting Hind's Crimson Star.

"Hello!" A cheerful voice called through the kitchen passthrough separating the two rooms. Fairy lights framed the window-like opening, a whiter light shining beyond in the mini kitchen. Two absinthe fountains sat on a ledge beside the fridge—one red, the other green—ready for the evening's guests.

In front of the fountains stood a woman in her sixties wearing a tan peasant blouse and black leather pants. Rainbow suspenders and military boots completed the outfit. Her pixie length hair was bright pink, spiked up in front and tilted to look like a faux hawk. When she saw Alard, her eyes widened. "Prince Alard! I wasn't expecting you today."

Alard waved his head, blushing. "You don't have to use my title, Monique."

"Yes, don't embarrass the princeling," James mocked from where he had sunk into the couch. "Everyone knows he hates that."

"I don't hate it. I'm just not a prince when I'm here." Alard walked into the second room and gave the older woman a hug. The kitchenette and lounge were brighter with an orange bulb over the wooden picnic bench of a table. A chandelier lit the kitchenette, adding to the charm of what served as a bar.

"First, you're a prince no matter where you are, Alard." Monique stepped back and touched his cheek. "Even if you've resorted to associating with humans like that one."

"Aw, I love you too, Moans." James raised his whiskey glass in salute.

"And second?" Alard asked.

"I might live here, but I'm still one of your subjects," Monique said. "It would be rude not to address you properly when you enter the room."

Laughing, Alard slid onto a barstool at the passthrough window. "I'm going to miss you both," he stated.

"They gave you a date?" Monique put a glass in front of him, the green absinthe adding an earthy scent to the rose and licorice in the air.

Alard nodded, picking up the glass, whirling the liquor around in it. "One human week."

"I'm sorry." Monique placed her hand on Alard's free one, squeezing gently. "I know being here means a lot to you."

"They couldn't have waited until we at least finished the Morrison case?" James groaned.

"Oh yeah, that would have gone over well," Alard said. "Mom, Dad, yeah, can we put off the wedding until after I finish this human divorce case? The kingdoms have been divided for over a thousand years, what's two more weeks?"

James lifted his head. "You think they'd go for it?"

Alard shot a glare at his best friend. "Seriously?"

"Ignore him." Monique leaned on the windowsill. "Are you ready for this?"

"Not in the least." Alard sipped his drink, savoring the taste of wormwood and fennel. "I understand why Meyda and I have to do this, but neither of us really wants to."

"I can understand her not wanting to marry you," James stated.

Monique gave James a look. "How much has he had to drink?" she asked.

"Not enough." James held up the empty glass. "Al owes me one more."

Monique walked around and handed James a bottle that had three fingers of whiskey left. "Knock yourself out." She turned and sat on the other barstool beside Alard. "Meyda doesn't want to marry you?"

"She doesn't want to marry anyone," Alard said. "We've been best friends since we were kids. She's never once been interested in anyone romantically or sexually, and that's fine. She's happy with her books and her pets."

"But?"

"When we marry...I know I can honor her choices, but our parents, hell, the entire kingdom, will expect an heir. We've talked about adoption, since you know, it worked for me becoming the heir. But her parents...everything is just so complicated." Alard rested his forehead in his hands, taking a deep breath. "And that's not even considering that I very much enjoy being intimate, but if I do so with someone not my wife, I dishonor my marriage to her."

"But you two do love each other, right?"

Alard drank the rest of his absinthe. "Like friends. Siblings."

Monique reached over to squeeze Alard's knee. "There have been generations of royalty that have never had the luxury in choosing who they married. Give it a few years, and once you've settled into your rule, the two of you can work to modernize the ideas in the court to compensate for both your preferences."

Alard ran his hand through his hair, sighing. "I don't know if the fairy realm will take well to human definitions of sexuality."

"You'll be their king. Also, I think you should have more faith in your subjects."

"Probably."

Shadows outside the French doors made Monique stand up. She caressed Alard's cheek before leaning in to kiss the top of his head. "You have spent too much time among the humans, Alard. It's given you much, but I think you may have forgotten a part of yourself in the process."

Alard leaned into the affection. "I needed to know who the human I could have been was."

"And he is a good person." Monique made her way back behind her absinthe bar, readying herself for customers. "But you're more than human, my lord. Don't forget that."

The shadows formed into a group of three women through the glass panes. One tried the French doors, but it didn't budge. She knocked, trying to peer in.

"Pet the damn cat!" James slurred from where he was slumped on the couch.

Alard reached over to take the empty bottle from James. "I think you've had enough."

"Never." James looked up at Alard with bloodshot eyes and a lazy grin. "You got a week left, buddy. There's no such thing as too much. Time to live it up and make some bad choices."

"Right, like that will ever end well."

Chapter Two

Razi Miller hadn't expected New Orleans to look the way it did. He'd heard so much about the jazz, Mardi Gras, and the party atmosphere that he expected the city to be dead during the days and a paragon of neon and sin once the sun set.

He did not expect a normal-looking city outside his hotel window. If it wasn't for the architecture, Raz could believe that he was on Canal Street in New York City—just with less Chinatown and more palm trees. There was even a Starbucks two blocks away on the corner.

Maybe it looks different at night, he mused as he pulled out his suit from the closet. There was a social event that night on Bourbon Street, so he would hold his judgement until then. Right now, he just wanted a hot shower and the largest cup of coffee he could acquire.

The line at the coffee bar in the hotel was wrapped around the lobby, dozens of twenty-something zombies staring at their phones until it was their turn. Raz smiled to himself, wondering how many of them were either brides or grooms recouping from bachelor or bachelorette parties.

Bypassing the horde, Raz stepped outside into the sunlight. He watched a streetcar pick up passengers across from the hotel. A little girl looked at him through the window. Raz smiled and waved at her. A tiny hand moved up, fingers opening and closing in a fist to wave back as the streetcar took off towards the cemeteries.

Raz walked up another block, then crossed the street to the entrance of the cafe. He expected to be flooded with the mellow rock that makes up a coffee house ambiance but was pleasantly surprised when smooth jazz greeted him at the door.

Hanging from the ceiling were old brass instruments—trumpets and trombones with a tuba taking a central place in the display. The walls gleamed of polished wood and tile while the slate floors reflected the light back up into the room. If it wasn't for the fresh smell of brewing coffee, Raz could be in a 1920s jazz club.

The line was short compared to that of his local one back in Washington, DC a dozen or so people needing their fix before heading off to work. It didn't take long for Raz to put in his order, then join the unorganized clump waiting for their drinks. Raz pressed himself against the archway separating the coffee bar from the seating area and took in the second room while he waited.

A long table made of driftwood filled the center of the lounge, with chairs on both sides at intervals. A chandelier made of more brass instruments and Einstein lights hung above it. Smaller tables formed another row beyond it, and a wooden bench running down the length of the wall provided their seating.

Three homeless men sat on the bench pressed against the bay of windows.. One was charging his phone with the outlet under the window seat, his fingerless gloves flipping through a newspaper paper. The second was stretched out, a jacket tucked under his head as a makeshift pillow.

The third man was inches from the sleeper's feet. He leaned over a small table, a pile of papers in front of him. Across the table sat a man, his back to the rest of the room. The suit jacket and briefcase made him stand out from his three companions. A tablet rested in his hand, a finger scrolling through what looked like a document.

"Now I know this must be confusing to you Jacob, but I guarantee it's real. Your sister Wynette left you as the benefactor to her estate." Putting the tablet down, the man, a lawyer to Raz's assumption, turned sideways in his chair. "Why don't you look this over while I get us some coffee, okay?"

Seeing his face, Raz recognized the young lawyer as the man he met in the hotel the previous evening. It was the hazel eyes, ones that now took in the sleeping man. There was a softness in them while evaluating the others.

"How about you two?" The sleeping man didn't respond. The one with the newspaper looked up and nodded, a hint of a smile showing through the graying scruff along his jaw.

The lawyer turned around and headed for the line, almost colliding once again with Raz. The hazel eyes widened a bit in surprise, jumping back a step to avoid contact. "Sorry." The apology was quick and automatic. Raz saw the moment the man realized who he was. "...again," he added, trying to hide his embarrassment by pushing a lock of brown hair behind his ear.

"We have to stop meeting this way." Raz grinned, then held out his hand. "I'm Raz."

"Alard." The pale, delicate hand gripped Raz's with unexpected strength. "It's a pleasure to actually meet you this time."

"Yeah, sorry about yesterday. I'm normally not that clumsy." The barista called Raz's name, and he snatched up the cup before someone mistook it for theirs. "But to be fair, that lobby was crowded. Is there some kind of bridal convention going on in town I wasn't aware of?"

Alard laughed, motioning for Raz to follow him to the end of the long line. "From what I heard, there's a mass wedding happening tonight on the first floor of the convention center."

"Like that cult...the Moonies?" Raz asked.

"Unification Church," Alard corrected. "Their Blessing Ceremony is very specific and takes place over a few days. The news this morning talked about an international organization that helps folks who can't afford to get married have a real wedding. Seems they do this around the world multiple times a year." Alard grinned, the brightness of his face causing his eyes to light up. "I dropped them a few bucks on their donation site."

"That was nice of you," Raz said. Alard shrugged, and Raz sipped his coffee. "So, from what I overheard, you're some kind of lawyer?"

"That's me. Alard Fairchild, attorney at law and defender of the poor all over New Orleans."

Raz laughed. "You fit all that on your business card?"

"I use tiny text." *That grin again*. It was contagious, and Raz felt himself smiling back. "I do have a real office, but some of my clients are easier to find when I go to their spots."

"Like the trio in the back."

Alard nodded. "This Starbucks is right where the trolley on Canal turns onto St. Charles. Easy to find and the staff here doesn't fret over their presence. Gotta love this city." They reached the front of the line and Alard ordered four coffees, then looked at Raz. "Can I buy you a refill?"

"Sure."

Alard paid and then dropped a five into the tip jar. "I take it you're not from around here."

"What gave that away?"

"Checking into a hotel, first off." They walked to the archway between the main part of the coffeehouse and the back area, waiting on their drinks. "Since you didn't know about the mass wedding ceremony, the idea of you being a groom no longer works."

"I'm here for the Business Leaders of America conference. They asked me to come down and give a few lectures on using social media as an avenue to connect with clients and build up a business."

"TikTok for MBAs? Sounds exciting." Alard raised his eyebrows. He was about to ask another question, but the barista called his name. He excused himself to grab the coffees, then stopped and looked at the five cups and his two hands.

Raz laughed. "Here, let me help." Downing his current coffee, Raz slid one of the coffees into his old cup, then picked up two more. Alard held two in his smaller hands and motioned for Raz to follow him.

"Gentlemen, this is Raz," Alard introduced him as they handed out the coffees. "Raz, meet the Three Musketeers of St. Charles."

"*Bonjour*," the man with the phone smirked as he took one of the coffees from Raz. He then elbowed the sleeping man, who jerked up and grabbed the offered coffee. "I'm Nick, and this is Logan."

"Pleasure is all mine." Raz shifted to sit on the windowsill as Alard went back to the table with his client.

"Do you have any questions about your inheritance, Jacob?"

"Only one—can I split this up between the three of us?" Jacob's eyes slid to look at his two friends.

Alard smiled. "Once the estate is settled and everything is officially under your name, you can do what you want with it. Just be aware you'll have an inheritance tax to pay, and anyone you owe money to will pop up again once they know you have assets."

"Ah, took care of all of them in the bankruptcy. When you're living on the streets, ain't really hard to stay out of debt."

"Yeah, no one wants to loan us money," Nick added with a gruff laugh.

Raz let the conversation slip into the background, his focus just on Alard. His hands wove through the air as he explained the will to Jacob. There was confidence in his stature, pride in what he was doing. Not everyone who became a lawyer would make a career helping those who couldn't pay, but it was clear that Alard loved his work.

"There you are, Raz." A voice snagged Raz's attention, and he turned his head. Marcel Savion made his way through the growing morning crowd. The businessman was dressed in a sharp navy suit with a powder blue shirt and silver tie. "What are you doing hanging out back here? First lecture is in twenty minutes."

Raz shook his head. "I was having a nice conversation with these gentlemen."

Marcel looked over the group of three homeless men, then at Alard. The lawyer was watching them both, his eyes narrowing at the judging look Marcel gave them. "I see." He turned to Raz, as if the others weren't there. "Well, come on, we don't want to be late."

"I'll meet you outside." Raz stood up, giving his colleague a pointed glare. Marcel rolled his eyes and slid his sunglasses back on before exiting out the side door. "I'm sorry about him," Raz apologized to the group.

Nick scoffed. "You're the one stuck with him for the day."

Raz laughed at that. "That I am. Anyway, I should go. It was nice meeting all of you."

Alard stood up, holding his hand out. "Nice to actually meet you this time. If you want to chat again, you know where my morning office is."

"I may just become a regular then." Raz shook Alard's hand again, feeling the smooth skin against his own rough hands. He looked at the lawyer's face and saw that grin, and for a moment, Raz debated staying and missing the lecture so he could study those enticing eyes.

"Razi!" Marcel shouted through the door, and Raz dropped Alard's hand and stepped back.

"Yeah, I should go. See you tomorrow?" Raz grabbed his coffee and sunglasses.

"I'll be here," Alard promised.

Raz turned and left the coffee shop, falling into step beside Marcel as they started back towards the convention center. "You're an ass, you know that?" Raz didn't look at his friend as he sipped his coffee.

"I'm just making sure you stay focused. We don't want a repeat of San Francisco."

Rolling his eyes, Raz looked over his sunglasses at Marcel. "San Francisco was three years ago."

"Right, but that didn't stop you from checking out Mister Lawyer in there and his tight pants."

Raz stopped short, confused. "He had tight pants on?"

Marcel laughed. "You seriously didn't notice? Hell, I'm not gay and even *I* was checking his ass out. It was like they were painted on."

"Damn."

"Your loss. Anyway, you don't need another convention fling, my friend. That last one ended in a disaster that I was barely able to rescue you from."

"Don't worry, it's not going to happen." They reached the convention center, and Raz opened the door. "I learned my lesson."

CHAPTER THREE

"If you drag me to Fritzel's again, Al, I swear to God I'm going to get a new best friend."

James stood with his arms crossed, refusing to move from his spot on Bourbon Street. The sun had set, bathing the five blocks in the neon lights of the bars. A cornucopia of music echoed out from the open entrances, drowning out the conversations of passersby.

Alard rolled his eyes. "Fine, we'll go someplace else tonight. Where do you want to go?"

"Oz."

Alard's head fell back as he sighed. "You know I hate club music."

"And I put up with your jazz all the time, so tonight you can handle club." James grabbed Alard's hand and dragged him down a block. The décor changed on the 800 block of Bourbon Street as pride flags hung off every lamppost. A techno beat emitted from Oz's doorway; the interior bathed in a pink glow. The glass bar top in the center of the establishment was surrounded by more people in leather pants than Alard felt was necessary. To the left of the door, a local band stood onstage, prepping for their soundcheck. The bar tables were full, and along the back wall there were three women taking selfies in front of the branded walkway banner that hid the supply closet.

It took a moment for his ears to adjust to the deafening bass track from the deejay. He had learned to deal with loud places, but the acoustics in the bar kept sounds rebounding in a way that put Alard on the fast track to a headache.

James pushed him into an open spot at the bar and ordered them drinks. Plastic cups with an orange drink appeared in front of them. "We can divvy up at the end of the night. I've already got a tab here."

The band started their soundcheck. Alard winced at the offkey guitar and took a sip of the mystery concoction. It had a gentle burn with the alcohol disguised behind a sweet fruit flavor. "This is good," he shouted over the crowd. "What is it?"

"I don't know!" James smiled at the bartender and gave him a thumbs up. "It's the bartender's special, and I've yet to squeeze the recipe out of him."

"You've yet to charm your way into his confidence? You're slipping."

"I've charmed my way into other places with him," James said with a wink. "But his recipe book is off-limits when it comes to sharing."

"Just keep at it. I'm sure you'll find out eventually."

"Oh, I don't plan on stopping. You won't believe what he can do with streamers..."

James continued to gossip about the bartender and his cunning use of discarded decorations while Alard scanned the crowd. He saw a few acquaintances on the dance floor, their bodies moving in time to the techno beat, gyrating against each other as they lost themselves in the moment.

Alard wished for a distraction like the dancers found in the music. With his days in New Orleans numbered, finding solace from the inevitable didn't come easily. Every moment in the city could be his last before being called back home. He should be enjoying himself, but instead, he felt the last parts of his freedom slipping away.

Caught up in his brooding moment, Alard missed five men entering the club, all in various forms of button-downs and khakis. They huddled in the doorway, debating on whether they should stay or move on.

"Alard?" one of the men spoke. Alard turned and smiled as Raz pushed past the four other men to join him at the bar. The blacklight made his skin darker, but his teeth glowed with his smile. "I thought that was you."

"The one and only." Alard felt the other man's presence disintegrate his lackadaisical mood. "Lectures done for the day?"

"Yes, thank God. I can only handle so many conversations about the current state of the job market before wanting to jump through the window and end my suffering."

Alard just nodded his head. "Yeah, that does sound like a painful way to go."

"So, what's good to drink?" Raz inspected Alard's drink.

"No idea. My friend James ordered this." Alard turned to look at James, who was talking to two drag queens. "James!"

"Give me a second!" James held a finger up in Alard's general direction, his focus not leaving the top of the neon yellow-haired queen's corset.

Raz snorted and reached for Alard's drink. "How about I just take a sip?"

"Only if you buy me the next one." The words rolled off Alard's tongue easily, a common exchange between him and James when they would finish off each other's drinks. Heat came to his cheeks as he looked at his hands, hoping the blacklights hid the blush.

Sipping the drink, Raz chuckled. "It tastes like a Hurricane, but there's something else in it," he remarked, taking a longer drink and motioning to the bartender. When he had the man's attention, Raz pointed at the cup, then at himself and Alard.

"You don't actually have to…"

Raz held up his hand as he finished the drink. "I know, but I want to. Can't come to New Orleans and not buy someone a drink at the bar."

Two more cups were put down in front of them, and Raz gave the man a twenty in return. "You come here often?"

"Not really. I'm more of a jazz fan, but James," Alard jerked his thumb over his shoulder towards James, "well, it was his night to pick."

"Looks like he's found some new friends."

Alard turned to see James with his tongue down one of the drag queen's throats, then sighed. "Seriously? We haven't even been here an hour."

Raz pulled on Alard's sleeve. "Why don't you show me your favorite place? I'm sure he can find you later."

"He always does." Alard noticed the other men in Raz's group had left. "Where'd your friends go?"

"Not really friends—business associates. They left looking for a bar with people more their type."

"And your type?" Alard held his breath, hoping he already knew the answer. Raz looked him up and down as he sipped his drink; Alard felt like the man was undressing him then and there.

"Why do you think I bought you a drink?"

The heat intensified along Alard's cheeks as he licked his lips. He grabbed his cup and downed it, building up his courage to respond. He wasn't used to getting hit on like this, especially by a man as beautiful as Raz.

"Thank you." Alard started to say more, but his words were drowned out as the band started their first song and the volume went up. The audience cheered. "Must be one of their hits."

"What?" Raz leaned closer to be heard over the music.

"Let's get out of here." Alard grabbed Raz's hand and led him to the door. He looked back to find James, but his friend had disappeared into the back of the club. *He knows where to find me.*

———

The moment they stepped out onto Bourbon Street, the noise dropped as the band's electric guitar and bass were replaced with the sounds of revelry from the street. Tourists walked from bar to bar, most drunk with plastic cups in their hands and beads around their necks. Musicians sat on street corners, playing trumpets and drums with hats out waiting for tips. It was hectic and loud; the music fighting for dominance over the peoples' conversations.

This was the New Orleans that Raz was expecting.

"This is beautiful," Raz stated standing by Alard's side, taking in the view. "I mean, you see it all the time on TV, hear the stories about vampires and voodoo magic...this morning, the city felt like any other city, but now? Can you feel the energy?"

"Yeah." Alard closed his eyes, humming in time with the sax player across the street from them.

Raz watched Alard in this unguarded moment, how the edges of his lips curled up at a change in melody. He smiled. "You still want to go to that jazz club?"

"We could," Alard replied, and Raz found himself staring into the other man's eyes, "though I wouldn't complain if we just walked around and talked."

Raz nodded, forcing himself to break eye contact before he got lost in the swirls of hazel and gold. "I think I'd like that."

They strolled side by side away from Bourbon Street and back to Canal Street. As they walked past the convention center, their feet took them to the park just beyond it. There were more street performers along the park perimeter, joined by artists with easels offering to sell caricatures or landscapes.

The paths wove through trees and grassy patches, all leading to the large statue in the center. Old iron streetlights provided more than enough light for them. Raz stopped at the statue to look at it, reading the engravement before rejoining Alard.

"Have you always lived here?" Raz asked.

"No, I grew up a long way from here." Alard's fingers danced along a bar on the nearby fence. "This city, though, I fell in love with it the moment I set foot here."

"How long ago was that?"

Alard stopped to think. Raz watched as his lips moved—very distracting lips, he noticed—while muttering as he counted numbers in his head. "Six years, I think. Yeah, six years. I did law school here, then started practicing."

"Nice."

"What about you? Where are you from?"

"Right now, it's DC. Next year could be different." Raz looked up at the stars. "It's hard staying in one place these days—at least for me."

"What keeps you from settling down?"

Raz shrugged. "I think it's that I've yet to find the right community."

"Yeah, well, humans are weird." Alard laughed, then added, "I mean, not you, of course."

Raz laughed at his efforts. "No, you're right. We are weird."

"But sometimes weird is good," Alard added, rubbing the back of his neck.

Raz noticed that Alard looked uncomfortable now, and he wasn't sure what had provoked that kind of response. "Everything okay?"

"Yeah, fine. Why?"

Raz shrugged. "You just seem distracted."

"I'm not distracted." Raz raised an eyebrow, trying to hold back a snort, and Alard sighed. "Okay, I'm a little distracted. I was just thinking about the future."

"You already thinking about a future with me?" Raz couldn't help but smirk at that. *You're not supposed to be having a fling*, the little voice in his head that sounded too much like Marcel reminded him. "Isn't that sweet?"

A sharp laugh echoing in the night. "I don't know you, Raz. Hell, you barely know me."

"Well, I'm in town for about a week. It could give us some time to get to know each other."

Alard shook his head, all mirth leaving his face. "As much as I wish to entertain the idea, I've got other responsibilities that keep me from acting on it."

Something about his voice made Raz suspicious of his excuse. His words dripped with melancholy, almost as if Alard had given up on having any chance of being in a relationship. He couldn't be more than his late twenties if his face was anything to go by. Raz didn't know what the cause of such a depressing thought could be, and he found himself wanting to fix it. "Like what?"

They came up to a bench and Alard flopped down onto one, resting his head in his hands a moment. "Let's just go with my parents are retiring, and I'm expected to go home and take over the family business."

"Is that what you want to do?"

"Of course." Alard snapped his head up, his eyebrows narrowed as if the idea of not going home was insulting.

Raz sat next to him, and after a second, scooped up Alard's hand. The other man didn't pull away—a good sign. "Why? I mean, if it's taking you away from a place and job you love, why give in to them?"

Alard hesitated, and Raz knew the other man was hiding something more to this story. Something that Alard couldn't talk about. "It's expected of me. I just...I can't not go."

"Then I guess you just need to enjoy your last few days here." Raz nodded to himself, then shifted to look at Alard. "Make a few last good memories before you go."

"That's what I've been trying—" Alard's words were cut off as Raz cupped his cheek and leaned forward. *You shouldn't be doing this,* Marcel's voice warned again, but he ignored it and carefully kissed the man beside him. Alard went still against his lips a moment before he pressed back, a hand sneaking up to hold the back of Raz's neck to keep him close.

Alard's lips were soft, his kiss gentle before deepening into a pressure betraying both desire and need. Raz responded, inviting him to press harder, to take more. The fact he was desired fueled Raz, and he ran his teeth along Alard's bottom lip. There was a soft moan as Alard's fingers dug into his skin.

After a moment, Raz pulled back, his eyes looking into the bright green ones only inches away. "I was hoping I read the situation right," he breathed against Alard's lips.

Alard's answer came from a tightening of his grip on Raz's neck, pulling him forward for a harder kiss. Raz moved closer to Alard on the bench as they kissed so he wasn't leaning across the space between them.

Raz let his free hand slide up Alard's back, gentle pressure along his spine until he reached his shoulders, then just kept his hand there. Another moment and Alard pushed away, out of breath as he leaned his head back. Raz wasn't done yet, and he pulled Alard closer and kissed along the man's neck.

"We...we shouldn't..." Alard closed his eyes, moaning as Raz nibbled at a spot where his neck met shoulder. "In public."

Raz leaned back, his eyes looking around until he saw the doors to the convention center. The lights were still on, and he could see people moving around inside. "Come on, I know where we can go."

He took Alard's hand, pulling the man up. Alard's eyes darkened and nodded his consent to following Raz. Holding hands, they made their way into the convention center's lobby. The room door furthest from the lobby was propped open with a sign outside of it. The sound of music and conversation spilled out into the stone and glass hallway.

Raz instead went to the first door and opened it. The room beyond was dark, the noise from the event in the next conference room dulled from the half wall that still stood between the rooms. Extra chairs, garment bags, and piles of white ribbons and flowers were visible in the light from the hallway. "It's empty," he whispered to Alard, pulling him in.

The door was still closing behind them when Raz pushed Alard up against the half wall. His hands pressed the wall just over Alard's shoulders, pinning him in place as he leaned in to kiss the man again. Alard's hands were in Raz's hair within seconds, pulling him closer while threading their way through his luscious locks.

Any semblance of patience was gone, and Raz's kiss was devouring, opening to run the tip of his tongue along Alard's lips, begging for entrance. He stepped closer, pressing his body against Alard's. He rocked his hips up, letting Alard feel just how much Raz wanted him, and then he moaned as Alard slid one hand free from his hair to press against the forming bulge.

Lust took over Raz's mind, and he focused just on his senses. The feel of Alard's hand, the sliding of their tongues over each other. The growing smell of sweat mixed in with a hint of the flowers in the room. Alard's soft moans when Raz's hips pressed harder to rub against his thighs as well as the hand. The taste of rum and tropical fruit filled his mouth as he sucked Alard's lips playfully.

It had been a few years, Raz realized, since he wanted someone this much. His hands slid down along Alard's hips, pulling his shirt free before sliding along the heated skin of Alard's stomach. Alard gasped, his head leaning back against the wall at the touch. Raz started on the buttons, opening his shirt to the cool air of the room, and then ran his hands along each ridge of his abdomen before running along his shoulders to push the shirt off.

"Please," Alard whimpered as Raz nipped his shoulder.

"Please what?" Raz asked, shifting to kiss along Alard's jaw. Alard moaned as Raz thrust his hips again.

"More," he breathed, his eyes fluttering closed.

Raz chuckled at the request. "As you wish," he whispered into Alard's ear. He reached down to move Alard's hand away, then used his own to grab Alard's ass. It was a quick lift, and Alard instantly wrapped his legs around Raz' hips. He walked them to the left, sliding behind a curtain to protect them in case someone came into the supply room. In the darkness, he found a solid wall to press Alard back up against.

Another thrust, this time with only their boxers between them, had

Alard whimpering in pleasure. "I got you," Raz muttered as he set up a slow pace between their hips. Something in his head tried to warn him against doing this, but he ignored it. Instead, he went back to kissing Alard, slower this time. He didn't want this to end too quickly.

In the periphery of his hearing, Raz could hear bits and pieces of the ceremony from their new position. Words like *everlasting bond* and *do you*.

"Yes," Alard hissed as Raz started to quicken their pace. "Oh my god, *yes!*"

"Almost there," Raz groaned.

Now pronounce...

A cry of completion rose from Alard's throat, and Raz leaned over to kiss him to keep him silent. He wasn't far behind, moaning against Alard's lips as he fell over the edge into pure ecstasy. There was a glow on the other side of his eyelids, a white light that flashed for just a moment, like a door opening somewhere in front of him. He ignored it, daring anyone to disrupt them in that moment.

The room beyond filled with applause a moment later, and Alard leaned his head back to laugh. "I hope that's not for us," he stated.

Raz helped Alard back to his feet, smiling. "We should probably go before they start leaving." He reached over to push the sweaty hair from Alard's face. "Come back with me?"

Alard nodded, taking his hand. "Yes."

CHAPTER FOUR

S unlight hitting his eyes was the first thing that woke Alard up. As his senses came back, he could feel an arm wrapped around his waist. The body attached to it, solid and warm, lay pressed against his back. The soft breath of someone sleeping tickled along the skin behind his ear.

Memories of the previous evening returned. Drunk just enough for their inhibitions to be lowered and needing more than a dry hump on a wall, they had crashed back into his hotel room in a tangle of arms working to remove clothing. It wasn't easy, seeing that they were still connected by tongue, but soon they separated enough for Alard to drop to his knees.

"Let me," Alard said with a mischievous grin as his fingers pulled down Raz's fly. Before he could answer, Alard had shoved his hand inside Raz's boxers and stroked along his hardening shaft. It was already a sticky mess, but Alard could fix that.

Laughing, Alard pulled it out, stroking it with ease. "You really made a mess in there," he added. "Let me clean you up." Raz gasped as Alard licked the top of his cock before sliding it into his mouth. He teased the rim and slit first, then ran his tongue along the throbbing vein of Raz's cock while taking it deeper into his mouth.

"Oh fuck," Raz breathed, trying to press further down his throat. Alard took his time, licking along his dick while working Raz's pants the rest of the way down. Alard's fingers scratched up his thighs, making Raz's legs vibrate until he sat down or risk collapsing on top of the other man.

Raz sitting down allowed Alard to shift his position, sitting back on his feet between the other man's legs. He grabbed the base of Raz's dick, rubbing it before he took all of Raz into his mouth. He sped up, arching his back as he tried to suck Raz's life out through his dick. Raz matched his pace, fucking Alard's throat as he held Alard's head in place. It wasn't long before Raz squeezed Alard's hair. "I'm gonna come if you don't stop."

Alard replied by sucking harder and cradling his balls in one hand. That set Raz off, and he groaned, falling back onto the bed, rolling on the mattress as Alard continued to suck down pulse after salty pulse from his dick.

When he finally stopped, Alard leaned over Raz and smirked. The man was a beautiful mess, glowing from his orgasm. "I take it you liked that," he teased, licking a stray drop of cum from the side of his lips.

"That was incredible, best head of my life." Raz said.

"I learned that in the back room at Oz." Alard stripped off his shirt and pants, then crawled up onto the bed naked. "Want to see what else I learned?"

"Gladly."

The night became a blur of hands and tongues, feeling that wonderful duplicity of pain and pleasure as Raz fucked him so hard into the mattress that he was in tears when he came, and then their soft breath against each other's skin as they came back from their collective orgasm.

But it was after that he remembered most; softly talking about everything and nothing as they dozed off to sleep, wanting to know more about the other than just how compatible they were in bed.

Time wasn't on his side. He only had days left here, then he would be gone, and no chance to see where this could go. He shouldn't have let Raz kiss him, but *damn*. Just the thought of it made him snuggle closer to Raz, refusing to acknowledge the arrival of morning.

"Hey," Raz's husky voice whispered into his ear, bringing a smile to Alard's lips. Just five more minutes...

Alard rolled over to face Raz, giving him a soft kiss. "Hi."

"I could get used to this," Raz chuckled, pulling Alard closer until their foreheads touched.

"I wish I could too, but we both know it's not possible."

Raz's smile dropped, and he pulled away to roll onto his back. "Yeah, I know."

Letting out a sigh, Alard sat up on the other side of the bed. "I'm sorry, I just don't think it's going to work." He closed his eyes, then turned to look at the man behind him. Raz stared at the ceiling, a frown darkening the beautiful face. Alard wished he could take it back, but wishful thinking wasn't going to solve the major problem looming over his head. Alard was too honest, even when it worked against him. "Mind if I use the shower?"

"Go ahead."

Alard watched him a moment longer, but when Raz didn't move, Alard stood and shuffled to the bathroom. He didn't jump into the shower right away, however. Instead, he stood at the sink, arms on the counter as he focused on his breathing.

"Hey Alard, do you remember us stopping for fake tattoos on our way back to my room?"

"What?" Alard moved back to the doorway. "I mean, no, I don't think we did. Why?"

Raz rubbed his forearm, then turned it to face Alard. The soft skin was marred with a tattoo that Alard knew for a fact hadn't been there last night. He stepped closer, trying to get an idea of what the design was, then froze.

The tattoo was of two hearts on their sides, interlinked near their bottom points. One heart was a chocolate brown, the other a mossy green. A silver infinity loop wove through it all. It was a symbol of two hearts united for eternity. Alard snapped his own arm up, finding the same design embedded in his own flesh.

"Shit."

He ran back into the bathroom, shoving his arm under the sink and rubbing the tattoo. "No, no, nonono," Alard muttered, his chest tightening as the mark refused to fade. He was aware of Raz appearing behind him a moment later, watching him.

"Alard, calm down. Breathe."

"This can't be happening." Alard looked at Raz's confused reflection in the mirror.

"What can't be happening? Alard, stop." Raz's hand reached over to turn the hot water off, then wrapped Alard's arm, red from scrubbing, in a towel. Raz turned Alard to face him, still holding his arm. "What's going on?"

The lump in Alard's throat, along with the tightening in his chest, made it hard for him to speak. Not being able to speak jumpstarted his panic attack, and he started to hyperventilate. Raz put a free hand on his cheek, guiding his face to lift, but Alard kept his focus on the floor.

Raz rubbed a thumb over his cheek. Wetness traced the path as Raz wiped along his cheek, and Alard realized he was crying.

"Talk to me, Alard. What does this tattoo mean?"

He had fucked up, bad. Alard focused on pushing the panic away—it wasn't going to do him any good. He had to tell Raz, but he doubted that the other man was going to believe him. No one did, which was why Alard stopped confiding in his friends.

"It means we're married," he whispered, unable to look Raz in the eye.

The silence that followed stabbed Alard's heart. He didn't dare look up, afraid of what Raz's face would show with this revelation. Then Raz spoke up, his voice almost as soft as his. "What did you say?"

Alard looked up and into Raz's brown eyes, darkening in what Alard assumed was confusion or anger. Maybe both? "Where I'm from, it appears on a couple after they are married."

The other man's hands dropped, and Raz took a step back. "The fuck it does? I think I'd remember getting married. We're not in Vegas."

"I know, and it sounds crazy—"

"Just a bit." The venom in Raz's voice was not subtle. Alard sighed, rubbing his hand over his face. Raz stared at him, but where Alard expected menace, he found the man almost pleading, as if hoping this was all a big joke.

"I'm sorry. But we can fix it, I think."

"You *think?*"

"It's not like I go around doing this every weekend!" Alard snapped his jaw shut, releasing the fists his hands had curled into. "Sorry. I didn't mean to yell."

"And what, you think *I* sleep around like this?" Raz threw his hands up in the air. "I can't believe it. Marcus was right."

"Raz?"

The other man started pacing the room, picking up clothes as he muttered to himself. "Just so stupid. I should have known better."

"Raz!"

"What?!" Raz pun, his own breathing picking up.

"Please, can we just talk about this for a moment?"

Raz took a deep breath, his hands clenching the clothing in his arms. "And just what can you say that will make this any better?" He gave a curt laugh. "Damn it, Alard, I thought you were different from the others," he added, then went back to picking up clothes.

"I am, in a way..." Alard said.

"Yeah, you're nuts, right? This is exactly why I need to stop having convention flings. The crazies always seem to find me."

"I'm not crazy."

"Then what are you?" Raz's voice went up an octave, his eyes wide. Alard could feel the waves of confusion coming off Raz and shivered. "We had an amazing night, the best sex I've had in years, connected on a level I've never experienced, then wake up with a tattoo I don't remember getting, and you telling me we're married. That's not how relationships work, Alard!"

"That's how it works where I'm from," Alard stated, taking a deep breath. He had to tell Raz the truth. There was no way he couldn't. If this was a fairy marriage bond—and he was ninety-nine percent sure it was—then spilling a few secrets was the least of their problems.

Raz crossed his arms. "Where you're from...if the next words out of your mouth are that this is some kind of voodoo ritual bullshit, I'm going to toss you naked out of my room."

"Not voodoo."

He fumed, and Alard was waiting for Raz to start screaming. "Some other kind of magic, then?"

"Kinda?"

One of Raz's perfect eyebrows lifted, but beyond that, he stood perfectly still and spoke with the slow, eerily calm clarity of a man about to break. "Kind of?"

"It's complicated."

"Make it uncomplicated."

They stared at each other for a moment, and then Alard closed his eyes as he took another deep breath. "I'm from the fairy realm. I've been crossing into the human world for the last decade because everything over here is so broken that I'm trying to look for ways to fix it, or at least help the ones who don't have any power to change their circumstances."

Silence filled the room for a moment, and Alard snuck a look at Raz. The other man hadn't moved, his jaw set. "Get out."

"Raz—"

The pile of clothing struck Alard's chest as Raz stormed across the room and threw the door open. "Get the hell out of my room or I'm calling security."

"Raz, I'm not—"

"Now!"

Alard huffed and held his hand out to the side. A gust of wind circled in the room and then buffeted the door, slamming it shut. Raz jumped back, looking at the door, then Alard.

"Not until we figure this out," Alard stated, his arm held out as white wisps of clouds circled his wrist, and his eyes glowed in the dim room.

———

It had been an amazing night, and the morning had all the makings of a great day. Raz couldn't remember the last time he woke to a warm body pressed against his chest. His body ached in that good kind of soreness, the kind that comes from a long night of sex. It couldn't have been more perfect.

Then Alard had to open his mouth and out spilled the crazy.

Now, on the opposite end of the room from Alard, the door ripped itself from Raz's hand and slammed shut. Alard remained near the bed; his hand outstretched. He refused to meet Raz's eyes, staring at a spot near Raz's shoulder.

Not until we figure this out.

"How did you do that?" Raz whispered, the pounding of his heart audible in his ears. That wasn't normal. Doors don't slam shut on their own except in horror movies. He *really* needed to stop having conference flings.

Alard sucked on his lips, then looked up at Raz. "Like I said...magic," he stated.

Raz wanted to laugh at the absurdity of it, but the look in Alard's eyes kept that laughter in his throat. The man was serious.

The man was crazy. "Magic? That's it?" *But doors don't close on their own, and eyes don't glow like that.*

"You need more proof." Alard moved to the windows, flicking the floor lamp on before he closed the two layers of curtains, darkening the room to where it was difficult to see each other. "I can do that."

Alard approached Raz, holding out his hand. "I need your arm."

Raz hesitated, unsure if Alard was about to drug him or something, but Alard was still naked. If he wanted to hurt Raz, there were ample opportunities last night. Reluctantly, Raz held out the tattooed arm.

Warmth spread from Raz's arm to his head as Alard traced the brown heart. Raz saw it shimmer for a moment before it and the warmth faded back to normal.

Still naked, Alard took two steps back. Raz saw Alard's eyes glow again. His eyes had changed: no longer hazel, they shone with a mossy light color, as if the irises gave off their own light. The glimmering light then spread across Alard's face and body, bathing the room in a green glow.

Alard's face started to pale, then took on an iridescent shine. The change spread down his body until the pearly complexion was from head to toe. Behind him, two wings, just the length of his arms, spread out into the space. Green flesh, dark as a forest canopy, outlined their shape. Between the folded lines a smoky almost transparent film filled the space. Colors appeared in them, as the light from the floor lamp shone through, like the stained-glass wings of a hummingbird.

When Raz looked back into Alard's eyes, Raz saw fear in them. Alard's teeth bit into his lip, and he still refused to meet Raz's eyes. It took Raz a moment to realize why. *He's afraid of me.* Alard's sharing of his identity, of who he really was, must come with a price or punishment. Something that had backfired on him before, yet he trusted Raz enough to reveal it.

Raz looked at the tattoo on his arm, then the matching one on Alard's.

So this is what going crazy feels like.

No, whatever Alard was showing him *had* to be real. There was no way he could create all this in one night as some ultimate illusion. He wasn't crazy, and neither was Alard. The world around them, yes, totally crazy, but what they had felt last night? That was real, which meant so was this, and Raz wasn't sure he could handle what all of that meant right now.

Because...Holy. Shit. Magic is real.

But why was Alard still avoiding his eyes? Raz wondered. It was obvious that Alard revealing his secret was only happening because of this tattoo—a fairy marriage bond—but there was a vulnerableness to it. A moment later, Raz realized why: *He's waiting for me to reject him.*

He knew the feeling of rejection all too well. In these "modern" times, Raz still felt the eyes of others prejudging him based on his features or his faith—or lack thereof. Their fear came from lack of understanding and a refusal to learn. He refused to do that to anyone else, especially someone as beautiful as Alard was in this form.

Breaching the space between them, Raz placed his hand gently against Alard's cheek. His thumb ran along a reflection of pink and green from the opalescence, then along Alard's lips.

"You're beautiful."

The tension broke in Alard's face, and he smiled. He pressed his cheek against Raz's hand, then turned to kiss his wrist. "You aren't scared?"

"Scared? No. Confused, hell yes. You have a lot of explaining to do." His thumb traced from Alard's pink nose to his pale cheeks, and he felt the heat from Alard's face warm his fingers. "But right now, I'm just mesmerized. How is this real?"

"I know it's a lot to take in." Alard pulled back from Raz and guided him back to the bed. "The short of it is that magic always existed. When humans started to use magic to gain power over others instead of caring for them, the King of Fairies divided the realms so that magic was cut off from everyday use in the human realm. Humans worked to create words to explain, to identify, and to quantify what magic was left. What could be explained was attributed to the will of a higher power to some.. Some call is paranormal phenomenon, because to call it magic brings up the ideas of witches and devils and none of the beauty that it actually is."

"So, science is magic that can be explained?" Raz rubbed his head, feeling a headache coming on.

"Sorta. It's difficult to explain here. It makes more sense in my realm where you can see it."

"And most people can't see magic?"

"Only children, unless you're born with the ability to continue to see magic beyond childhood." Alard stood up, his wings receding into his back as he shifted into his human appearance. "I gifted you a small touch of magic through the tattoo so that you can see me when I shift into my real form."

Raz pinched the bridge of his nose. "I'm so confused."

"I know." Alard knelt in front of Raz, taking the darker hands in his pale ones. "But right now, we need to figure out what happened last night so we can remove this bond."

There was something in Alard's voice that made Raz lift his head and stare into the now hazel eyes. "What happens if we don't, or can't?"

The hint of a smile on Alard's face dropped away, and he swallowed. "War."

CHAPTER FIVE

"War?" Raz looked incredulous, as if he were at a point where his brain would go into shutdown mode. "What do you mean *war*?"

Alard knew there was still a lot to explain, and he needed caffeine if he was going to continue this conversation. "Why don't we get dressed and go get some coffee, and I'll explain on the way?"

Raz stared at him, lips parting as if to say something, then he shook his head and rubbed his eyes. "Fine. I don't have any sessions this morning so no one will miss me."

Once dressed and leaving the hotel, Alard explained. "My status—whether or not I'm married—is a political matter as much as an emotional one. It'll be fine, and we'll figure this out long before it gets to that." He hoped so, at least.

"I hope so," Raz said, echoing Alard's thought. "So, the first thing we should do is retrace our steps, right?" Raz checked the street for cars before crossing, Alard following in his wake. "We can start at the bar."

"We didn't do anything there that would create a bond. I don't think." Alard knew he was supposed to focus and not be enjoying the view from behind Raz at this moment, but in his opinion, it was all Raz's tailor's fault.

They reached the middle of Canal Street and stopped, waiting for the traffic to stop on the other side. "What *are* the conditions for this bond?" Raz asked.

"Um, an exchange of affection, like a kiss."

"We did that."

"We did a lot of that," Alard pointed out, smirking. "And a bit more."

Raz turned to look at Alard, his eyes narrowed in thought. "Does consummation come into account for this bond?"

Alard shook his head. "No. Some fairies are genderless and can't do that, but they can form a bond. The exchange of affection is decided upon by the couple."

"That's very progressive," Raz commented as the traffic lights changed, and they could finish crossing the street.

"I'd say so, but that's how it's always been for my realm. Humans are the ones who feel the need to identify and classify."

"Touché."

Alard and Raz beelined for the coffee shop and got in line. It had been their first agreement before they left the hotel: acquire coffee. The wait line wasn't as long as it had been the day before. Raz bought the coffee this time and as they waited, a thought came to Alard. "We didn't drink from each other's cup at all, right?"

Raz leaned his head back in thought. "No...no wait, I did at the bar. Why?"

"It's a Scottish thing. Two people drink from the same quaich cup during a wedding ceremony as a symbol of becoming one."

"I'm not Scottish," Raz pointed out. "Far from it. I barely knew you at that point, anyway. I don't think sharing a drink with a stranger could represent lifelong commitment."

Alard shrugged, focusing on the floor. "Just a thought."

Their drinks arrived, and they slipped back out on their way deeper into the French Quarter. Raz took in the scenery as they walked. "I don't think we jumped over any brooms, and I'd remember if we tied each other up."

Choking on his coffee, Alard looked up at Raz in horror. "What culture has marriage via bondage?"

"A lot, when you look into it." Raz's eyebrows rose, then laughed as Alard's cheeks warmed. "But not like bondage in the bedroom. Handfasting. Two ribbons wrapped around joined hands..."

Realization dawned and Alard shook his head. "Handfasting. Yeah, that I know. You had me worried there for a second."

Raz snorted. "Sorry, but I mean, if people like it like that, why not?"

They turned onto Bourbon Street. It was dead; the revelers returned to their morning lives of jobs or sleep. The bars were still open, but most were serving breakfast and mimosas from their tiny kitchens. Street cleaners were working on cleaning up the remains of cups, cigarettes, and other discarded items.

Not the beads, though. The men who were selling them walked the streets, inspecting the strands left behind to see which could be resold. If not, they were either tossed into the trash or up onto the crisscrossing lights over the street to hang between bulbs. Strands for years of celebrations hung there, left to add to the atmosphere until their weight threatened the light strand and they were removed.

"This is what I thought the entire city would look like," Raz said more to himself than Alard. "Streets like this, and the cemeteries."

"Not everything is as it seems." Alard closed his eyes, taking a deep breath. The breeze carried the scent of coffee, chicory, beignets, and sausage. Softer jazz music, piped through speakers instead of musicians, continued the city's heartbeat until the evening would bring the brass back to the bars. "This city has many faces. It's magical like that."

"So, you say." Raz smiled, though, throwing a knowing look at Alard. Alard blushed, hiding his smile behind the lip of his coffee cup. "You said something about humans not being able to see magic. What does this street look like to you?"

Alard thought about that for a moment. He wasn't one to show off his skills to others, especially in the human realm. He'd never shed his human shell either, but he had to keep Raz from throwing him out into the hallway before he could make him understand.

"Well, right now I see it the same as you." It was the truth, but Raz's raised eyebrow showed that the man saw the dodge in his answer. "If I use my true eyes, I can see more."

"Can you show me? Like you did in the hotel room?"

"You still have the magic I gifted, but I can't do it for you." Alard shrugged. "It takes practice, and it's rare that a human adult retains enough of a connection to the other realms as they exit childhood."

Raz stopped in his tracks, taking a deep breath. "Okay, we're going to return to the phrase 'other realms' later." Alard blinked, realizing that he let slip something more that Raz might not be ready for. "Right now, explain what you mean by connection."

The club they were at last night, Oz, was coming up on the next block. Alard debated how long of a conversation that was going to be and decided it would have to wait. "Not something to talk about in the streets. Later, though, I promise."

Raz watched him. Alard assumed that Raz was evaluating him. He'd seen similar looks on opposing counsel trying to determine if Alard was a lawyer that would pose a challenge to them. Normally it made him nervous, as if they had the ability to look inside him and see the parts that weren't normal. Now, with Raz's focus, Alard wanted him to see deep inside and find the truth to his words.

"Fine, but you can't hide the truth from me forever."

"I won't."

They walked to the next block where Oz sat, the neon signs turned off but doors wide open. Alard stepped in, scanning the room. Only yesterday he had been here with James—one of dozens of visits—but now the room felt different. Calm. Peaceful, even.

"So, what are we looking for?" Raz asked.

"No idea, but something magical."

Raz sat down at the bar. "Well, that's your department. Have at it."

Alard sighed, resisting the urge to roll his eyes. Instead, he took one last scan of the room, memorizing its features that were only visible to humans. He blinked, shifting just his eyes back to his true mossy green glow. He heard Raz gasp. Alard didn't turn to him; instead, he walked away from the bar to see the magic in the room.

The room lit up in shades of pink and red. Small streaks of green flittered around his head, and he laughed. Of course, there would be sprites in the LGBT bar; a sprite's main purpose was to ensure happiness and love. An LGBT nightclub strives to provide that more than any other bar Alard's been to. *Why haven't I noticed this before?*

Alard whistled a quick tune, holding his palm upright in front of him. The green streaks, the sprites, stopped moving, hovering in place. He listened to them communicate with each other in a series of keys higher than most humans could hear. Alard knew how to hear them, but he respected their privacy and just waited.

One flew forward, landing on his palm and kneeling to him. "You wish to speak to us, my lord?"

"You can call me Alard." He spoke softly in their language, not wanting to let anyone in the bar overhear them. "I didn't know there were sprites present in this bar. I would have brought you proper offerings on my visits."

"We do not wish to be known, my lo—Alard." The sprite giggled nervously. "We are here just to bring joy."

"You all do a remarkable job." He looked up at the other sprites, still hovering in their group. Their giggling sounded like windchimes, and Alard saw Raz look up in their direction from the bar as there was no loud music playing to cover the sound from humans.

"What is it we can do for you, Alard?" The sprite bounced in his palm, the green dust from her wings gathering in his palm.

"Were any of you here last night? I'm trying to find the origin of some unexpected magic."

The green bundle of energy shook her head, her dragonfly wings beating fast enough to make her hover over Alard's hand. "Not here. Except for us but that magic is normal. We want to make people feel welcome and loved. Happy. We didn't do anything wrong, right?"

Alard smiled. "No, you're doing exactly what you're supposed to. I'm not mad at any of you."

"Oh, good." She relaxed, her toes touching his palm again like a ballerina on pointe. "We follow the laws. We are happy here."

"Oh, trust me," Alard laughed and felt Raz's eyes on him, "I enjoy being in this realm too."

"But not for long."

The joy left his smile, and Alard took a deep breath. "Yes, not for long."

"Oh, I didn't mean to make you sad, Alard!" She was hovering again, her glowing hands covering her mouth. "Please don't be sad."

"That is not something you can help me with." Alard nodded to the group of sprites and then to the one in his hand. "Thank you. I'll let you go back to work."

"You are most welcome." She flew up and kissed Alard's forehead, a sparkle of green dust falling and tickling his nose before the sprite shot off back to the group.

Alard walked back to Raz and slid onto a stool beside him, as Alard's eyes lost their glow. "Nothing happened here."

"You know you looked like a crazy person talking to your hand," Raz chuckled.

"Welcome to life as a fae in the human realm." Alard shook his coffee to see if there was anything left in it, then sipped it.

They sat quietly for a minute, sipping their coffee while listening to the coffee house jazz playing on the internal radio. Raz broke the silence first. "I have to return to the conference this afternoon before Marcel comes looking for me."

"Well, that's where we went after here. I can look around while you do your lectures."

"Don't you have any clients to meet with?" Raz asked.

Alard shook his head. "I've been shuttering my half of the practice over the last month. I've got one client left, but once he decides to accept the estate, he can get a lawyer on retainer and doesn't need my advice any longer."

"You weren't kidding when you said you were heading home."

Alard stood up, reaching across the bar for a shot glass and two sugar packets. "If I didn't have to, I'd stay here forever."

"I can see why. Compared to DC, this city is relaxing."

"You're only seeing the major tourist district. You'd think differently if you went further downtown."

Raz watched Alard open two sugar packets and dump them into a shot glass. "You need a sugar rush?"

"No, it's an offering." Alard walked to the door.

"Let me guess. You'll explain later." Raz tossed his cup in the trash and followed Alard back out into the street.

Alard grinned. "I must sound like a broken record."

"You do. But you have a nice ass so I'm willing to put up with you...for now."

———

The convention center was packed by the time Raz and Alard arrived. Men and women in business attire walked the halls as the men peeked into open conference room doors. Others huddled in small groups along the walls, talking adamantly with their voices and hands. Organized chaos, Raz mused, the typical convention experience.

They walked to the branch of the convention center where they had snuck in the previous night. It was closed off, a velvet rope blocking most of the doorway.

"We went this way," Alard said as he slipped around the rope stanchion.

"We can't go in there now," Raz hissed. He checked behind them to see if anyone was paying attention to them.

Alard paused, holding his hands out to his sides. "Are you serious right now?"

"The sign says not to go back there."

"I can read it just fine."

"I would like not to get kicked out of the convention on the second day." Raz checked over his shoulder again. "There are too many people."

Alard licked his lips to hold back his laughter. "We're not breaking into Fort Knox here, Raz. The worst thing they will do is drag us back out, which will happen the longer you stand there and make a scene."

"I'm not making a scene."

"Oh really? Let me also remind you that you weren't so rule abiding last night when you dragged me in here the first time."

Raz wanted to wipe the smirk off Alard's face. He wasn't wrong, but Raz also didn't want to draw too much attention to what they were doing. It's not like he could explain it without lying, and Raz hated lying.

Raz took one more look over his shoulder. When he was convinced that no one was watching them, he skirted past the stanchion and sped after Alard to the conference room door. The door was closed but unlocked so it was easy to open it far enough to slip in.

The lights were on in the room, a stark fluorescent that took a moment for Raz's eyes to adjust to. It was too bright and now too big, Raz realized. The wall partition was down, and he could see through the entire hallway's worth of conference rooms. White chairs were being stacked against a wall, mounds of white ribbon on flowers being tossed into shipping crates. No one noticed their arrival; the workers too caught up in their duties while earbuds played their preference of distractions.

Alard walked to where the room divider was folded back, then turned and traced the wall's normal placement with his steps. As he moved, the scaffolding for what looked like a concert stage blocked his path. The steel bones went from floor to ceiling, stage lights hanging from the top, and a skirt of black velvet blocked the space under the stage floor from view.

Raz moved to join him as Alard put his hand on the steel pole in front of him. His hazel eyes closed; Alard's face scrunched up in concentration. "What are you doing?" Raz asked.

"Trying to sense residual magic."

Alard's fingers tightened on the pole, lifting his chin as he took a deep breath. Raz watched, enraptured, waiting for something to spark in the air. He had no idea how magic would appear but growing up with books about schools of magic and adventures made him envision a white mist wrapping around them, whispering secrets in some ancient tongue to them.

But none of that happened.

"Anything?" Raz asked. Perhaps the magic was invisible to his human eyes.

Alard shook his head, dropping his hand to his side. "Nothing."

"What do you two think you're doing?" A voice boomed out from across the room. Raz and Alard turned to find a security guard walking over to them. "You're not supposed to be in here."

"Sorry, we got lost." Alard chimed in, throwing on his charming smile. The guard stopped a few feet away and crossed his arms over his chest. "We're looking for the MBA conference. Isn't that in this wing?"

"One floor up." The guard wasn't taken in by Alard's smile, his eyes laser focused on them.

"I told you," Raz hissed, more about getting caught than the location of his conference.

"Yeah, I know, I'm sorry. What's happening in this room? Looks like you're setting up for a big concert." Alard's smile brightened, and Raz couldn't help smiling along with him.

"Breaking down an event from last night. Some mass wedding." The guard stepped forward, pointing at the door. "It's off limits, so you need to leave."

Raz and Alard exchanged a quick glance. *Of course,* their eyes told each other.

"Yes, we can do that. Sorry for disrupting you." Raz grabbed Alard's hand and dragged him to the door.

"You don't by chance know where the people who run the event went to?" Alard asked, looking back as Raz pulled him away.

The guard scoffed. "Not my job. Go ask the event coordinator."

As Alard thanked the guard, Raz pulled him out of the room and back on the right side of the rope stanchion. They kept moving until they exited back out into the convention center's park. Raz found a bench and sat down with his head in his hands. "So not only were we hooking up against the stage of a mass wedding ceremony, but they have also already disappeared from town with no way to get them to undo this."

He watched Alard's feet through his fingers. The man was silent, but his red Converse spoke volumes. The toe of his left foot dug into the ground, kicking at the loose stones. When it stamped down, planting itself in the ground, the right started to vibrate along with his leg.

"Damnit," Alard growled through clenched teeth. Raz looked up and saw Alard was vibrating with frustration. His hands were balled into fists, his eyes squeezed closed, and Raz watched as a glow appeared behind the lids.

"Whoa, hey, hold on." He jumped up and held Alard's face. "You need to calm down."

"I can't. I really fucked up, and I don't know how to fix this." Alard opened his eyes, his irises glowing, tears threatening to spill onto his cheek.

"Hey, we're going to figure this out. Just need a little more time, that's all."

"We don't have a lot of time." Alard reached up to press his hands over Raz's.

"That war you were talking about? Is that why?"

Alard nodded. "And..."

Raz closed his eyes. "And?! What's worse than war?"

"I'm supposed to get married—" Raz's eyes widened in horror "—a strictly political marriage, next week."

Raz pressed his forehead against Alard's. "This just keeps getting better," he muttered. "Next thing you'll tell me is that you're marrying a troll or something."

"Oh man, don't let Meyda hear you call her that."

"Let me guess—she'll order some beast to eat me and eliminate the competition?"

Alard bit his lip lower lip, trying to smile. "Just keep remembering I have a nice ass?"

Raz chuckled and leaned forward, pressing his lips against Alard's and sighed as the kiss was returned. Warm softness enveloped his senses, and he pressed closer, letting the warmth against his lips push away all the frustration that had been building up between them.

When he pulled back to breathe, he opened his eyes and found Alard's hazel eyes staring at him. The nervous energy in the other man had disappeared, replaced with a small smile. "Better?" Raz asked.

"Yeah."

"Good. Now let's get something to eat and figure out a new plan" Raz traced his thumb along Alard's cheek, then dropped his hand to take his, weaving their fingers together. "We've still got options. We just need to keep clear heads until we find them."

Alard took a deep breath. "Right. Okay, breakfast. You up for beignets?"

CHAPTER SIX

The line at Café du Monde wasn't outrageous, and Alard got them seated in under ten minutes. The café itself was simple—open air covered patio with dozens of metal tables, bent iron chairs that looked like they came out of eighteenth-century France, and a shaker canister of powdered sugar full and waiting next to the napkin dispenser. Fried dough and coffee permeated the furniture, columns, and the tablecloths, making any visitor hungry long before they got to their table.

A plate of beignets and two café au laits later, they sat back and relaxed for a moment. "You have some powder here," Alard told Raz, his hand brushing along his own chest. Raz looked down, laughed, and patted away the powdered sugar.

"These things are messy. So worth it though. And the view is incredible." Raz watched the park across the street from the café. Artisans were setting up tables along the exterior fence, hocking their art while continuing to work behind the table. The closest to them was an older gentleman, skin dark from years out in the sun, setting up an easel on the side of his display. Paints were scattered on the bench behind him.

"It is," Alard smiled. "I've sat here for hours some days, letting the atmosphere seep into my bones. The art, architecture, music, and even the people create their own kind of magic, in a way."

"I believe it."

They relaxed, focusing on their coffees and the murmur of the crowd. Chuckling, Alard motioned toward the painter. "You know, before I decided to study law, I thought about doing that."

Raz followed his eyes, then smiled. "I could see you as a painter. You see things differently than most people. Literally."

"That's what I wanted to paint. I wanted to show the city, and how the magic weaves its way around everything."

"Were you any good?"

"Not in the least," Alard laughed.

Raz joined in with the laughter. "Good thing you stuck with studying law then." He opened his mouth to say something else, but his cell phone alarm went off.

"What's that?" Alard asked.

"My next workshop partner wants to meet and go over our presentation," Raz said, staring at his phone before popping off a reply.

He reached for his wallet to leave a tip. "We should get going."

Alard stayed in his seat. "But we still haven't figured out a plan."

"We can figure one out as we walk back to the convention center." Raz stood, checking the time on his watch, then flashed him a smile.

"Don't you think that we've got more important things to deal with than practicing a speech?" He lifted his forearm, showing the tattoo. "I mean, I don't think there's a seminar there on removing this."

"That would just be too easy." Raz grabbed Alard's arm and dragged him away.

When they were far enough away from human ears, they stopped at the mouth of an alley. "I have a life too, you realize. I can't just drop everything to figure out this problem." Raz reminded him. "But we will figure this out, together, and you'll get to go back and get married without anyone knowing about what happened. I'm still going to be here, and if I flake out on this conference, people are going to talk. I'm still building my business, so that's my reputation at stake. You get that, right?"

"I'm...I'm do." Alard chastised himself for his comments. He should have thought about what kind of problems this was going to cause Raz. "I didn't think."

"You may want to fix that before your next marriage." The fondness in

Raz's voice was still there, but Alard could see some tension remained in his shoulders.

Alard snorted. He shifted behind Raz and reached up to massage his shoulders. It took a moment, then the tension dissolved under Alard's fingers, and when Raz's shoulders and arms dropped, Alard pressed his forehead against Raz's back. "I'm really sorry."

Raz groaned and leaned his head back to rest on top of Alard's. "I just keep reminding myself of how nice your ass is."

They both dissolved into laughter now that the tension had broken, and Alard placed a kiss on Raz's shoulder. "Let's go back to the convention center. You do your thing, and I'll try to research the wedding organizers and see if I can track them down."

Raz smiled, and Alard felt the warmth return to his own face. "Meet up after to see where you're at?"

"I can work with this plan."

They walked back to Canal Street hand in hand. Raz ducked into the hotel to change and grab his briefcase, leaving Alard to get more coffee for them at the hotel coffee shop. He returned to his bench from yesterday to wait.

"Oh, it's you!" A woman ran over to him, beaming while dragging a young man behind her. "I didn't think I was going to get to thank you for the other day."

It took Alard a second to remember the young bride, Shelia, from two days ago. "Oh, it was nothing. I take it this is your fiancé?"

"Husband, now. I'm Davin." The man's Eastern accent was thick, holding out a hand. "It was a beautiful ceremony."

"I heard." Alard hoped he wasn't blushing as he thought of where he and Raz had been at that time. "Too bad I couldn't see it."

"Oh, you can!" They sat on the bench next to Alard, and Shelia pulled out her cell phone. She pressed a few buttons on the screen and then turned the phone sideways. "They live stream the weddings online so that our families can watch."

Crowded around the tiny phone, Shelia showed Alard the moment where they were exchanging their vows. It was beautiful, even if it was hard to make out any faces when the camera shot showed the couples.

When the officiate came on the screen, Alard was so focused on listening to the words that he almost missed the rustling of the curtains to the left of the stage. He sucked on his lips, sneaking a glance at the happy couple, but they made no comment about the curtain disturbance.

"It looks like a beautiful ceremony," Alard said as Shelia put her phone away and then the couple stood. "Now how long are you staying in New Orleans?"

"Our flight to California is tomorrow morning," Davin said. "We are spending today playing tourist."

"Well, I'm a local, so let me give you pointers on the best places to go." Alard gave them a small list of places to go including Café Du Monde, Fitzel's, and Mother's Restaurant just past the casino. They thanked Alard and headed off on their day as Raz returned.

"Friends of yours?" Raz asked.

Alard stood up, enjoying the cut of the suit and how it clung to Raz's body. "Um, kinda. I met Shelia two days ago looking for her fiancé in the crowd of people in the lobby."

"Looks like she found him."

"Davin looks like a good man." Alard grinned. "I think they're going to have a happy life together."

Raz barked in laughter. "You know, you're an optimist for everyone but yourself."

"Family trait." Alard handed Raz his coffee, then leaned over to straighten Raz's tie. "The couple also gave me a place to start on my research today."

"Did they now?" They left the hotel and waited to cross the street to the convention center.

"They did. There's a website that streamed the wedding last night." Alard took a long sip of his coffee as the streetcar cut them off from crossing completely. It was easier to just wait than go around. "I figure I'll take a look at the site, see if there's anything about the details of how they officiate the weddings, or where they are going next."

Raz nodded. "Good. I'll find you at three?"

"I'll meet you at the Starbucks."

"You have a coffee addiction, don't you?"

Alard grinned over the rim of his cup. "I'm a lawyer. Of course I do."

Raz missed the first set of classes that morning while he was eating beignets with Alard. The second set was just starting when he rushed into the convention center, struggling to find his lanyard in his bag. He found his presentation partner, and they got to work practicing since their lecture was set after lunch.

The guest of honor lunch was only an hour long. Other than Marcel, Raz only knew the other men in passing from the convention circuit. Life for them was the same as it had been three months ago when they met in Miami. Nothing changed, time moved on, and they kept reminiscing on the same stories of the good old days before marriage and mortgages.

It was sometime during his second lunch beer that Raz realized how much he hated this part of the business—the convention circuit. Raz spent years working on his business degree, and even more years building a resume, a company, and a reputation. Barely in his thirties, he was considered old among entrepreneurs in the social media marketing world. Technology changed faster each year, and keeping up on Facebook policy changes and whether consumers were using Instagram or TikTok was time consuming. He earned enough to live well, but at each convention, hearing these men and their stories, he felt the desire to be a Fortune 500 company slip further and further away.

It was a dream, though, and dreams didn't always end the way he'd hoped. So why did he keep doing it? He worked himself to death to meet his projected budget needs while dealing with older white men who had no idea what social media even was—the same ones who attended his lectures every year and learned nothing.

When lunch was over, Raz excused himself to use the men's room. As he washed his hands, the edge of the tattoo peeked out from his sleeve. He shook his hands dry, then pulled the sleeve up so he could observe the entire image.

His finger traced the lines of the infinity symbol linking the two hearts. The skin on his forearm tingled, and Raz smiled to himself. He was about to trace the green heart when the bathroom door opened. Marcel walked in and headed straight for the urinals. "Hey, Raz. I was hoping to get some time with you today."

Raz rushed to push his shirt sleeves back down and focused on buttoning the cuffs. "I had an interesting morning," he replied, turning back to check his reflection.

"That's what I've heard." Marcel finished his business and joined Raz at the sink to wash his own hands. "Rumor has it you broke your convention fling promise."

Raz closed his eyes. "Who told you that?"

"Couple of the guys saw you walking to the hotel last night with a handsome young thing." Marcel fixed his tie and winked at Raz's reflection. "Said that you two had your hands all over each other, not that I'm surprised at all."

Placing his hands on either side of the sink, Raz took a deep breath. "Marcel..."

"Hey, you don't have to explain yourself to me, Razi." Marcel pat Raz on the back. "I didn't think you were serious anyway when you said you were going to avoid getting some ass. I just wanna know how good it was, and if he's got a friend."

Raz sighed. "It was a mistake."

"Well, of course it was. You have the worst taste in men that I've ever seen. But if you had a good time, you just need to take it at face value and remember you'll be leaving here in a few days and won't see this guy ever again—unless you were stupid and gave him your business card." Marcel narrowed his eyes and stood up straight, turning to face his friend. "You didn't do anything that stupid, right?"

The warmth of the tattoo now felt like fire against his skin, or at least that was what Raz believed it to be. "Of course not."

"Why don't I believe you?"

Raz laughed, moving away from the sink. "Trust me, Marcel, I'm pretty sure if I tell you about last night, you won't believe half the things that happened."

Marcel tilted his head, and Raz could feel his friend trying to find the truth in his words. After a moment, a bright smile broke out on Marcel's face. "Ha! The sex was good!"

Shaking his head, Raz led them out of the bathroom and back to the convention. "Yes, I can confirm that the sex was good. Amazing, even."

"Was it worth the trouble?"

As they entered the hallway leading to the seminar rooms, Raz spied Alard sitting on a bench with his laptop. He was focused on his typing, his earbuds in as he talked on his cell phone that peeked out of his back pocket. Alard seemed oblivious to the world around him, and Raz smiled at the intense focus he had on his work. "Yeah," he told Marcel, pulling him into a room a few feet from where Alard sat. "Even if it was a mistake, he was worth it."

CHAPTER SEVEN

The afternoon of research got interrupted when James called for an emergency consultation on a client case. Alard caught the streetcar to his office and scanned the documents his partner needed. Later, back at the convention center, while sitting with his laptop waiting on Raz to finish his lectures, James called again with notes to be dictated.

"Why can't you do this yourself?" Alard asked, plugging his earbuds in.

"Because I only have a tablet, and its swipe function can't tell a divorce from a divination." James's voice was quiet, which told Alard that James was still in the courthouse. "God help us if I have to try and swipe my client's name."

"You know you can pick up your fingers and type onto the screen keyboard, right?"

"I know how tablets work, Alard. That just takes too long."

"So, you called me as someone to dictate your notes to instead?"

"I'm making you feel like you're a part of the team!"

Alard laughed. "You suck, you know that right?"

"Yes, I know." Alard could hear the smug grin over the phone.

It took ten minutes for Alard to type the information into the court document, reading back each paragraph to make sure he got it correct.

"Alright, I'm emailing it to you now," he told James as he attached the document to the email.

"Thanks. I owe you."

"Yeah, you do." A stray thought came to Alard's mind, and he blinked. "Hey, James, does Catherine still work as an event coordinator for the city?"

"Sometimes." There was hesitation in James's voice. "Why?"

"I need information about a recent event there." Alard shoved his laptop back into his bag. "Think she could hook me up with contact information on the people?"

"You could ask her."

"She doesn't like me."

"Bullshit. She treats you like a lost puppy she found on the street," James pointed out. "She's my ex-wife—she *really* doesn't like me."

Alard sighed. "You know I wouldn't ask if I didn't need it."

There was a moment of muffled noise on the phone. Alard assumed James covered the mic so that he could talk to someone. When it cleared up, the background noise had changed to elevator music. "I'll text her and see if she's available for a drink after work. If we buy, she may actually use her words and not try to bite you."

"She does have a nasty bite." Alard's throat tightened, remembering the last time he and Catherine Wilson had gone toe to toe. He and James had stood in the backyard as Catherine threw James's possessions over the stairwell railing to feed the pile of clothes already on fire. Alard had tried to mediate to end the screaming and burn party before the cops arrived.

Alard was pretty sure it was the Xbox that nailed the back of his head, giving him a concussion that lasted for two days. He couldn't be sure, though, since that last part was a bit fuzzy. He did remember, however, that she had sent a large bouquet of flowers as an apology for hurting him.

"Part of why I married her, until she turned her temper on me. I'll let you know what she says."

"Thanks."

Alard hung up and took out his earbuds, draping them around his neck. The hallway was empty now that the next session of lectures had started. Alard thought he had seen Raz walking into a room out of the corner of his eye but wasn't sure.

A quick look at his phone screen told Alard he had about two hours until he was due to meet back up with Raz. He checked his email, calendar, and social medias in turn on his laptop to pass the time. His leg bounced under him and when he checked the time again, only fifteen minutes had passed.

He almost wished he had something to do—a case to work on, friends to meet up with, anything to occupy the next hour and forty-five minutes of his mind from the nervous energy coursing through his body. His schedule was barren, the result of tying up loose ends before leaving New Orleans for good. James was in court, so even going to the office to sit across from his best friend and annoy him wasn't possible.

Alard didn't need to get *another* cup of coffee.

His phone dinged, a bird chirp that he had assigned to only one contact in his phone. Alard checked the hallway, seeing if anyone was paying attention to him, and then opened the messaging app.

> When are you arriving back home?

Alard smirked, then replied:

> Soon. Got one more thing to settle before I cross over.

The tiny face in the contact bubble was smiling, pink eyes sparkling with delight. He had gifted his betrothed, Princess Meyda, a human cell phone to be able to contact him when he was in New Orleans. It wasn't always reliable—it depended solely on his makeshift Wi-Fi router wired through the passage between the two realms—but if she was visiting his parents, she was able to get a signal to send him messages. Otherwise, she had a few games and a handful of songs that she could play.

Meyda was addicted to Candy Crush. Alard found it adorable.

> Our parents are discussing the parade route again. They're worried that the trolls will act up when we hit the bridge.

Alard slid his laptop into his bag and went out into the courtyard. He didn't want to have to explain to anyone who asked what he was laughing about.

> I'm not surprised. Has anyone thought to offer them food as part of the celebration?

He found a shaded bench near the fountain and sat down. The faint spray of water that the breeze carried was refreshing against his face.

> Too bad you're not here to suggest it.

> Is it really that bad?

The answer didn't come right away. Alard closed his eyes, imagining his parents and Meyda's sitting across from each other in the parlor. Both trying to be regal while trying not to scream to get their own ways. The two families had been connected ever since their children had been betrothed to each other at the tender age of three. Alard and Meyda grew up together, bouncing back and forth from the two kingdoms so they could form a bond early on. Their parents, however, seem to grow more distant every year. Two kingdoms not united for a thousand years because of discussions just like this for generations.

> No one has pulled a weapon yet.

Alard laughed.

> That's impressive. I'm so proud of them.

> I miss you.

> I miss you too. It's just for a few more days.

> When this is over, I'm spending a week in the library. No visitors, no parties. Just me, my books, and my music.

> What will you build out of them this time?

The image of Meyda hiding in the huge library made Alard smile. He remembered as kids when she used to build herself a cave of books, and he would guard the cave while she read stories to him.

> A pirate ship like in that book you brought me back last time. You can be my parrot.

> I thought you wanted no visitors.

> You don't count.

> THANKS!

He laughed again, the nervous energy fading from his body.

There was a lag in her response. Alard stood up and paced around the park, shading his eyes when he came out of the shadow on the other side of the fountain. Sometimes Meyda's family left the castle before she was able to say goodbye—the phone was also hidden from her parents as they both disapproved of Alard's fascination with the human realm. Meyda could take care of herself, and Alard knew her parents wouldn't let anything happen to her, but he still worried. The reaction was just that of a big brother fussing that his little sister was getting herself into trouble again.

Which, of course, was the center of the problem in their betrothal. Except he was the one known for getting in trouble.

The phone dinged again.

> I chose pink for the floral arrangements.

He grimaced.

> What kind of pink?

> The kind you hate, obviously. It is so obnoxious. I hope it will scare away half the kingdom.

> Which was your plan all along?

> Of course.

There was a pink poop emoji at the end. Alard shook his head, laughing to himself.

> Time to go.

The second text came immediately after.

> I'll talk to you soon.

> Don't do anything stupid until then.

Alard looked at his forearm, the tattoo hidden under his light blue button-down shirt. The guilt ate at his stomach. While he and Meyda both knew each other's opinions on this marriage, he couldn't help but worry about how she was going to take the news.

No, she wasn't going to hear about it. Alard and Raz would solve this before he had to go home, and he could tell her later when the wedding drama was over. Maybe then she would only throw something at him about his stupidity.

He hoped no one in the fairy realm would ever learn about this. Alard didn't even want to think of all the ramifications it would cause. He wasn't lying about starting a war; he just hadn't told Raz that war was just the start of the problems.

The end would be death, and if they didn't solve it soon, that death would be Raz's.

CHAPTER EIGHT

When the lecture was over, Raz sprang from the room like a child heading to recess. There were no other lectures he had planned to attend that evening, and except for walking around the vendor room, he had done almost everything he came to the convention for. He had one last lecture to give Thursday afternoon, and his flight home was that night.

It wasn't a lot of time to get some kind of fairy annulment, but he had yet to fail on anything he worked on...well, mostly. He didn't count the "teach your ferret to swim" marketing campaign he had taken on for a friend of a friend. That campaign—and the actual program—was doomed to fail from the get-go.

Alard had been sitting in the hallway earlier, and Raz hoped that he hadn't left. The chair Alard had occupied was vacant now, which left Raz wandering the lobby to rout him out.

Three women leaned against the glass window overlooking the courtyard. Raz followed their line of sight to see Alard leaning against a tree, laptop bag behind him, eyes closed, and fingers laced behind his head. They whispered to each other about the "gorgeous man" out there and what they would do to him if he was in their bed.

Avoiding them—even if their ideas were good and he could offer details

—Raz exited the conference center. He walked to Alard's side and nudged his leg. "You alright there?"

Alard opened his eyes, looking up at Raz with a beaming smile. "I'm super, thanks for asking."

Raz held out a hand to help Alard up. "You get any further in your research?"

"I'm waiting for a phone call to discuss it over drinks." Alard stood, dusting the dirt and leaves from his pants. "It shouldn't be long now."

"So, do we have enough time to go back to my room so I can change?"

"Yeah, sure."

They made their way back to the hotel, the lobby seeming deserted now that the brides and grooms were married and had returned to their homes. There was no fight for an elevator, and Raz loosened his tie as they rode up to his floor.

"Would you mind if I left my laptop here?" Alard asked as they reached his floor, and he followed Raz down the hallway. "I don't really want to trek back to the office to drop it off at the moment."

"Do we need it for this meeting?" Raz opened the door for Alard to precede him into the room, letting it shut behind them.

"No, I can do almost anything we'd need on my phone. I only needed it for a quick project with James while you were being lectured."

Raz made an affirming noise with his throat as he hung his suit jacket in the closet, followed by the tie. Alard went to the hotel window and stared out, but as Raz watched in the reflection, Alard kept his face forward while his eyes focused on the reflection of Raz's hand pulling down a zipper and pushing his pants off his hips.

"You okay over there?" Raz asked, walking to the closet to hang his pants up. He stood in just his unbuttoned top and black boxers. Even with the window reflection, Raz knew it didn't do justice to the details of his body. He put a lot of work into keeping himself healthy, mostly to enjoy the feel of eyes taking him in. It balanced out the looks of hatred he still got occasionally.

"Yeah," Alard said, a roughness to his voice. "Just thinking."

"About what?"

"What to have for dinner." The answer came fast, and Raz suspected that dinner was the last thing on Alard's mind.

A smirk came to Raz's lips, and he looked towards the window, catching Alard's eye. "Oh really?"

Alard blushed, turning around and rubbing the back of his neck. "I just, I wasn't trying..."

"You can look, you know. It's not like you haven't seen it all already." Raz dropped his shirt into an open suitcase, a few other pieces of crumpled laundry already piled inside. "I don't mind."

"I wasn't sure if you'd be comfortable with it."

Standing in just his boxers and socks now, Raz held his hands out to his side. "If I wasn't, I would have gone to change in the bathroom."

"Point taken." Alard took a step closer. "Though I will admit, we really didn't get to appreciate this part last night."

Raz watched where Alard's gaze crept along his body. Raz checked the time on the bedside clock, seeing how late it was getting. "See, here I'd usually make a joke about how if you want it, you should put a ring on it."

The song quote hit Alard, and he looked up and laughed. "I already have."

Raz watched Alard a moment later. He wasn't sure if he wanted Alard to touch him or not. The previous night had truly been wonderful. Most of the time, these flings were over in a day, and someone else would step into their place in a long line of bedfellows. A part of him wanted to grab the lawyer, throw him on the bed, and try to recreate that electricity. Even now, he could still feel how his body tingled while Alard's hands had slid down along his stomach, teasing about going lower. The way they guided each other in their pleasure. The softness of Alard's hair as he stroked it, easing Alard back from his orgasm. The soft whispers against each other's lips, breathing promises to one another in their moment of passion; promises that the stark light of reality had turned into lies.

The other part of him, the businessman, knew it was the worst thing he could do. They were trying to find a way to break this bond. Succumbing to carnal desires would only make the separation harder—not to mention the added guilt they'd both feel over how it would complicate Alard's *other* betrothal. Raz was already imagining a life if they could stay married, a dream that couldn't...shouldn't be realized.

He couldn't keep Alard. Chasing this fantasy would do neither of them good, so he needed to control himself and his desires.

"But it's probably best we don't." Raz walked to the dresser, reached for a polo shirt, and shrugged it on.

"Yeah." Alard went back to staring out the window—actually staring this time—as Raz hunted for a clean pair of jeans and slipped them on as well. When the headboard thumped as Raz sat down on the bed, Alard turned back.

"I'm sorry. I didn't mean to be presumptuous," Alard assured him.

"You weren't." Raz pulled on his sneakers, focused on the laces. "Honestly, if we weren't in this particular situation, I would be all for calling room service and spending the rest of the night in bed with you."

"But not now."

Raz shook his head. "I don't sleep with married men." Alard snorted at that, and Raz chuckled when he realized what he had said. "I meant you and your..."

"I know." Alard moved to sit next to Raz and put his hand on Raz's knee. "I would too, if I didn't have to leave."

Raz slid his hand on top of Alard's. "So why did you?" he breathed.

Alard stared at their fingers, then threaded them together. "I don't know. I wasn't planning on it."

"Neither was I. In fact, I swore to my friend Marcel that the last thing I would do was have a convention fling."

"But...?"

Raz took a deep breath. "But...I felt like my running into you three times in twenty-four hours was some weird sort of sign. I mean, how were you in the same lobby of the hotel I was staying in? The same Starbucks? The same nightclub? The probability in a city this large, I can't even compute."

A hint of a smile graced Alard's face. "Magic?"

They both laughed, stopping only when Alard's phone rang. He reached into his back pocket and saw CATHERINE on the screen. Alard swiped to answer it and then put the phone on speaker. "Hey Catty Cat."

"Why am I on speakerphone?" The pinched voice sent chills down Raz's spine. He could feel the flames of her annoyance licking each word. "If James is there—"

"He's not," Alard replied quickly. "But someone is. Raz, this is Catherine. She's the best event coordinator in New Orleans."

"Damn right I am." The flames died down to a soft, pleased rumble. "How can I help you boys?"

"Were you involved with that huge mass wedding down at the convention center last night?" Alard shifted to put the phone on the bed between himself and Raz.

"No. Hold on though, I can find out who was." Catherine hummed to herself. "Do I want to know why you're looking for this?"

"Probably not."

"Wouldn't have anything to do with rumors of an illegal fairy marriage in town yesterday, would it?" Raz and Alard looked up at each other in shock. Catherine's laughter followed. "I'm going to assume that is a yes from the jump in both your heartbeats."

"You can hear our hearts?" Raz choked out.

"I'm a vampire, of course I can," Catherine replied matter-of-factly.

"Vampire?" He glared at Alard, because *of course* vampires were real. What was he thinking?

"Oh, sweetie. Alard, tell me you didn't marry a *human* last night."

Alard shrugged at Raz, mouthing *I'll explain later*. "It wasn't intentional."

"Have you told Meyda?"

"Hell no! I'm trying to figure out a way to fix this mess so she never has to know."

Catherine clicked her tongue at them. "First, that's the wrong thing to do. She will gut you if you hide this from her. Second, you know things like this ripple through the lay lines. It won't take long for the news to leave this realm and get back to yours."

Alard flopped back onto the bed with a big sigh. "Which is why the faster we fix this, the better."

Raz shook his head, getting up from the bed while Alard and Catherine continued to talk fairy world politics. He knew he should pay attention, but with each new revelation, Raz felt his head pounding.

Vampires were real. They were in New Orleans. His eyes flit around the people on the street below. The sun was out, so these people couldn't be vampires. Right?

Raz shouldn't be surprised by this after learning about magic and fairies already, but there was a limit to what his brain could take, it seemed. What's next, werewolves?

No, werewolves were probably real too. He might as well just admit it now and be happy if he was proved wrong.

"Huh, this is more complicated than I thought." Raz tuned back in as Catherine's voice took on a curious tone. "I may have to go down to the conference center to get the information."

"Will that take long?" Alard asked, his hands tapping against the bed.

"I don't think so. I'm over here at Harrah's finishing up a project, so it's not a long walk."

"Thank you, Catherine," Raz said, returning to stand beside the bed.

"Oh, he has manners. That's new." The purring in her voice was back. "How about this, Alard—you two meet me at the speakeasy around nine tonight. It'll give me enough time to finish up here and work my magic."

"We can do that." Alard looked up at Raz, who nodded. "See you tonight."

Alard ended the call, and Raz snickered. "So, vampires?"

Groaning, Alard hid his face behind his hands. "Yes, vampires are real. Fairies, trolls, witches..."

"Werewolves?"

"Yup."

Raz grinned to himself. "So pretty much every myth and fairy tale?"

"Not the Loch Ness Monster." Alard held one arm in the air in objection. "That's a bunch of drunk ancient Scots screwing with the English to keep them out."

"Makes sense." Raz reached down and grabbed Alard's hand to pull him back up. "Come on. Sitting around here isn't going to get us anywhere. Let's get some dinner while we wait."

Alard stood, and for a moment, they stood pressed against each other. Alard lifted his chin to look into Raz's eyes. Neither moved, unsure of where they stood with the other with all that had happened. Alard's warmth heated the space between them, and Raz remembered just how hot it could become. The feeling of Alard's body pressed against his, the firm chest hidden behind the clothing. Raz longed to press his lips against the skin, tasting the salt as Alard's heart thumped against the kiss.

As he leaned forward to kiss Alard, the other man stepped back and away from Raz. The green eyes stared at the floor, Alard's shoulders slumped. "We should go," he whispered.

You can't keep him, he reminded himself. The spell now broken, Raz took a deep breath and nodded. "Any suggestions for dinner?"

"What form of New Orleans cuisine are you thinking about? Tell me the food, I'll tell you the place."

Raz thought for a moment, then shrugged. "You're the local. I'm open for anything, just make it good."

"Then I think I know just the place."

CHAPTER NINE

"When you suggested choosing the place for dinner, I was expecting something a bit fancier than a deli."

"You wanted something authentic, where all the locals go. I'm just giving you what you want."

Alard knew he shouldn't enjoy the frustrated look on Raz's face, but he did. The wrinkles that formed above his nose, sliding down between the nose and eyes—they were cute. It was not the right word; he needed something more masculine than "cute" to express it.

It was hard to find the right words to describe a lot of things about Raz, but the hardest right now was what they were to each other. A fun one-night stand turned into marriage was not at all how Alard had pictured this going, and yet there was a small part of him that was...happy. It was like this was where he was meant to be, with *who* he was meant to be with.

He knew it wasn't, though. Alard's whole life had been planned out for him since he was born. At least, that was how it felt. Yet here he stood next to one of the sweetest men he had ever met, and Alard knew for all his wealth and power in the fairy realm, he couldn't keep him. Well, he technically could, but Raz deserves a life better than a human consort of the future king. He'd just be seen as an object to be toyed with, one that could be used to manipulate him.

All that work for a career that Raz had mentioned would be wasted, and Alard didn't want Raz to resent him for it. That would destroy both of them.

The line inched closer to the counter, and a waitress walked by with menus. Raz took one before leaning into Alard. "So, what's good here?"

"Everything." Alard's answer was automatic. "However, in accordance with our terms, you're going to want either the muffuletta or the original po'boy."

"We could get one of each and share?"

"Yes," Alard agreed, "but I'm not a big fan of olives."

Raz stood up to look over the menu. "Which one has olives?"

"Muffuletta. But no, it's fine, I'm good with this plan." Alard took the menu out of Raz's hand and put it down on a table piled high with dirty dishes. "Trust me."

When they reached the front, Alard did the ordering and added fries and sweet tea to the order. They were given a table card and told to find a seat. However, every seat was taken except for the one table covered in dishes.

"I guess we wait," Raz said.

"Nope." Alard walked over to the table with the dirty dishes. "Sit," he told Raz as he gathered up the dishes and walked them back towards the kitchen. It took him two trips, plus a quick stop in the bathroom, before he returned to the table.

Raz just stared at him, and Alard knew his ears were turning pink. "What?"

"I've just never seen someone help like that to get a table."

Alard laughed. "I wasn't always a lawyer. Bussed tables just like everyone else when I first got here. These guys have more customers than help, so why not lend a hand?"

"You just keep surprising me," Raz stated.

The food arrived, a large pile of fries between two sandwiches on the tray. In the corner was a large slice of pecan pie that they hadn't ordered. "I just want to help people, that's all." He pointed out the pie. "Though it doesn't always go without its own rewards."

Alard cut the two sandwiches in half and they both dug in. Raz made delightful noises in the back of his throat when he took his first bite of the muffuletta. They reminded Alard of the sounds the other man had made while Alard had kissed his way down Raz's body once they were back at the hotel. Alard had never heard it before—a mix of a gasp, whine, and groan—and he couldn't get enough of it. He spent the rest of last night seeing how many times he could get Raz to make that very noise. Hearing it again brought back the memories of the pleasure from last night. Alard wanted nothing more than to drag Raz back to his hotel room and see what spots his lips missed. Yet he knew he couldn't.

If Catherine knew about what happened, even before she had the faces and names, Alard had no doubt that the rest of the supernatural community was in on the gossip. When it reached home, his parents...

No, he couldn't think of that right now. He needed to free Raz from this bond before Alard pulled him into something the man hadn't asked for. No matter how *right* this felt between them, there were things more important than his happiness at stake. That was why he had pulled away from Raz in the hotel room; he couldn't risk letting himself get too attached.

"You okay?" Raz asked, wiping his mouth.

Alard snapped out of his thoughts. "Yeah. Just thinking, that's all." Raz didn't reply, just watched him as he nibbled on a fry. "I'm trying to figure out how far these rumors might have gone in a single day."

Raz nodded. "You're worried about Meyda finding out?"

"Yes, but not as much as my parents."

"I see. Your parents wouldn't be happy that you married a human."

"No, it's not that." Alard didn't want to have this conversation, least of all here. It was long, complicated, and sounded just a bit crazy to anyone who hadn't lived among fairies for a time. "Honestly, I think my parents would both love you, circumstances notwithstanding."

Raz smiled at that. "That so?"

"Yeah. My mom would be thrilled with your manners and good taste. My dad would love your business sense."

"And Meyda?"

Alard's breath caught in his throat a moment. "She, uh...actually, I'm not sure what she'd think right now. It'll be somewhere between highly amused and extremely pissed."

Raz hummed around his bite of sandwich. "Sounds about right."

"What about your parents?" Alard asked. "What would they think about me?"

"I don't know. I haven't seen them since I graduated college." Raz's eyes focused on his sandwich, and Alard cursed himself for bringing up what seemed to be a sensitive topic.

"I'm sorry, I didn't know."

Raz shrugged. "When I started to find myself, a lot of what I discovered went against our faith." He grabbed a fry but just stared at it while he talked. "They immigrated here from Egypt, and the idea of having a gay son went against the Quran. They were more than happy to send me to a college away far from home, especially since my younger sister was hitting her teens, and they didn't want me to influence her."

Alard took Raz's hand as he explained, giving Raz an anchor out of the memories. "When I finished college," he continued, "I came home and found that my parents had made arrangements for me to marry a woman from Virginia. She was previously divorced and wanted children badly."

Alard hummed at that. "Sounds familiar."

Raz gave a sad laugh. "Yeah, it does. We had a big blowup, and I left home and moved into the district. The woman tried to reach out, but I didn't want anything to do with her. Looking back, I wish I had done it differently so she wouldn't be hurt, but I was young and stupid and didn't know any better. But because of this, I haven't talked to my parents in over ten years. I keep tabs on them through my sister, though."

At the end, Raz looked up, and Alard saw the hint of tears being held back. "I'm so sorry, Raz," Alard said, squeezing his hand.

Raz squeezed Alard's hand back once before pulling back. "Now my sister...that's someone you'd have to win over."

The change in conversation was so abrupt emotionally that Alard wasn't sure if it was proper to laugh at that. He did smile though, curious about this sibling now. "Is that so?"

"Yeah." Raz wiped the escaped tear away with a hand, a smile coming to his face as well. "She didn't care if I was straight or gay, just that as long as I was happy...and married someone who would treat me well or she would come kick their ass on my behalf."

They both laughed at that, drawing stares from the other diners. Others glared, watching them like hawks wanting their table. Mindful of them, Raz and Alard finished up their sandwiches and left, taking the napkin-wrapped pie slice with them.

They nibbled on it as they walked towards the river. The sun was setting, casting the sky in shades of orange, pink, and purple. The steamboat chugged along the Mississippi with its load of tourists, blowing its whistle when Alard and Raz waved at it.

Alard was going to miss this place when he was gone. The river that ran between his and Meyda's kingdoms might be lush and better smelling, but it didn't hold the same history that this one had. Coffee and beignets were foreign to the fairy realm, and Alard couldn't cook a hot dog, let alone try and fry his own dough. The scents of home were comforting, but they weren't New Orleans.

"You've got that brooding look on your face again," Raz spoke, crumpling up the now empty napkin and putting it in his pocket. "What's on your mind?"

"Just thinking about what I'm going to miss when I'm gone."

Raz took Alard's hand, weaving their fingers together. "You do that, and you're going to sacrifice the time you have now to enjoy it."

Alard snorted. "True."

Raz looked at his watch on the other wrist. "We still have two hours before meeting Catherine. What do you suggest we do?"

Alard thought for a moment, his eyes taking in the river before looking up into Raz's. "Back in the hotel room, did you want to...you know?"

Raz blushed. "Maybe. Did you?"

"Yeah, but I didn't think it would be a good idea. Seeing that we're trying to get rid of this." He motioned to their tattoos, which, coincidently, happened to be on the arms that had their fingers linked. "I didn't want to take advantage of you."

"*So* not taking advantage here." Raz tugged him closer. "I'm more worried about ramifications you might have to deal with."

"Well, until this is undone, we're married. We can't get any more married by sleeping together."

"But you'll feel guilty anyway."

Alard nodded at Raz's correct assumption. "I'm just worried that we may get too attached, and it will be harder for us to separate. As it is, I'm already said that I'll never see you again after I leave."

"And remember, I don't sleep with married men," Raz added.

"Except the one you're married to, right?"

Their laughter was drowned out by the jazz band starting to play along Chartres Street in front of the cathedral. Raz looked at the musicians, and Alard pulled him closer to the makeshift band stage. They sat on a bench, arms linked, listening to the songs as the sun set and the stars stared to wink into existence. Couples walked by, tossing money into the open saxophone case near the band. Some stopped to listen, and one took a moment to pull his wife into his arms and sway to the slow, romantic beat.

"I wish I could see the magic around us like you do," Raz breathed against Alard's ear. "It must be beautiful right now."

Alard smiled, turning his head to lean in and press their cheeks together. "Not all magic is fairy made. It looks beautiful right now because the city and people are making their own kind of magic."

The band switched songs, still on the slow side, but more cheerful. On a whim, Alard stood, then held out a hand to Raz. "Care to dance?" Raz looked around, but Alard knew no one would pay attention to them at this time of night. He motioned again, and Raz took his hand and let himself be pulled up.

"You sure?" Raz asked.

"Wouldn't ask if I didn't want to." Alard guided Raz's arms around his shoulders, then slipped his own around Raz's waist.

They swayed in time to the music, stepping closer to each other unconsciously with each key change in the song. It wasn't long before Alard realized they had moved close enough that he could lay his head on Raz's shoulder.

"Why do we keep ending up here?" Raz asked.

It took Alard a moment to realize that Raz wasn't talking about the pavilion. "I don't know. But it just feels right."

Raz started to respond, but was cut off as Alard tilted his head to kiss him. Their lips ghosted against one another, testing the waters after a long day of frustrating dead ends. Alard felt a spark of happiness ignite in his heart, and he shifted to get even closer to Raz, a hand rising up to cup his cheek so that he could pull the other man in and deepen the kiss.

They were aware of the applause when the band finished their song and quickly separated. Raz took a quick look at his watch. An hour had already passed while they enjoyed the riverside. "How far is it to this speakeasy?" he asked, his face flushed.

"Not far." Alard wanted to lean back in for another kiss, but Raz moved another step away. It was a stark reminder that what he'd just done was going against their agreement. He just found himself unable to resist.

"We should probably go," Raz said, his eyes looking at Alard's lips. "We don't want to be late, and I could use a drink."

Alard nodded, tearing his eyes away from the other man. He realized that getting drunk was a great idea. "How do you feel about absinthe?"

Raz gave him a confused look. "I don't think I've had absinthe before. That's the drink with the green fairy, right?"

Alard laughed. "Yes, that would be it, but the only green fairy you'll see is me, I promise."

"I'll give it a try. What's the worst that could happen?"

Alard dropped his head and sighed. "Now you're just tempting fate."

"What? Why?"

"What's the worst that could happen?" Alard made air quotes with his fingers as he repeated Raz's words. "There are times when you just don't want to say that, like when dealing with magic, vampires, or, say, hand grenades."

"Hand grenades?" Raz asked, chuckling.

"Yeah. I mean, that one should be obvious."

Raz just shook his head. "Sometimes the strangest things come out of your mouth. You know that, right?"

"Then make me shut up." Alard smirked, trying to tempt Raz into giving him another kiss.

"Later," Raz winked, then blushed and looked anywhere but at Alard. "Drinks first."

"Right." Alard took a final look at the river and saw a tiny shadow moving in the distance. It reminded him of something. "You're not allergic to cats, right?"

"No...why?"

"You'll see."

Raz motioned for Alard to lead the way, and they linked arms again as they walked away from the river and back to the French Quarter. Streetlights were on, and the neon glow in the distance called to them, inviting them back into the never-ending party.

CHAPTER TEN

"So, the cat's the bouncer?"

"Yup."

"And I need to pet her to get in?"

"That's how it works."

Raz stared down at Misty. Misty licked her front paw, the pink tongue a contrast to the tawny fur. Alard, the smug son of a bitch, sat on the stairway's top step next to the cat.

"What happens to people who are allergic to cats?" Raz asked, crouching down to look at Misty at her eye level. Intelligent orange eyes lifted to watch him while continuing to clean herself. "Or have a fear of them?"

Alard tipped his head to the side, a look Raz linked to the other man trying to decide on the right words to answer with. *Must be a lawyer thing.* "I don't know. Misty?"

They both looked at the cat. Misty lowered her paw, stood up, and arched her back high into the air as she stretched. She gave a rumbling purr and pressed the top of her head against Alard's arm, which he automatically lifted to scritch behind Misty's ears.

Raz waited a moment longer before holding out his hands in acquiescence. "What did she say?"

"She's a cat, Raz. Cats can't talk," Alard laughed.

The French doors behind Alard opened and a woman with a mohawk poked her head out. "You two going to loiter on the steps all night or come in?"

Misty padded away from the men to jump on top of the bureau on the landing. She laid down, then turned her attention back to Raz. Her reflective eyes flashed, making Raz feel as if the cat had passed judgement on his being with Alard.

"Who was that?" Raz asked, nodding his head toward the woman.

"Monique. She's the bartender here." Alard tugged on Raz's sleeve to get his attention. "Come on. First drink is on me."

"I think all drinks are on you," Raz stated as he crossed over the threshold and squinted as his eyes adjusted to the dim atmosphere lighting. "You're enjoying this a little too much, aren't you?"

"Enjoying what?" Alard turned and walked backward further into the room.

"Torturing me with my lack of knowledge of all thing fairy."

Alard gave a quick look around the room, but the three occupants in the lounge weren't paying attention to them. Alard smirked. "Okay, maybe a little bit."

"And that is why you're buying."

Alard led them to a pair of stools at a kitchen window counter. A lit kitchenette faced them, highlighted by two beverage dispensers; one filled with a green liquid, the other red. Raz leaned forward to read the tiny handwriting on the signs next to them. "So that's the absinthe?"

"Handmade and better than anything you'll find in this country." Two fingers, long with pointed red nails, walked along Alard's shoulder, and Raz jumped. He hadn't heard anyone approach them.

"Catherine," Alard said as Catherine ran her hands down his shoulders and chest to hug him from behind. A flash of jealousy gripped Raz's mind, making his jaw clench as he took in the tall woman. Her blonde hair was pulled up into a messy bun, tendrils curled and resting on the shoulders of the sharp red jacket that matched her nails and heels. The suit gave her trim figure a professional look, the red standing out from the white blouse and black slacks.

She pressed her cheek against Alard's head affectionately. "What am I to do with you, child?" Her voice held a fondness that wasn't of a lover, but that of a mother or older sister. The jealousy faded a bit, and Raz rubbed his jaw to ease the soreness from having clenched it.

Alard looked up at her as he tried to look innocent. "Pet me and tell me I'm pretty?"

Catherine laughed and pushed herself back up, ruffling Alard's hair as she turned to face Raz. Her eyes, a silver gray, cut right into him as her red lips pursed together. "Well, I have to say, you do have fabulous taste, Alard. He looks delicious."

"You're not serious, right?" The urge to run away from a predator took hold, but Alard put a hand on Raz's knee to steady him.

"No, she's not." Alard gave Catherine a look. "She's just teasing you."

"I wasn't joking about Alard's taste, though." Catherine smiled, holding her hand out. "Pleasure to meet you...Raz, right?"

"Yes." He shook her hand, feeling the tight grip of her hand. "So, were you able to find any answers?"

"Straight to the point." Catherine made her way around the kitchenette wall and pulled three glasses from a wire rack. "I was able to get the name of the company, which, sadly, is based in India." She filled two of the glasses with the green absinthe, then set them on the counter and reached for something under the counter.

"Can we get in touch with them though?" Alard asked, reaching over to take a glass.

Catherine slapped his hand without looking. "Not possible. They are traveling across South America this month, and reception is spotty at best where they are going." She held a carafe of a fruity smelling concoction, which she then poured a small measure into each glass. Tiny bits of fruit floated in the absinthe before Catherine stirred each one, then topped them with candied flowers.

"Guess that means we can't reverse the ceremony." Alard sighed as Catherine handed him one of the wineglasses.

"So, where does that leave us?" Raz took the other glass and had a small sip. The flavor of wild berries burst against his tongue, the alcohol then coating everything with a smooth warmth. He looked at the glass in shock, then Catherine. "This is amazing."

"Thank you." Catherine sipped the red absinthe she had poured herself straight. "As for what else you boys can do, I'm not going to pretend I know how to help."

"No magical answers?" Raz asked.

"Magic is not my forte." Catherine looked over her shoulder to the lounge where Monique, her hair now a bright blue, sat on the coffee table across from the three patrons on the couch. "If you want to use magic to get out of this mess, she's the one to ask."

"Magic is what got us into this mess." Alard pointed out. "I was hoping not to use it to get out of it."

"You may not have a choice." Catherine leaned on the counter, giving Alard a smile full of perfect white teeth. "Last time I checked; divorce wasn't an option in your realm. I can talk with James, do some research to see if we can find a way to word a divorce petition that might negate the ceremony, but I wouldn't lay all my hopes on it."

"Back up a moment—divorce isn't a thing in your realm?" Raz asked. While listening to the conversation, he was building up a list of facts in his head. When he was in over his head in a situation, the list helped keep him afloat.

His mental notebook on Alard's world was almost full.

"Divorce is a human thing." Catherine ran her finger along the lip of her glass, a soft hum filling the air between them. "But Alard isn't human anymore." She looked at Raz, leaning closer and taking a deep breath. "And you are pure human. A very nice representation, indeed."

"You're not his type," Alard spoke, and Raz heard a growl in the words. Catherine jumped up, putting distance between her and Raz.

There was something else in Catherine's words that Raz needed more information on. "What do you mean by Alard not being human anymore?" he asked.

Catherine grinned, then looked at Alard. "Ah, looks like it's story time."

Alard was still glaring at Catherine, but he then took a deep breath and looked back at Raz. "It's not a long story. I was born human and abandoned at birth. It was during that time that the king and queen in the Kingdom of Earth and Sky asked the pooka to bring them an unwanted human child. They found me first, brought me to the fairy realm, and the king and queen, my parents, gifted me with enough magic to change me into a fairy."

Raz logged that information in his "fairies are real" file folder in his brain: *Enough magic can turn a human into a fairy.*

He was about to speak again when Monique walked through the archway into the kitchenette half of the speakeasy. In the other room, the three patrons were leaving through the French doors. "You all realize that your voices carry in this place, yes? I don't like hypnotizing humans to make them forget their time up here."

"Better you than me," Catherine stated, sliding out from behind the windowsill bar and walking into the living room. "Your way doesn't leave marks."

Alard stood up and hugged Monique. She kissed Alard's cheek, then looked at Raz. "Who is your friend, Alard?"

"Raz," Catherine answered from her velvet armchair before either man could speak. "Alard's husband."

Alard and Raz both glared at Catherine, who shrugged innocently. Monique continued to stare at Raz, then held out her hand. "Can I see your palm, Raz?" Raz looked at Alard, who nodded. He hesitated, but rested his right hand in hers, palm up. Monique leaned forward, her fingers starting to brush along the lines.

Her touch tingled, a tingling sensation that Raz struggled not to laugh at. It shifted quickly to a warm touch, almost as if a blanket was wrapping around him to keep him warm and safe. Any doubts Raz had about Monique's intentions faded away. Instead, he believed that Monique would protect him from any harm—which was crazy since he had just met the woman—yet Raz knew it was true.

Monique murmured to herself, no discernable words that Raz could make out. Her gaze left his palm, staring right into his eyes. The gold flecks of her eyes drew him in as she caressed his cheek. Raz smiled and leaned into the touch. The warm safety increased like a protective shell forming around him.

"You have a good heart, Razi Miller," Monique whispered, a soft smile shared just between them. There was a bond between them now, something Raz couldn't explain, similar to the marriage bond, but he knew that if he was in trouble, Monique would be there to help.

She patted his cheek and stood up. The warmth faded, and Monique winked before she walked behind the bar. "I want to know more about this marriage," she stated while fixing herself a drink.

Alard led Raz to sit on the velvet couch next to Catherine's chair. It was comfortable, sinking in just enough to relax, but not something to stay in for long periods of time. Monique joined them a moment later, dragging the piano bench over to sit around the coffee table with them.

Alard explained what had happened, leaving out the more colorful moments in the last two days. Monique nodded occasionally but, otherwise, her face didn't reveal what she was thinking. When "story time" ended, Monique took a long drink from her glass.

"You boys have gotten yourself into a big pickle," Monique stated. "Bonding magic is very old magic, going back before the separation of the realms. I mean back in the days of djinns, oracles, and fairy godmothers old. That kind of magic is almost extinct these days, since it was tied to both realms. I haven't seen a djinn or oracle for centuries."

"Centuries?" Raz asked. "Just how old are you?"

Catherine laughed. "It's never nice to ask a woman their age," she pointed out.

"Let's just go with *old*," Monique stated with a smile.

"What about fairy godmothers? Has anyone seen them?" Alard asked.

Monique shook her head. "Godmothers are very rare. They started dying out as more and more generations believed that fairies weren't real, just characters found in children's stories. Children stopped wishing with serious intention for overcoming problems, and instead just wished for material things. By the time children become adults, they've lost their belief in magic, and the godmother moves on to watch over another child."

"Do you know of any?" Raz asked.

Monique gave Raz a small smile. "Part of the rules of a fairy godmother is that they can't reveal themselves, or others like them. So even if I did, I wouldn't be able to tell you. They only reveal themselves to their chosen child in their time of greatest need."

"Guess that kills that option, since you're an adult now and all," Alard sighed.

Raz reached for his drink while shaking his head. "I really should have skipped this conference," he stated before taking a gulp of his drink. "I could have been at a food and wine festival instead."

"You know I didn't intend for this to happen," Alard said. The hurt in his words made Raz look over. Alard stared at his hands, not meeting Raz's eyes.

"I know," Raz told him, taking Alard's hand and squeezing it. "And I don't regret my time with you. I'm just not a fan of scenarios that I can't control."

"Unfortunately, I have a feeling it's going to get worse before it gets better," Alard stated. There was an apology in the look Alard gave him.

"Why's that?"

Before Alard could answer, there was a scratch on the kitchenette window. Monique walked over and looked out, then opened it. A hummingbird flew in, then did three circles around Alard's head before dropping something into his lap and flying back out.

Alard picked up a walnut from his lap. He looked at Monique first, but the older woman shrugged. Catherine gave a sharp laugh, grabbing Alard's glass and going to refill it.

"Do I want to know what that is?" Raz asked.

"It's a message." Alard twisted the cap off the acorn and pulled out a folded piece of paper. Raz stood up and walked to his side. The message had a set of symbols in green ink the color of Alard's eyes.

"What does it say?"

"It's from my father." Alard's shoulders slumped, and he took a deep breath before looking up at Raz. "I'm being ordered home. Now."

CHAPTER ELEVEN

They walked along a street in the Garden District just as the church bells tolled midnight. Streetlights, metal ornate tops with flower baskets hanging off prongs, guided their way. Alard gripped Raz's hand, not because of the hour, but because he needed reassurance that everything was going to be alright.

"These houses are amazing," Raz stated, taking in the unique southern architecture that the district was known for. Everything from modern designs to 1800s plantation homes had planted their roots in the blocks northwest of the French Quarter.

"I like how each one of them is different." Alard stopped them in front of a large green and white home. "There are so many places where the community homes look like they were made with a cookie cutter. Here, you get to see personality. It even shows the history of the city as it grows when you gauge where the city boundaries were."

"So, when in history are we now?"

Alard laughed. "I think somewhere in the nineteen forties. Though this house was built about ten years ago."

"Oh? How do you know that?"

"Because it's mine." Alard pulled Raz along and opened the white picket fence gate. A series of large, flat stones created a path from the gate to the front steps of the house. A row of flowers lined either side of the path, the bright colors standing out from the simpler color scheme of the exterior.

Large white pillars rose from the porch to the second-floor balcony of the plantation-styled home. Dark brown hardwood floors made up the porch, complete with white rocking chairs on one side, a planter with flowers on the other. The door was made of frosted glass with dark green wood for inserts and a frame. A two-person porch swing was further down the right side of the porch, swinging gently in the breeze.

The second-floor balcony had a metal railing along the edge, the design more at home on the balcony in the French Quarter. The plantation pillars were set back from the edge of the balcony on the second floor, more decorative as they held up the roof. Flower baskets hung between each of the pillars on both balconies.

"This is yours?" Captivated by the details, Raz slowly walked up the path. Alard enjoyed the fascination on his face, watching the stress melt off and almost reverse his age. Raz looked so much younger when he smiled; more innocent than Alard had seen in a human his age.

"Technically, it belongs to both James and me. We run...ran most of our law firm out of my office here." The sign for their firm was gone from the front yard, having moved with James to the downtown closet of an office that he rented.

Raz looked up at the porch ceiling, watching fans slowly turn when a firm breeze drifted over them, the swing creaking a moment later as it was also buffeted by the wind. "It's amazing. What'll happen to it?"

"No idea. We were thinking of turning it into a vacation rental." Alard sat on the porch steps, patting them for Raz to join him. "I'm hoping that I'll still get to come back now and then to see my friends, and I'll need the place."

"Why wouldn't you be able to?"

Alard looked up at the stars, watching them for a minute before speaking. "I should probably tell you what we're walking into. You see, the whole reason I'm betrothed is because I'm the heir to one of the two fairy kingdoms in our realm."

Raz blinked. "Come again?"

"You heard me." Alard turned his head, catching the wide-eyed look on Raz's face.

"When you said that the King and Queen were your parents...I didn't realize that you were their only child."

Alard nodded. "My mother had troubles getting, or staying, pregnant. My father was the one who urged my mother to consider adoption so she wouldn't have to go through any more loss."

"So, a fairy prince..." It wasn't a question. Alard could see that Raz's brain was connecting the dots from the last two days, so he waited for a barrage of questions from Raz. "Does that make me your fairy princess?"

Alard laughed so loudly that he slapped his hands over his mouth before he risked waking the neighbors. Tears pricked his eyes as he watched Raz's lips turn up into a smirk. "No," Alard gasped when he regained his ability to speak. "No, I already have one of those."

"Meyda, right?"

"Yeah. You're more like my knight in shining armor."

Raz shrugged, but a hint of pink came to his cheeks. "Well, we are told in business school to treat our suits like battle armor when going in to work a deal."

"You do look charming in those suits." Alard stood up, holding his hand out to Raz. "Come on, we should get this over with."

Raz stood, then looked down at the flower bed near his foot. "I take it that's the door?"

Alard looked around Raz to see what he was talking about. Tucked into the flowering bush was a small child's fairy garden, complete with a tiny cottage. Alard laughed. "Honestly, I have no idea where that came from."

"You should bring your new neighbors a housewarming gift," Raz teased, indicating the fairy house.

"Maybe I can ask them to bring in my mail." Alard snorted, but he reached into his back pocket and pulled out a tiny tin of mints. He knelt and placed a few under the window. As he stood up, Alard noticed that Raz tried unsuccessfully to hide a smile behind his hand. "What?"

"I was just kidding," Raz explained.

"No, it was a good idea. I don't need to piss off the neighbors, and, I mean, they *are* my subjects. Or will be." Alard tugged on Raz's shirt and started up the porch stairs. "Come on, I can at least give you the grand tour first."

They entered an expansive foyer, the hardwood floor from the porch continuing into the home. Alard found it a bit pretentious, but James assured him that it would impress their actual paying clients—the ones they used this office for. A marble table was in the center of the entranceway, with a planter of lavenders and lilacs on top. It filled the room with a relaxing smell, putting anyone who entered instantly at ease. Beyond it, a stairway wound upwards in a wide spiral to the second floor. Near the front door was an empty metal coatrack and an umbrella stand with two umbrellas and an aluminum baseball bat.

"You have a bat with your umbrellas?" Raz asked.

Alard nodded. "Can't be too careful. Mardi Gras can get crazy around here."

To the left was a closed door with the top half a frosted window and black lettering: *Fairchild & Wilson; Attorneys at Law.* A sitting room filled in the room on the left, fancy antique couches with new cushions surrounding a large coffee table covered in magazines. A child's table sat in the corner with two plastic chairs, a bucket of coloring books and crayons on the tabletop.

"This is what's left of the firm," Alard said as he walked to the waiting room. "I'd show you the office, but it's mostly just boxes now."

"I'm surprised your partner doesn't want to continue using this place." Raz's fingers slid along the top of a couch. "It's very impressive. I know a lot of people who would kill to have an office space like this."

"I'm pretty sure they wouldn't want to deal with the portal." Alard kept moving, opening a set of French doors on the side wall of the sitting room. They revealed a dining room. In the center of the room sat a long wooden table that at least a dozen people could eat at. It was stained dark brown, and the edges had a Celtic knot that traveled along all the edges, blending so that there was no indication where it started or ended. The chairs were a mix of black metal and matching dark wood, the wood for the back and seat, the metal thick with black ivy leaves accenting the legs and supporting the wooden back. There were no place settings out, the chandelier above the table glowing in the otherwise empty room.

"Have a lot of dinner parties?" Raz asked.

"To be honest, I don't think I've ever eaten in this room." Alard shrugged. "I mean, who uses a dining room anymore?"

"So why didn't you change it into something else? I mean, it's a nice sized room. This could be a good media room, or an indoor gym."

"The media room is in the basement." Alard thought about the question for a moment, then chuckled to himself. "Oh yeah, we didn't change it because we couldn't get the table out of the room and didn't have the heart to chop it up."

Alard waved to Raz to follow him, and they headed for the kitchen. "Now this is where I spend most of my time." It was a smaller kitchen than most people expected when looking at the size of the house, at least that's what guests usually told Alard. He didn't mind, because everything was within reach when cooking. The gas stove was the centerpiece of the room, built into an island with a breakfast bar on the opposite side. A large, bronzed vent hung above it. One wall behind the stove was lined with cabinets, the other was a butcher board countertop workspace with a ceramic sink.

"So, you know how to cook?" Raz wandered over to look out the window. The bottom sill was a shelf filled with cookbooks.

"Yeah. James and I would work late some nights, and you can only eat so much takeout. I spent a weekend watching The Food Network and tried out a few things." Alard stood next to the stove and caressed the clean metal cook top. "I don't get to do a lot of that back home."

"Yeah, that wouldn't help the princely image." Raz leaned back onto the counter and watched Alard. "All I know how to use is a microwave. There's a lot of restaurants in DC so it's easier to eat out than lug groceries home on the metro."

"I could see that." Alard gave the stovetop one last pat. He was going to miss his home in the human realm. "So, second floor are the bedrooms and the portal to the fairy realm. Shall we?"

"It is what we're here for."

Alard led Raz up the stairs. At the top stood the main set of doors leading out onto the balcony. The landing had some furniture, but their details were lost under the white sheets covering them. They walked to the end of the hallway and Alard put his hand on the black metal door handle. "Welcome to my bedroom," he declared as he opened the door.

The bedroom took up the entire side of the floor above the sitting and dining room, the white shiplap walls giving a cozy appearance of the entire space. Two-thirds of the way into the room was a wall partitioning off the master bathroom. A rail sat above the doorframe and a sliding barn door was against the wall in case someone needed to separate the two parts of the suite.

Despite its size, the room was sparsely furnished, the wood and metal motif present here as well. A large platform bed sat under a trio of windows that overlooked the neighbor's house. The ceiling fan was still, the dark wooden blades matching the hardwood floors. The dresser and vanity sat opposite the window with two piles of white linen waiting to be thrown over them.

"Impressive," Raz said as he wandered over to the bed.

Alard watched him, and for a moment envisioned them laying together in that bed, their limbs tangled under a disheveled sheet. Sunlight would stream into the room as the sun rose, highlighting the lighter tones in Raz's hair as he slept in Alard's arms...

He shook his head. It was a nice dream, but it wasn't meant to be. Alard walked to the bathroom door, careful not to trip on the orange cord that ran under the barn door against the doorframe. "You ready?"

"Doubt it." Raz joined him at the bathroom entrance, confused. "I don't see another door in here."

"You wouldn't. It's hidden at the moment." Alard pulled Raz into the bathroom, then grabbed onto the edge of the barn door. "Before I close this, did you forget anything? Got your toothbrush?"

Raz patted his backpack strap. "Everything for a three-day visit, check," he saluted.

Alard laughed. "And you have no lectures to give tomorrow, right?"

"Nah, my last one is Thursday afternoon."

"Great." Alard pulled the door across the bathroom entrance. It covered the entire empty space, stopping only when it hit a rubber insert on the rail to keep it from going too far.

The other side of the barn door was anything but wood. The rustic planks framed a large mass of swirling colors. Raz took a step back, and Alard reached to take his hand. "Hey, it's just the portal. You'll be fine going through."

"So you say." Raz ran his fingers through his hair, tugging on it as he stared at the entrance to the fairy realm. "I mean, I think I'm handling this whole 'fairies are real' thing pretty well and then I see this, and this is some real wizard magic type shit right here."

Alard bit his lip, trying not to laugh at Raz's distress. "And you're only on *this* side of the portal." He reached over and threaded his fingers through Raz's. "Trust me, nothing's going to hurt you as long as I'm around."

Raz tilted his head to look at Alard, one eyebrow up. "That makes me feel so much better," Raz said, his tone dripping with sarcasm.

Alard lifted Raz's hand to his lips and kissed them. "What good is a fairy prince if he can't protect his knight?"

Raz laughed and tried to pull his hand away, but Alard gripped it tighter. They stared at each other a moment, and Raz licked his lips before tugging again. "Not here," he whispered, the mirth slipping away. "You're already in trouble."

Alard nodded, and reluctantly let Raz's hand go. "Sorry."

Raz looked back at the portal, and then down at the ground. "What's the orange cord for?" It came to the inside edge of the door, then vanished.

"Wi-Fi signal." Alard stood at the door and pulled down two handles along the track that hung behind the barn door. Two clicks followed, and Alard tugged on the door edge, but it refused to move in either direction. "I needed to be able to get work emails whenever I traveled home."

"And that?" Raz looked at the handles.

"Locks the door in place. You can only unlock it from in here, so it makes sure that if James or Catherine visit, they don't accidently trap me in the fairy realm."

Raz nodded. "Smart."

"Thanks. If they did, the only other portal is in Meyda's kingdom, and it opens to New York City. Airplanes and I don't get along well, and I'm not a fan of flying in general."

"Wait a sec." Raz held up a hand, interrupting Alard's train of thought. "How can you hate flying? You have wings! You don't even need an airplane."

Alard shrugged. "Airplanes are too small, and I panic in them. As for my wings, I had a bad accident when I was learning. My wings are smaller than most flying creatures, and I struggled with stopping. I would keep hitting trees, but I thought I was getting better. Then, one day, I tried to fly to the library. I got through the window but couldn't stop and crashed right into a bookcase on the second floor. I fell, and then the books crashed down on top of me, followed by the bookcase."

Raz's eyes opened wide. "That sounds painful."

"It was. I broke my arm and my left wing and had horrible tears in my right wing. I recovered, but ever since then, I don't use them if I don't have to. I'll stick to the trolley and trains, thank you."

Raz nodded, looking at the portal, and Alard watched Raz lick his lips. He reached across and took Raz's hand. "You can still back out if you don't want to face this."

"No, I can do this. I just never imagined I would leave Earth before."

"Still Earth, different realm," Alard pointed out. "You ready?"

"As I'll ever be."

Alard watched Raz, seeing the emotions rippling across his face. "Fuck it," he muttered, reaching for Raz's cheek and pulling him in for a kiss. Raz squeaked in surprise, and he made to pull away, so Alard snaked his hand around to hold the back of his neck. His fingers played with the hair at the nape of Raz's neck.

After the shock passed, Raz melted against Alard. He hooked his fingers into Alard's belt loops and pulled their hips closer. It was Alard's turn to groan as Raz ground their hips together, and in return, Alard teased Raz's lips with his tongue.

He took a few steps back, looking for a surface to lean against. Three steps back, and suddenly he was weightless, a warping in his stomach as he fell away from Raz and landed on the other side of the portal. Bright sunlight burned his eyes as he looked around the small field he now lay on.

He started laughing, only to get cut off with an "Oof!" as Raz fell through the portal and landed on top of him. "That's one way to portal jump," Alard groaned as Raz rolled off him.

Raz stared at the canopy above them, eyes wide on his flushed face. "Are you okay?"

"Oh, I'm fine. But that wasn't the effect I was looking for."

Raz jumped up, then helped Alard stand back up, brushing the dirt and grass off him. "I'm sure," he drawled with a smirk.

"Feel better now?"

Raz hesitated. "Yes...?"

Aland took his hand. "Good, then we can go."

CHAPTER TWELVE

T hick, tall trees stood like giants around Raz, reminding him of a spring break he spent hiking through the redwoods in California. He could almost taste the earth in his mouth with how it permeated the air.

Feeling tiny and insignificant compared to the trees, a rush of doubt raced through his brain. He was barely able to handle the vortex without accidental groping turned accidental portal jump—how would he handle an entire realm of magic?

Maybe he should leave Alard alone to face his family and fix this. There was nothing Raz could do until a solution was found. His presence would only serve to remind Alard's family of the illicit night that led to their current situation.

Part of him wondered if, after the bond was broken, would he even remember all of this? Raz hoped so. For all the insanity of the last two days, Raz enjoyed Alard's company. A lot. And didn't want to forget a single moment of it.

"You need a hand?"

Alard hovered over Raz, a hand extended between them. Raz saw concern in the hazel eyes, and he wondered how long he had been kneeling on the ground. "I'm fine," he told Alard, taking the other man's hand and standing up.

"Good. Now, unfortunately, I didn't have time to summon a carriage so we're going to have to walk a bit," Alard said. "The good side is that the view is spectacular."

Raz moved to stand next to Alard and gazed beyond the edge of the forest. The forest sat on top of a hill. The dirt trail beneath their feet continued down the gentle decline while trees gave way to a prairie filled with tall grasses and wildflowers. Blues, purples, and yellows pushing their way through the sea of green could be seen down the hill and beyond.

The grassland ended at a stone half-wall not far beyond the foot of the hill. Raz guessed it was about three feet tall with a break in the wall where the path continued through. Raz could make out some homes past the wall, but they were few and far between. The open areas beyond the wall had geometric shapes plowed into the ground, some only showing dirt, others with dots of color between green leaves.

Farms, he realized, and that bit of familiarity helped him relax. Fairy tales always painted worlds with great differences when compared to the human world: houses made of candy; castles surrounded by lava with dragons guarding the sleeping princess...yet what Raz saw looked more like medieval England.

Perhaps the two realms weren't so different after all.

The dwellings started to blend together further down the dirt path towards the castle. The homes were dwarfed when compared to the castle—Raz wondered now if perhaps actual dwarves live in them—and the wall that surrounded it.

Castles in books and vacationing websites were Raz's only exposure to castles. Now, as he looked at the structure that dominated the horizon, he realized they were nothing compared to this building of gray and brown stones.

Green banners hung from every arched window as the castle spires disappeared into the clouds. A design in the center of each one—a long, dark line cutting through the middle of the banner and gray swirls on either side—caught Raz's eye, and he wondered what details he would notice as they got closer. What did each part of the design signify?

Birds flew up from the castle walls as a dark shape moved by. It looked about the size of a brick on the side of the fortress from this distance. A large wooden drawbridge sat in the exact center of the side facing them. As Raz stared, the drawbridge began to lower.

Raz felt Alard's stare and turned to face him. Alard's lips carried a smug grin. "You're getting enjoyment at watching me take this all in, aren't you?" Raz asked.

"What of it? You look adorable...like a kid at Solstice."

Shaking his head, Raz pointed at the castle. "Looks like the drawbridge is going down."

Alard's face shifted from merriment to confusion as he squinted towards his home. A minute later he groaned and dropped his head. "Of course," he muttered to himself.

"Of course, what?"

Alard threw out his hand, finger pointed at the opening in castle's defenses. Barely a second later, Raz saw a white covered carriage barrel through the opening and continue on the dirt path in their direction.

There was nothing pulling the carriage or steering it. "Um, Alard, where are the horses?" Raz asked.

"That's right. I forgot." Alard stepped closer; his eyes glowing. He placed a hand on either side of Raz's face. "This won't hurt."

Raz leaned back. "Whoa. You know, explaining things before you do something to me would be greatly appreciated."

Alard sighed, then nodded. "I need to give you more of my magic so you can see the world properly and talk to others here."

"But I was able to see you before."

"I only gave you enough to see me, and only when I wanted you to. Here, no one is going to do that for you, so you need a bit more magic to open your mind and truly see this realm."

"...Okay." Raz nodded, then smiled. "Now was that so hard?"

Alard didn't answer, but instead leaned in and kissed Raz. His lips tingled as a cool breath slipped through his mouth and seemed to drift up towards his brain. Raz took a deep breath through his nose, and the earthy scent seemed sweeter. His tattoo felt warmer against his skin, and when he pulled back, he saw that the two hearts were glowing.

"It's never done that before," Raz told Alard.

"Not for you."

Raz looked back up at Alard, then stopped to examine his face. The pale skin was iridescent again, and there was a slight aura of green along Alard's edges. Raz reached out to trace Alard's cheek, smiling as Alard closed his glowing eyes to lean into the touch.

While still holding Alard's cheek, Raz looked past his shoulder to spot the carriage approaching. He could now see two feathered creatures pulling the carriage behind them. Their plumage started with tan along their bodies, brightening to red tips that made them look like they were on fire as they ran. One had a head that resembled a bald eagle, while its partner had all tan feathers along its scalp.

"Wow," Raz breathed, and Alard opened his eyes.

Alard turned to see what Raz was looking at and smiled. "They're fantastic, aren't they?"

"Just a bit." Raz replied. "What are they?"

"Griffins."

The carriage pulled up beside them. There was no driver, and Raz was about to ask Alard about that when the griffins bowed their heads and spoke. "Hail Prince Alard, son of Earth and Sky."

Alard chuckled and walked over to the bald-headed eagle griffin, tapping his shoulder. "You know you don't have to bow to me, Sirus. Stand back up." He looked around at the other griffin. "Melody, how are you doing? Keeping Sirus in line, I hope."

The tan griffin, Melody, chortled in laughter. "You know that is impossible, my lord."

Sirus puffed up; Raz could only assume he was insulted as he ignored Alard and Melody's banter.

"Here, let me introduce you to Raz." Alard turned to Raz and smiled, beckoning Raz over with a wave of his arm. "Raz, these are the captains of our air force; Sirus and Melody."

"It's a pleasure." Raz stumbled over his words, his mind wrapping around the knowledge about griffins being real and able to talk. "I was telling Alard I've never seen a griffin before. You're beautiful."

Sirus twitched his head like any eagle would, staring at Raz with an intensity that reminded Raz how fragile his human body was. Melody, however, cooed over him. "Such good taste. You have a very polite human friend."

"This is Razi Miller," Alard continued his introductions. "He and I—"

"The rumors of your illicit marriage have already traveled through the kingdom, my lord," Sirus spoke, eyes never leaving Raz. "Your father is enraged."

Alard sighed. "I have no doubts. I guess there's no use in delaying the inevitable."

Raz reached over to squeeze Alard's hand, reassuring Alard that he was on his side of the court. "Perhaps we can take the long way? See a bit of the countryside before whatever happens next?"

"We are under strict orders—"

Melody brought a wing over Sirus's head. "I think we can arrange that."

The carriage door opened on its own, beckoning Alard and Raz to enter as a set of stairs folded down from the inside. As Raz approached, he realized that the vehicle was made of crystals, which reflected rainbows onto the ground around it. The inside had a couch that ran along the entire circumference of the carriage's interior—except for where the door was, of course.

Alard stood at the side of the carriage and held out his hand. Raz slapped it away. "Still not a fairy princess," Raz muttered as he climbed into the carriage, and he could hear Melody's soft laughter as Alard climbed in behind him. Alard pulled the carriage steps up, the velvet stairs completing the couch circle.

Sirus and Melody turned as one, and Raz fell back into the cushions as the griffins took off toward the castle. Alard sat across from him, his eyes taking in the countryside as they moved. Raz closed his eyes, focusing on his breathing until his lungs adjusted to the speed so he could catch his breath.

"Damn, they move fast," Raz gasped, adjusting in the couch to get comfortable. "Felt like I was in a plane without the pressurization."

"I wouldn't know." The edge of Alard's lip lifted in a smirk but dropped almost instantly.

Raz knew something was wrong. Alard's gaze was distant, not even seeing what he was looking at. He waited another minute, watching the scenery himself as the fields changed to farms. "Are you okay?" Raz asked, leaning forward to take Alard's hands in his.

"I'm nervous," Alard said, his hands squeezing Raz's tightly. "My father has never been angry at me before. Not at the level Sirus described."

"He was probably just exaggerating."

Alard laughed, a harsh snap between them. "Does Sirus look like he exaggerates?"

Raz smiled at him, ducking his head to get Alard to look at him. "Does it look like I know the behavior and whims of a griffin? All I have so far is that he comes off like a British butler you see on *Downton Abbey*."

Alard laughed again, more earnest this time, and Raz watched the tension melt from Alard's shoulders. "Yes, he does come off that way."

Raz squeezed Alard's hands again, trying to reassure him. "Everything is going to be okay. We can fix this."

"I hope so. If we can't reverse the magic, I fear what may happen to you."

"What do you mean by that?"

Alard bit his lip, his eyes leaving Raz's to stare at their hands. "There are stories about fairies who have mated with undesirable partners. This realm also has its own set of social classes and structures, and if a bonding happens that breaks those rules..."

Raz closed his eyes. "You're a prince. I'm a commoner."

"In layman's terms. So, if there's going to be a punishment or a violent breaking of the bond, it will fall on you."

The truth hit Raz's chest like a gunshot to the heart. He took a deep breath, then glared at Alard. "By violent breaking, you mean being killed to free you from the bond, don't you?" He should have realized that this was a possibility, but Alard hadn't told him. "You should have mentioned that earlier."

"I'm sorry," Alard whispered. "I never intended for this to happen."

"Yeah, I know. Still doesn't excuse you for forgetting this *tiny* detail."

"And I swear, I won't let anyone hurt you. I'll give up my title and let Meyda have my kingdom before that."

Raz hummed his uncertainty at Alard's words as he looked up to see the carriage race along the drawbridge into the inner courtyard of the castle. "So, I take it my going back to New Orleans is out of the question, huh?"

Alard shook his head. "I mean, we can go back and forth, like for your lecture on Thursday. But you're safer if I'm with you. After that, depending on my parents, they will probably order that you remain here until we find a solution."

"Because?"

"Part of it is that you could return to your realm and disappear in a way that I can't find you..."

"I wouldn't do that."

"...and because there may be threats placed upon your life if you return, and I can't protect you."

"Oh." Raz sighed. "Well, that's just wonderful."

The carriage pulled into an alcove and stopped. Melody looked over her shoulder and through the window at them. "We're here, my lords."

"Thank you, Melody." Alard sat up, straightening his spine and schooling his face to a flat, emotionless look. Raz figured that Alard was trying to mask his emotions from the castle residents now that they were under their scrutiny. It made sense, but Raz didn't like the resting bitch face that removed all the light from Alard's eyes.

Alard made no move to open the carriage. Raz started to, but Alard cleared his throat and gave a shake of his head. It took Raz a moment to realize that, being royalty, there were servants that would do these kinds of tasks.

As the thought passed through his mind, the carriage steps were released and lowered. Raz looked out to see a small creature looking up at them. The little man had white hair, a wrinkled face, rosy cheeks and nose, and bright blue eyes. Dressed in a navy-blue jacket and pants, his outfit was capped off with a large, pointed red hat.

"Hello, David," Alard said, nodding at the little man.

"Welcome home, my lord," David answered.

Alard climbed out of the carriage first. His presence caused the servants in the yard to stop what they were doing and kneel. Raz watched as Alard blushed at the attention, then cleared his throat and nodded. "You can all rise," he said before turning back to look at Raz and held out his hand. Raz took it, allowing Alard to guide him down the steps to stand beside him.

The yard stood still; the bustle silenced as the castle residents got their first look at Raz. He could feel their stares and wondered how rare it was for a human to be in this realm. Was he the first human some of them had ever seen?

Raz straightened his back as some unconscious thought to stand up and represent the human species proudly flew through his brain. He heard Alard snicker at his side. "Relax," Alard whispered in his ear while threading their fingers together.

"Why are they staring at me like that?" Raz whispered back.

"Because you're new," Alard said. "It's not every day that they see an outsider to the realm within the castle limits. Plus," Alard gave Raz a quick once over and grinned, "you are very easy on the eyes."

A group of creatures like David hopped over to the carriage and reached inside for the backpacks the men had brought. Raz kept himself from stopping them when Alard made no notice of them. "They aren't stealing my stuff, right?" Raz asked.

David, still in front of them, huffed at the comment. Alard held up his hand at David to stop the little man from speaking. "He's still learning, David, and doesn't mean to insult," Alard stated. "You will need to tell the others to be patient and help Raz understand our customs."

David bowed his head. "Yes, my lord."

"Good luck with that," Sirus said to David as the griffins pulled the carriage away and disappeared around the side of the castle wall.

Alard turned to Raz, and the resting bitch face was back. It was going to take a lot to get used to it. "Raz, the gnomes of our kingdom have been loyal servants for centuries. If you need anything, they will be more than happy to help. I'm pretty sure our household wouldn't function without their presence."

"My apologies," Raz said. He looked back at the small group of gnomes that had stepped away from the bags after the accusation. "I didn't know. I'm sorry."

There was a chittering of words between them that Raz couldn't understand. *I guess seeing and hearing fairies are different skills.* One gnome in a red and green suit stepped forward and bowed to Raz. "We accept your apology, my lord," she spoke. Then, as if the incident hadn't occurred, the gnomes picked up the bags and carried them to a side entrance of the castle before stopping, waiting on something or someone.

David cleared his throat. "Your lord father demands your presence in the throne room immediately, Prince Alard."

"I guess we can't avoid it much longer." Alard reached out to take Raz's hand again. "You ready?"

"As I'll ever be." Raz squeezed Alard's hand to show his support.

"Actually, my lord," David interrupted, standing up taller, "the king wishes to see you...alone." Raz saw the side-eye glare from the gnome, and his worries about this world dripped back into his mind.

"Did he say why?" Alard asked.

"He did not, my lord. The guards are waiting to escort you to him."

David looked over to where two guards stood. Up close, Raz saw that the guards were some form of tree person. They wore moss covered bark as armor with golden helmets of solid amber. Vines snaked down their arms and legs, pulsing like veins beating in time to the heart. Black eyes were locked on Raz, leafy beards hiding the rest of their expression.

Alard shook his head. "I want to at least get Raz settled in my rooms—"

"I would not risk increasing your father's rage, my lord." David looked at the gnomes holding Raz and Alard's bags. "We will show your...consort... to your wing."

Raz squeezed Alard's hand again. "Go, I'll be okay."

"You sure?" Alard asked. Raz felt his skin prickle at the nervous look on Alard's face.

"Yeah. As long as 'your wing' doesn't mean a dungeon or something, I'll be fine." He tried to push bravado into his voice, hoping that it would relax Alard's nerves.

"If you're sure."

Raz nodded, releasing Alard's hand. "I'd rather we start this trip off not ostracizing ourselves from your parents."

"I'll be there soon. Hopefully with my head still attached." Alard took a deep breath, put his resting bitch face back on, and turned to follow the guards into the castle.

Raz watched him go—taking just a moment to enjoy the view—and then looked down at David. "So, where do you want me?"

From the look that passed over David's face as he walked past Raz without a word, Raz was pretty sure he didn't want to know the gnome's answer.

Chapter Thirteen

The pair of dryad guards marched Alard from the carriage receiving entranceway towards the center of the castle. They flanked him, walking as if Alard was a prisoner that they feared would escape them.

"You can relax," Alard stated. "I'm not going to try and run away." He grasped his hands behind his back as he walked. Alard refused to show his nervousness while in the castle. He learned a long time ago to hide them this way so his hands wouldn't fidget in sight of those Alard was talking to. It also helped push his chest out, improving his posture to a more royal posture.

"We are only doing as the King has ordered," the dryad to his left spoke without turning his head.

"You should be grateful he hasn't ordered us to put your pet human in the dungeon," the other dryad muttered.

"Halt." Alard stood still, seeing that both guards had stopped walking as well. He moved to stand in front of them both, staring up at them. His eyes glowed, and the glow escaped from the sides of his eyes to spiral along his face like delicate swirls in lace. "Until such time that this is resolved, that *human* is my *husband*. That makes him part of this royal family, one you have sworn an oath to serve under and protect. You will treat him as such, or you will be dismissed from your posts. Do you understand me?"

"Yes, my lord," they replied in unison, their gazes averted to the floor.

Taking a deep breath, Alard focused his anger away and pulled his magic back into himself. The tendrils faded away until only his eyes held their mossy glow. "Good. Now show me to my father."

The rest of the journey was silent except for the sound of Alard's shoes on the marble floors and staircases. Alard used the quiet to plan his defensive strategy against his father. The ramifications of this unintended nuptial would be vast if Alard and Raz weren't able to find a way to dissolve the marriage.

He had to assume that Meyda's family either knew or wouldn't be far off from learning. Alard would need to keep Raz hidden from their view, or they might demand immediate action be taken. If it came down to that, Alard would abdicate his throne so that Raz wouldn't bear any punishment.

Though doing so could reignite the war, which would cause countless deaths and suffering. Was it right of him to do that to his people? Was there even a right answer to this conundrum he had created?

They reached the throne room doors. Two slabs of redwood reaching from floor to the top of the vaulted ceiling at least twenty feet above Alard's head. A tree was carved into the center, growing along the seam with thousands of branches arching away to the edges of the door. When they reached the walls, the carving turned into embedded green jewels, a canopy that sparkled when the sunlight hit it just right from the skylights above. The dryads each pushed a door open for Alard, taking up post at the doors once he had walked through.

The throne room was a mixture of the Earth and Sky in their kingdom —the two elements that were dominant in their half of the fairy realm. The marble floor curved around the fruit tree trunks that lined the perimeter of the room. Each tree bore a different fruit, pollinated by the hummingbirds that flittered above them. Shadowed balconies extended on either side of the room, allowing for easy picking from the trees as one passed.

Gusts of wind entered the room from knotted designs that were carved through the marble walls to the outside. Crystal and metal pipes hung like chandeliers from the frosted glass ceiling, hitting each other to create a constant undertone of tinkling music in the room.

In the center of the room was a fountain that sprayed water into the air that rained down on a carpet of flowers. The flowers' bright colors were planted into a design that matched the family crest of a green tree growing with blue spirals of wind buffeting it on either side to keep it standing straight. Alard stopped at the edge of the flowers and knelt, inhaling the gentle scents of lavender, chrysanthemum, and daisy. Honeybees worked among the blooms, and below them, brownie men and women tended the snails and worms that kept the soil fertile.

One of the tiny women noticed Alard and gasped, the drop of water falling from her hand to the ground. She tugged on the arm of the man next to her with one hand, pointing at Alard with the other. In moments, dozens of brownies removed their green caps from brown haired heads, wiped the dirt from their dark orange faces before going to one knee and bowing.

"Rise, please," Alard whispered, not wanting to hurt their sensitive ears. "I just wanted to give my greetings."

"We are pleased you have returned, Prince Alard," the first woman spoke, smiling brightly. "We have missed you."

"As have I." Alard returned their smile, taking them all in. At least someone was happy to see him. "Have I missed anything important while I was gone?"

The brownies told Alard about who had gotten married, had babies, and the overall status of their tiny work. Two men brought up a problem about the lack of shells for the new snails, and Alard swore he would have someone help fix it.

"Well, my father calls," Alard told them as he stood back up. "You can return to what you were doing."

"Yes, my lord." There was a chorus of goodbyes, and the brownies returned to work as Alard walked around the side of the fountain.

At the other end of the room, two crystal thrones sat on a stage with marble steps leading up to it. Gold threads ran through the crystals on the larger throne, the one for the king, while silver threads ran through the queen's throne.

His parents weren't there. Alard looked around, confused. Surely, they would have been informed he had returned and was being escorted to this room? He had been preparing for his father's booming voice to vibrate off the walls the moment Alard had rounded the fountain. Their absence wasn't a good sign, and Alard wasn't sure if he should wait or escape while he had the chance.

Deciding it was better to wait, Alard lowered himself to sit on the first step leading up to the thrones. The windchimes tried to soothe him with their music but, as the minutes passed, Alard felt his anxiety grow. Just when he was about to stand up and go to his parents' quarters, a side door to the throne room opened.

Queen Norah entered first, her silver wings fluttering as she glided through the air. Her ice blue dress floated around her like a cloud, her silver hair braided up around her head with green and gold ribbons. Alard's skin tone came from her magic, the iridescence of her skin reflecting blue and pink tones as she landed a foot away from him.

"Welcome home, son." Norah held her arms open as she closed the distance between them on foot. She pulled Alard into a hug, both her arms and wings embracing him.

Alard leaned his head against her shoulder, soaking in the warmth of her love. "I missed you, Mother."

"I missed you too." Norah pushed Alard back, her hands on his arms as she examined him. "You look healthy. The human realm hasn't damaged you too much."

"Mom." Alard resisted rolling his eyes. "I'm fine. Where's Father?"

"I told him to meditate for five minutes before coming back into the room." Norah sat down on the stairs, pulling Alard down with her. "I didn't want you to come home to anger."

"I swear I tried to find a way to resolve it before we came here."

"What happened, Alard? How did you get caught up in this?"

Alard explained to his mother the series of events that led up to his and Raz's unintended marriage—leaving out the more personal aspects of the night. He saw the disappointment in her eyes and lowered his gaze. "You know I would never do something like this on purpose. I'd never hurt Meyda like that."

Norah caressed his cheek, her thumb wiping away a tear that betrayed Alard and ran down his face. "I know, my love. Neither of you would want to hurt the other. But this has happened, and you will have to take responsibility for your actions."

"Yes, Mother." Alard rubbed at his eyes, then looked at the door Norah had flown through.

A shadow stood in the doorframe, watching Alard and his mother. He couldn't see the face from the sun's halo around the person, but Alard knew his father's posture anywhere. Alard shifted from sitting on the stairs to kneeling and bowed his head. "Father."

King Quin strode across the room. His coal-colored skin lightened by the strands of clay that made up his hair and beard. A robe of green leaves went from his shoulders down to brush against the ground. His pants and vest were both leather, embossed with trees and animals running through the branches. Quin's bare feet were covered in moss, and on his head sat a crown of gold with emeralds embedded on each pillar around the circlet.

"Stand, Alard." The gravel in his voice caused Alard to wince as he stood up. Quin inspected his son just as Norah had, then placed a hand on Alard's shoulder and squeezed. "I don't know what I'm supposed to do with you, boy."

"I'm sorry, Father." Alard kept his gaze on the marble floor. "It was an accident."

"An accident?" Quin's voice rose, and Alard shut his eyes.

Norah stood. "Dearest, you promised—"

"I know what we agreed to, Norah," Quin interrupted, raising his hand to stop her. "However, I would be an inept king if I didn't deal with the matter at hand."

"It was an accident." Alard raised his head, meeting his father's mossy green eyes. "We didn't know that a marriage ritual was taking place in the next room. If Raz and I had been anywhere else, this wouldn't have even happened."

Quin looked at his wife, and Norah nodded in agreement with her son's story. The hand on Alard's shoulder squeezed tightly, but Alard refused to acknowledge the discomfort. Finally, Quin released his son. "You will end this relationship now."

Alard wanted to promise his father that he would, but the words refused to leave his throat. Annulling the marriage was the reason Raz had come with him. It was the goal, yet in that moment, Alard hesitated. It only took a moment of self-reflection to realize why.

"You care for him, don't you?" Norah asked.

"I do," Alard said, and his heart felt lighter with the admission. "We both know what needs to be done, but I don't want him hurt in the process."

"That is the last thing we want," Norah said, then glared at her husband when he didn't agree with her.

"I have had Elan working in the library to find any record of dissolving a bond outside of death," Quin stated. "You will go to him and comb the archives for a solution."

Alard took a deep breath because he knew his next question wasn't going to go over well. "May I bring Raz with me?"

"Absolutely not!" Quin roared. The hummingbirds, shocked by the sudden change of pitch, flew off into the balcony alcoves. The sound echoed off the marble walls, and Alard felt the ground beneath him vibrate with rage.

"But Father—"

"I will not allow a human into the archives of our realm." Quin pushed away from his son and stormed up to his throne. "You shouldn't have brought him here in the first place."

"He needs to be here!" Alard stated, his hands curling up into fists. "If we find a solution, we will most likely need him here to execute it. Having to go back to New Orleans to retrieve him would just delay the process."

Norah walked up the stairs to stand at her husband's side. "Your son makes a good point."

"Humans chose to separate the realms in the early days of their existence," Quin pointed out. "Their presence here is unwanted. If those in town learn of his existence, we could have a riot."

"Not if they know he is my friend," Alard said.

Quin pounded his fist against the throne's arm. "Especially if they know he's your friend! They will think he has corrupted you, compelled you to be his lover to gain control of the kingdom."

Alard scoffed. "We both know that's not true."

"But do they? Alard, my son, they will see this and not want you as king. Your people will revolt against you. The power will shift to King Eldren, and when he learns of your bond to a human, he will forfeit this marriage arrangement and instead overtake our kingdom and rule all of the realm."

"You're exaggerating, Father." Alard rubbed his forehead, trying to ignore the headache he knew was brewing behind his eyes. "Our people are smarter than you give them credit for. They will listen."

"And you, the bleeding-heart optimist, give them too much. You have spent so much time being the hero lawyer in the human realm that you've forgotten how your subjects react to change in this realm."

"That's not true!"

"There is still animosity among them towards those of Fire and Ice origins. Remember, it was not that far back where the people of Earth and the people of Sky did not want to join as one kingdom. We, along with Meyda's parents, had our own obstacles to face when our parents began this unification process, just as you now face. It will not end even in your rule, but in your children's children." Quin shook his head. "And now, you have put all of this at risk, Alard, for what...a moment of passion? Is the ruination of this fragile balance we are walking worth it?"

"And what would you have me do, Father? March him off to the gallows?" Alard ripped his sleeve back to show them the bond tattooed and how the colors glowed. "Can you assure me that killing him won't kill me in the process, even if I would ever consider that?"

"Enough!" Norah held up her arms, pushing most of the air from the room. Alard and Quin gasped, trying to breathe in the thin level of oxygen that remained. Alard fell to his knees, pulling at his shirt collar as if it would help.

The queen strode down to Alard, cupping his face in her hands. "Calm your heart, my child. We will not order your friend to his death." She kissed his forehead and allowed the air to swirl around Alard.

She turned to her husband, still on his throne. "And you, husband, will do best to remember that you were just as passionate about our people when you were his age. You need to realize where your fear truly comes from if we are to conquer it."

Quin took a deep breath, closing his eyes but not speaking. Alard looked up at Norah, still regaining his breath. "What are you two afraid of?" Alard asked.

"The same thing we've been afraid of for the last thirty years, Alard." Norah sat next to him, taking his hands into hers. "When we told you of your human origins, we were afraid you'd go into the human realm and never return. Now you return with a human consort..."

"Mom, you saved my life with your magic." Alard looked up at Quin. "Both of you. My human mother, whoever she was, left me in a dumpster to die. I am fairy, the son of Earth and Air. Yes, I sympathize with the humans, connect with them, love them even—but I will never abandon this realm for the one that abandoned me."

Norah smiled, lifting their hands so she could kiss Alard's knuckles. Quin left his throne and sat on Alard's other side. The hand he placed on Alard's shoulder was gentler this time, a comforting squeeze to match a relieved face.

"We're all in agreement that this marriage problem isn't what we wanted, and we will find a way to break it, I swear. We just need some time to find that solution." Alard looked between his parents. "But please, for me, keep an open mind when it comes to Raz while he's here. He's a good man, and I think you'll like him."

"I don't know how much time we can give you, son," Quin said. "The wedding ceremony for you and Meyda is already being set up. But we will give you every second that we can."

"Thank you."

The clacks of tiny wooden shoes on marble had the royal family looking up as David entered from the side door. "My lords, my lady, the captain of the guards is here to go over the security plan for the wedding parade with you."

"Thank you, David." Quin stood before holding his hand out to his wife. Norah took it to stand as well. "We will be ready in a moment."

Alard joined them. "I'm going to make sure Raz is settling in okay, then we'll go find Elan at the library."

"You both will join us for dinner, yes?" Norah asked.

"Of course, Mother." Alard leaned in to kiss her cheek.

Quin received a kiss from Alard next. "Are you sure you don't want to be a part of this meeting?" Quin asked.

Alard shook his head. "Meyda has been keeping me in the loop, and I'm more than certain you both can handle this." He took a step away from his parents, a smirk coming to his face. "Just remember to take care of the trolls. I've never had a problem with them myself, but remember that when in doubt, offer goats."

Chapter Fourteen

It was two days ago when Raz was ignorant of the existence of magic and fairies. In those two days, Raz had learned much about magic and creatures. Yet as he walked through the hallways of Alard's castle, he realized that what he knew was just a drop in the bucket.

Alard had been called the Son of Earth and Sky by Sirus when the griffins had picked them up from the forest, and the décor of the palace reconfirmed the title. Carved wooden furniture formed gathering spots along open-air walkways. The marble walls should have made the hallway cold, yet a warm breeze surrounded him. As the walls rose to the second floor, the tops of trees peeked over some of these spots, offering fruits to those resting there.

He paused in front of a tapestry hanging on the wall near a second staircase. On the tapestry, he was able to see the details he couldn't make out before on the castle banners. A tree grew in the center of the tapestry, a chocolate brown trunk reaching up until it split into almost a hundred branches. Orange, yellow, and red leaves hung to those sticks, trying to keep from blowing away in the silver swirls that Raz could only interpret as wind. Other leaves, not so lucky, danced in the air.

"David, what does this represent?" Raz asked the gnome who waited at the bottom of the stairs.

"It is the bond symbol of King Quin and Queen Norah," David explained. "The sigil of the Kingdom of Earth and Sky."

"Is that what their arm tattoo looks like?" Raz reached out to trace a finger along the tree.

David cleared his throat. "I would not touch the tapestry, my lord."

Raz stopped his finger just before touching the brown threads, yet a breeze through the corridor ruffled the tapestry, and his finger connected with the fabric. It felt like an electric shock danced from his arm and down his spine. Raz jumped back, breathing hard.

"Some magics and humans do not mix well," David stated, then motioned to the stairwell. "Shall we continue?"

"Yeah, sure." Raz rubbed his tingling hand, then followed David up another set of stairs that emptied into another open-air balcony hallway. Raz looked over the edge to see the garden paradise that made up the center of the castle.

A tree rose above the courtyard walls, the canopy providing shade for all. Flowering vines and ivy climbed the outer walls, dancing along the opening of each window to create a rim of greenery around them when looked at from outside in. Animals played among the branches above and in bushes below. Some Raz recognized—rabbits, deer, squirrels—and some he didn't.

At the end of the hallway was a large door, already opened by the gnomes that had proceeded them. "Here is Prince Alard's private wing," David spoke as they entered. Raz could tell that there was a story carved on the door, images of a baby in the arms of a fairy being carried to the castle. Raz followed the gnomes with their travel bags into the main sitting room.

One wall was a double fireplace burning fragrant logs. A door stood on either side of it. "You will be staying in this room," David stated as he walked to the closer of the two rooms. The door bore Celtic knotwork, similar to the style around the edge of Alard's dining room table. David opened the door, and Raz could see a few things beyond the frame: the edge of a mattress, a wardrobe, and a green plush chair with a blue blanket draped over its back. Raz imagined that the fireplace would be near the chair if it was linked to the one in the main room.

His bag went into the room with half the gnomes while the other half made for the door on the other side of the fireplace.

"I take it Alard's room is the other door," Raz said.

"That is Lord Alard or Prince Alard to you," David reminded Raz sharply. "But yes, it is, and you best stay out of it when the prince is not here." David summoned the gnomes to leave. "Do you require anything?" David asked, his tone sharp, demanding that Raz dismiss him.

"No, I'm fine. Thank you, David."

David turned at the "no" and was almost out the door when Raz offered his thanks. The gnome turned back to look at the human, his head tilted in confusion. The sharp edges around the gnome's features faded a bit, and Raz smiled. "You're welcome, my lord," David murmured before leaving and closing the door behind him.

Raz spun around slowly in the front parlor, letting himself take in the space. Vaulted ceilings with strong wooden beams cut across the open space so light fixtures could hang off them. A chandelier swayed in the center of the room. Each light was a small glass oil lamp with a burning wick—a ring of six lights hovering above a larger ring of eight lights. Black metal wrapped around the wooden rings, reminding Raz of some of the fixtures in Alard's home.

A suit of armor stood on either side of the fireplace. In the left arm of each, a small shield was strapped to the arm bracer, covering the wearer from wrist to elbow, heart to stomach in an oval. Sword sheaths were tied with a belt around the armor's waist. Raz pulled one out, admiring the looping cage of the hilt before the thin blade of the small sword began. He carefully sheathed the blade before moving on.

On the fireplace mantle sat a series of pictures in frames. As Raz came closer, he realized that they were all recent pictures with Alard looking the same in them as he looked now. Pictures of who he assumed were his parents, the king and queen, stood in the center. Next to those were a few scenic shots of NOLA, others of him with Catherine, Monique, and even one of Misty laying on her back in a patch of sunlight. There was one of James, this time smiling instead of making out with a drag queen, and Alard standing in front of the house with their shingle for the law firm in their hands.

One picture held a person that Raz didn't recognize, and he picked it up to look closer. The woman was young, her skin an icy blue that reminded Raz of the morning sky when it was snowing. Library shelves made up the backdrop, and the woman was curled up in a cushioned window seat. She was comfortable, pillows behind her and a thick woolen blanket covering her lap and shoulders. Pink eyes were focused on the book in her lap instead of the picture taker.

This must be Meyda, Raz thought. He traced a finger along the white hair in the picture, wondering if she was as cold to the touch as she looked. She held an ethereal beauty that even Raz found enticing and Raz felt like a pale comparison to that level of beauty.

Raz put the picture back and turned away from them to examine the tapestries and furniture. The dark-stained wooden tables, desk, and chairs would impress the most professional Amish carpenter. The tops had scrolling ends to make it look as if it was made from paper instead of wood. The Celtic knotwork theme continued along the wood, right down to the tiny footstool next to the fireside chair.

The desk sat in front of a window—one of two in this room. Raz laughed as he saw the orange cord that had started in the NOLA bedroom sneaking in the window and plugged into a wireless router. *That had to take a lot of time and digging to lay.* Pens, pencils, and journals covered the desk surface, trinkets from NOLA imbedded in the clutter. A coffee cup with a saxophone held multiple pens. Tiny statues acted as paperweights: a Mardi Gras mask held down a pile of six folders; a sugar skull in blues and greens had a letter opener stuck in one eye and scissors in the other rested on top of a leather portfolio; and two black coffins sat on either end of an unrolled scroll.

Realizing he had only been looking at the walls and furniture, Raz looked down to see the details of the floor. The marble was covered in a layer of dirt and mossy grass like a large natural carpet. He sat down on a purple velvet couch—identical to the one at the speakeasy—and stripped off his shoes and socks. When he returned his bare feet to the ground, he felt the softness of the moss. His toes dug into the ground, shifting the dirt to feel the texture.

Of course, Alard would choose that moment to enter the room. He looked deflated, and Raz sat up. "Are you okay?"

"Yeah. It's just been a long morning." Alard joined him on the couch, flopping down and closing his eyes. "How about you?"

"You mean, am I worried about gnomes sneaking in and slicing my throat in the middle of the night?" Raz held back his laughter as Alard opened one eye to stare at him, eyebrow raised. Raz reached over and let his fingers thread through Alard's hair. "I'm good. I think David might even come around to my charm sooner rather than later."

"David is a good man, he's just old and unfailing in tradition." Alard closed his eyes and shifted to put his head on Raz's lap. Raz's fingers continued to comb through the soft locks, and Alard tried to push his head against the feel of Raz's hand. "Give him time."

"Easier said than done. Meanwhile, when you said you were a fairy prince, I was not imagining all this." Raz examined one of the tapestries across the room. It was a deep forest green with silver knotwork along the edges. In the center was an image of the castle. The tree from the center courtyard grew over the top and spread its branches out in multiple directions. Many branches ended with a display of leaves and flowers.

Symbols were etched above the ends of each branch, and it took Raz a moment to realize he had seen that type of lettering before. "What's on this tapestry?" he asked.

Alard opened his eyes and followed the direction of Raz's gaze. "That is the royal family tree of the realm," he replied.

"I've never seen one that works this way," Raz said. "Normally, the tree branches extend out with each generation, but yours looks like it's doing the opposite now."

"That's a very astute observation." Alard sat up. "The castle represents the start of the realm—the house of Oberon and Mab. The pillars represent the four elemental regions. The tree began after the four elements broke away from a united realm when Puck wove deceit among the elders of each region after the fading of Oberon and Mab." Alard motioned to where the tree trunk split into four smaller trunks. "Each main branch follows the line of succession in that kingdom. The branches follow the other children and their families."

"And now the branches are arching back towards each other."

"They are. You can see the generation before Meyda and me—our parents—merged four trunks into two. When Meyda and I marry, it will merge back into one, as it should be."

Raz stood up and walked closer to the tapestry, then pointed up at the trunk on the left side, careful not to touch it this time. "What does the dead branch stand for?"

Alard sighed, then joined him beside the tapestry. "That was the true son of King Quin and Queen Norah. He died in childbirth, and the whole kingdom was devastated. Then I arrived, but I wasn't introduced until after I was turned into a fairy. Most people learned of my heritage when I started traveling between realms, but the people in my kingdom loved me by then so they didn't balk at the revelation."

"Which explains why David accepts you."

Alard laughed. "You'll need to ignore fairy prejudices like that if you don't want to go crazy. There are plenty of people in Meyda's kingdom who hate me because of my origins."

"Isn't that going to be a problem for your future?"

"No, because Meyda will be queen. They all love her, so she and I believe they will come to respect me after a few years."

Raz thought about his reaction to just seeing a photograph of her and cleared his throat. His eyes went back to the tapestry looking for a distraction, and he noticed a bird was being etched into the tapestry before his eyes. "This thing updates itself?"

Alard laughed. "Fairy realm. Everything is magical."

Raz pointed at the limb where the magical embroidery was happening. "So, what does the bird mean?"

"Birds represent humans." Alard looked back at the tapestry, then cursed. "Oh no, this isn't good."

"That's me being added to the tapestry, isn't it?"

"Yes." Alard strode to his desk and grabbed a fresh piece of paper, then started writing.

"Well, I guess that's to be expected. Will it go away when we break the bond?"

"It should. But that's not the current problem."

Raz joined him at the desk. He felt the tension flowing off Alard and put a steadying hand on Alard's shoulder. "Then what is?"

Alard whistled and held out a hand toward the window. "This isn't the only tapestry of this tree."

A raven flew into the room, landing obediently on Alard's arm. He rolled up the paper and tied it to the bird's leg. "Take this to Meyda immediately. Do not let anyone else in the household take it from you."

The raven bobbed its head and took off. Raz looked from the window back at Alard. "What's happening?" Raz asked.

"Meyda's family also has one. Between whatever rumors people have spoken based on the ripples in the magic lay lines, and *that*," Alard pointed at the tapestry, "Meyda's family will figure out what's happened."

"And that's not good."

"No. It will lead to war."

Chapter Fifteen

T he Grand Library of the fairy realm was housed in a small stronghold at the border of the two kingdoms. The single tower rose into the clouds. Window arches wound around it in a spiral that matched the staircase that lay on the inside. There were no guards, no gates, no security of any kind to stop Alard and Raz from entering the building.

"I'll summon you when we're ready to go back," Alard told Sirus. The griffin nodded and flew off, leaving the small carriage behind at the entrance.

"So, we're looking for someone named Elan?" Raz asked. Alard nodded, watching Raz's face carefully. After the discovery of the tapestry addition, they rushed from the castle to the library. The timetable they believed they had was drastically cut short, and Alard worried that they wouldn't find a solution in time.

"Yes. He has been the grand librarian here for a few hundred years." Alard reached for the door, opening it for Raz. "If anyone is going to know how to reverse this bond, he will."

As they entered the reception room, torches along the wall sparked to life. Alard smiled to himself. He spent days walking through the rooms, educating himself on everything from the laws of the kingdom down to basic magical spells. The library was as much a home to him as his own palace but, in this home, he was free to be himself and not a prince.

"Where do we start?" Raz asked.

"Probably in the law section." Alard motioned with his head to a door on their right. "Elan should be in there if he is researching for a solution as my father asked him to."

"Maybe he's already figured it out?"

"One can hope."

Alard pushed open the double doors into the law library. The musty smell of old parchment wafted out to meet them. Alard took a deep breath, enjoying the scent, as Raz coughed into his elbow. "You okay?" Alard asked.

"Yeah. It's just a bit dusty."

"Well, it is an old library. Dust is expected." Alard chuckled as he pulled Raz further into the room. The torches were already lit, an indication that someone was in the room. "Elan?" Alard called out, looking for a shadow between the rows of bookshelves with rolled up scrolls and handbound books.

"Is that you, Prince Alard?" A voice spoke, followed by the sound of books and scrolls hitting the floor. "Oh gonads!"

Alard ran to the noise, followed closely by Raz. Three rows over, a pile of scrolls covered an old man with a bald head. One scroll perched perfectly on his head, both sides unrolling down to give him a big curl over each pointed ear. Alard slapped his hand over his mouth to keep from laughing.

Raz shook his head and stepped forward, offering the old man a hand. "Here, let me help you."

Elan took the hand, letting Raz pull him up. He shook his head to get the scroll off, then looked over his shoulder to see another one covering a blue butterfly-like wing. The scroll flew off the wing with a wave of his hand, rolling itself back up and landing on the empty shelf.

"You didn't tell me you had Jedi in your world," Raz whispered into Alard's ear.

Before Alard could reply, Elan huffed and patted the dust off his long brown cloak. "Child, I don't know what this Jedi is that you speak of, but I am not that." Looking at the mess, Elan lifted both his hands into the air. Raz and Alard stepped back as the books and scrolls lifted off the stone floor. When Elan swept his hands to his sides, the scrolls and books took off, reorganizing themselves on the shelf in an orderly fashion.

"Damn. I could use that kind of power to clean my house," Raz spoke, his eyes wide as he watched.

Alard smiled at that. He continued to be amazed at how quick Raz was to adapt to the fairy realm. There would come a breaking point, a person could only handle so much after all, and he would be at Raz's side when it happened.

"Magic like this is not used for simple chores..." Elan admonished, then looked at the clean shelves near him. "Er, not for one untrained in the life force."

"Ha, I knew it. The Force." Raz grinned.

"It's *not* the Force," Alard replied.

"Toe-may-toe, toe-mah-toe."

Elan cleared his throat. "My lords, please. You came here with serious business, correct?"

"We came to see how you've progressed in finding a solution to this." Alard pulled his sleeve back to show the bond mark.

Elan leaned in to look, humming as he poked at the tattoo. "Interesting." Elan held out his hand, and a book flew across the room to him. He started to flip through the pages. Alard saw the pages were filled with symbols. "Every bond mark is different. One needs to know the nuances of the symbology to see what kind of bond was created from your union."

Raz shifted to read the book over Elan's shoulder. The librarian ignored him, flipping until he stopped on a two-page spread covered in hearts. Elan placed the book on Alard's wrist, and Alard spread his fingers out to support the book.

"This heart is special. The open edge that fills with a color shadow isn't something I have seen before." A quill appeared in Elan's hand, and he started drawing the heart into the book.

"Do the shadows have significance?" Raz asked.

"Shadows signify secrets. Something hidden from the one carrying the shadow." Elan finished his sketch, and the quill disappeared. "The fact that you both have them is troubling."

"Well, we don't know each other that well," Alard pointed out. He'd only known Raz for three days now, most of which was spent dealing with the bond mark.

Elan snapped his head up to look wide-eyed at Alard. "You don't even know the man you mated?"

"It happened so quick!" Alard's voice jumped in pitch as he defended himself. "I didn't even know it happened until I woke up the next morning!"

"And what were you doing that distracted you so?" Elan narrowed his eyes, the shock shifting quickly to judgement.

Alard shot a look over at Raz, begging with his eyes for the businessman to save him. "We were...mating?" Raz offered.

"That much is obvious," Elan huffed.

Raz moved to Alard's side, leaning between them so that Alard no longer felt Elan's glare on him. "We didn't know that we were standing behind the stage of a mass wedding. I still think this bond is illegal. There was no mutual consent given in the way of marriage."

"Fairy mating doesn't work with any of your human logic." Elan snapped the book shut and left the racks, heading for a large standing desk in the center of the rectangular room. The torches adjusted to where the people were, lighting their way and extinguishing as they passed by.

Raz sighed and looked at Alard. "Yeah, I gather that."

"Do you, my lord?" Elan slammed the book onto the desk, opening it again while pulling a parchment out of thin air and placing it on the desk beside the book. "You understand that fairy deals with a human always end badly for the human. It takes an intelligent person to get out of them, and the only ones I have seen broken were all done so by women. Therefore, my *lord*, you are at a disadvantage here from the start. But please, continue to tell the one being with all the knowledge of the realm how magic works."

Alard blinked, looking between the men. Elan was shorter than them both, his fiery red eyes just able to see over the desk as he glared in their direction. Raz, no longer staring Elan down, looked like he had no idea what had just happened between them.

A laugh escaped, and Alard bent over with laughter. Both men turned to watch him, but he couldn't stop. "You two," he tried to speak between laughs, holding his stomach as it started hurting, "are both being...so stubborn...I don't know...oh god it hurts." Alard crouched down, trying to ease the stomach pains. Warm tears escaped his eyes, and he wiped them away.

Elan walked over to Alard and pressed his palm to Alard's forehead. Comfort flooded through Alard's body, helping the laughter fade away. Breathing again, Alard fell back onto the stone floor, a grin still on his face.

"You get all your laughs out?" Raz stood above him, concerned.

"I'm sorry. A human and a Sidhe in an argument over knowledge of the fairy realm—it's like a priest and a mobster walk into a bar situation on Earth." Alard sat up, rubbing at his face.

"Sidhe?" Raz helped Alard back to his feet, brushing the dirt off him.

"Fairy of the mounds—though these days it is of the stacks." Elan stood with crossed arms, not amused. "Gifted with supreme knowledge from the four elements to provide counsel to anyone who seeks it. I believe your human mythology would call me an 'elf.'"

"So, elves have wings now?"

Elan rolled his eyes and looked at Alard. "You got a real genius here, Prince Alard."

"Okay you two, stop it." Alard moved between them. "Raz is still learning about the fairy realm, so instead of berating him, you should help educate him."

A loud screech interrupted the argument. All three men turned to face the doorway. A drake towered over them from just inside the room, balancing on two legs while its tail thrashed about behind it to help keep balance. The drake's black eyes watched them, a snarl of warning on its black lips.

Raz took a step back, but Alard grabbed his arm to keep him from moving further as the drake narrowed its vision on the human. "Don't move," Alard whispered, shifting Raz behind him.

"Shoo!" Elan stepped forward, moving his arms to back the drake out of the room. "You know you're not allowed in here." The drake gave a warbling cry, then lowered its head and whined. "No, none of that," Elan continued. "You don't want to set the books on fire, right?"

"He knows better than that."

Alard stood up straighter when he heard Meyda's voice, watching as she slid off the orange-red drake's back and landing gracefully on the stone floor. She was clad in her riding gear, dirt on her face, and looking nothing like the princess in fancy dresses and glass slippers she showed to her kingdom. Black riding boots were laced up to her knees over the brown leather pants. A white tunic billowed out from the bottom and sleeves of the canvas vest; the sleeves tucked into her black riding gloves. A hemp woven black skullcap covered her head, a hole cut in the back letting her ponytail fly free behind her.

Meyda patted the drake on his chest and clicked her tongue twice. The drake warbled again before shrinking down to the size of a ferret. Black bat-like wings spread as he flew up to sit on Meyda's shoulder.

"Is that Timmie?" Alard asked. "I didn't recognize him all grown up."

Meyda nodded, stroking Timmie's chin. "You've been gone three years," she stated. "He isn't a fledgling anymore."

"I can see that."

"Is that your human?" Meyda tilted her head to look past Alard to where Raz stood.

Alard rolled his eyes. "Meyda, this is Razi Miller. Raz, this is Princess Meyda, heir to the Kingdom of Fire and Ice."

"It's a pleasure to meet you," Raz said, moving to stand at Alard's side.

Meyda hummed as she removed her cap and gloves. "And it is true that you two are mated?" She looked down, and Alard realized his bond mark was still visible.

Alard rolled his sleeve back down. "Meyda, I can explain—"

Meyda held up a single hand to stop him. "I don't want your explanation, Alard." She walked past him and approached Raz. She circled him for a moment, then reached out her hand to him. "May I?"

Raz looked from her hand to Alard, who nodded to let Raz know it was safe. Raz put his hand on Meyda's, and she gripped it, turning it over. Her other hand traced along the lines in Raz's palm.

Timmie leaned in to sniff the air, then took off, hovering in front of Raz's face. He stuck his lizard tongue out, wiggling it along Raz's cheek. A tiny arc of electricity flew between them, and Raz winced. Alard wasn't worried; he knew that it would only shock like static when Timmie was that size.

The drake hovered a moment longer, then returned to Meyda's shoulder. He cooed in her ear as Meyda let Raz's hand go. "Do you believe yourself a good man, Razi Miller?"

"I try to be a good man," Raz said.

"If this bond can't be broken, will you be true and faithful to Alard?"

Alard shook his head. "Meyda—" Her hand covered his mouth to shut him up, her pink eyes never leaving Raz's.

"Alard and I have only known each other for a few days. So, it's hard to say. But in general, I'd like to think I would be that way with whomever I married."

Meyda nodded. She looked deeper into Raz's eyes, then smiled and leaped in to hug him. "I am so happy to meet you, Razi Miller!"

Raz blinked, then laughed as he hugged Meyda back. "The pleasure is all mine, Princess."

"Please, call me Meyda."

"Only if you'll call me Raz."

"Deal."

Meyda turned and faced Alard who stood next to Elan with matching looks of confusion. "Now you. Why are you still in your human guise, Alard?" she asked. "You're back home!"

"I've only been back half a day," Alard said. "Plus, I didn't want Raz to feel like he's the only human here."

"But I am," Raz pointed out.

Meyda patted Alard on his cheek. "Is that the only reason?" She leaned in close and kissed his nose. Alard hummed softly as the warmth from her lips spread across his body. "Because if your husband there likes you this way, I could get used to it."

Alard shook his head. "Why aren't you angry about all this?"

"Why would I be angry that you found someone special?" Meyda asked. "I mean, really, Alard, you're my best friend. I want you to be happy."

"I know, but what about us? *We're* supposed to be getting married and reuniting the kingdoms. I can't do that married to Raz."

"Oh yeah, that's going to be a problem." Meyda paced the room. Her hand went to twirl with Timmie's tail. "We've still got two weeks. I did what you said and took the tapestry down. As I told my mom, Timmie might have scared me, and a glass of wine went flying up high and stained it." She smiled, all teeth, as the drake chirped a complaint.

Alard laughed. "This is why I love you, Meyda. Thank you."

"It'll buy you some time, but not much. My mom has spies everywhere."

"Then we shouldn't waste any more time." Alard faced Elan. "Tell us where you haven't looked yet, and we'll help with the research."

Elan snorted, then waved into the air. "Meyda, there's a section on courtship rituals somewhere in the tower shelves. Alard, you're the lawyer. Go back into the law library and look up any case history about broken contracts."

"What about me?" Raz asked.

"You could check in mythology. That's where the books about human rituals are."

"Mythology?" Raz raised an eyebrow.

Elan smirked. "Where else?"

CHAPTER SIXTEEN

M eyda sat on the spiral staircase. Two piles of books were on the step below her, thrown open on specific pages that she had written down notes on in her phone. Alard had presented the cell phone to her as a birthday gift five harvests ago. She kept it in this "airplane" mode that Alard insisted would keep it powered up longer. As long as it still played Candy Crush, she didn't care what setting it was in.

Timmie was asleep on the windowsill at her side. The drake had learned when he was just a fledgling to keep away from Elan's books. The fried scrolls were still in Elan's office. One day he would rewrite them, but for now they existed as something to threaten to hit Timmie with.

The tiny phone screen had a long list of notes about what she uncovered in the different books. Stories of marriage bonds created in multiple ways. She was especially intrigued by the broom jumping tradition. *Maybe Alard and Raz could jump backwards over one to undo the bond.*

Probably not, but it would be fun to watch.

"Princess Meyda?" Raz's voice echoed from the bottom of the tower.

Meyda poked her head over the inside railing and looked down. She was up at least twenty feet from the ground. "I'm here, Raz. What can I help you with?"

"I found the mythology section—I think—but I can't read any of these." Raz held up two books.

"Did you ask Alard?"

"He's busy with Elan, and I don't want to deal with that elf's attitude."

Smiling, Meyda waved her hand for him to join her. "Let me see if I can help."

Raz climbed the stairs of wood and steel. The outer circumference of the wall was covered in bookcases. Each stair corresponded with a shelf so that not an inch of space was wasted. Even where the windows broke up the stacks of books, the shelves framed them with scrolls around the curved edges.

Meyda watched how carefully Raz climbed, his hand gripping the banister with white knuckles. The human was interesting; he was a proper gentleman, but she sensed he was hiding a facet of his personality from everyone, or at least from her.

When he reached her, Raz sat on the step above her, inching away from the open side. "I think they are what Elan told me to find." Raz handed the books to her.

"What made you think that?"

Raz rubbed the back of his neck. "I may have been muttering to myself and they started to glow." He shrugged. "So, I figured maybe they heard me."

"Books have a way of finding you when you need them most." Meyda pushed her book aside and opened one of Raz's in her lap. "Let's see what found you."

The symbols glowed a faint blue, lifting off the page to shimmer between them. Meyda leaned in, her finger touching one. "This one here, it's the glyph for human."

"I wish I could read them." Raz reached out to poke at a different symbol. "It would make things easier."

Meyda looked up at him. "Alard didn't give you the ability?"

Raz shook his head. "He gave me enough power to see the magic, but that's about it."

"Hmm, I don't understand why he wouldn't give you more. Give me your hand."

Reaching out, Raz almost took her hand, but pulled back at the last minute. "This isn't going to cause another marriage bond, is it? Are poly relationships even legal in fairyland?"

"I have no idea what you're talking about, but no, this won't marry us." Meyda took his hand into hers. Her pink eyes glowed brighter, and she sent a tendril of energy down her arm. Timmie lifted his head as the scent of magic woke him.

The pink energy swirled around her arm, then up Raz's. Meyda squeezed Raz's hand as he tried to pull back. "Just let it flow into you, Raz. It won't hurt."

Raz watched the energy climb his arm and shoulder. As it slid along his cheek, Raz groaned, a smile forming on his lips. The magic danced around his eyebrows before dipping into his eyes. The brown orbs contracted, the black center turning into a tiny dot. Pink lines moved like veins through the muddy pools, and Raz gasped.

"Meyda, no!" Alard ran up the stairs, and Meyda quickly broke the contact. Raz leaned back against the stairs, eyes focused on the ceiling as he caught his breath.

"I wasn't hurting him, I swear," Meyda said as Alard reached them. He hovered over Raz, checking his eyes and then the rest of his body. "He wanted to be able to read the books, that's all."

"He's human, Meyda." Alard looked at her, his fear evident in his eyes. "If we push too much magic into him, he'll change into one of us."

"Oh." Meyda bit her lip, inching away towards the books while Alard straddled Raz and cupped his face with his hands. The space around them became hazy, and Meyda schooled her features to keep from smiling at the sight of the white glow around their tattoos. It was rare to see a glow like that, but it confirmed what she had been thinking about the two of them.

"Raz, come back to me," Alard whispered.

Meyda noticed that the bond mark on Alard's arm looked as if it was blistering. "What happened there?" she asked, pointing to the tattoo.

"It started to hurt. I looked down at the brown part and my flesh was turning red. It felt like someone had hit it with a flaming torch." Alard shrugged, his eyes never leaving Raz. "Its placement only meant one thing to me, so I came running."

"I'm sorry, Alard. I just wanted to help." Meyda pulled her legs closer to her chest. Timmie jumped onto her knees and nuzzled his head against Meyda's cheek.

"I know. I'm not mad."

Meyda knew that. She had seen Alard angry many times during their childhood. Her mother explained that it was due to his human origins. Humans were emotional creatures, more so than any other creature known to fairies. If she was going to marry Alard, she needed to understand these emotions and how to handle them. It was why they spent so much time together here, at the library, when they needed to escape from their families.

"You're worried," she whispered.

Alard nodded. "Our magic gives them a drugged feeling if not controlled. I only gave him enough to see our world, knowing anything more could do this."

"Is he in pain? Did I hurt him?"

"No, he'll be okay." Alard rubbed Raz's cheek, trying to elicit a response. "But he shouldn't be this zoned out."

"Can I do anything to help wake him up?"

"No. But let me try something." Alard leaned forward and pressed his lips against Raz's. Meyda watched as a white haze brightened around them as Alard continued to kiss his husband. A moment later, Raz's eyes opened wide, the brown iris glowing brightly as he took a sharp breath.

Alard sat back on Raz's lap and smiled. "There you are."

Raz blinked, looking around for a moment before focusing on Alard. "Hey, I know you."

"You better," he teased, shifting off Raz and helping him sit up. "You're married to me."

Raz chuckled, then looked over at Meyda. "What's wrong?" he asked her.

"I didn't mean to give you too much," Meyda said. "I'm sorry."

Raz shook his head. "I'm fine, Meyda. I mean, the lights seem a bit brighter, but other than that, I'm good."

"You'll get used to the brightness," Alard said. "Side effect."

Raz nodded to Alard but held his hand out to Meyda. "I'm okay, I promise."

Meyda uncurled her legs. Timmie took off into the air and resettled himself on top of Meyda's head. When she took Raz's hand, there was a feeling of warmth there that hadn't been there before, and she scooted closer to him. "You should be able to read the books now," she told him, putting one of them on his lap.

Raz looked down at the symbols. A hint of pink freckled his brown eyes then, and he nodded. "Yeah, I can understand them now. Thanks."

"Just don't take anymore magic in, Raz." Alard stood up.

"I won't."

Alard started back down the stairs. "I'm going to check in with Elan. Let me know if you find anything."

"Oh wait," Meyda reached for her phone and pulled up the list. "Did you guys happen to jump over a broom the night you got married?"

"No," Alard said slowly, and Raz shook his head. "Why?"

"It was one of the rituals I came across that had links to the magic down where you lived in the human realm. I figured it was worth a try."

"Never hurts to try." Alard nodded to both and jogged down the stairs.

It wasn't until Alard was out of sight before Raz turned to Meyda. "Ok, spill, what actually happened?"

Meyda fidgeted, unsure of what she could tell him. The last twenty-five years, before Alard even took his first trip to the human realm, Meyda had found Alard obsessed with learning about his origins. Having human origins made sense for how different Alard was from all the other men in the kingdom. In a way, it also made it easier for Alard to understand how Meyda was different from most of the ladies.

In his obsession with researching and living among humans, he had neglected his studies in fairy marital relations. He was lucky that Meyda took detailed notes, but she wondered how much of it he had read. Did Alard know about all the powers a marriage bond possessed?

"I gave you magic, and you smiled and leaned back on the stairs and wouldn't respond to us."

"I'll admit, it felt good. Like you had wrapped me in a warm blanket."

Meyda smiled. "Your hands do feel warm. I guess that's another side effect."

"One I don't mind. I was starting to get cold."

Raz held out one arm, and Meyda immediately pushed herself over to cuddle against the warm human. Timmie warbled at the sudden movement, flapping up into the air. He hovered between them, then landed on Raz's head this time and made a nest in the dark hair before settling back down.

"I think he likes me," Raz said with a grin, wrinkling his nose as Timmie's tail hung down in front of his face.

Meyda laughed. "That's a good sign."

"That he won't eat me?"

"No. That you're a good person." Meyda looked up from her book at Raz. "Alard deserves to have a good person in his life."

"He has you," Raz countered.

"Yeah, but we don't love each other like that. Not romantically. More like siblings." Meyda shook her head. "I don't want anything romantic. If I didn't have to get married, I'd be ecstatic."

"But what would happen if you didn't? I mean, say you told your parents you didn't want to get married. What would happen then?"

Meyda snorted. "Knowing my parents? After disowning me and throwing me out of their kingdom, they would declare war on Alard's family. I'm an only child, and I don't want to have kids. That means the family line ends, and Alard's family takes over the realm."

"Couldn't your parents adopt like Alard's did?"

"My mother despises humans. Even if they changed them into a fairy child, they would still be half human. As it is, my mother hates that I'm going to marry Alard."

"Because he's human."

"I only agreed to it because Alard knows how I feel about relationships and would respect my choices. Not that I'd tell my mother that. She thinks I'm madly in love with him."

"She's going to see me as a threat, huh?"

Meyda nodded. "That's why Alard asked me to hide the tapestry. But that won't keep my mother at bay for long."

"Well, I guess we better get back to researching then." Raz shifted his weight to lean back, letting Meyda press her back against his legs. She stretched out, her feet lifting to rest on the windowsill, and she propped her book on her stomach to read.

As she turned the pages, skimming the different marriage rituals through time, she thought back to the concern Alard had over Raz. There was something more between them than just friends at this point. She wondered if they even noticed how much they cared about each other; how purely their bond glowed around them.

An idea formed in her head, something she would wait until later to ask Elan about in private. Maybe if there wasn't a way to break their marriage bond, perhaps there was a way she could marry them both? She didn't know of something like that happening before, but Elan might. It'd be a backup plan, but if Alard and Raz were starting to fall for each other, then this plan would give all three of them what they want.

Chapter Seventeen

It was dark when Raz, Alard, and Meyda left the library. No solutions were found, but they had a few ideas to try. They read through almost a hundred books before it was too dark in the library. Elan complained about the number of books he needed to reshelve while pushing them out of the library before they could reshelve the tomes themselves.

Raz stared up at the sky. It took him a moment, but he realized that the stars were the same here as they were back home. The only difference was that they were brighter here, sparkling like diamonds.

Alard appeared at his side and looked up. "Making a wish?"

"No. I just realized that it's the same stars...look, the big dipper is right there." Raz pointed to where the seven stars hung in the indigo sky. "Wouldn't you have a different sky?"

"We're still on Earth, just in a parallel plane of existence on it. There are multiple layers of reality that exist." Alard took Raz's hand and squeezed. "You've just started to learn the real wonders of our world."

Raz chortled, giving Alard a sidelong look. "You think?"

They laughed, and Alard pointed at a bright shooting star. "Now, will you make a wish?"

"Why? It won't change anything. I mean, Monique said that the creatures that grant wishes are long gone."

"She said she hasn't seen them. That doesn't mean they are gone."

Raz looked at Alard, a confused expression on the prince's face. "Wishes don't come true, Alard. Trust me, I made my fair share of them as a kid."

"You also thought fairies, vampires, and werewolves weren't real until two days ago," Alard countered. "Maybe you just didn't wish on the right thing?"

"Oh, so there are also rules on how and what you can wish on?"

"Monique already covered the difference between material and needs-based wishing. Wishing for a Nintendo to appear won't happen unless you're in the Make-A-Wish program." Alard pointed at Polaris, the North Star. "Wishing on the first star you see at night won't work. Stars don't have the power to create change. They are the ones that change."

Meyda joined them in the clearing, tucking her ponytail back into her riding cap. "I have to get home before my parents summon me for dinner."

Raz held out his hand to say goodbye. Meyda ignored it, instead pressing close to hug him. Her warmth relaxed Raz, and he rested his chin on her head. "It was a pleasure getting to know you, Meyda."

"Same here, Raz." Her arms tightened just a bit more. "I just hope it isn't the last time I see you."

"I'll make sure Alard swings me by before I return to my realm."

"You better."

Meyda released Raz, then turned to face Alard. "I will see you soon."

"I'll be the guy in green and gold by the ancient tree." Alard kissed Meyda's cheek. "Unless I see you sooner."

Meyda smiled, then tapped Timmie on the snout. The drake stood up on her shoulder and stretched his neck out before lifting into the air. He rapidly grew to his larger size—the one Raz had first seen him as—and resettled on the ground beside Meyda. She swung herself up onto his back, tucking her hands and feet between scales to stay secure.

"Fly safe, I guess," Raz said.

Meyda nodded. When she clicked her teeth, Timmie took off into the air, flying in the opposite direction of how Alard and Raz had arrived earlier that afternoon.

"Sirus or Melody should be here soon," Alard said, watching Meyda and Timmie disappear over the horizon.

Raz watched Alard carefully. His sad eyes stayed on the horizon line long after Meyda disappeared, hands shoved deep into his pants pockets. After everything in the library, Raz shouldn't be jealous of Meyda and Alard's relationship. Alard said friendship, but there was an intimacy between them Raz witnessed more in deep, committed relationships.

Even knowing that what he and Alard shared between them was going to end, Raz bristled at the idea of Alard marrying her. A part of him wanted to grab Alard, bring him back to the human realm, and destroy the portal to keep him there forever.

Whoa, hold on. Raz shook his head. No, he didn't want to do that. Did he? It was the bond talking, Raz mused. The longer they were bonded, the stronger the possessive feeling would grow, right?

If so, why doesn't Alard act the same way?

"We could get there faster if you flew," Raz suggested.

Alard huffed, turning back to face Raz. "Like I said, I don't like flying."

"I was teasing."

"Oh." Alard blinked, then sighed. "Sorry, I was just thinking about something."

"Want to share?"

Raz watched Alard think, unsure of what he would say next. Just as Alard opened his mouth to speak, his eyes opened wider, and he nodded with his head. "Sirus is here."

The griffin created a breeze with his wings as he landed near the carriage that had brought them to the Grand Library. "My lords."

"Welcome back, Sirus," Alard said as he walked over to Sirus and went to work getting the harness straps into place.

"Sirus." Raz joined them, not knowing what he could do to help.

"Were you able to find a solution to your...situation?" Sirus ruffled his feathers after the leather straps were in place.

"No," Alard replied first as he climbed into the carriage. He held his hand down for Raz to help him up before they both settled on the cushioned bench. "There may be a few things we can try, but nothing solid that promises results."

"I'm sure the answer will come to you." Sirus clawed at the ground a moment before he started galloping back to the palace.

When they arrived, David informed the men that dinner would be served in thirty minutes. Raz walked with Alard back to their living quarters.

Alard went into his room, heading straight for his wardrobe. "We should wear something more formal."

Raz examined the layout of Alard's bedroom, realizing that it was a mirror reflection of his guest room, yet larger and more extravagant. Like the bed, Raz had a beautiful four post bed with green, blue, and silver layers of fabric draping down from the metal canopy. Alard's bed was completely hand carved. The headboard rose at least six feet into the air before curving over the top half of the bed. Tree branches and ivy were embedded in the wood. Air swirls covered the base, a final large gust curling up to make the footboard at least ten feet from the headboard. It could fit at least three or four people on the mattress and had enough pillows against each wooden end for them.

It filled half the room, leaving little space for the wardrobe just past the door and the chair in front of the fireplace.

"You didn't tell me to pack a suit." Raz leaned in the doorway, arms crossed. Everything in the castle was breathtaking. Nothing he had brought in his bag could come close to matching it.

"I know. I don't mean formal in your style." Alard stepped back, holding out two tunics. One was silver, shifting from bright to dark as the fabric moved under the candlelight. Green tendrils of ivy were embroidered into the fabric, creeping up both arms, across shoulders, and joined together around the edge of the turtleneck collar. The other tunic was almost the exact opposite in color, but the ivy was silver spirals that looked like a wind symbol on a weather station's map. "Pick one."

Raz walked into the room, his fingers feeling the edge of the fabric. The green one was velvet-like, soft to the touch like the moss that made up the rug in the main room. The silver one was silk, slippery and cool to the touch.

"I think you'd look better in the green one," Raz said. He took the silver tunic from Alard, draping it over his arm. "Now do I get pants?"

"I think your black pants would work just fine." Alard grinned, tossing the tunic onto his bed before starting to pull off his shirt. "I'm going to be barefoot, but the marble is cold so you may want to keep your shoes on."

"Will it insult your parents if I did?"

Alard thought a moment, then shrugged. "I don't know. You're the first full-blooded human to dine in our home."

"Well, when in Rome." Raz kicked his shoes off and leaned down to pick them up. "You can just rub them warm later by the fire."

"Maybe." Alard laughed, shooing Raz out of his room. "Go change."

Raz went to his own room, the warmth from his side of the fireplace embracing him. Shutting the door to keep the heat in, Raz started to undress. As he unbuttoned his shirt, Raz noticed that his arm was glowing. It wasn't just the brown and pink of the tattoo—he'd seen that before— now a white halo hovered over the infinity symbol connecting the two hearts.

He raised his arm closer to his face, and as it got closer, the haze shifted into fairy symbols. Now that Raz could read it, he tried to suss out the meaning of them. Raz sat on the bed, his lips moving as he worked to translate each symbol into a human meaning. Without Meyda nearby to help, it took him a bit.

"Why aren't you dressed yet?"

Raz snapped his head up. "Sorry, I got distracted."

"I couldn't tell. Have you been sitting there all this time?"

"I just left your room."

"No, you left my room almost thirty minutes ago." Alard walked closer, and Raz watched as his eyes went from admiring Raz's chest to focusing on his arm instead. "What's going on?"

"Was this writing on the tattoo earlier?" Raz poked his finger at the symbols.

Alard leaned closer, then shook his head. "Raz, I don't see any writing there."

"The infinity symbol...it's all lit up. You really don't see anything?"

"I'm sorry, no." Alard put his hand over the tattoo, smothering the light that only Raz seemed to see. "We can worry about that later, ok? Right now, you need to get ready to meet my parents."

"But what if this means something?"

Alard's grip tightened. "I'm sure it does, but we can't focus on it this second. After dinner, I promise."

Raz didn't want to drop it. When you had an opening, some dangling offer for "more", a successful businessman grabs that string and pulls until he receives the prize. His brain screamed that these symbols—ones only he could see—held an important clue, but until he was able to translate it, Raz was stuck back at square one.

"Fine. Grab my bag for me?" Raz undid his travel pants and dropped them to the floor. Alard left the bag on the bed, and Raz pulled out black slacks. He tossed the tunic on next. The fabric flowed across his skin, a texture that Raz wished he could get bedsheets made from. He could live in this tunic for the rest of his life and be happy.

Alard reached into the top drawer of the dresser in the room. He pulled out a black sash and brought it over. "What's that for?" Raz asked as Alard whipped the sash to the side with one hand, then whipped it again so it wrapped around Raz's waist before he caught it with his other hand.

"It keeps you from swimming in your tunic." Alard smiled as he tied the sash. "There, now you look dapper."

"I can pull anything off." Raz took a step back, admiring himself.

"We should go then. We're already late."

Something Meyda said earlier jumped back into the forefront of Raz's mind. "Before we go, maybe you should...you know, shift back?"

"What do you mean?"

"Meyda pointed out that you're still in your human guise." Raz shrugged. "You sure you want to go to dinner like that?"

"My parents have seen me in my human form many times." Alard shrugged. "It's fine."

"Alard, are you staying this way so I don't feel like an outsider?"

It took a moment before Alard lowered his head with a sigh. "You're the only human here. I thought it would be easier for you."

"You don't have to do that. I'm very confident in my humanity." He tried not to laugh, but Raz couldn't hold back a smile. His grin was infectious, and Alard joined him until they were both laughing.

"But for real," Raz said, catching his breath. "Please, be yourself here. You're just as beautiful to me either way."

Alard nodded. His eyes started to glow, and his human skin tone faded into his fairy iridescence. The wings stretched out, pushing through the tunic like a hot knife through butter.

Raz walked over and stroked Alard's cheek with his thumb. "So beautiful," he whispered before leaning in for a kiss. He felt Alard's lips press back, and for just a moment Raz forgot the rest of the world and the situation they were in. He savored the intimacy, only to lose it when Alard took a step away, a blush on his cheeks.

Alard took Raz's hand and pulled him to the door. "Come on, we're really late now. We can focus on *that* after dinner too."

CHAPTER EIGHTEEN

Alard held Raz's hand just until they walked into the royal dining room, then released it in case his parents were already inside. A large table stretched the length of a room created from tree trunks that arched overhead and wove together in a spiral that ended in the middle of the room. From the spiral's end, branches spread out with glowing orbs that provided light in the otherwise open space.

At one end of the table, the royal seats for the king and queen acted as the head of the table. Attendants stood at either side, a few steps behind the chairs with their heads bowed.

"Are we supposed to do that too?" Raz whispered.

"No. Right now, you are royalty, so we don't have to." Alard motioned for Raz to follow and guided him to the queen's side of the table. Two more royal seats—not as extravagant as the king's and queen's—were waiting with their own set of attendants.

When Alard and Raz arrived, two beetle-like men stepped forward, their shorts and sashes a mixture of blues and greens. Each grabbed a chair and pulled it back so that Alard and Raz could sit. Raz started to sit, but Alard shook his head. "Not until the King sits," he said.

"Oh."

Two members of the royal guard arrived through the same doorway

Alard and Raz had, taking posts at the entrance. The tinkering of bells accompanied Alard's parents as they entered the hall arm in arm. They hadn't changed from their afternoon gowns, but the crowns had been removed. It was hard to eat with a crown on your head—Alard knew this personally from dropping the half-crown of the prince into his dinner too many times in his youth.

They chose to approach from the side of the table that Alard and Raz were on. Alard looked at Raz. "You ready?" Raz nodded and Alard slipped out between the chairs to intercept his parents.

"Good evening, Mother. Father." Alard bowed his head in greeting.

Queen Norah stepped to her son, lifting his chin up before leaning in to kiss his cheek. When she stepped back to King Quin's side, she looked in Raz's direction. "Please introduce your guest to us."

Alard held his hand out to Raz, motioning for Raz to stand at his side. "Mother, Father, this is Razi Miller from Washington DC in the United States of America in the human realm."

———

If King Quin could incinerate Raz where he was standing, it would have happened the moment Alard's parents walked into the room. Raz felt the stony glare the moment the royals entered the room, and it continued even as Alard introduced him.

Raz spent almost a decade in various businesses until he made his own. He'd gone toe to toe with corporate leaders, the "rock stars" of the business world, and cutthroat colleagues who vied for the same rung in the corporate ladder. It was one of the reasons he decided to go solo, but those survival skills continued to help him through life in general.

Like dealing with ignorant people in general. Raz had spent decades receiving glares just because of the color of his skin. He was born in Arizona, but no one asked for the birth certificate until you tried running for political office, and even then, they sometimes wouldn't believe it. School was rough, but he melted every barb and built a steel cage around himself. He refused to let the bullies win.

Raz hoped it wasn't the case with Alard's parents, but from that glare, Raz stood prepared for it.

Queen Norah got his attention first, letting her arms spread out in the universal sign for giving a hug. "Welcome, Razi Miller. We are honored with your presence this day."

Raz looked at Alard for guidance. Was he supposed to hug the queen? Alard nodded. Raz smiled and hugged Norah, sighing at the feel of her arms and wings wrapping around him in a welcoming embrace. "The honor is mine, Queen Norah."

When Norah released him, Raz turned to confront King Quin. The king's skin was darker than even Raz's, and his green eyes were darker than Alard's. It was at that moment Raz realized that only Alard and Norah shared a skin tone. Raz continued to be amazed at the differences in everyone he had met so far, and yet they treated each other with respect.

So far, the fairy realm wasn't that bad of a place.

The king stood at his full height, built with the bulk of an ancient oak tree. Silence stretched between them until Norah cleared her throat. Quin sighed and held out his hand. "Welcome, Razi Miller."

Stalemate. Raz reached in and gave a firm handshake. "Thank you, Your Highness."

All noise in the room died in that instant as Quin dropped Raz's hand. Something was wrong, and Raz didn't know what he had done. Alard cleared his throat, stepping forward. "Father, this is my mistake. I did not convey the nuance of court greetings to Raz."

Quin looked down his nose at Raz, then turned his attention to his son. "You best fix that immediately, Prince Alard." Taking Norah's arm, the King and Queen moved to the head of the table.

"What was that?" Raz whispered as he and Alard went back to their seats.

"My parents use the lord and lady honorifics. Meyda's parents use highness. I should have reminded you about that before we came to dinner."

They took their seats after that, and the attendants brought silver domed plates to the table. When each was placed in front of the respective person, all four lifted the hoods and stepped back.

In hindsight, Raz should have asked what the food in the fairy realm consisted of. He would try most things at least once, but would he be able to? If there was a giant cooked fairy bug in front of him, guts spilled open— nope, he would claim to be a vegetarian even if it wasn't true.

Instead, Raz was pleasantly surprised to see a hunk of meat on a bed of greens with fruits and berries interspersed on the plate. Cups of wine and water waited in front of him, and a bowl of candied nuts was set down between him and Alard.

"This looks wonderful," Raz stated, looking at Alard's parents.

Norah smiled at the compliment, but Quin huffed. "What did you think we would serve you? Twigs and bugs?" he asked.

"Father." Alard closed his eyes as he spoke. "Please."

"No, I am curious about what the human was expecting." Quin put his wooden fork down.

"I wasn't expecting anything," Raz spoke before Alard could. "I never thought to ask what foods in this realm would be like. One of my hobbies is attending food and wine festivals around the world. I enjoy seeing the diversity of cuisine across cultures and will try most things out of curiosity."

Quin tilted his head, his glare starting to lose its sharpness. Raz smiled. "Though to be honest, if you had served me a roasted bug, I probably would have had to leave the room. At one festival in the Philippines, I decided to try some of their bug delicacies and was sick for a week. I was never able to go fishing with my friends after that."

Alard turned his head to face Raz, his eyes wide. Raz was about to apologize, but Quin's booming laughter filled the hall. Norah joined in with the laughter, her wings twitching in time to her breaths. Raz gave Alard a triumphant grin, and Alard started laughing as well.

The tension in the room melted away, and when the laughter died down, Quin had a smile on his face. "I will make sure our chef knows to avoid them during your stay here, Razi."

"Thank you, my lord. And please, call me Raz."

"Very well, Raz."

They started to eat, and Alard reached under the table to squeeze Raz's thigh. Raz put the hand not holding his fork on top of Alard's, and they exchanged a quick smile.

"Raz, why don't you tell us how you met our son?"

Alard choked, and Raz was quick to pat Alard on his back to help him dislodge whatever he had swallowed. "Well, we actually had two first meetings," Raz explained. "We ran into each other in the lobby of the hotel I was staying in."

"Literally," Alard added. "I was on the phone with James and not watching where I was walking."

Quin hummed and leaned back in his chair. Raz felt the king's eyes on him again, but when he looked at Quin, the look was more thoughtful than judging. It was a welcome change, but Raz wished he knew what Quin was thinking.

"So, the next day, I was getting coffee, and Alard was there working with some of his clients," Raz said.

"Starbucks?" Norah asked.

"That's the name of the coffee shop I meet my homeless clients in," Alard explained. "The one with all the brass instruments on the ceiling."

Norah's eyes brightened in recognition. "Yes, you showed us pictures of that place. They use their earthly resources well."

"It's a beautiful sight," Raz continued. "I stood there watching Alard with his clients for a few minutes before he noticed me. Your son is very passionate about his work."

"Alard always cares for others less fortunate than he. I think that is one of his human qualities he maintained when we blessed him with our powers to become fairy," Norah spoke fondly of her son. "I hate having to pull him away from his passion, but we always knew it would end one day."

Raz's heart tightened, making him gasp a moment and press his hand against his sternum. Next to him, Alard's shoulders fell while he picked at his food. *He doesn't want to stay here*, Raz realized. "Well, perhaps he and Meyda can figure out an arrangement that will let him continue to do both."

"We had talked about that," Quin stated, sitting back up to his full height. "Being king isn't a part-time job. It is a lifelong commitment; one he has been raised to take. Splitting time between worlds would weaken the kingdom, as well as put doubt into the minds of the fairies that he isn't committed to them."

Raz shook his head. "Not necessarily. I mean, the kings and queens in my realm take vacations all the time."

"Yes, but among your own people," Quin pointed out. "Leaving them for another realm is perceived differently."

"It's okay, Raz," Alard spoke softly. "I've come to accept this realization."

Acceptance isn't what they were really talking about. The tug in his heart was the bond helping Raz understand what Alard truly felt. *Trapped.*

Silence hung in the room before Norah cleared her throat. "You were telling us about watching Alard at the coffee shop," she prompted, pulling the conversation away from the tangent it had taken.

"Yes," Raz nodded in thanks to the queen. "I was able to spend a short time there, but we got a proper introduction in that time. The third meeting was at a bar..." *How do fairies handle sexuality?* Raz realized he had no idea. "...Alard looked lonely, so we took a walk. At about that time, I realized I liked him and wanted to get to know him better."

Alard coughed, his ears turning red. "They don't need all the details."

"There are things parents don't need specifics about," Quin stated, amused at his son's embarrassment while Norah reached a hand across the short distance to pat her son's hand.

"I wasn't going to go into details. I was thinking about sitting in the park."

Alard leaned his head back, laughing. "Thank goodness."

"And after that, we kissed for the first time." Raz smiled at the memory of Alard's warm lips on his. The prince was just as passionate in romance as he was in his work.

"And we woke up the next day with the bond mark and have pretty much spent the time since trying to find a way to dissolve it," Alard said quickly, finishing the story for Raz.

"Did you find any solutions in the Grand Library?" Quin asked.

"There's a few things Raz and I will try tonight, but Elan wasn't confident on them working," Alard said. "If they don't, we'll start researching in the family archives down at the temple tomorrow."

"In the meantime, I will send a letter to the Kingdom of Fire and Ice informing them of the situation," Quin said.

"My lords," David entered the hall from a separate entrance behind Alard. They all looked to see the gnome standing like a soldier, an emotionless mask on his face. "That may not be necessary."

"And why is that?" Norah asked.

"King Eldren, Queen Willa, and Princess Meyda have arrived with their army. They demand an audience with the royal family immediately or they will order their soldiers to seize the kingdom."

CHAPTER NINETEEN

Alard stashed Raz in a dark alcove on the second floor of the throne room. He wanted Raz to be within earshot so that he could use his business sense to evaluate everything said and look for where negotiations could be made. Then Raz could convey that to Alard who, in turn, would use his lawyer skills in parlaying a temporary ceasefire.

If they survived this encounter.

Norah and Quin sat on their thrones, looking down at Meyda's parents. King Eldren was dressed in ceramic plate mail armor, painted red with orange flames etched in to make it look as if he was on fire. His dark red skin made it nearly impossible to distinguish how angry he was, but the explosive boom of his voice hid nothing.

"How dare you hide your son's maleficence from us?" Eldren loomed at the bottom of the stairs to the throne. "He has dishonored my daughter and the terms of our ceasefire!"

Alard lowered his head and sighed. He stood on the first floor almost directly below where Raz stood. The marble pillar behind him felt colder than normal where he leaned against it. He knew that the chill in the room emanated from Queen Willa's anger. Alard didn't have to look up to know her ice-white eyes glared in his direction. Willa remained silent, letting her husband release his anger as she stood at his side, an ice sculpture of a woman wrapped in a seaweed dress adorned with coral snaking up her sleeves.

"The Prince did not intend to harm either the Princess or our terms," Quin stated. "What happened is a mystery; an accident that he is working with the Grand Librarian to find a way to reverse. He still has every intention of marrying your daughter..."

A warm hand slipped into Alard's, and he lifted his head to see Meyda at his side. "I'm sorry," she whispered. "My chamber maid went to retrieve the tapestry from the cleaner and saw the bird and branch."

"It was bound to happen." Alard tried to smile, and Meyda squeezed his hand. "I wish it could have delayed this longer, but it couldn't stay hidden forever."

"Next time, I'll just get Timmie to set it on fire." Timmie, sitting on her shoulder, spit a tiny bolt of lightning into the marble in agreement.

"Thank you both." Alard chuckled at that and reached over to pet the drake. "So, how did they react? I mean, your father isn't creating a volcano in the throne room, so it's not that bad...right?" The volcano Eldren created when he learned that Alard was born human had nearly destroyed the griffin quarters. The King of Fire had a short temper, and when he got royally pissed, his top would blow. Literally.

"No, this time he left the volcano in my bedroom instead of the main chamber. I feel sorry for the servants—it's going to take weeks to get the ash out of my sitting room." Meyda nudged Alard to move over so they could share the pillar, only half listening to the quarrel between the kings. "Where's Raz?" Meyda whispered.

"Above us, behind the tapestry."

Nodding, Meyda turned her head to whisper into Timmie's ear. The drake warbled a reply and took off, heading to where the tapestry ended in the next archway and slid behind it. Alard tracked the tiny lump as it continued to rise, then disappeared when it got to the second floor.

"What'd you tell him to do?" Alard asked.

"Raz is unprotected, and I don't trust my parents when they are in a fury like this." Meyda stopped talking when Willa turned her head pointedly to stare at her daughter.

Alard leaned closer. "Your mom still scares me."

"You're not alone."

Willa smirked at that, confirming to Alard that the Queen of Ice could hear them over the raised voices of the kings. "Gentlemen," Willa spoke, turning back to face the kings, "perhaps it is Alard who should speak to his own defense?"

"I think that is a good idea." Norah stood, catching her son's eye and waving him forward.

Shit.

Alard let go of Meyda's hand and slunk forward to join the four royals. "Your Highnesses," he greeted his future in-laws, bowing.

"Prince Alard." Eldren crossed his arms, pushing out his chest to intimidate Alard into obedience. "I demand an explanation for your actions."

"Yes, Your Highness." Alard took a deep breath, then explained what happened in New Orleans in a similar manner that Raz spoke during dinner —just with less romantic detail. "I still don't understand how the bond formed in the human," Alard finished, "but we won't stop working on this until the bond is released. I intend to honor the terms and marry Meyda."

Eldren nodded, then looked at Quin. "Three days," he spoke, then looked back at Alard. "I will give you three days to find a solution. If you are unsuccessful, you will claim responsibility for breaking the ceasefire and abdicate your heirship to the Kingdom of Earth and Sky."

"What?" The worlds were out of Alard's mouth before his father had a chance to respond. "You can't be serious?"

"He is very serious, Prince Alard." Willa moved to link her arm with her husband. "Our daughter has no part in your actions beyond trying to hide the truth from her parents. If in three days you cannot break the bond, you will abdicate to her, and Meyda will become Queen of the Four Kingdoms, reuniting this realm once more."

"And what happens if Alard refuses?" Meyda asked, sliding to Alard's side and taking his hand again.

"Then we will break the ceasefire and will take their kingdom by force." Eldren stated. "And we won't stop until the Prince's head is on a pike."

"Father!" Meyda shouted her dissent but was drowned out by the shouts of outrage from Quin and Norah. Alard tuned it out, looking at his arm and the bond symbol and then over his shoulder. Raz stood in plain view on the balcony, his hands gripping the marble ledge to match the shock on his face. Timmie sat in a nest in Raz's hair, his wings beating against the air as he hissed.

"Quiet," Alard murmured, turning to face the chaos. When the argument didn't stop, he cleared his throat and straightened his bearing. "*I said quiet.*"

Silence filled the room; even Timmie's wings stilled. Alard walked up the stairs to stand between the two sets of parents. "I will find a way to break the bond. Until then, you and your soldiers are welcome to stay here. You can choose to help in the endeavor, or I will keep you informed of our progress. But hear me: You threaten my life, or my kingdom, once more, and I will not be responsible for my actions."

Alard looked at Meyda. He wasn't surprised to see her nod in agreement with his statement.

"The goes the same for me." Meyda moved to Alard's side, taking his arm. "I trust Alard to find a solution or an alternative that will allow the unification to proceed as planned. But Alard is also my friend, and if you try to kill him, I will disavow you, and you will have to find yourself another heir."

"Seriously?" Alard asked her quietly.

"Absolutely."

Willa's face hardened. She pressed a hand to her husband's chest. "Let us discuss this again tomorrow when tempers have settled."

"I second this," Norah said. "I will have David get your wing freshened up for your stay with us."

"Thank you, my lady," Willa said.

Quin looked at his son, then motioned with his head towards the balcony. "You are dismissed, Prince Alard."

Alard bowed in acknowledgement and started to move away with Meyda on his arm. She tugged him to a stop. "Let me go with my parents," she said, squeezing Alard's arm. "I'll try to make my father see reason."

"Thank you, Meyda. For everything." He took her hand and kissed her knuckles. "I will see you in the morning?"

"With bells on."

Alard gave her a short bow, then strode away from the thrones and into the hallway. He started up the stairs that led to the second-floor balcony but found Raz already halfway down them. "Are you—" Raz started to speak but Alard pressed a finger on Raz's lips.

"Not here. My rooms." Alard looked at Timmie, still nested on Raz's head. "Thank you for protecting him, Timmie," he told the drake, rubbing him under his chin. "Go back to Meyda now." The drake trilled and took off, heading downstairs before he disappeared around the corner.

Alard took Raz's hand and tugged him along as they walked back to Alard's room. He didn't trust talking outside of his rooms where Meyda's people might be lurking and could overhear them. He also didn't trust himself not to lose his composure until he was in his safe space.

When they reached the large door of his suite, Alard waved them open. His magic made them burst wide open, and he rushed Raz inside before slamming them shut with another wave. For added safety, Alard waved at the ceiling. A large, thick wooden beam lifted from where it was resting on two stony outcroppings. He focused, lowering it until it slid into steel hooks halfway up the door, creating a barricade between them and the rest of the castle.

"Alard?" Raz asked, his voice filled with concern in the single word.

Alard shook his head, feeling his lungs clenching. He fell backwards onto the floor, gasping for breath as his body trembled. His wings retracted inside of him, unconsciously shifting into his human form.

Raz knelt beside him, reaching for Alard's shoulder. "Hey, deep breaths. You're hyperventilating."

He knew that. Alard felt the panic cutting off oxygen to his brain, but he couldn't stop it. *They wanted to kill him!* It was worse than Alard thought. He royally screwed up this time and, so far, all signs were indicating that there was no solution. A strangled cry escaped his lips, and he wrapped his arms around his legs, pulling them tightly to his chest, trying to make himself as small as possible.

"Alard, breathe!" Raz's voice was so far away now. Why did Raz still care so much about Alard? It was his realm's magic that bound the human to him. Raz could have picked anyone in all of New Orleans to pick up at the bar, but no; he chose the one person who would screw up his life irreparably.

Alard never should have kissed Raz. Never let himself fall for a human.

His love was going to get them both killed.

The warmth of hands pressed against Alard's shoulders. Raz was trying to hold him. Alard knew he should push him away, stop whatever this was between them, but all he could do was lean into Raz's embrace as tears escaped Alard's eyes and washed down his face into Raz's shirt. The sound of Alard's sobs echoed off the walls, the only noise breaking the silence of the night.

Raz pulled Alard closer before standing with Alard in his arms bridal style. He walked them both to the couch in front of the fireplace. It was then, as the warmth from the fire caressed his skin, that Alard realized how far his temperature had dropped from sitting on the floor. He shivered, clinging tighter to Raz, unable to stop his sobbing.

A blanket wrapped around them as Raz sat on the couch, keeping Alard in his lap and pressed close to his body. Raz's hand rubbed small circles along Alard's back, and soon after, a soft humming lulled Alard down from his panic attack.

Alard clenched Raz's tunic in his fingers, desperate to hold on to something. As the sobs abated, Alard took a deep breath. "I'm sorry," he whispered, looking at the fire instead of Raz's face.

"For what?" Raz kept his voice soft, his arm keeping Alard from moving away. "None of this is your fault, Alard."

"Of course it is. If I was normal, none of this would have happened."

"You are normal."

Alard shook his head. "If I was a human, we wouldn't be bonded. If I was full-blooded fairy, I would never have been in the human realm."

"And if you weren't who you are, we never would have met."

Forcing his head to look up, Alard stared at Raz's face. "Is all this worth having met me?"

Raz tilted his head a moment, then shrugged. "I could deal with less talk about people dying, but yes, it is." Raz stroked Alard's cheek, brushing the tears away. "I would never wish to not have met you."

Alard chuckled, struggling not to start crying again. "You're crazy."

"Maybe." Raz thread his fingers through Alard's hair. "But I can't help it. You really do have a great ass."

Alard's eyes opened wide, and he laughed. Raz smiled at the sound, fingers continuing to play with the mess of hair on Alard's head. Fresh tears came to Alard's eyes, but these were happy ones. When the laughter faded, he nuzzled closer to Raz's chest.

"Raz," Alard whispered.

The blanket wrapped tighter around them. "Yeah?" Raz said.

"I think I'm falling for you."

The fingers stilled in Alard's hair for a moment. Alard looked up at Raz. There was a fondness in Raz's eyes and, without saying a word, Raz leaned down to kiss Alard. Shifting to let Raz lay on top of him, Alard kissed him back, his hands snaking around Raz's shoulders to keep him close.

He loved kissing Raz, tasting the spice of his lips and feeling the wet slide of their tongues dancing to music Alard could hear only in his head. He never wanted to stop kissing this man, to be lost in his arms in a world without marriage contracts and blood wars.

Alard groaned as Raz pressed his hips down against Alard's own. His body responded, his cock hardening at the friction to press back up. "Raz," Alard moaned softly against his lips.

"Alard?" Raz replied, his lips leaving Alard's and trailing down along his jaw.

"I want you," Alard admitted, and Raz looked up to lock eyes with him. The brown orbs questioned him, probably thinking of the threats from earlier. "I *need* you," he begged.

Raz nodded and pulled off his shirt quickly before leaning back over Alard and kissing his neck. As he did so, Raz's fingers went to Alard's pants' zipper and pulled it down. Alard lifted his hips so Raz could pull them off, leaving Alard in just a shirt as he kicked the clothing away.

He was already leaking from his cock, so Raz's hand slid along it easily. Unlike last time, he moved slowly, pumping up and down in time with their breathing. In moments, their breathing synced up, along with the beating of their hearts.

Alard fumbled, pawing at Raz's pants before the man undid his jeans and pushed them to his knees. Raz guided Alard's hand to his shaft, and

Alard joined in, stroking in time to their heartbeats, feeling Raz's cock grow hard and thick in his hands with each pump.

"Please," Alard begged, widening his legs on the chaise to fit Raz between them. He heard Raz spit into his hand, and then two fingers were at Alard's puckered hole, slowly pushing inside of him. He groaned, arching his back as he welcomed the stretching, and he moaned when a third finger joined.

"Raz," he cried, his hands holding onto Raz's arms to keep him from sliding off the couch. "Oh damn, please..."

"Don't let go," Raz whispered into his ear as he shifted around. A hand stroked along Alard's ass, then guided one leg up onto Raz's shoulder. The fingers left, only to be replaced by something bigger and firmer stretching him. He whimpered as it worked past his ring of muscles, then moaned as the shaft filled him so deep that Raz's hips pressed against his own once more.

Alard guided Raz's lips down for another kiss as Raz started thrusting in and out. This wasn't a race against getting caught, or a drunken tumble. It was more, something unspoken on the tips of their lips that neither would speak aloud, but their bodies made clear.

Each thrust drew a beath into Alard's lungs, and its withdrawal stealing the air back. His other leg wrapped around Raz's waist, trying to keep him deep inside with shallow thrusts hitting all the right spots. His arms wrapped around him, running along his back to feel each muscle as they flexed.

He had to memorize each moment so he could hold on to it in the cold and lonely days to come.

Raz groaned, and his thrusting picked up the pace. Harder and faster, his sweat dripping onto Alard as those brown eyes clouded in the lust of the moment. Alard hung his head back and instantly Raz was kissing and sucking along his neck. He clung to the man, then gasped as Raz started to stroke him in time to their thrusting.

Moaning, Alard thrust into the hand, chasing the euphoria waiting for him. As Raz gasped and stilled, his cock thickened before pumping burst after burst deep into Alard. The idea of being filled like that set off his own orgasm, releasing all over Raz's hand and stomach.

As they came down, Raz kissed his way up to Alard's lips, then pressed their foreheads together again. They didn't speak, just shared the oxygen between them as their heartbeats settled back into a matching rhythm. Still connected, Raz guided Alard's leg from his shoulder, then shifted to meld against his body. Alard held him, their fingers gently stroking each other's sides in the quiet afterglow. They were still royally screwed but in this moment, Alard refused to let the panic return. Instead, he focused on the man he was falling in love with, swearing silently to them both that he would find a solution that made everyone happy.

CHAPTER TWENTY

Raz left Alard's bedroom halfway through the night to relieve himself. The fire had died down, making the temperature in the suite drop. Unconsciously, Alard had rolled into the warm spot Raz left behind in the bed, making Raz smile in the darkness.

Oh, he was so screwed.

Pulling back on the pants from dinner, Raz shuffled across the marble floor to keep his feet from freezing in place. In the morning, Raz needed to thank Alard for having a human style bathroom in his suite. Tonight was not the night Raz wanted to learn the art of the chamber pot.

When he exited the bathroom, he saw a red light buzzing around the room. "Hello?" he whispered. "Can I help you?"

A tiny fairy zoomed into his face. The first thing that came to Raz's mind was a Treasure Troll toy with a fire opal embedded around where the belly button would be, and the orange-red hair sticking straight up and waving like fire.

"Are you Prince Consort Razi Miller?" she asked.

"Yes. Who are you?"

The fairy looked around the room, her hands twisting with nervous energy. When she focused back on Raz, she was biting her lip, and he wondered why this creature was so nervous. "I'm sorry about this," she said as she took a deep breath, and then blew a cloud of pink smoke into his face.

Raz waved his hand between them, trying to clear the smoke. He could feel it settle on his face, pink stardust clinging to his hand as well. "What are you..." Raz started to ask, but his head fogged over, and he stumbled back a step. As every second passed, his body grew more numb and heavy.

The fairy began to grow until she was the same size as Raz. "I'm really sorry, my lord, but I can't disobey my master." She gently guided Raz to the floor where a blanket was already spread. How had he not seen that?

Raz tried to speak, but he felt like he was engulfed in a marshmallow lulling him to sleep. The smell of a forest campfire and smores overtook him. The last thing he remembered was the fairy cocooning him with the blanket and kissing his forehead. "I promise I won't drop you."

He had no sense of how much time had passed. It had to be at least a few hours as the sun was rising, its rays waking Raz from his slumber. He tried to move but was still restrained by the blanket.

The forest floor beneath him was wet. Turning his head, he could see dew sliding down the blades of grass that rose high above his head.

Wait.

"What the hell?"

"Oh, you're awake!" The red fairy landed next to him, a bright smile on her face. "I was worried I used too much dust on you." She dropped to the ground, her legs crossing in a meditative pose. "I was told specifically to knock you out, not to kill you. Killing you isn't my job."

Raz freed his hand to rub his head, trying to massage away the growing headache. "Who are you?" he asked. "And why is the grass so tall here?"

"Firenze! Oh, but you can call me Fi. Everyone does because Firenze is long and can be a tongue twister to the ogres, and you don't want to do anything to make ogres mad." Fi bounced where she sat, her wings flittering with pent up energy. "And you're Razi, but people call you Raz? Why do they do that? Razi is pretty, and it isn't a tongue twister at all."

"Less exotic and easier to get through school with." Raz wiggled the blanket around his shoulders loose and tried to sit up, but the world spun.

Fi pushed him back down on his back. "You shouldn't get up too fast. I don't know how my dust works on humans. I've never met a human before.

I mean, I've seen Prince Alard when he dresses like one, but you're a real human. Really human. Do all humans look alike?"

"No, we don't." Raz had a feeling the headache wasn't going away anytime soon. He looked at Fi a moment, seeing the red tattoos that wound along her flesh like vines of thorns. "You didn't answer my question about the grass."

"Oh! I'm sorry." Fi's smile disappeared. She jumped up and went to put her hands on a blade. The dew slid down along it, and she cupped the drop in her hand. "Are you thirsty?"

She was deflecting, Raz realized. He'd come back to it later. "Yes."

Her smile back, Fi brought the drop to Raz. "Drink it from the top or you'll burst it all over yourself."

Raz sat back up—slower this time—and Fi handed him the dew drop. It wobbled in his hands, cold to the touch. Carefully, he leaned his head over the top and drew a sip from the bead of water. The freshness of the water excited his mouth, and he could detect a faint hint of the grass it had been resting upon. It was better than anything bottled he had ever tried.

"Thank you." When he had his fill, there was only a tiny bead of water left. He clapped his hands and let the water burst over his fingers to clean some of the dirt off them.

"You're welcome!" Fi bounced on her toes. "I can show you around the swamp now, if you want."

"I'd rather return to Alard," Raz stated. "I don't think he would like to know you took me away from him."

"He doesn't know. My master wanted me to make sure he was deep asleep before I brought you here." Her wings started to beat, making her hover a few inches off the ground.

"So, you used your dust on him too?"

Fi nodded vigorously. "When you left into the other room. He was so cute, clinging to the pillow you had just left. I could smell you on it, so I bet that's why. I wouldn't know. I never had a mate before."

"I'm pretty sure it's wrong to kidnap mates from each other."

"I know, but I had to do what I was told." Fi bit her lip as her wings stopped, dropping her back down. "Please don't be mad, Razi...I mean Raz. If I wasn't told to do it, I wouldn't have done it."

Raz thought about those words for a moment, and how Fi's energy disappeared when he brought this up. Something was wrong here. "Who told you to do it?"

"My master."

"Who is?"

Fi turned around, wrapping her arms around herself. "I can't tell you that."

Raz slowly stood up. The water seemed to have cleared the dizziness from his head. "Can you tell me why he had you bring me here?"

Fi shook her head. "I'm sorry. I only know he grabbed a raven from the sky to eat, and it had a letter attached. He asked me to go after he ate."

Raz sighed and took a good look at their surroundings. His mind now clear, he realized that the grass wasn't the only thing towering over them. Trees reached up into the heavens, disappearing in a layer of morning mist. A bird was sitting on a branch, a hundred times larger than it should have been.

He blinked, remembering how small Fi had been in the bedroom. Maybe it wasn't her that grew. "Fi, did you shrink me down?!"

She nodded in confirmation, her wings drooping further. "It was easier to carry you. Full size people are too heavy for my wings."

"I'd like to go back to my real size now."

Fi shook her head again. "If I do, my master will see you."

"Wasn't taking me to him the whole reason you kidnapped me?"

"I'm really sorry, Raz!" She turned back to him, tears in her eyes. "That's why I kept us small. Ogres can't see tiny things. As long as you're small, there's a chance you'll be rescued."

Raz narrowed his eyes, scenarios of rescue spinning in his head. They all had a common factor. "The ogre wants Alard?"

"No, he wants you. But you have this." Fi took his arm gently and traced a finger along the bond tattoo. "Your prince can find you with it. You can too, but you'd need more magic gifted to you to feel it like that."

"Yeah, Alard told me I can't take any more into me or I risk no longer being human." Raz looked at the tattoo. The glow was there, faintly, and the words on the infinity loop were hidden in the radiance.

"He's right." Fi said. "And you have magic from both kingdoms in you. Anyone could become master over you if they asserted enough energy into it."

"Like the ogre does with you?" It was a guess, but as Fi's eyes opened wide, Raz knew he had nailed it. "Can you break that kind of magic?"

"There are a few ways. The King of Fire can, and the Princess. They have the royal bloodline of fire creatures. They can cancel any fire magic spells."

"Beyond them, anyone else?"

"Someone who is willing to fight my master for me and wins."

"What if your master dies?"

Fi nodded. "Yeah, I'd be free then too."

Raz nodded, his mind working on a solution that got both him and Fi free of the situation. Maybe he could ask the bird to take a message to Alard. He'd watched Alard send a scroll to Meyda via bird, so he should be able to.

Before he could voice his idea to Fi, a shadow fell over them. Both he and Fi snapped their heads up to see a gray face with veins of lava looking down at them. "There you is, pretty Fi. You get us Prince Consort. Good. Now grow big."

Swallowing, Raz turned to see Fi reaching down to touch her opal. "I'm *really* sorry."

CHAPTER TWENTY-ONE

The warm nose of the fire drake brought Meyda out of her dreams. It had been a good dream of just sitting on a beach along the southern edge of the salt rivers, a book in hand and endless refills of the strawberry tea she adored. No one for miles except for Timmie who was supposed to be asleep in a sunspot.

The nose was persistent. Meyda opened her eyes to see the two tiny black orbs looking at her. Timmie whined in the back of his throat, nudging her again.

"What is it?" she asked before yawning, sitting up and stretching her arms above her head.

The drake warbled, flying up to hover in front of her face. He was going too fast for Meyda to understand. "Slow down and tell me again."

A spark of lightning left Timmie's mouth. Meyda could see he was upset. The drake warbled again—slower—and when he was done, Meyda whipped her head to look at her pillows.

Pink dust. A fire fairy's sleep smoke they exhaled when needed. It was against the laws of the realm to use it on royalty, but the evidence was right there.

Before she had time to question it, her father's booming voice came from the other side of the door. Meyda grabbed her robe and rushed to the door dividing her room from her parents in the guest wing.

Eldren and Willa stood near the fireplace as castle gnomes rushed into the room. A small contingent rushed past her as well when the door opened. Her parents walked over to her, checking Meyda for any signs of foul play.

"Did you have dust on your pillows too?" Meyda asked.

"Yes," Willa replied. "If it wasn't for your father's snoring, I don't think we would have awakened this early."

"How dare they turn one of my own subjects against us!" Eldren shouted. "I will have their heads for this!"

Meyda placed her hands on Eldren's chest. "Father, please. Let us first figure out what happened before we lay blame."

"It is clear, my daughter, who is to blame," Eldren stated. "We stand in their castle. They find someone from our own realm to do this—"

"But what benefit would come from putting us to sleep, husband?" Willa interjected. "We were all kept safe and warm in our beds. If they wanted to harm us, they wouldn't have just put us to sleep."

The logic deflated the raw anger in Eldren. "You do speak the truth, wife."

"We should check on Quin and Norah," Willa said. "It could be an attack on them, and the fairy was to keep us asleep so we couldn't aid them."

Meyda gasped, tying her robe tightly. "Alard." She whistled for Timmie. "You two check on the king and queen, Timme and I will check on the prince."

Timmie arrived from the other room. He landed in the hallway just beyond the suite doors and started to grow until he was about the size of a horse. Meyda ran to him and jumped onto his back. "To Alard's rooms, quickly!"

They flew through the castle, swerving to avoid statues and guards. Meyda knew her parents would be following in her wake, so she didn't turn into the wing where Quin and Norah lived. Instead, she and Timmie dove down a staircase, twisted through two more hallways that overlooked the central garden, and landed in front of Alard's large wooden door.

Meyda dismounted and went to open the door, only to find it locked. "Alard!" she shouted, banging on the door. There was no answer. She kept trying, knowing that Alard's room was the furthest from the main entrance. He rarely slept with his bedroom door closed though, so he should be able to hear her.

When the silence in the room continued far longer than Meyda's patience, she took a few steps back and looked at her hand. *I can't burn down the door. It's protected from fire. I could freeze it, but it would shatter and destroy the artwork.*

Meyda tried to remember where all the hidden passages in the castle ran. There was one that led to Alard's room from the servants' quarters. That same doorway also connected to his parents' bedroom. There was a spell needed to open the doors; one she didn't know.

"This fucks!" she shouted. *Or was it sucks?* Alard said both a lot. She wasn't supposed to use the human words, but it felt right in the moment.

"Fine, ice it is." She pressed her hands together to start the spell, but Timmie tugged on her robe. "I need to get in there, my friend."

Timmie tugged again, pulling her to the hallway. She tossed a look at the door again, then followed the drake as he flew around a corner. He stopped on the sill of a window arch looking out over the courtyard.

Meyda smiled. "You beautiful boy. Take me there."

Unable to grow back to the horse size because of the window size, Timmie grew large enough to wrap his arms around Meyda's shoulders. He picked her up and carried her the short distance to the window of Alard's suite.

The door from the balcony into Alard's bedroom was open. Once Timmie released her, Meyda ran into Alard's room and to the bedside. The prince was still fast asleep in his human form. His pillow and hair covered in dust—much more than Meyda had found on herself. She sat next to him, out of reach of the dust, and shook his arm. "Alard, wake up!"

He didn't stir.

Meyda rolled Alard onto his back. She saw his chest rising and falling, so he was still alive. There were tales of fairies who could put others to sleep indefinitely. Meyda hoped this wasn't the case.

She leaned over his face, blowing the traces of dust away from his nose and mouth. "Come on, Alard, you need to wake up."

Timmie jumped on Alard's chest, now back to his tiny size. He bumped his head against Alard's breastbone, helping Meyda wake her best friend. When it became clear touching and shouting wasn't working, Meyda pressed her hands together.

"Sorry, my friend, but this may be the only way." She muttered a few words to herself and held her hands over Alard's face.

Then the rain fell.

———

Alard jerked away as the freezing water stung his face. He sat up, his head smacking into the pair of hands above him. Meyda squeaked, fisting her hands to stop the water from running out of them.

"What the hell, Meyda?" Alard pushed his wet hair off his face.

Meyda summoned a towel to her hand from Alard's basket of linens near the bedroom fireplace. It was warm. She leaned forward to dry his face. "You were under a sleeping spell."

"A what?" Alard's brain was still booting up. He took the towel from her and rubbed his hair.

"We were attacked...if you call sleeping spells an attack." She whistled for Timmie and ordered him to let her parents know that Alard was awake, then sent him off. "Do you remember getting hit with it?"

"No. After meeting with your parents, I came back here and had a small breakdown. We went to bed after that."

"Where's Raz now?"

"He was just here." Alard looked at the other side of the bed, but it was cold. Raz hadn't been there for hours. "No, no, they wouldn't."

Alard pushed away the drenched covers and jumped out of bed. He slipped on the wet floor but regained his balance quickly. Both he and Meyda ran into the main room, then knocked on Raz's closed bedroom door. "Raz!" Alard shouted. "Are you in there?"

No answer. Alard opened the door and looked around. The bed was still perfectly made, Raz's bag on top with some clothing pulled out from when they had been deciding on what to wear to dinner.

"Where could he go?" Meyda asked. "The door was barred from the inside."

Alard moved back into the main room, rubbing his arms from the cold of the room and his wet hair. Meyda waved her hand to bring the fire back to life, wood flying into the stone opening. His eyes focused on the floor, looking for any sign that might reveal where Raz had disappeared to.

As he scanned the floor outside the bathroom, he saw the hint of pink outside the door. "Meyda, what kind of sleeping spell were we hit with?"

"Fire fairy," Meyda replied. "They breathe a pink smoke made of sleeping dust."

"Shit." He approached the door, avoiding the dust with his feet, and opened the door.

The bathroom was empty. The floor and sink were covered in dust, and there was a smear in it that looked like something dragged through it. The drag was short, and Alard assumed that Raz was picked up to keep the evidence of the abduction to a minimum. "He was knocked out and taken," he told Meyda, turning to look back in the room. "But like you said, the door was barricaded."

"Alard, fire fairies have wings. They're part fire, part air." Meyda pulled him to the window. "They had to have come and gone through the window."

"Depending on how long we've been asleep, Raz could be anywhere in the realm." Alard threw a clay pot across the room. It shattered against the door, the pieces spraying back into the room from the force of the impact. "He could be hurt...Meyda what if they killed him?"

"You'd know." Meyda put her hand on his shoulder. "You'd feel it."

"I don't feel anything from the bond." Alard looked at the tattoo, willing it to give him an answer.

Meyda shook her head. "All I know about the bond is what Elan's books said, and I saw it yesterday when you ran to Raz's side when I gave him some of my magic. If he was hurting, you'd *know*."

"Books." Alard pushed past her and went to his desk. The piles of books he had borrowed from the library sat undisturbed. He opened one, flipping through the pages, then closed it and repeated the steps with each of them. "We took a book about how the bond operates. Raz was going to email a friend a hypothetical design of it and see if their experience in operating systems could find any similarities to codes."

"Codes?" Meyda asked, standing at his side.

"How computer programs run." He stopped at a specific page and started to read the symbols. "There was something here...there it is."

Meyda leaned over his shoulder to read along with him. "Bonds and Location Spells."

"It talks about the emotional connection, but there's a way I can have it nudge me towards where he is." Alard started to write down a list of ingredients. "I hope this isn't just a way to cheat in hide and seek."

Meyda moved behind Alard's desk, pulling down the ingredients from the various decorative boxes that sat in front or on top of books in the bookcase. "Here, I'm better at magic than you. Tell me what to do."

They worked in tandem, Meyda putting the ingredients in a gold bowl from the top of the bookcase while Alard focused on the pronunciation of the verbal component. When everything was ready, Alard nodded to Meyda. She snapped her fingers, and the ingredients burned from an internal flame. Green smoke rose into the air, and Alard waved his hands to have the smoke move to him so he could inhale it. The scent of pine, soil, licorice root, and Raz's cologne assaulted him, but Alard pushed past the overload and focused his eyes on the tattoo. He spoke the incantation, then blew the smoke out over the bond symbol.

His heart tugged towards the window. He walked to it, watching as a magical line extended from his arm and curved around the castle and onto the path leading back to Meyda's kingdom. "I see the path," He told Meyda, unfolding his wings and stretching them out.

"I'll summon Timmie—"

Alard shook his head. "I don't know how long the spell will last. I need to leave now."

"But Alard, you and flying...?"

"I know," he said, looking into her eyes as his eyes glowed, his transformation back to his real appearance complete. Meyda knew how much Alard hated to fly, how out of control he felt when he couldn't stop his forward momentum. The determination in his eyes told Meyda that he didn't care about the risks this time. "He needs me now. Follow me when you can."

"Wait!" Meyda ran to the fireplace and pulled the sword and shield from the armor that stood by the fireplace. "Take these at least."

Alard nodded, strapping the shield to his arm and tied the sword belt to his waist above his pants. He leaned in to kiss her forehead, then took off flying out the window, over the courtyard wall and disappearing around the curve of the tower.

He held his arms in front of him, flying just above the tree line as he aimed for the swamplands. The brown line glowed, showing him the way.

I'm coming, Raz. Just hold on.

CHAPTER TWENTY-TWO

The rapid growing, along with the empty stomach and recently drugged brain, had Raz on his knees, gagging as he coughed up the dew water. His head spun. He closed his eyes to prevent the dizziness from making him gag further.

Even back to their normal heights, the ogre towered over Raz and Fi. The fire fairy hovered just off the ground with her arms twisted in front of her body.

"Prince Alard's human wench." The ogre rumbled with laughter, the ground shaking. "Weak. Stand up!"

Raz raised his head, glaring. "From what I've been told, until I'm no longer mated to Alard, I'm royalty in this realm."

"Grah say no human be prince." Reaching down, the ogre—Grah—grabbed Raz by the back of his pants and lifted him into the air. Raz flung his arms around the ogre's thumb to keep from tipping forward, then lifted himself a bit to keep from having his pants slice him from crotch up.

"I think decisions like that are out of your control, Grah." Raz wrapped his legs around the thumb next, feeling like a pygmy marmoset.

"Grah answer to no king. Only clan." Grah tried to shake Raz off, but Raz just clung tighter.

"So, if you don't answer to the royalty, why does it matter whether I'm a prince or not?"

Grah didn't answer, just raised his hand so that Raz was in front of his face. Raz did his best to not gag at the smell of rotting wood and ash coming from Grah's open mouth. "Human bad for realm. Destroy everything for themselves."

"Trust me, that's not a new one," Raz said. "Is that why the fairy realm split from the human realm?"

Grah laughed. "We kick human out. Let them destroy own realm."

"If it makes you feel better, I plan on returning to the human realm once Prince Alard and I are no longer bonded."

"Bonds don't break. You be here forever. Make human baby. Destroy fairy realm. Grah no let happen."

There were a lot of things in that statement Raz knew were incorrect, or at least he hoped so. He also assumed that Grah didn't know of Alard's human origins, so he wasn't going to bring that up. "Maybe not, but I can't live in this realm, Grah. I know I don't belong here, and I want to go home."

Grah kept watching him, making Raz nervous. All he wore was a pair of pants. He had no weapons. If Grah wanted to kill him, Raz was certain that it would happen. *Alard, if there was ever a time to find me through this bond, that would be now.*

"Maybe we could make a deal?" Raz asked. He took a moment to look for Fi, finding her peeking out from behind a tree. "Is there something you want that maybe only a human can do?"

"Human has no magic. Human worthless." Grah laughed again. "Human only good as lunch."

"Actually, I've been told eating human flesh drives people insane."

"Grah take chance." The ogre lifted Raz above his head, leaned his head back with his mouth open, and released his grip on Raz's pants.

Raz tightened his grip on Grah's thumb. The stench intensified, drool escaping between Grah's rotted teeth. Raz gagged, fingers slipping from their grip.

"Release him at once!" Alard's voice cut through the swamp. Raz turned his head as Alard flew out of the tree line and straight at Grah's face. Alard pulled a sword off his belt, slicing it across Grah's face. The ogre screamed, flinging his arms out to stop the attack.

And in flinging his arms out, Raz went flying.

Shouting for help, Raz tried to flip around to see where he was going to land. He was almost there when hands grabbed him under his arms. "I got you!" Fi said, her voice strained from suddenly taking his weight.

Losing altitude with Raz's extra weight, Fi landed them both near a large boulder, then pulled him behind it. "If we stay here, Grah can't step on us," she told him.

Raz nodded. "I approve of this plan."

They peeked out from behind the boulder and watched as Alard flew back and forth, slashing at the ogre with each pass. Neither spoke as they fought, not stopping to notice that Raz was out of harm's way. Each time the sword cut the ogre, sparks would burst from the impact point, the crash of steel hitting stone reverberating in the air. The cuts were shallow though, and lava formed to fill the space, cooling the instant it hit the morning air.

Grah swiped at Alard, but the fairy prince was too fast when in flight. For someone who didn't fly much, his wings worked like a hummingbird with how fast Alard moved. It now made sense why Alard had a hard time stopping. At that speed, Raz could barely make out Alard's form beyond a streak of bright green in the air. Instead, Alard arched through the air with each pass, rather than stopping to turn around. It worked, but Raz wondered how long Alard could last in the air; his wings were smaller than average, and he rarely used them.

Before Raz had time to wonder further, Grah managed to grab Alard's leg. The ogre gave a grunt of satisfaction. "Fairy Prince try hurt Grah. Fairy Prince fail." With that, he flung Alard against a tree. Alard cried out as he hit it chest first, then fell to the ground and lay still.

The spike of pain hit Raz hard. He stumbled back from the rock, hands around his waist, trying to cover the painful spot. "Alard!" Raz moved from his hiding space toward where Alard lay, then looked up as a shadow fell over him from above. Grah reached down, intending to pick Raz up again, but stopped as he was hit with a bolt of lightning from the tree line.

Just above the trees hovered an enormous fire drake, his black bat-like wings causing the trees to bend with each flap. It wasn't until he saw Meyda standing on the drake's back, holding a rope with one hand to keep her balance, that Raz realized the drake was Timmie.

"That was just a warning shot, friend ogre," Meyda shouted. "You best step away from my friends, or the next one will shatter you into pieces."

Grah looked back and forth between Raz and Meyda, then growled and walked away. The ogre sat back on a fallen tree trunk, mumbling to himself. Timmie landed a moment later in the center of the clearing, his black eyes never taking their sight off Grah.

"It's the princess!" Fi landed on Raz's shoulder. She was back in her shrunken size. "She is not going to be happy with me!"

"Just stay with me, and I'll explain everything to her," Raz said as he headed to where Alard lay. "Meyda isn't a cruel person."

"Okay." Fi hid herself behind Raz's ear, and Raz resisted the urge to scratch the spot as her wings and hair tickled his neck.

Kneeling next to Alard, Raz checked for a pulse. "Wake up, Alard. It's over." Raz felt a strong pulse and sighed in relief. Alard was alive. His panic abated; Raz noticed that Alard's back was also lifting every few seconds; he was also breathing. *Good.* "Come on, pretty boy, I need you to open your eyes. I can't roll you onto your back to see if I can wake you up with a kiss."

"How is he?" Meyda knelt beside them.

"He's alive, just unconscious." Raz ran his fingers through Alard's hair. "I just can't seem to wake him up, and I don't want to flip him and hurt his wings while they are out."

"Here, I'll help." Meyda gently pulled one of Alard's wings out, keeping it from getting crushed as Raz carefully rolled Alard over. She then held Alard a few inches off the ground as Raz shifted the other wing out from under him.

The spot on Alard's chest where he had connected with the tree was already turning purple. He had no armor or tunic to pad him during the impact. There were also bits of bark embedded into his flesh, tiny puddles of blood gathering under his iridescent skin waiting to exit once they picked out the wood.

"Some of those are too small. We won't be able to get them all," Meyda said, reaching for a larger splinter.

"I can help with that." Fi shifted out from behind Raz's ear and fluttered down to Alard's chest. "I can pick out the little ones."

Meyda narrowed her eyes. "You're the one who knocked us all out."

"I know, and I'm sorry. I didn't have a choice." Fi bit her lip, trembling under the gaze of the princess.

"That ogre is her master," Raz explained, throwing a glare at Grah.

"Is that so?" Meyda's eyes deepened to a dark red color. "After Alard is awake, we shall fix that."

They worked in silence, removing the splinters piece by piece. Meyda summoned water to her hands and washed away the dirt and blood once they were certain they were all out. Not even the cold water on his chest brought Alard out of his unconsciousness.

"Should I try kissing him now?" Raz asked.

"It doesn't work that way, I'm afraid," Meyda whispered as she stroked Alard's cheek. "Kisses are powerful, but only against magic and then only if there is a strong bond between the two."

"It helps break sleep spells," Fi spoke up, back on Raz's shoulder. "Is that how you woke him up from mine?"

Jealousy tugged at Raz's heart again. He knew Alard and Meyda were free in their affection for each other, but he had yet to see them kiss each other. Was this something they did? If she didn't want to be married, why would Meyda be that affectionate with Alard?

"Ow," Alard groaned before Meyda could answer. He reached up to rub his eyes. "Whoever is squeezing my head, please stop."

Raz and Meyda sighed in relief. Raz continued threading fingers through Alard's hair as Meyda stroked Alard's cheek. "There you are," she said softly. "You had us worried."

"What happened?" he asked, staring up at her.

"You got thrown into a tree." Meyda smiled down at him, and that pang of jealousy in Raz flared again. Alard groaned and squeezed his eyes again. "You should have grown your armor before flying off like that."

"Yeah, remind me to do that next time."

"There's going to be no next time," Raz stated, tugging on Alard's hair a bit to make his point.

Alard rolled his head to look at Raz, and he smiled. "Did I at least look impressive before I got my ass kicked?"

Raz chuckled. "Yes, you did, my personal prince charming."

The tension eased, and soon Meyda and Raz helped Alard to his feet. Alard kept one arm wrapped around Raz's waist for extra balance. Fi, forgotten once Alard had woken up, landed back on Raz's shoulder. He turned his head to look at her. "Thank you," he whispered to her, and Fi blushed.

They walked across the clearing to where Timmie was staring down the ogre. Grah hadn't moved, but instead held a stick. He was digging it into the swamp floor, making designs in the mud.

"I believe you owe us an explanation, Ogre," Alard said.

"His name is Grah," Raz told Alard.

Alard nodded, then pushed himself up to his full height. "Why did you have my husband kidnapped, Grah?"

"Grah got letter," the ogre growled. "Want know how break marry bond. Grah know bond go away when dead. Grah do what asked, Highness. No hurt him. Be quick dead."

"You will address me as Lord Alard. Princess Meyda is a highness."

"Sorry, m'lord," Grah huffed.

Fi left Raz's shoulder and grew to her normal height in front of them. "It's true. He didn't want the Prince Consort hurt." She kept her head bowed as she faced the two royals. "I was under specific orders to make sure that anything I did would not cause pain or harm."

Alard watched Fi a moment, then looked at Raz. "You believe her?"

Raz nodded. "If Grah wanted to hurt other people, she could have killed any of us in our sleep."

"He *did* want to hurt you," Meyda pointed out.

"Grah was trying to solve a problem...in his own way." Raz looked up at the ogre, seeing the fiery eyes watching him carefully in return.

"If this letter had not gone out, would you have done this?" Alard asked.

"No, m'lord," Grah said. "Grah not know human here until letter say so."

"Fi?" Raz asked, wanting her confirmation.

"I told you, I never met a real human before," she explained to Raz. "I only knew you were here because my master asked me to fetch you."

"Speaking of that." Meyda stepped forward to get Grah's attention. "You will release this fairy from your hold."

Grah moaned. "Not pretty Fi."

"Either you do it or I will." Meyda's eyes started to glow. "And you don't want me to do magic over you when I'm angry."

Huffing, Grah reached into a crevice of his chest. He pulled a steel ball from inside himself and dropped it on the ground. "There, Highness. Fi free."

Meyda nodded to Fi, and she flew forward and pressed her hands to the ball. It cracked open and a silver mist exited the cracks and wrapped around her. Silver and blue scarfs wrapped themselves around her naked body while blue streaks of color pushed into her wings in spots that had been clear.

She turned back to look at the group, and Raz swore it was a different fairy. Fi held herself still, looking specifically at Raz for approval. "So, this is really you?" Raz asked.

"Yes. I have my air essence back." Fi started to bounce again on her feet, and Raz smiled. "I really am sorry for my part in this."

"You are absolved of the crime, Fi." Alard released Raz, able to stand on his own now. "Grah, consider this a warning. Try to interfere in royal business, and next time there will be no leniency."

Grah grunted and spat on the ground. "Grah under-stand." He stood up, casting a sad look at Fi before skulking away.

When the ogre was gone from sight, Alard slumped. Raz rushed over to support him before he fell over. "I think it's time we head back home," Raz suggested.

"I agree," Alard said. "Timmie, think you can handle three of us?"

The drake snorted and lowered his belly to the ground. Meyda helped Alard climb up first while Raz turned back to face Fi. "Well, you're free. What are you going to do now?"

"I don't know," Fi said, bouncing in place. "I do owe you though. Is there something I can do for you?"

"You owe me nothing, Fi. Just go be free and find a life that makes you happy."

Fi bit her lip, looking over Raz's shoulder to check where Alard and Meyda were, then leaned forward to hug Raz tightly. "Thank you," she whispered into his ear, her body vibrating against his.

Fi pulled away and smiled, then took off flying into a different part of the swamp from where Grah had disappeared. Raz watched her go, then rejoined Alard and Meyda. Meyda helped Raz climb onto Timmie's back, and when she followed him up, Raz found himself sandwiched between Meyda and Alard.

Raz wrapped his arms around Alard's waist, and Alard leaned back against him in return. "I'm sorry," Alard murmured.

"You're not at fault in this at all," Raz told him. "Now let's get you home so we can make sure you didn't break a rib rushing to my rescue."

Alard rested his head on Raz's shoulder, a sleepy grin on his lips. "Would've been worth it."

CHAPTER TWENTY-THREE

Alard had fallen unconscious on the ride back. There were a lot of questions that needed answering about the abduction and the origins of this letter. Yet while in the warmth of Raz's arms, knowing that they were safe, Alard decided it could wait a few hours while slipping into a healing sleep.

When consciousness returned, the cushion beneath him was not the warm body of his husband, but the familiar embrace of his bed. Someone was stroking his hand—a coolness that didn't come from a warm-blooded human or a daughter of fire. Alard opened his eyes and saw his mother sitting at his side.

Norah smiled when Alard opened his eyes. "Good evening, my darling," she said. "How do you feel?"

Alard took stock of his physical state. His head still hurt, but not nearly as bad as before. The pain from his chest and back was almost gone. "Better," he told his mother, just before his stomach growled. "And hungry, it seems."

"I will ask David to send up your tray." She shook her wrist, the sound of bells coming from her sleeve. "The others are in the dining hall having dinner, but I'm sure they will rush up once they know you're awake."

"Thank you, Mother."

A warm breath across his cheek drew Alard's attention to the side. Timmie was curled up on the pillow. He stretched then, rising and walking over. He licked Alard's nose with his forked tongue and then purred his greeting.

"Let me guess, Meyda told you to stay here and watch me." Alard reached up with his free hand to scritch Timmie behind his ears.

"He is a very loyal drake," Norah said. "I see why you and Meyda love him so much."

"He is a very good boy," Alard said, chuckling as Timmie pressed his head into the affection.

David arrived and left to fetch Alard food, leaving mother and son alone once again. "What happened when we returned?" Alard asked his mother.

"Nothing much. David and his gnomes spent the day cleaning up the fairy dust from the bedrooms and your bathroom. You can take a shower later, but I gave you a cloth bath so that you wouldn't go to bed covered in swamp."

"I appreciate that," Alard said with a yawn, leaning back into his pillow. His hand dropped from Timmie, and the drake flew to curl up on Alard's chest.

"Your father has talked with Meyda's parents and kept the peace. Raz and Meyda had been waiting for you to wake, at least until David served dinner. I believe they are eating in the kitchen as so to keep Raz from meeting Eldren and Willa."

"Did they tell you about this letter the ogre mentioned?"

"Indeed. Your father and Eldren spent the afternoon trying to track down the source. So far, they have been unsuccessful."

"Perhaps Elan may know."

Alard started to sit up, but Timmie growled at the sudden movement. Norah put her hand on Alard's shoulder to press him back down. "You have not finished healing yet," Norah said. "You must rest until morning."

"I feel fine."

"Mother's orders." Norah gave him a stern look, and Alard sighed in defeat.

"Can I at least sit against the headboard? Otherwise, I will make a mess eating."

Norah helped rearrange his pillows so he was sitting up when Raz and

Meyda arrived with the food tray. "I see your companions have returned," Norah said as she stood up. "Remember, rest until tomorrow." She turned to look at Raz and Meyda. "I will leave that up to you two."

"Yes, my lady," Meyda replied, giving a half-curtsey. Raz was a second behind with a bow.

Smiling, Norah leaned forward to kiss Alard's forehead. Then, after a quick pet along Timmie's muzzle, the queen left the room.

Meyda moved to take her place sitting beside Alard on the bed. Timmie flew up to her shoulder, warbling. "Yes, you were a good boy," she replied, rubbing under his chin.

"You know, you two keep spoiling him like that, and he's going to become fat and lazy," Raz said as he placed the tray of food on Alard's lap.

"He's my baby," Meyda said as Timmie hissed in Raz's direction. "And I'll spoil him if I want to." She finished her statement by sticking her tongue out at Raz, causing the other man to laugh.

Alard shook his head, amused at their antics. "I'm happy you two get along so well," he said.

Raz pulled the chair closer to the bed and sat down. "No one can say you don't have good taste. Plus, I'm pretty sure Meyda is the nicest person I've ever met, even when she's riding into battle like a Valkyrie intending on death and destruction."

"Thank you, Raz."

While eating his dinner, Meyda and Raz told Alard their version of the aftermath of the kidnapping. Meyda kept her parents from meeting Raz; there was a chance Eldren or Willa had sent the letter to Grah. "Security will be upgraded for the overnight hours—guards at each suite doors and in the courtyard to watch windows," she explained. "Speaking of which, I told my parents I would spend the evening in their suite before bed. I should go and honor that."

"We'll see you at breakfast," Alard assured her.

Meyda left, taking Timmie with her. Raz leaned forward, watching as Alard ate. There was a heaviness in the air that Alard couldn't place, focusing on his food instead of Raz's observant eyes.

When the plate was empty, Alard knew he had to address the uncomfortable silence. "What's wrong?"

"We both almost died today because of this," Raz said, the lightness of his voice gone now that they were alone. "If you hadn't shown up, I would have."

"Raz..."

"No, let me finish." Raz stood up and removed the tray from Alard's lap, leaving it on the bedside table. "I knew coming here was going to be risky. I'm used to being the focus of someone else's hate. But things Grah said...that went beyond simple bigotry. What happened to make your people hate humans so much?"

Alard motioned for Raz to lay down next to him. Raz moved around the bed and sat cross-legged on top of the blankets. "It's a very long story, going back thousands of years to when both our realms existed as one."

The story was easy to understand. Magic and man had existed as one during the early millennia of the Earth's lifespan. Neanderthal walked the Earth then and both respected and feared magic. Clans had members that learned how to use magic for healing and protection. Nature and life were respected by both.

Then Homo sapiens arrived, and the balance shifted.

"Oberon was King of the Fairies during that time, and his was the last rule in the coexisting habitat," Alard explained. "That's why a lot of your myths mention him. He saw what the humans were capable of and feared that their traits would spread to other species. Then he watched as humans started to kill each other—for power.

"The split was supposed to prevent the idea of murder for power from taking root. It was only generations later, centuries after the split, that the kings of old realized they had been too late." Alard slid down a bit further into his bed. "The worst example being when this realm split into separate kingdoms."

"Which you're trying to fix now." Raz sighed.

"Trying to." But would he be able to? Finding an answer was getting less probable as each day passed. There was going to be a time—sooner rather than later—where they would have to admit the bond wasn't going to go away. A moment where either he or Raz, possibly both, would end up dead amid the coming war.

Yet, as Raz shifted to lay beside him, pulling Alard into his arms so that they could sleep, Alard knew he would give his life to keep Raz safe.

He just hoped that wasn't going to be the only option.

CHAPTER TWENTY-FOUR

"Now, when you enter the dining hall, do not show affection to each other," Meyda warned from the doorway of the dining hall. "You can't let my parents think for a moment that you are anything more than stuck in this situation, Raz."

Meyda watched as the two men took a step further away from each other. She hated putting them into this situation, but decorum required it.

Breakfast with her parents. This could go wrong in so many ways. Meyda just hoped everyone survived it with all limbs attached. "In fact, let me sit between you two. I mean, I'm supposed to sit next to Alard anyway, but the extra person will give the illusion—"

"Meyda, relax." Alard put both hands on her shoulders. "We got this. It isn't my first rodeo with your parents, and I doubt it will be the last."

Raz raised his hand a bit in the air. "Um, it is my first one."

"This is going to be a disaster." Meyda dropped her head into her hands. "My mother is going to chew you up and spit you out alive."

"Don't worry about me," Raz stated. "I've stared down CEOs scarier than her."

"I don't know what a CEO is, but you don't know my mother."

David joined them in the doorway. "Your parents have entered and are at their seats, my lords, my highness." He motioned for the three of them to enter.

"Here goes nothing." Alard let go of Meyda and motioned for her to lead them.

They followed proper protocol with Meyda entering first, followed by Alard, and Raz at the end. They silently walked to the set of three plush chairs now set up on Quin's side of the table. Eldren and Willa stood behind the chairs on Norah's side, both watching the heirs enter but with their attention on Raz.

Please don't kill anyone, she prayed towards her parents.

Alard pulled out the middle seat for Meyda to sit at before the boys flanked her. Quin nodded and moved to sit, signaling everyone else to join him.

"You appear to have recovered well, Prince Alard," Eldren stated as he pushed Willa's chair in. Alard did the same for Meyda, and she took his hand and squeezed it in thanks.

"I feel better. Thank you for your concern, Your Highness."

"And I see your consort was not harmed in yesterday's debacle," he continued. There was an edge to the comment. Meyda sighed, knowing that her father was trying to stir up an argument; her father lived to create arguments. It was due to his fire spirit, Meyda knew, but she felt he enjoyed it a bit too much.

"I thank you for your concern as well, Your Highness." Raz spoke, his voice a mixture of firmness and friendliness that had Meyda turning to him with a smile. "I was not harmed, thanks to both Alard and your daughter. I am truly in their debt."

Compliments, manners, and not wilting at a backhanded insult...he's good. Meyda relaxed, seeing that Raz wasn't intimidated and could handle himself just fine after all.

Eldren stared at Raz. Meyda knew that her father was seeing him for the first time, and Raz stayed relaxed in his seat as he sipped from his glass flute of orange juice. This was going better than she hoped.

Of course, it wasn't her father she was worried about this morning.

"So, Alard, how has the search for a dissolvement of the bond progressing?" Willa didn't spare Raz a look; her dagger eyes narrowed at the prince.

"Well, yesterday was a bit of a setback on the research side. However, we have a few possible solutions that we are going to try out today," Alard said. "It will, of course, require us to travel back to the human realm."

"The human realm?" Willa raised one perfect eyebrow. "Why would you travel there for this? Surely you could work this magic on our purer grounds."

Meyda heard both Alard and Raz take sharp intakes of breath. Insulting them was one thing, she realized, but insulting the human realm was another thing to them. "Seeing that the bond was formed there with the magic in the human realm, I felt that it was only proper to use the magic there to undo it," Alard explained.

"And if that doesn't work?" Eldren asked.

"Well, Your Highness, if it doesn't work, we still have two days to return to the library and keep hunting for a solution," Alard said.

"It is safer for them as well, returning to the human realm." Everyone at the table looked at Meyda when she spoke up. Her father's jaw was gritted, not liking his interrogation to be interrupted. Willa just turned her head slowly, her expression unreadable, but her eyes held a warning not to defy her. "What I mean is that since someone sent letters throughout the realm asking for any known solutions to ending the bond, we've already seen what kind of miscommunication it can cause." Meyda continued. "Raz and Alard can work safely in the human realm. Meanwhile, I'll work with Elan to review any suggestions the people send in response and see if they are viable."

"We just all need to have patience," Raz said. "The end goal *is* to break this bond so Meyda and Alard can be married. We all know how important this union is, and we're going to make it happen."

"Are you willing to bet your life on that, Prince Consort?" Eldren asked.

Raz nodded. "I have great respect for both Alard and Meyda, and I do have my own life I plan to return to. So yes, I am, because until we do, I'm just as trapped as the rest of us."

Alard lowered his head and Meyda sighed. She was certain Raz hadn't meant his words to come out as if he hated going through all this, but she also knew Alard. He'd add the inflection to the words and blame himself.

Norah cleared her throat and smiled at her son. "When will you two be leaving?" she asked, changing the direction of the conversation gracefully.

"Sometime this afternoon," Alard said. "It'll be in the middle of the night so we can slip back in, take a small nap until sunrise there, and then while Raz takes care of some business he has, I'm going to see if Catherine and James have found anything on their end."

"And how much time will pass here while you do that?" Norah asked.

"At most, three days."

"Three days?" Eldren slammed his hands on the table, the dishes clattering as they bounced to the vibration. "You don't have three days—you two are supposed to be married in two! Do you know how much planning has gone into this? They are already setting up the decorations in both kingdoms for the celebration!"

"I understand your frustration, Your Highness—"

"This is not frustration, boy." Eldren pointed his finger at Alard. "You plan to leave for another realm while we are left to explain your lack of responsibility and fidelity. How many of your subjects will you disappoint before you even take your royal vows?"

Alard stayed calm, but Meyda reached a hand out to squeeze his thigh. "Father," she said, "you are making too much of this. Alard is taking responsibility for his actions—which were accidental in nature—and I have never doubted his fidelity to me or our people. If we must delay the ceremony a day or two, the people will understand."

Quin smiled at Meyda, then turned his attention to Eldren. "Your daughter is very wise, Eldren. We can solve this easily by turning the celebration from a day into a week. We have more than enough from the harvest this year to support it, and it will allow more time for subjects from the further reaches of the kingdom to arrive."

Willa put her hand on Eldren's arm. "I think that is a wonderful solution. The more here to celebrate, the faster the entire realm will come to love our daughter."

Eldren took a deep breath before sitting back down. "You had better find a solution to end this bond by then, young prince, or I will."

Breakfast was silent after that, the ultimatum hanging over all their heads. When Quin and Norah rose to signify the end of the meal, Meyda grabbed Alard and Raz and rushed them all back to Alard's room.

"I'm so sorry about my father, Raz," she apologized, wringing her hands.

"But you two know when he makes statements like that, his pride won't allow him to deviate. You need to come back with a solution."

Raz nodded, understanding the severity of the moment. "I do have a question—since we all know this was an accident, why don't you two just get married while we're still working for a way to remove the bond?"

"It won't work." Alard moved behind his desk, picking up a book from the library. "Part of the marriage ceremony involves blessing the bond mark. It will become the emblem that represents the kingdom...well, realm now, as to our leadership. It won't appear on Meyda, and the people will know something is wrong."

"We can only have one bond mark. As far as we know, it only disappears when one member of the bond dies," Meyda added.

"And we're back to all the death talk." Raz pinched the bridge of his nose between his eyes.

"There has to be another way." Alard flipped through the book. "Are there any possibilities we found that we haven't tried yet?"

"We deemed the reversing of the ceremony impossible," Meyda said, sitting on the edge of the desk.

"And I refuse to eat the entrails of a dozen swans until it's the very last option," Raz added, his skin taking on a greenish tint as he swallowed.

"Then we're back where we started." Alard shut the book. He brought his hands up to his face, digging the base of his palms into his cheek while resting his elbows on the wooden surface of the desk.

Raz walked behind Alard and rubbed his shoulders. "You're not alone in this. I'm just as responsible. I'm the one who picked the room."

Meyda watched the boys comfort each other. She could have done it as well, but she still wanted to see what their relationship was like. She didn't need to know the intimate details—mainly because she found them gross—but the more she saw, the more confident she felt that she would enjoy a life with both of them. Theirs was an intimacy that she neither wanted nor wished to receive. It could belong to just them, and she would be happy for them.

Reading Raz's hand when they first met helped alleviate a lot of her fears about whether she could trust Raz. She knew her parents hated humans, and for some time, she did too, even if she had never met one...or thought she hadn't. When Alard's parents told him the truth, she was the first one he told. At first, she recoiled at the knowledge, but sanity caught up and reminded her that Alard had always been that way, and nothing had really changed.

Her parents, of course, refused to see it her way.

Raz was more formal than Alard, showing confidence that he needed in the face of the realm. But his anxiety rolled off him in a way that Meyda was familiar with. He wasn't going to hurt her, and that, along with Alard's ringing endorsement, made her comfortable enough with the human to extend trust and some basic affections. Time would tell how much further she would let him in.

Raz wasn't the first person Alard had been intimate with in the human realm. Meyda had pictures on her phone showing the many lovers he had been with during his years away. But none had been serious. None had learned Alard's secret.

None had given Alard such a pure glow of love when they were together in moments like this.

She hated being the reason they had to separate. If it wasn't for the reunification, she would happily break their engagement so Alard and Raz could stay together.

Her thoughts were interrupted as Timmie flew into the room. He landed on the desk in front of Meyda and warbled, his draconic words holding an annoyed edge to it.

"What's he saying?" Raz asked.

"My mother is summoning me." Meyda sighed and picked Timmie up, settling the drake on her shoulder. "It's probably to discuss the rescheduling of events. If I don't see you two before you leave, please be safe."

Alard looked up from his chair, leaning back towards Raz. "We will."

Nodding, Meyda left the room. She took one last glance back at the boys, seeing Raz kneeling to be at Alard's height as they spoke softly, fingers entwined.

There must be a way we can all have what we want, she told herself. *And I'm going to figure it out.*

CHAPTER TWENTY-FIVE

Alard and Raz arrived back in New Orleans just past three in the morning. The Garden District was quiet, the residents sleeping the last few hours before having to wake up for work or school. They were able to slip out of the house and find a car service to get them back to Raz's hotel. The "Do Not Disturb" sign was still on the door handle, making Raz's disappearance for the day go unnoticed.

"And you're sure we were only gone a day?" Raz asked as he opened the hotel room door.

"I've made this trip many times between realms," Alard told him, having answered this question three times since breakfast. "A day in the fairy realm is only eight hours in the human realm. Don't ask me how—that level of cosmic magic is beyond my understanding. Even Elan struggles with understanding those ancient texts."

"So, if you're twenty-six here...that makes you seventy-eight there." Raz laughed, entering the room. "Wow, you're a cradle robber."

"And yet I still look younger than you." Alard smirked, watching as Raz's mirth turned into a pointed glare. "But then again, being a fairy gives me a longer life span naturally. My father is in his three hundreds, and my mother is about to turn four hundred."

"They look forty."

"Yup."

Raz was quiet a moment. Alard watched as Raz's shoulders slumped before he turned back to face Alard. "So even if we had to stay bonded, you'd end up just watching me grow old and die before you even appeared to age a bit."

Alard nodded. "The bond might let you live longer. As far as I saw in my research, you're the first human to ever bond with a fairy this way. And if you stayed in the realm, you'd age faster. Let's say you have fifty years left in life. That doesn't change no matter which realm you're in. If you stay in the fairy realm, barely seventeen years would pass here."

"And if we stayed here, a hundred and fifty would pass in your realm."

"Which would just create war, and I doubt I would recognize it when I'd return. That's if the doorways aren't closed to me by then."

"Meyda wouldn't do that to you."

"It wouldn't be Meyda in charge. It'd be her parents." Alard sat on the edge of the bed. "Even though I'm a fairy now, they know of my human origins. But this reunification effort started when my father and Meyda's mother were children. The realm was in four kingdoms then. Then it became two when they married, and with Meyda and me, it would become one."

Raz joined him on the bed. "If your parents never told you that you were human...none of this would be happening, huh?"

Alard shook his head. "My father still regrets telling me, but my mother was determined that I know exactly who I was before I became king. She encouraged me to spend time in the human realm. When I learned about the time difference, I used it to my advantage while getting a GED, then college, law school. I created an entire identity and life here, forgetting for a moment that I would have to give it up."

"You don't have to, you know." Raz rubbed Alard's back. It helped ease the stiffness from Alard's shoulders, and he leaned into Raz's side.

"I know. I have the right to abdicate, but I have no other siblings, no one to take my place." Alard closed his eyes, turning his head to press into Raz's shoulder. "In the end, I only have one choice—marry Meyda and unite the realm, or don't and watch all the hard work from generations of ancestors dissolve into flames and bloodshed."

Raz huffed, then kicked off his shoes and stretched out on the bed.

"Come on, let's take a nap before second breakfast. The wedding drama can wait a few hours."

Alard chuckled, letting himself be guided under the covers and then spooned from behind by Raz. He wasn't tired—all his traveling back and forth made it that he didn't need a lot of sleep. That, plus the extra rest he got from being forced to stay in bed the previous day would make it nearly impossible for him to clock out.

It wasn't long before Raz's breathing slowed. His arms loosened their hold on Alard, but the prince didn't move. Alard wanted to soak in as much affection as he could before his bond with Raz ended.

Alard knew he would have many nights curled up in Meyda's arms. She enjoyed cuddling with him and trusted him to respect her wishes on intimacy. He would never try to change her or ask her for something he knew she was uncomfortable with. He loved Meyda just the way she was.

That said, Alard was aware that moments like this, nights wrapped in this level of intimacy, were coming to an end. When Raz kissed him back in the park, Alard realized he had never known true passion. Sure, he had dated in the human realm, far from the prying eyes of his and Meyda's parents—Meyda knew about it and understood—but none of his other partners ever impacted him so emotionally.

Alard didn't want to lose Raz, but he knew he would. It was only a matter of time.

The hours passed while Alard continued to lay in bed, watching the sky through the window as the indigo brightened through the blue spectrum. Only when it reached the gray that came right before sunrise did he nudge Raz awake.

Raz groaned, nuzzling his head against Alard's neck. "Too early," he muttered.

"I know, but we were going to do breakfast again before you wrapped up your convention," Alard reminded him, rolling in Raz's arms to face him. "And I need to figure out a time James and Catherine are free so I can see if they found out anything further."

"And we're meeting back at your house after everything?" Raz asked.

"Yeah. You can catch a nap in the bedroom if you need one before we cross back."

"Sounds like a plan." Raz ran his fingers through Alard's hair. "I guess we just have to figure out what we want for breakfast."

"Coffee," Alard replied. "Lots of coffee."

Raz laughed. "Is that all?"

Alard thought for a moment, then tossed all reasoning to the side and leaned forward to kiss Raz. There was no stillness, no confusion from the other end as Raz kissed back, rolling them so that Raz was on top of Alard, leaning down to kiss him while pressing their bodies together. Alard reached up, his arms reaching past Raz's shoulders to wrap around his neck, pulling Raz closer.

When they separated to breathe, Alard looked deep into Raz's brown eyes. They weren't glowing now that they were in the human realm, but they still had a light of their own. A light he could get lost in forever.

"I wish I could keep you," Raz said.

Alard's lips spread into a smile. "I know," he said, then pulled Raz back down to him, kissing him deeply. His fingers gripped the back of Raz's neck, keeping them together. Today could be the last day they had this, and Alard didn't want to end what they had without one more intimate moment that was just between them.

He realized Raz wanted the same thing as the man's kisses traveled from Alard's lips, along his jaw, and down to his neck. Alard moaned as he felt Raz nibble on the skin where his neck met shoulder. His body arched up to press along Raz's, wanting to feel as much of the man against him as he could.

Raz's fingers drifted to Alard's shirt, starting to inch it up. Alard helped, tossing his shirt to the floor. Raz kissed down his chest, and Alard closed his eyes, focusing on his sense of touch as Raz's fingers slowly traced his ribs, across his stomach, and eventually to start playing with his belt.

Then Raz's lips were back on Alard's lips, kissing him deeply while his hips pressed against Alard's. Alard groaned, his head falling back into the pillows as a flash of pure pleasure hit his brain.

"Yes?" Raz whispered directly into Alard's ears.

"Yes."

Alard let himself get lost in the sensations. Somewhere along the way, they shifted so that Alard could worship Raz's body the same way he had just experienced. Time didn't matter in this moment, the idea of breakfast gone even as the sun rose, bathing them in sunlight that added to the warmth between their bodies.

They made love as the city awoke around them. Alard clutched the headboard, willing time to stop just so he and Raz could hold on to this moment forever; so that they could stay connected in body and soul until the end of time.

But, like everything, it would come to pass. Alard felt tears track down his face as their moment of pleasure reached its peak, Raz clinging Alard against his chest, his head buried in Alard's hair to muffle the strangled cry of completion.

After, with both gasping for breath as the world around them returned to their ears, Alard curled up in Raz's arms, listening to his heartbeat while it thundered from their exertions. Raz didn't loosen his grip, clinging to Alard as if to never let him go.

The alarm on Raz's cell phone broke the silence. Alard watched Raz look over his shoulder at it, reaching for it.

"Five more minutes?" Alard asked, looking up at Raz, begging not to let the moment end.

Raz tossed the phone back on the side table, the alarm silenced. "As you wish."

CHAPTER TWENTY-SIX

R az felt odd returning to the conference after the last few days. He couldn't tell anyone where he had been or what he had been doing. They'd put Raz in a straitjacket and padded room for even the suggestion that magic was real, let alone that he was married to a fairy prince.

It'd be easier to convince people he'd spent the last thirty-six hours lost in a haze of sex and alcohol. Raz realized that spoke a lot about his life up until this moment, or at least his life while at conventions.

After parting ways for the day with Alard at the coffee shop, Raz strode the three blocks to the convention center. His gray suit blended into the rest of the businesspeople walking through the double doors and heading straight for the stairs to the second floor.

Raz hesitated, looking down the hallway leading to the ballrooms. He could hear the grumbling of people dragging tables across the carpeted floor. The *clanking* of chairs being removed from stacks. Silverware being jostled. They were setting up for a meal, and Raz recalled that it was the Farewell Luncheon for the convention.

That was going to be awkward, sitting for lunch feet away from where he and Alard groped their way to matrimony. Maybe he could beg off—

"Razi!" Marcel's voice jarred Raz out of his thoughts. Before Raz could turn, Marcel had his arm strung across Raz's shoulders. "I must have been so busy yesterday because I never saw you—unless *you've* been the busy one."

Raz snorted. *If only you knew.* "I was distracted with something else, so I took the day off."

"Something or *someone*?" Marcel teased, pulling Raz closer. "Please tell me it was that cute piece of ass you nailed on Monday."

"His name is Alard. And yes, but it wasn't like that."

Marcel laughed. "Of course not. But Razi, if it was, no one would blame you. Hell, I'm insulted you didn't call me so I could join in."

Raz narrowed his eyes at his friend, and he bit back the snarl that tried to escape his throat. If he had thought his jealousy over Meyda was bad, just the idea of Marcus with Alard had him bristling.

Noticing the drop of temperature in the conversation, Marcel removed his arm from Raz's shoulders and backed up a step. "Whoa, Razi, it was just a joke."

"Sure it was." Raz took a deep breath, pushing away the sudden urge to kill from his mind.

"Hey, the last time we tried that, it ended with us having to file a joint restraining order against the dude. Never again."

Having focused on steadying his breathing, Raz nodded. "Alright."

Marcel dropped his jovial tone, pressing his lips into a line. "Wow, you've got it bad. Should I be worried?"

Raz laughed. Yes, Marcel should be worried; this relationship might be the death of him—literally. All Raz could do was shake his head. "It'll be okay. Let's just say I've bonded with Alard a bit more than I have with anyone else."

A smile creeped onto Marcel's face; a genuine smile that Raz didn't see often. "You've really got a thing for this lawyer." Raz nodded to Marcel's question. "Well, it's not like your business needs to be set in DC, you know. You could always take a month and see how it works while running the business out of a hotel. I'm sure there are businesses around here that would hire you in an instant."

"True." Raz took another breath, his shoulders drooping.

"How about we discuss this during lunch?" Marcel offered. "Go grab something down along the river and hash out a plan."

He couldn't tell Marcel that any kind of plan was doomed to failure, but his friend was trying to be supportive for once. They could make a plan for a dream that would always remain just that. "Yeah, let's do that."

———

Alard texted James while at the coffee shop to see if he had any morning appointments. His friend didn't, so Alard got himself a refill and grabbed another for James before heading down to the office James was hanging his shingle at. It was located between an art shop and a pub on St. Ann Street.

James had given him a spare key, an invitation to come in anytime Alard might be able to sneak back to the human realm. It was a small gesture, but one that meant the world to Alard. He'd always have a home in NOLA.

The window shades were down over the windows, so Alard wasn't sure if James had beat him to the office or not. Juggling the two coffees in his hands, he freed one up enough to get his key out and open the door.

"James?" Alard called into the building as he stepped into the waiting area and closed the door behind him. The lights were on in the tiny space painted a boring tan color. Two loveseats comprised the entirety of the room; one on each side of the door. Another door was opposite the main one, the name "James Wilson, Attorney at Law" embossed on the frosted glass insert.

To the right were two more doors. One said "Employees Only" and the other had a generic restroom sign on it. Alard pushed open the first one, seeing that it led to a kitchen area. It was empty, but as he walked further in, he noticed two empty mugs on the counter near the full and steaming coffee maker.

A tendril of fear danced in the back of Alard's head. What if someone in this realm tried to kidnap and kill Raz like Grah had? There are enough supernatural creatures in NOLA that had contacts in the fairy realm to make it a real possibility. Would they be able to tell the difference between Raz and James?

A *thunk* against the kitchen wall made Alard jump. He left the coffee cups on the counter and ran out of the kitchen and to James's office. He threw open the door, ready for a fight to save James. What he found, however, was the last thing he expected.

Catherine was sitting on James's desk, her back pressing the hutch into the wall, her business skirt up around her waist. James's shirt was open, Catherine's hands scratching down his chest as James's hips thrust up against hers. Two small rivulets of blood ran down James's shoulder from the bite mark on his neck.

They had been kissing roughly but broke apart as the door slammed open. Alard stared at them with wide eyes, knowing their shocked expression had to match his. "Oh. OH. Um, sorry. I'll be, uh, in the kitchen." Alard said, quickly grabbing the door and closing it behind him as he snuck out to the sounds of their giggling.

There was a tiny balcony off the kitchen looking into the alley that ran behind the building. Alard waited there, sipping his coffee and trying to scrub what he had seen from his mind. Even trying to think of him and Raz in the same situation wasn't helping, and eventually Alard just groaned and lay his head down on his crossed arms resting on the balcony banister.

He barely heard Catherine as she joined him. She nudged him with her hip, then sighed. "So, yeah, we're on again."

"No, really?" Alard turned his head to look up at her. "Couldn't tell at all."

Catherine smiled. "Brat."

"You guys couldn't wait until after I left?"

"I was hungry." She put a small whine into her voice and pouted.

"Oh god, stop it." Alard left his coffee to balance on the banister while covering his ears. "I don't need these images in my head."

"Stop acting like a scandalized virgin." Catherine swatted his shoulder. "Come inside and let's talk."

She opened the balcony door, beckoning for Alard to enter. He grabbed his coffee and walked into the kitchen where James was waiting. James at least had the decency to blush and look at his hands when Alard caught his eye.

Alard went to the coffeemaker and refreshed his cup, then leaned on the counter across from James. "You told me you had no appointments."

"Come on man, you know Catherine—she never makes appointments." James winced as Catherine slapped his shoulder before nestling into his side. "But I'm sorry. I should have put a do not disturb sign on my door."

Shaking his head, Alard chuckled. "No, it's fine. I'm just relieved it was that and not something worse."

"Something worse?" Catherine asked.

"Yeah, I should fill you in on what's happened while I was back home." Alard proceeded to tell them about the problems between his and Meyda's family, the threats of war and heads on sticks, and the kidnapping. James and Catherine just listened, not moving except when Catherine grabbed James's hand when Alard talked about his battle with Grah.

"I was afraid that was another kidnapping attempt, and that they had mistook James for Raz," Alard said, rubbing the back of his neck.

"I've never been so relieved to be having sex," James stated.

Catherine released his hand and ran it along her skirt, flattening a non-existent wrinkle. "Well, I haven't heard anything about that kind of plan in my circles, but if I do, I will stamp them out before they even think about trying it."

"Thanks," Alard said.

"It looks like it's becoming less and less of a chance to find a positive solution," James stated as he reached for one of the two file folders behind him. He held it out for Alard. "I looked in every law book for every state on divorce proceedings. The best I could come up with is dissolving a religious or Common Law marriage, and they both require a legal divorce through the courts."

"Great," Alard spat.

"Let him finish," Catherine said.

"Sorry, continue."

James grabbed the second file folder. "It's worth a try to see if the act of signing and notarizing an uncontested divorce petition will work. Monique, Catherine, and I drafted this last night. It's worded like an unlicensed religious ceremony, with the speculation of the religion being..." James looked at Catherine for help.

"Somewhere between being wiccan and a cult," she explained. "Neither single template fit completely, but we think this will."

Alard put the first folder down and took the second. The divorce petition was five pages long and laid out the basic framework of how the marriage happened. There were a few specific details that made Alard pause. "You sure this is what happened?"

"We found the YouTube video of the ceremony, and I got the translation of the exact wording," James said.

"Alright." He finished reading, seeing sections about the dissolution of Raz's ability to claim any gains, monetary or not, that would have come through their continued marriage. "This is where you're trying to dissolve the bond?" he asked, pointing at the language.

"Monique suggested it," James said with a shrug.

Catherine gave Alard a soft smile. "She wasn't fond of helping with this. She felt you and Raz were great for each other. Even if it meant turmoil in your realm."

"Yeah, she's not the only one," Alard muttered.

"Excuse me?" Catherine tilted her head. Alard knew she was trying to get a read on him from the way her eyes were squinting.

Alard sighed and rubbed the back of his neck, feeling his cheeks warm. "I think I'm in love with him. And I'm pretty sure he is with me too."

"Oh Alard." Catherine walked over to pull him into a hug. "I'm sorry."

James took the folder from Alard so Alard could hug Catherine back. He pressed his eyes against her shoulder, willing himself not to cry. She rubbed his back, pressing a kiss against his head. "It's not fair," Alard muttered. "It wasn't supposed to be like this. I never let it get this far. I always made sure my partners knew that nothing would come out of us being together. But now I'm the one running towards him, refusing to let go while knowing it's the last thing I should do."

"We know," James replied, his hand gripping Alard's shoulder.

"I don't want to go through life never having this feeling again." A few tears escaped Alard's eyes, creating a damp spot on Catherine's orange blouse. "I love Meyda, but not like *this*."

"What does she say?" Catherine asked.

"We did discuss a three-way marriage but figured it wouldn't work because of the bond being between only Raz and I. She wouldn't be able to just join in."

"And we're back to needing the bond removed, preferably in a way that keeps Raz alive. Then we convince both sets of parents to let the three-way marriage happen. And BAM, everyone gets their happy ending!" James licked his lips, then looked at Catherine. "We've accomplished harder tasks."

"Okay." Catherine pushed Alard back, her hands holding his biceps. "Let's focus. Why don't we try this document first? If you sign it, I'll go to the conference and talk to Raz between lectures and get his signature. Then we can go down to the courthouse and file it, making it official through the court. If it works, problem solved. If not, we'll look at other options."

"You have another option?" Alard asked.

"You won't like it," James said.

"What is it?" Alard stared at Catherine; his gut unsure if it wanted the answer.

Catherine licked her lips. "I could turn him. He'd technically die before the transition, so it might work."

"No!" Alard snapped back, then thought about it a moment before looking back at her. "I mean, even if we entertained the idea, it needs to be his choice."

"Of course. What did you think I'd do—sneak up behind him and drain him without asking?" Catherine huffed. "I'm classier than that. Plus, I don't want any children if I can help it. Raz would be an extreme exception to that."

"Let's table this idea for later," James stated, pulling a pen out. "Alard, sign. I want to get this in fast enough so that if it doesn't work, we still have time before you need to cross back."

"Right." Alard flipped through the divorce petition before signing his name at the bottom. "How much do I owe you?" Alard's lip curled up in an attempt to lighten the mood.

"Consider it Pro Bono. I need a few hours to get a CLE credit." James snapped the folder shut and held it out to Catherine. "My lady."

Catherine plucked it out of his hand. "I'll meet you at the courthouse," she said, kissing James on the cheek before turning and leaving.

"What will you do now?" James asked Alard.

Alard shrugged. "Probably grab a few beignets and then enjoy the view from my porch while I still can until Raz is done with his conference."

James nodded. "Catherine and I will meet you at your place then."

"Thanks. Let's hope that this works." Alard pulled James into a hug, then whispered, "And you may want to zip up before you enter the courthouse."

"What?" James looked down, then growled and reached for his zipper. "Damnit."

CHAPTER TWENTY-SEVEN

When Raz exited from the lecture hall, three men were huddled by the door whispering.

"Check out the legs on her."

"You kidding me? I'm still staring at her breasts."

"I don't even go to this show, and I want her."

Curiosity got the better of him, and Raz followed their line of sight. At the end of the hallway, Catherine stood with a compact mirror while fixing her lipstick. She was dressed for work in a tight leather skirt and a silk orange blouse, a gold necklace plunging just between her cleavage to draw attention to it.

"Fellas, she'll eat you alive," Raz spoke, pushing past them to approach Catherine. She smiled as he got closer, closing her mirror with a click. "Hello, Catherine."

"Raz." She leaned forward to kiss his cheek and all the hallway conversations ceased. "How are you, darling?"

"As well as can be expected, especially now that I'm the center of attention."

"Sorry they're all still staring at me." She slipped her arm through his and guided him down the hallway. "Think you can spare a few minutes to buy a girl a cup of coffee?"

"I could be persuaded." Not that she couldn't get that from any man—or woman—that she asked. "As long as it's just coffee."

"Mmm, I've already had breakfast." Her smile grew as they exited the conference center and turned in the direction of the coffee shop.

Raz let out the breath he didn't realize he was holding in. "That's good."

"Alard and James sent me to get your signature on something." Her free hand tapped her red leather messenger bag.

"Then why isn't Alard here?"

"He knew he'd be a distraction to you."

Raz opened the door to the cafe, motioning for Catherine to proceed him. Like everywhere else she appeared, Raz watched as all eyes took her in. "So, do you have some kind of superpower that makes everyone stare at you?" he asked with a chuckle.

"Somewhat." She grinned at him over her shoulder as they stood in line. "But most of it is training."

Training? Raz blinked, unsure of the meaning of that. "What kind of training?"

"The kind you get a few hundred years ago to be a proper lady of high standing."

They reached the register and Catherine ordered for them both, "letting" Raz pay for their drinks. As they moved to the barista side, Raz felt compelled to look in the seating area. The three homeless gentlemen were not in their corner. Instead, a few customers in business casual attire sat behind laptop, earbuds in and ignoring the world around them.

"Why don't you find us a seat, Raz? I'll wait on the drinks." She winked while making a shooing motion with her hands.

He snagged them the table near the window and stared out it at the street corner. Technically, it was his last day in NOLA. Raz had an evening flight back to DC scheduled. His travel bag was already packed and just waiting for him at the hotel when he returned from lunch to check out.

Of course, Raz didn't *have* to get on that plane. Depending on the bond, he may not be able to. Things were still up in the air and the deadline set by Eldren was a noose around both his and Alard's necks.

And after the conversation in the predawn hours, knowing that they were on the same page in how much they cared for each other, Raz wanted to find a different solution. He had been called the prince consort, but that was only due to them being married. Without the bond, he'd just be a royal mistress...or whatever the male equivalent was. He tried to Google it during the last lecture with no concrete answer.

"You look like a man deep in thought," Catherine said as she sat across from Raz, putting a cup in front of him.

"I've got some decisions to make before I return to DC," Raz told her, his hands wrapping around the cup, enjoying the warmth against his palms.

"Like what?" She sipped her coffee, her eyes watching him like a cat stalking a mouse.

"If I want to return to DC." Raz rotated the cup in his hands. "I mean, I'll have to go back eventually, but—"

"You don't want to leave Alard." Catherine nodded, reaching into her bag. "This is going to be awkward then."

"What do you mean?"

"I'm here to serve you divorce papers."

Raz's heart clenched at the words, and then took a moment to remember that this is what they were trying to do. They were still working toward this...right?

Catherine smirked as she put the folder between them. "James and I scoured through videos and legal documents to create this. We're thinking that perhaps if the bond was formed from a human wedding ceremony, then maybe it can be broken by a human divorce."

"The one thing we haven't tried." Raz chuckled, his breathing evening back out. "Could the answer be that obvious?"

"If it is, drinks are on me tonight."

Catherine walked Raz through the document and the legalese of the terminology. When he understood it all, Raz signed his line on the document under Alard's signature. "So, what now?"

Reaching into her bag, she pulled out a logbook and a stamp. "Well first, I notarize this bad boy, then I'm going to meet James at the courthouse to file it. He's going to try and get it in front of a judge quickly, claiming safety issues from those who married you. After that, we're going to meet up at Alard's place to get dinner."

Raz nodded. "Well, I guess I should let you go then."

"One thing first." Catherine put her coffee down. "Let's go back to the whole discussion on if you want to return to DC."

"I'm still thinking about it."

"Sometimes talking it out to someone else helps."

Raz sipped his coffee as he thought. "I think I'm in love with him. We've been skirting around saying it, since we can't keep going on like this with everything in his world on the line. , But I realized this morning I couldn't...I don't *want* to let us go."

Catherine leaned back in her seat, shaking her head. "Ah, the joys of young love. What do you really want, Raz? I know what Alard and Meyda need to do, and I know Alard always sacrifices his own needs for that of his people. But you haven't said anything about how you want this to go."

"That's what I'm still trying to figure out. I just know I don't want to lose Alard."

Catherine leaned forward, dropping her voice. "You know that when he marries Meyda, he will probably never return to this realm. He made sure he only spent a lot of time with James before he met you because of that."

"So, if I want to stay in his life, I'd have to leave this realm behind forever." Raz put his coffee down before crossing his arms on top of the table.

"Exactly. You'd lose all your friends, family...you'd be the lone human in a realm that hates your kind."

"Catherine, look at me." Raz held his hands to the side. "I'm dark skinned. I'm already in a realm that hates my kind."

Catherine winced at that. "I'm sorry, I didn't mean..."

"It's okay." Raz sighed. "I'm more worried about the long run. I have my own life, my own business. Is giving all that up going to pay off in the long run to be Alard's...male mistress?"

Chuckling, Catherine smiled. "I can't give you that answer. I don't think anyone can—not even Alard. This is one of those leap of faith moments in life. You just have to close your eyes and jump, hoping there aren't jagged rocks waiting at the bottom of the waterfall."

"I hate doing that," Raz said. "I've had to make plans for every moment of my life to get to where I am today. I needed to if I wanted to survive my childhood, get into college, build my business."

"You've never taken a chance at love?"

Raz shook his head. "Don't get me wrong, I've jumped into my share of flings without thinking, but they always ended without attachments. I never wanted an attachment like this...until now."

Catherine was watching him with that predatory look again, and Raz rubbed his eyes. She then clicked her tongue against her teeth. "Oh, baby, you're so afraid to let someone in. Why?"

Raz thought back to his first boyfriend when he was fifteen. It was confusing, and knowing he was going against his parents, it felt dangerous and exciting. One day they were holding hands between classes, and the next they were giving each other blowjobs under the bleachers. It had been wonderful, everything he thought he wanted.

Then they were caught by the gym teacher, and the principal called his parents. They said nothing to him at school, but his father had thrashed him the moment they returned home. His mother cried while his father called him a deviant, a stain on the family, and a blasphemous child.

Everything changed that day. He was moved to a strict private school and had a curfew to be home afterwards unless given permission. His cell phone was a basic phone for phone calls only—no text or internet. His laptop was for homework only, and his television and video games were taken away. Anything that could lead him back down that path of deviance was removed as to not tempt him again.

After he left home, he tried again with a boy in college, but he felt the guilt and disappointment hanging over him. He heard his father's voice call him a deviant and felt the pain from the beating. So, he ended the relationship before it became anything. It didn't matter, in the end his parents disinherited him anyway.

Since then, he was careful who he slept with and ended it before the guilt crept in. It wasn't going to change his relationship with his parents, but that didn't stop him from feeling like he was going against them each and every time.

"I've lost too much already," Raz whispered. "I don't know what I'll do if I choose him, and his parents take him from me."

Catherine reached across the table, taking one of his hands in hers. "Loving anyone is always a crapshoot, Raz. Love is a game in that way. But if you want to experience it, to have it forever, you also need to be willing to risk losing."

Raz squeezed her hand. "I don't want to lose him."

"Then you know what your choice is. Everything else comes after that leap."

"Then let's hope there are no rocks at the bottom."

Chapter Twenty-Eight

The door to Alard's home stood wide open. There were no signs of forced entry, the light on in the hallway just beyond the entrance. Music floated through the door, all but inviting the two people on the porch to enter.

James turned to look at Catherine. "He doesn't do that," he told her. "Not even in the summer or when hosting parties."

Catherine looked at the door, then tilted her head so that her right ear was directed toward the house. "I don't hear any heartbeats," she told him.

"Not even Alard's?" It had been four hours since Alard left James's office for his home in the Garden District.

"None." Catherine straightened back up and took a deep breath through her nose. "But I smell magic...and some kind of chemical"

"Magic and chemicals mixed together, and I wasn't invited."

"Pretty sure this isn't a welcoming party."

Catherine nodded and walked to the door, dropping her briefcase just inside the threshold. She splayed her fingers out, her nails growing into claws. The sting of her canines extending was barely noticeable as she shifted. It was going to ruin her manicure, but she wasn't going to leave herself or James unprotected.

The *cu-chunk* of a gun loading a round made her head spin around.

James stood there; his briefcase open as he checked the gun in his hand. "What the hell, James?" she asked, her voice growling now in her vampire form.

"You really think I'm not going to carry living on Bourbon?" James tucked his briefcase behind a planter near the steps.

"I hope you have a permit for that." Catherine turned her attention back to the open door. "Let me go first."

"Go ahead. You're the one with the healing factor."

That was the one thing she loved about James—no matter how much of an asshole he was, he was practical and knew when to listen to her.

They entered the house, and after assuring themselves no one was in the front entranceway, Catherine ran to do a quick recon of the living room and kitchen while James checked his old office. They found nothing and started upstairs.

Halfway to the landing, Catherine stopped James. She took another sniff of the air. "Something's wrong."

"Wrong beyond Alard missing and a possible explosive in the building?" James turned to make sure there was nothing on the stairs following them.

Catherine glared at him. "I'm starting to hear a heartbeat, and just got a whiff of latex."

"What does that mean?"

The padding of paws on wood, followed by a deep canine growl made both look at the landing. A black wolf, its fur short and slicked back against its body, focused its gold eyes on Catherine. Its jaw snapped in their direction, shifting in preparation to jump.

"Shit, of course it had to be a werewolf."

———

Raz arrived at Alard's house just past four. Lunch with Marcel had gone longer than expected, but his friend wanted to make sure Raz had at least three options on what to do if the relationship went sour. "A relationship can be like a business," Marcel explained. "Always aim for success but have a few backup plans in case the first attempt falters."

The closer the cab had gotten to Alard's house, the more excited Raz became. He wasn't going to give up his business, just move it to an online platform using the internet that Alard had set up in his realm and get a PO Box in NOLA that he could check once a month. Set bills up on autopay, and he was set.

If it didn't work out in the end between him and Alard, he would be able to transition back to the human realm and move on.

After thanking the driver and grabbing his suitcase from the trunk, Raz started for the front door. Everything looked normal to him, but when he tried to open the front door, he found it locked. Raz knocked, trying to look inside the hallway. "Alard, it's me. Open up!"

A minute passed with no one answering the door. Raz knocked again, then looked around the porch in frustration. Had Alard gone out with James and Catherine to do something? Was he too early?

Raz dropped his briefcase by the door and went to the large porch swing. He sat down, melting into the wooden beams as he kicked off from the floor to start swinging. *It's not that cold to wait out here for a while*, Raz told himself. He closed his eyes, enjoying the moment of relaxation.

He was knocked out of his Zen moment by a car backfiring on the street. A quick check of his phone told Raz that a half hour had passed since he sat down. He checked his text messages, but there was nothing from Alard.

Maybe there was a holdup at the courthouse? Raz peeled back his shirt sleeve to look at the bond mark on his arm. It looked like a normal tattoo again thanks to Alard teaching Raz how to control his fairy vision before they returned.

Raz tried not to play with the magic sight while he was at the convention that morning, but it had been too tempting not to. After he left Catherine at the cafe, he had put on sunglasses to hide any glow from his eyes.

Take a deep breath and focus, Alard had said. *Imagine that your brain has an eye of its own, and that all the magic you can see is because that eye is open. Now, when you close your eyes, imagine that third eye closing as well.*

Raz discovered that it worked in the opposite direction, and he stared in awe at the magic that lit up Canal Street brighter than any neon light. Tiny streaks of light flew past him, twirling in midair with each other before turning onto side streets towards the river. The ground glittered with gold and silver sparkles, and the trolley arriving from the cemeteries had a few ghosts disembarking along with the humans.

There were so many questions in Raz's mind that he doubted he could understand the answers in his lifetime. It was scary, thrilling, and beautiful all at once, and Raz loved being able to peek behind the curtain to see it.

But right now, the question Raz had was where everyone was. He was about to text Alard when he looked over the top of his phone and noticed something behind the planter. He slid off the swing and knelt to get a better look.

It was a briefcase. Raz slid it out and examined it, seeing the initials JTW engraved into the leather above the gold lock. *This doesn't belong to Alard.* He fidgeted with the combo but was unable to open it.

Raz hummed to himself as he stood up, looking around the balcony. He took a deep breath and closed his eyes, thinking of the third eye and opening it as he opened his eyes again.

The porch was awash in a green glow. Raz ran his fingers through the glow, watching the magic swirl in his wake. It was a familiar magic, the same warmth that he had come to feel while in Alard's suite back in the fairy realm.

"Can he see us yet?"

"His eyes are glowing. He should be able to. Hey, human!"

Raz twisted to look back at the briefcase. Standing next to it, balanced on the edge of the lip of the planter, were two tiny men. They wore clothes that resembled the fur of a squirrel, and their pale skin was splotched with brown patches. "Who are you?"

"We're the neighbors." The first man was taller, his nose resembling the upper half of a robin's beak. "I'm Joe, and this is my mate, Gary."

"Hi. Or is it Yo? I hear the humans on the street use that word." Gary had silver hair and a beard that was filled with twigs. "I remember you. You were with the prince when he left us a housewarming gift."

"We have been putting his mail under the door every day," Joe added.

"Hi." Raz squatted down to be more at their eye level. "I'm Raz."

"Are you the prince's consort?" Gary asked.

Raz nodded. "I am. You two haven't seen the prince, have you?"

Joe pointed at the door. "He went inside a long time ago. Then the wolf came. Then the vampire and her human."

Alard, Catherine, and James. "Wolf?"

"He was covered in black fabric that made him not smell like a wolf," Joe explained. "He went in and there was a fight. Then quiet."

"The vampire and her human arrived later, and they went in," Gary continued. "There was another fight, then quiet."

"And then the wolf came downstairs and closed the door," Joe finished.

"But no one came outside?" Raz asked.

"Not this door," Joe said before looking at Gary.

Gary shrugged. "And not the lawn."

Raz clenched his jaw, standing back up. He went to the door and tried the door again, but it was still locked. Only the green glow of the house was on the knob. Raz took that to mean it wasn't locked by magic. "I need something to pick the lock with," Raz said, turning back to the brownies. "Do either of you have a paperclip, a hairpin...something long and metal?"

Gary and Joe looked at each other, then back up at Raz. "No. But we can go inside and look!" Gary stated.

Of course, they could.

"Do you think you can unlock the door when you're inside?" Raz asked.

"No, it's too heavy. That's why we slide the mail under the door," Joe said.

Raz stared at the door, trying to formulate a plan. "Okay, this is what I need you to do. The room to the left is an office. If you go in there, you should be able to find paperclips on papers in boxes, or on the desk."

They both nodded, then Gary raised his hand.

"Yes?"

"What's a desk?" Gary asked, completely serious.

Raz took a deep breath and resisted rolling his eyes. Instead, he sat on the ground and talked the plan over in more detail with the brownies. He wanted them to get into the office and find a few paperclips and bring them back to the door. Raz only had a small recollection of the office from his tour of the house, but it was enough to guide the brownies.

It took them ten minutes to fulfill the task, but they returned and started throwing paperclips under the door. Joe crawled under next, and once he was standing, he reached down and pulled a long silver letter opener out. When it was through, Gary joined them.

"You said something long and metal," Gary said. "Is this something that you want?"

Raz had been unfolding the paperclips but smiled as he grabbed the letter opener. "This will help, yes. Good job, you two."

Focusing on the door, Raz shoved three paperclip ends into the deadbolt and started fiddling with them. He wasn't proud to know how to pick locks —it was a time when money was scarce, and he was hungry—but now it was the only way he could imagine getting in without being noticed.

Which would be a moot point if the wolf was still inside, but Raz still had to try.

The paperclips kept slipping out of place, and Raz muttered curses under his breath. He felt the brownies climb up his shirt to sit on his shoulder and watch, then they climbed along his arm.

"We can see the stuff inside," Joe said. "Can we help with that?"

Raz grinned. "Yes, yes, you can." He explained to Gary and Joe what he was doing, and when he got one pick wrenched against the lock, Joe grabbed the paperclip and held it for Raz. Gary joined him, and Raz paused long enough to jam the letter opener between the deadbolt and the door handle before working each pin into place. When all five were in place, he took the clip from the brownies and twisted the deadbolt open.

"We got it," Raz stated, then pulled back on the letter opener to press open the entry latch. The door opened inward and the brownies—back on his shoulder—jumped for joy. "Good job, team," Raz added.

Moving carefully, Raz let the brownies climb onto his hand so he could return them to the planter. "I go on alone from here. When Alard and I come back, we'll throw you a real housewarming party."

Gary and Joe grinned. "We look forward to it," Joe said.

"Don't let the wolf hurt you!" Gary added.

Right, the wolf. Raz stood up, slowly opening the door further so that it didn't make any noise. He rolled the suitcase and the briefcase into the front hall. He saw Catherine's messenger bag on the floor and left the suitcase and briefcase there before closing the door again.

Next, he crept to the umbrella stand and pulled out the baseball bat among the objects Alard had collected over the years. He tested the weight, then started to move quietly through the first floor. The fact there were no voices, just the soft sound of a radio, told Raz that he'd quickly be found if he called out anyone's name.

The first floor was clear, so Raz headed back for the stairs. He was about to put his foot on the first step when a growl threatened him from above. Raz looked up and saw a black mass pressed up against the landing railing. Its teeth were bared, slate-gray eyes focused intently on Raz.

"What are you, some kind of ninja werewolf?" Raz locked the creature's gaze as he started to climb the stairs. The wolf jumped back to the floor, claws digging into the wood as it stalked closer to the top of the staircase.

"Not big on talking I take it?" Raz continued to climb as he formulated a plan. He'd taken on wild dogs in alleys before, but he doubted any of them had been werewolves. How does one handle them—silver bullet? Stake to the heart? Throw the bat and tell it to fetch? "Wanna give me a reason why you're here? Or where my husband and his friends are?"

The wolf snapped its jaws in the air, snarling as it made ready to pounce. Raz readied himself, calculating the trajectory of the wolf and how it would impact him. He made a slight adjustment to his stance, leaning towards the wall.

When the wolf launched itself in his direction, Raz swung the bat in an upward motion. His arms vibrated as the bat smashed into the underside of the wolf's muzzle. The change of inertia sent the wolf flying onto the stairs' railing. Raz followed up with a push of his foot, sending the creature down to the floor of the main hallway.

Knowing the wolf would shake it off and be on him soon after, Raz ran up the stairs and into the bedroom, slamming the door shut behind him. He pressed his forehead to the door, trying to catch his breath.

Until he heard the muffled voice trying to get his attention.

Raz turned and saw Catherine and James tied up on the floor, socks in their mouths and held in with ties. James wiggled to get Raz's attention, his eyes flicking from Raz to the door. "I gave it a good strike to the head," Raz assured James as he knelt to undo the gag. Catherine lay unmoving between James and the footboard of the bed.

James tried to shout against the gag again, and when Raz finally pulled the sock from his mouth, James took a deep breath. "Bomb!" he shouted, his head motioning to the bathroom.

Raz turned his head to look at the bathroom barndoor. The door was in its spot, blocking the entrance to the bathroom. The locks were engaged so it wouldn't move. Two sticks of dynamite were duct taped to the door, and a timer was on top of it.

Two minutes.

"Oh, fuck me," Raz stated, working on James's bonds. "Where's Alard?"

"They were taking him through the portal right when we got here. He was unconscious and tied up like this," James explained, watching Raz work.

"And Catherine? She okay?"

"The wolf bit her. It's like poison to her. She needs time to heal and work it out of her system." James wiggled as the rope around his arms and chest loosened, and with Raz's help they tossed the rope away.

"You know how to disable a bomb?" Raz asked James, standing up and going to it while James started to free his legs.

"No, I try very hard to avoid situations like this," James deadpanned.

Raz leaned close to the timer, trying to see if he could find an obvious off switch. "If this goes off, it'll destroy the portal," Raz stated.

"Yeah. The other one I know about is somewhere in New York City." Freed, James was trying to rouse Catherine as he untied her. They both jumped when the wolf arrived outside the bedroom, throwing itself against the locked door.

"We're not going to make it out in time." James stood up, Catherine in his arms.

"I need to get through that portal and find Alard." Raz looked at the door locks, realizing the ones on the bathroom side were locked in place. He cursed. "This thing is going to blow in just over a minute. Take her into the closet and duck down."

"That's not going to protect us much," James said.

"Would you rather open the other door and deal with the big, bad wolf?"

"You make a valid point." James headed to the door opposite the bed in the room, juggling his ex-wife while opening the walk-in closet. "What about you? What are you going to do?"

"Something really, really stupid."

Raz pushed on the barndoors, trying to get his arm through to grab the bottom door lock and disengage it. There was just enough room to get his hand in, let alone his wrist and a few inches of his arm. Wood splinters dug into his arm—not the little kind from cheap chopsticks, but the semi-impaling your body kind—and he felt the blood drip down his fingers. It also made the spot on the door slippery and easier to continue through.

The bedroom door started to splinter as the wolf dug into it, but Raz refused to acknowledge it. Instead, he bit his lip against the pain of the wood going further into his arm as he twisted his hand down to grab the handle and pull the lock back.

When the bottom was free, Raz was able to swing the door further into the room. He looked at the timer: fifteen seconds left. Raz looked at James and waved for him to get into the closet. "We'll call you when we get signal again!" Raz shouted.

As James slammed the closet door shut, the wolf crashed through the bedroom door. It shook its head, then turned to Raz. Raz ducked into the bathroom, locking the door back in place just as the wolf crashed into the bomb.

Raz jumped through the portal as the light in the bathroom brightened with a dangerous orange glow.

CHAPTER TWENTY-NINE

T he pair of werewolves had jumped Alard just as he was unlocking the door back home. They had slapped a patch onto his neck while holding him down. Alard tried to fight back, but within seconds, he felt the magic bleed out of him while his vision doubled. He was barely conscious when he was carried upstairs and into his bedroom.

"Send His Highness back where he came from," one of the werewolves spoke, shifting himself into a creature that was half-man half-wolf. His slate-gray eyes glared down at Alard. "I'll stay here and finish the job."

He passed out after that, and he woke up in his current predicament: hanging from the ceiling in a tower a few feet off the ground, tied up in a ball that kept him firmly in the fetal position. He swung in the breeze that blew through the open windows of the tower turret, which wasn't helping the vertigo he was still suffering from. From the sight of the green hills and clean air, he knew that he was home, at least.

It wouldn't be long until someone found him. Either someone on the ground would notice the shape of him hanging in what should be an empty battle station, or Raz would return and come looking for him. Or maybe Catherine and James? They were on their way over when he was attacked. What had become of them?

He screamed against the gag, hoping someone in the castle would hear. He had to get out of there and get back before they got hurt.

When an explosion echoed across the hills, the hope of Raz coming died. He knew in his heart that the explosion had come from the portal. If the pathway between NOLA and the fairy realm was destroyed, Raz would have no way to get back to him. There was another portal in Meyda's kingdom, but he doubted King Eldren and Queen Willa would grant him access to go find his husband.

It wasn't a way to end the bond, Alard knew, but it would make it impossible for their marriage to continue. Alard had a feeling that this was the plan. But who would do this, and how was it related to Raz's kidnapping by the ogre Grah?

"Prince Alard?" A fluttering of wings announced the presence of Fi, her tiny form moving in front of his face. "I saw something up in this turret and came to see if it was Raz. What are you doing up here?" Alard tried to explain, but the gag kept him from forming actual words. Fi realized this and grew to her humanoid size and stood on her toes to pull the gag off him. "Do you need help?"

Alard coughed, trying to get the taste of the gag from his mouth. "A werewolf kidnapped me from the human realm," he explained while trying to wiggle out of his bonds again, to no avail. "And yes, I need help."

"Let me see what I can do." Fi lifted a few inches up into the air, moving to look at the knots in the bondage. Alard arched his neck to keep her in sight. Fi reached for the ropes knotted above his wrists and tried to trace the paths the ropes took in and out of each other. "I've never seen something so tangled. I don't know if I can untie this."

"Try your magic," Alard suggested.

Fi bit her lip. "I don't want to set you on fire. Why can't you use *your* magic?"

"They put something on me that won't let me access it." Alard felt another wave of dizziness as the wind swung him again. "It's a film on my neck."

Fi looked closely at Alard's neck. "Oh, I see it. There's a spell on it."

"Can you take it off?"

Landing, Fi looked at Alard. "I think I can. Stay still." On her toes again, she reached up and placed a warm hand on Alard's neck. Fingernails scratched along the nape of his neck. Alard grimaced as he felt the patch ripped off, then gasped as his magic flooded back into him.

"Better?" Fi asked, the patch folded in half. "I think I got the spell contained for now."

"Good. I need that as evidence." Alard focused on his earth magic, communicating with the fibers in the rope to release him. The strands unwound, dumping Alard onto the floor of the turret. "Thank you, Fi."

"You're welcome, my lord." Fi bowed her head.

Alard took the patch from her and placed it in his back pocket. He would examine it later with Meyda and perhaps Elan to figure out what the spell was and if there was a signature to the magic. "May I ask why you were here to be able to help me?"

Fi bounced on her feet a bit. "You and Raz saved me from Grah. I just, well, I wanted to make sure you both were okay after the explosion in the forest."

Alard looked out the window arch to see smoke rising from the forest, but water creatures were flying overhead and trying to drench it with water from the nearby rivers. "I have no idea where Raz is."

Fi moved next to him. "You don't think he was in that explosion?"

"I don't feel any pain from our bond." Alard pulled his sleeve back to see the bond. "I think he's trapped in the human realm."

"Then you need to go back and get him!"

"I know, and I will." But he needed to talk to his parents first...and Meyda's parents. This was the second attempt to split Alard and Raz apart, and unless the werewolf returned to the human realm after leaving him in the turret, it remained in the realm and could reveal who was doing this. "Thank you again, Fi. I need to find my parents first."

"Can I do anything?" Fi asked.

Alard looked at her. "Do you know what a werewolf is?"

"Not really. I never saw one before."

"Then no. But if you want to look at the forest for me and tell me what's going on, that would be helpful."

Fi nodded. "I can do that, my lord!" She grinned, then shrank back into her tiny form and flew out the window toward the forest.

Alard watched her go, then proceeded downstairs to the main floor and the throne room. He heard the voices of his parents arguing with Meyda's parents inside. Without waiting to be announced, he stormed into the room.

Meyda saw him first and ran across the room. "Alard!" she said, wrapping her arms around his neck. Alard hugged her back, rubbing Meyda's back to calm her.

Silence filled the throne room as all four parents watched their children. Quin and Norah stood from their thrones, walking down the stairs and towards Alard. He released Meyda to embrace his mother and felt his father's arm drop onto his shoulder and squeeze it firmly.

"We were afraid you were caught in that blast," Norah whispered into Alard's shoulder, her arms pulling him closer. "I'm so glad you're safe."

"I am, but only because I was kidnapped and left tied up in the western tower." Alard looked at his father, seeing Quin's face darken with the news. Norah pushed back a bit, confusion in her eyes. "I'm certain it was another attempt to separate Raz from me."

Eldren moved to join them, any anger that he had from the previous argument with Alard's parents had gone from his face. "Where is your consort, Prince Alard?"

"I don't know. I can't feel him." Alard took a deep breath. His anger shifted into pain, feeling the loss of any connection to his husband. "I fear he's trapped in the human realm."

"Then we go back and retrieve him," Meyda stated.

"Are you two forgetting that you are to be married?" Willa stated, moving to her husband's side. "I understand wanting to find your consort, Alard, but if you return to that realm again, even for a day, you will miss your own wedding here and insult your people."

"I can't marry Meyda while I'm still married to Raz!" Alard pulled free from his mother to look at Meyda's parents. "The people will know it's a farce."

"It won't be," Norah explained. "We spoke with Elan, and there's a chance that just the act of marrying Meyda will dissolve your bond to Raz and create a new one with Meyda. However, we can't know for certain until we try."

Alard stared at his mother, the pain in his heart sharpening at the feeling of betrayal from her. "And I'm supposed to wait and try this while leaving Raz abandoned in the human realm?"

"You need to think of your people right now, Prince Alard," Eldren spoke. "Unite the kingdoms, and then if the bond with your consort remains, we will deal with the complication outside of the spotlight."

"This is crazy." Alard turned to look at Meyda. She was hugging herself, staring at the ground. "You can't agree with this, Meyda. We can't start a marriage based on a lie!"

Willa stared at her daughter, clearing her throat. Meyda looked up but refused to meet Alard's eyes. "We have to put the people first, Alard," Meyda whispered. "I want you to be happy—" she added before Willa's hand dropped onto Meyda's shoulder, silencing her.

"There, it's settled." Willa looked at her husband. "The marriage will proceed on schedule in two days."

"You will stay in the realm, Alard," Quin stated, and Alard heard the weariness in his voice.

"But Father," Alard started, but was silenced as Quin lifted his hand, glaring at Alard. There was no use in debating when his father had that look. The King had made his orders very clear. "Yes, Father."

"You're dismissed."

Dismissed? They hadn't even discussed the fact Alard had been kidnapped and needing to find the werewolf or whoever it was working for. "Father, you're not even going to—"

"I said that you're dismissed." Quin snapped.

Alard jumped at the finality in those words, then stiffened before bowing to his father. "I understand, my king."

Turning on his heel, Alard stormed out of the throne room. He made his way to the courtyard, aiming for the central tree. The sight of the forest burning was obscured by the four castle walls surrounding the courtyard. In this space, it looked like another beautiful, sunny day. The windchimes in the trees tinkled, the air stiller here than in the rest of the castle, while birds hopped from branch to branch while making their nests.

Reaching the tree, Alard punched the trunk for all his worth. The bark bit into his knuckles, and he shook his hand out, trying to focus on the pain instead of his anger. There was something wrong with his father; he never treated Alard like that before. Was Quin cracking under the pressure from the Kingdom of Fire and Ice? Or had the king finally reached the end of his patience with his son?

"Alard?" Meyda's voice came from behind him. Alard turned to see her just out of arm's reach, hands folded together in front of her. Her white hair was pulled into a quick ponytail, lessening the impact of regalness that she had been back in the throne room.

"What did I miss while I was away?" he asked, rubbing his arm across his face.

"The armies were...are getting restless," Meyda explained as she took a seat on the marble bench overlooking the garden between the castle and the walking path around the tree. "The original deadline passed, and their captains hadn't been informed of the extension. Some of the men got into a barfight and it extended out into town."

"Damn." Alard leaned against the tree, giving his entire weight to the sturdy trunk. "Was anyone hurt?"

"Just the soldiers, thankfully. My father has already sent people to survey the damage." Meyda patted the empty part of the bench next to her. "He is going to rebuild the tavern since it was his men who instigated the fight, but the damage is done. The people are on edge, having arrived for a wedding only to find two armies sizing each other up."

Alard joined her, and Meyda curled into his side. He put an arm across her shoulders, keeping her close. "And our parents think us faking a wedding will make it better?"

"It's the only choice left." Her fingers traced gentle circles over his chest, resignation in her voice.

"And what about Raz?" Even the thought of Raz no longer being at his side sent daggers into his heart. "He's still alive over there."

Meyda sighed. "I don't think my parents will ever grant you access to our portal. Even after we marry, it is still their castle."

They sat in silence, unable to soothe the other. The birds stopped chirping, and Alard could feel their eyes on them. "Do you believe the tales about bonded couples suffering when separated over long distances?" Alard asked. "I don't want him to suffer."

"I don't know. I've never seen my parents separated further than the distance of the castle." Meyda looked up at Alard. "Are you suffering now?"

Alard nodded his head. "It's like my heart is being torn to shreds."

Wrapping her arms tighter around Alard, Meyda pulled him to rest his head against her chest. His arm over her shoulders slipped away as they shifted, Alard going from the comforter to the one needing comforting. He tried to hold it back, but once the sob escaped from his throat, it was impossible to stop.

Meyda kissed the top of Alard's head, rocking him as he got lost in the pain. It wasn't just the loss of Raz either; Alard cried over being kidnapped, losing his home and friends, getting injured trying to rescue Raz from death, his parents turning on him when he needed their support most, and knowing he would never get to explore the love he felt for Raz.

Sobbing, Alard felt the dream he had started to build in his head rip away; seeing Raz in the morning light, sitting across the kitchen table on a lazy Saturday, or a snowy candlelit night snuggled up in blankets in front of a fire reading. The two of them kissing under the spray of his favorite waterfall south of the castle, hands tracing every inch of the other's body.

I should have told him that I love him.

He lost track of time. For all Alard knew, they could have spent the rest of the day in the courtyard, or only ten minutes. When he managed to get his emotions back in check, he felt drained of any energy he had left.

"Better?" Meyda asked, her fingers threading through his hair.

"No," Alard replied, not leaving her comforting embrace. "But I can fake it."

Meyda laughed softly. "I appreciate the honesty." She helped Alard sit up, using her sleeve to wipe his face dry. "I know it may not seem like it, but things will eventually get better. I know we both hate this arrangement, but at least we'll still have each other. You and me versus the realm, right?"

Alard smiled at that, taking her hand and squeezing it. "Always."

They settled back into comfortable silence, hands linked, lost in thought. "You know," Meyda said softly, "while you were gone, I was talking with Elan about a three-way marriage. I'd been thinking about it ever since I saw how well you and Raz fit together. I just didn't want to get your hopes up until I knew if it was possible."

"I thought about it too, but I didn't think it would be fair to you," Alard said, looking down at her.

Meyda scoffed. "Alard, I love you, but it will never be in that way. We both know that. What you and Raz have...that's true love. The kind of things humans write stories about."

"Yeah, but still, the people—"

"The people will be happy as long as their rulers continue to care for them. Whether it's just you and me, or the three of us, that part doesn't matter here."

Alard smiled at that, hugging Meyda close to him again. "What did Elan say?"

"He said it was possible, but we would still need to remove the bond between just you and Raz. A mate bond, once formed, won't change to add in another. That's why it fades away when one of the mates dies."

"Leaving us back at the beginning of the problem again."

Meyda shrugged. "It was just an idea."

"Thank you," he said, looking back at the sky again. "I knew you'd understand but thank you for being supportive like this."

"What are best friends for?"

Chapter Thirty

The walk from the forest to the farmland border of Alard's kingdom took two hours. Exhausted, Raz bent over the stone half-wall that protected the farms from small animals coming out of the forest. The castle still looked far away from where he stood.

At the rate he was going, it would be the middle of the night before he got to the castle. That didn't bode well for his body, needing food and water soon. He had also torn a strip from his shirt to bandage the puncture wound on his forearm, but if he didn't clean it out soon it would get infected.

He needed to find a faster method of travel.

A sensation, like the brush of feathers, traced along Raz's face. He turned, trying to find the source, then jumped back against the wall as Fi grew into her human size just inches from him. He gasped, a hand going to his chest to verify that his heart wasn't going to stop in shock.

"Raz! Hi!" Fi squealed as she pulled Raz into a tight hug. "I've been so worried about you, and Alard said that the portal was destroyed, and the forest is on fire, and it was thought you were trapped forever with the other humans, and it's so good to see you here and not hurt and Alard is going to be so happy to see you!"

Raz extracted himself from Fi's grip and pushed her back a few steps. "Alard's here?"

Fi nodded. "I found him tied up in the western tower. He's okay, but his parents are being mean to him, and they are making him marry Meyda and not caring about how you feel."

"They probably think I'm dead," Raz mused.

"No, Alard still has the bond mark. It would go away if you were dead."

Raz looked at his arm, then nodded. "You're right." He looked at the distant castle. "Hey Fi, think you can give me a lift to the castle?"

Fi grinned. "Of course." Without hesitation, she picked Raz up bridal-style and took off, making a beeline to the castle. "Where do you want me to drop you?"

"Alard's suite. I need to change first, then I'll go find him."

"Good thing I know what window that is!"

Flying was faster than walking. Fi dropped Raz off at the window, then realized she hadn't checked the forest for Alard and zipped back off to do her task with a promise to find him later.

Raz changed into clean clothes, taking a moment to wash dirt from his arms and face. He also rebandaged his arm after finding a travel first aid kit in Alard's desk drawers. When he felt ready, he left the suite and headed down the hallway, turning to the second story walkway that overlooked the courtyard.

He heard Alard's voice coming from the courtyard and stopped. It took Raz a moment to find where Alard was—directly across from him on the other side of the tree. Meyda sat next to him, and Alard was holding her. The pang of jealousy stabbed deep, and he was about to call out when a chill went up his spine.

"Aren't they beautiful together?" Willa asked, stepping around the other end of the walkway, her arms folded into the billowing sleeves of her ice-blue dress that covered her from shoulder to ankle, belted at her waist with a string of crystals. "Combined, they are the perfect balance of all four elements in the realm. It has taken generations of planning to bring them together like this."

Raz couldn't hear what Alard and Meyda were saying to each other, but the familiarity they had with each other was evident just by watching them. "Yeah, but he loves me," Raz whispered.

"I know, and it is unfair that he put this burden upon you." Willa stepped closer, her voice gentle. "Alard knew better than to let himself be romantically involved with anyone. His mother has spoken to me about a few other humans he has been with. Each time I feared something like this would happen."

"He should be allowed to find real love." Raz looked at Willa. "And your daughter should get to choose how she wants to live her own life."

Willa chuckled. "Their marriage isn't one of love. It isn't even something that we or Alard's parents' control. This arrangement was made by the parents before our own parents. Each generation brings us closer to unification, and now, the generation to follow Alard and Meyda shall represent the true beginning of a new era."

"So, they get no choice whatsoever?"

"I'm afraid so." Willa looked over at the prince and princess with a sad smile. "I'm just happy that they at least care for each other. Eldren and I were strangers to one another on our wedding day."

"Most royalty in my world have given up the practice of arranged marriages," Raz pointed out. "A few religions and cults still practice it, but love is one of the few gifts we're given that we can share with another freely."

"It sounds beautiful." Willa sighed. "Perhaps in a few generations, when the days of elemental wars of blood have passed, their children's children will be able to have a choice."

"Why wait that long?" Raz asked. "It can start right now, right here."

Willa licked her lips, and Raz wished he could read her mind. It was weird; everything Willa said was sincere and heartfelt, but the hairs on his neck refused to relax.

"How much of our history have you been told, Razi Miller?" Willa asked.

"Just the basics," Raz said. "I've been focused more on finding a solution to the bond problem."

Closing her eyes, Willa withdrew her hands from her sleeves and pressed her palms together. She chanted a few words, and as she pulled her hands apart, a clear ball of ice formed. Snow fell inside like a snow globe. Willa opened her eyes, looking at Raz, then the ice she held.

"When the human realm and this realm separated, there was peace for millennia, happy with our choices," Willa stated. "It was thought that we escaped before the human influence of greed and power overtook the land. In the end, we were wrong."

The snow swirled like a tornado, and then combined to create a miniature version of four kingdoms. Raz watched as large creatures on all sides battled, arrows flying, fairies aiming magic down on land-based creatures below them. The snow started to turn red, creatures falling on the castles, the red flowing from their wounds down on the ruins until the entire battle scene was covered in blood.

"Our harmony was ruined," Willa continued to explain. "We lost countless species of fae during the wars, relegated into tales that are seen as myth in our realm as well as yours. There was no way for any of the kingdoms to win, but they kept fighting because the urges to grab power held the hearts of the rulers."

"How did it stop?" Raz asked.

The snow swirled again, the red fading away as a throne room appeared. Raz recognized it as the one sitting just a floor below him. "It was a true gift from the creator. In one generation, each kingdom bore a son who showed no inclinations to greed and power. They gathered together, intent on finding a path forward together to breed out the thirst for power from their descendants while also building to a show of reunification that would bring a king to the throne whose blood carried all four elements in the realm."

"It still doesn't mean they should be forced into this," Raz said. "There are plenty of ways to unite two kingdoms that don't involve marriage. Treaties, unification edicts—"

"It may be that simple where you come from," Willa interrupted sharply, "but here, the elements need to work in harmony for there to be peace. Fire needs Air, and Earth needs Water. We've been without balance for too long, and their unification and eventual heir will bring the balance back. Then there will be no need to conquer each other, no path for power. Just peace."

Willa moved her hands over the edge of the balcony, melting her globe so that it rained down on the garden below them. "We have always been upfront to our children about why this is necessary. Even knowing that Alard has human origins, I see the humble soul he has grown to be. He hasn't let the need for greed or power into his heart, even from all his trips to the human realm."

She looked over at Raz, the soft smile returning to her lips. "I can see why you would be attracted to him from that alone."

Raz tried to hold back the tears stinging his eyes. "I love him."

Willa sighed. "I know, my dear. But you must also understand that this love will destroy him in the end, and his kingdom and the realm in its wake."

Forcing himself to break away from staring at Alard, he looked up at Willa. "I don't know how to stop it. We've tried everything."

"No, there is one option you haven't tried, but only you can do it." Willa held her hands out to Raz, guiding him to walk down the hallway to an alcove with a small couch they could sit on.

"What's that?"

"You are human, Razi Miller. All humans are born with a fairy godmother assigned to them. It is a tradition going far back to the times when the realms were one."

Raz laughed. "If we still had fairy godmothers, our world would be in way better shape than it is now."

"The reason you believe this is because your people have turned any evidence of our realm's existence into stories to entertain children." Willa ran a cold hand along Raz's cheek. "But there is evidence it exists when you look, mostly given to children who still have the purity in their hearts to see the magic around them."

"I'm not a child," Raz pointed out.

"But you believe, and you've been given back the sight to see magic." Willa motioned with one hand to the open space between them. "Try but believe in your heart that she will appear when you ask for her help."

Raz was skeptical, but after the week he'd had, he couldn't dismiss the idea. He closed his eyes, cleared his mind, and focused on his heart and sent a silent request into the world for someone to help him.

The smell of absinthe and flowers engulfed him, and Raz opened his eyes to find Monique standing in the space between Willa and Raz. He jumped up, but the feisty bartender put a hand on his shoulder and pushed him back into the seat. "Monique?"

"Hello, Raz," Monique said, pushing a strand of pink hair from her face. Her human façade was gone, and instead she wore a dress matching her hair color, the fabric glittering with pink and blue sparkles. "I was wondering when you would summon me for help."

"Wait, you've known about me the whole time?"

"I've watched over you since you were a little boy," Monique said. She waved a hand, and a footstool appeared for her to sit on. "I was the one who helped comfort you at night while you were made to deny your true self. The voice reminding you that you were perfect just the way you were."

Raz's eyes opened wide, unable to hold back the tears this time. "That was you?"

"Yes, darling. You were getting too old to believe in me, but my heart ached seeing you suffer so, knowing you would eventually find your path to Alard. That's why I came to New Orleans, so I could witness that moment and know you were safe and with the one you were supposed to be with."

"Thank you." Raz rubbed at his eyes with his sleeve.

Willa cleared her throat. "Godmother, I told Razi about how you may be able to solve the problem with the marriage bond."

Monique stared at Willa a moment, then she returned her attention to Raz. "I can dissolve the marriage," Monique explained, watching Willa from the corner of her eyes.

Raz narrowed his eyes. "If you knew that, why didn't you offer to help when we first came to see Catherine? You could have saved us from all this!"

"Because doing so wouldn't have kept you from your feelings," Monique explained. "You meeting Alard wasn't just an accident, child. The fact you bonded so fast is evidence of that."

Willa cleared her throat. "Accident or not, Raz wasn't given *his* choice in this bonding, and that fact seems to continue to be ignored, even if he wants him now. In fact, everything he feels now could be the influence of the bond, and not entirely on his own. And just dissolving the marriage would not solve the problem because you'd still desire him, but Meyda and Alard must still marry for the peace of the realm."

"So, I could wish that the marriage never happened?" Raz asked.

"No, you'd have to go back further," Willa said. "You would have to wish that you'd have never met him at all." Monique and Raz both looked at Willa sharply, and she sat up taller. "Otherwise you'll still remember all your feelings, and it will leave you forever wanting something that you can't have. You'd be in misery."

Monique nodded, looking at Raz. "She speaks the truth. I can't do something that would leave you in pain."

Raz looked at his hands for a moment, then to the overlook balcony where he knew Alard and Meyda waited just beyond. "Maybe I should ask Alard..."

"It would only add to his pain," Willa took one of Raz's hands, pulling his focus back onto her. "He believes you are still trapped in the human realm. He knows you're not dead or in pain through the bond. If the tattoo fades away, he can let himself believe that you found a way on your side the break it."

"James was trying to file for divorce to see if a human method would work..."

"Perfect." Willa squeezed Raz's hand. "Save him the pain and let him go. He can move on with a free conscience, believing that your plans worked."

"He'd never know?" The hairs on Raz's neck started to settle now that a solution was possible.

"Only myself and your godmother would know the truth. And I'm sure your godmother can make it so that she leaves you in a place leading to a happy and fulfilling life."

Raz looked at Monique, who took a deep breath before responding. "I *can* take away your memories of Alard and all that's happened so I can put you on a path to find true love...*if* that's what you really want," she added solemnly.

"It's what you want, Razi," Willa interjected. "You deserve to have a beautiful life free from this realm and its politics. To be with someone who makes you their whole world."

Raz took all this in, then stood up, walking to the open archway window to look at where Alard and Meyda sat. They were beautiful together, and Raz knew that Meyda would take good care of Alard. Raz knew he and Alard could never have this. He would be a human trapped in a realm that hated him, and war would break out from a broken arrangement. His continued presence in Alard's life, no matter how much they loved each other, could lead nowhere but ruin.

"Godmother, I wish to dissolve this bond between me and Alard. Please, take these memories of him from me, and take me home so none of us have to suffer anymore and for us both to find love and happiness, even if it isn't with each other." Raz felt the tears run down his face.

Monique glared at Willa, then walked over to Raz and put a hand on his shoulder. "Are you sure, darling?"

Raz nodded. "My heart's tearing apart with this decision. Just make it quick."

Willa stood, nodding her head in their direction. "It has been a pleasure meeting you, Razi Miller. You give me hope for the human realm's continued growth in compassion."

Raz nodded, then let Monique embrace him. The sparkles from her gown danced away from the fabric, surrounding them both before both human and fairy godmother disappeared.

And just before the fae realm melted away from his sight, he watched Willa's smile grow.

CHAPTER THIRTY-ONE

A lard knew something was wrong when he felt his arm start to itch. He pushed away from Meyda and grabbed his sleeve.

"What's wrong?" Meyda asked.

"My arm." As Alard pulled the sleeve back, they both saw the tattoo's glow fade away. Alard watched in horror as the ink faded as well until his arm bore no trace of the bond at all.

"Is he...does that mean?" Meyda looked up cautiously.

Alard shook his arm. "I didn't feel any pain," he said, his fingers tracing the spot where the tattoo had been. "If he had died, I would have felt that, right?"

"That's what the lore says." Meyda took his hand into hers. "Did you put anything into motion in the human realm that could have broken the bond?"

It took Alard a minute to move past the shock and remember what he had done hours—days?—before in the human realm. "We filed for divorce," he told Meyda. "James thought that it might work since the bond was forged in the human realm during a human ceremony."

"Then he was right." Meyda squeezed Alard's hand. "Your plan worked."

"I guess so." Something didn't feel right, though. Alard felt numb; cold. He knew he should feel some type of emotion like sadness, relief, *something* instead of just...nothing.

Was this how it felt when part of your heart disappears?

They were interrupted as Fi appeared off to their side, looking around the garden as she approached them. "I'm back. The trolls and sea snakes have the fire under control, but the dwarves say the portal is destroyed," she reported, continuing to look around instead of at Alard.

"Thank you, Fi," Alard said.

Meyda watched Fi a bit longer, then spoke, "What are you looking for, Fi?"

"Where's Raz? I thought he would be here with you." Fi asked.

Alard and Meyda exchanged glances, and then Alard sighed. "Raz was still in the human realm when the door exploded," he explained.

"No, he wasn't," Fi replied, shaking her head.

Meyda tilted her head. "What do you mean?"

"He was here. I left him in your suite before going back to check on the fire," Fi explained. "I found him on the road by the farmlands. He made it through just before it exploded."

Alard stood up. "You left him in the suite?"

Fi nodded. "He was really dirty and wanted to get changed before he came down to see you. Maybe he is still deciding what to wear?" she shrugged.

Without hesitation, Alard called out his wings and took off flying for his suite window. Fi followed behind, carrying Meyda with her, and they watched Alard stumble into one of the suits of armor as he tried to stop himself. Meyda and Fi stayed in the main suite as Alard went to Raz's room first, then the bathroom, and finally his own room. He checked each space, growing more frantic as they revealed nothing.

"He's not here," Alard told them, gasping for breath.

"But I left him right here," Fi said, pointing to an exact spot on the floor. "I swear to you, my lord, I know it was him."

"I believe you, Fi," Meyda said, putting a hand on Fi's shoulder as the fire fairy started to bounce anxiously. "Perhaps he is in the castle looking for you?"

"Maybe." Alard walked past them, striding down the hallways leading to the throne room.

As they passed the walkway overlooking the courtyard, Fi stopped. "Magic happened here," she said, grabbing Alard's shirt to stop him.

"Magic is done throughout the castle," he stated.

"No, I mean, very recent, and very powerful. The energy hasn't left yet." Fi waved her hands in the air and blue and pink sparkles lifted from the ground. "See, there's a trail."

Meyda knelt to look at the glitter. "It's fading fast, but if we collect some, we can find a spell to tell us who the caster is."

Alard nodded and leaned over the window. He chirped, and a sparrow flew over to him. "I need an empty nutshell."

The bird bobbed its head and flew off, returning moments later with a walnut shell in its beak. Alard thanked the bird and knelt beside Meyda, handing it to her.

"Make it swirl again, Fi," Meyda ordered.

"Yes, Highness."

Meyda caught the sparkles in the shell, trying to get as much as she could. "Okay, that should be enough."

"We need to get to the library fast. Where's Timmie?" Alard asked.

"Sleeping on my bed," Meyda stood up. "Come on."

The three of them snuck through the castle. If Raz had indeed returned to the castle, and magic was done in the hallway leading to his bedroom, Alard knew that it wasn't a coincidence. Whoever cast the magic could still be in the castle, and he wasn't sure what would happen if they were spotted.

Slipping into Meyda's room, they moved directly to the bed. Timmie was stretched out on his back, a beam of sunlight covering him and warming his belly. Meyda reached over and scratched the drake under his chin. "Timmie, wake up."

The drake opened his black eyes and looked at the three humanoids around him. He warbled a question before rolling to his two feet and stretched his chest straight up into the air, wings spread wide.

"We need you to take us to Elan," Meyda told the drake. "It's urgent."

Timmie sniffed the air, then looked at Alard. He tilted his head and chirped a question. "Yes, Raz isn't here," Alard replied. "We'll explain on the way."

Moving to the window that overlooked the western lands of Alard's kingdom, Timmie stretched out his wings again before flying out the window. It took him a minute to grow to his full size. Meyda used the time to find a handkerchief and wrap the walnut shell. Her travel belt was hanging over the chair, and she strapped it on, then slid the wrapped walnut shell into one of her pouches.

Alard and Meyda climbed onto Timmie's back and, along with Fi flying at their side, they went straight to the library. They caught Timmie up on what had happened since sunrise, and the drake growled, warbling something akin to how he can't leave them alone for a minute. Alard pat Timmie's shoulder, touched by his loyalty, to assure the drake that what happened was not in any way Timmie's fault.

Once they arrived, Timmie shrank down and landed on Meyda's shoulder before they all entered the library. "Elan!" Alard called, heading straight for the magic scroll section of the first floor. "We need your help immediately."

"If you have come to check on the status of my research, I still have yet to hear of a solution." Elan appeared at the top of the stairs, holding a mug in one hand and a pheasant leg in the other. "Now, unless it is a true emergency, I am in the middle of my midday meal—"

"Someone did powerful magic in my castle and now Raz has disappeared. I don't care if you are creating a cure for bone rot right now, come down here and help," Alard ordered, slamming his fist on the side of the bookshelves.

Elan blinked, then tossed the food over his shoulder and started down the stairs. He finished his drink on the way, leaving the mug at the bottom of the stairs, and he joined them. "Tell me what you know."

Fi moved forward, hovering a few inches from the floor as she kept looking around the library in amazement. "The portal to the human realm exploded," she explained. "I found Raz walking back to the castle and brought him back to Alard's room."

"I was kidnapped by a werewolf from the human realm and left tied up in the western tower before the portal blew up," Alard added.

"We were under the assumption Raz hadn't made it through the portal since Alard wasn't there to bring him," Meyda continued, "until Fi told us what she had done. When we went to find him—"

"I sensed big, powerful magic having been done!" Fi interrupted, holding her hand up proudly.

Meyda smiled at the jubilant fairy. "She did, and we gathered some of the residual energy to figure out who did the spell because we think they took Raz," she said.

"Oh, and during all this..." Alard pulled back his sleeve. "It disappeared."

Elan leaned forward and poked at Alard's skin. "I see. But wasn't the goal to get the bond removed so that you two," he motioned at Alard and Meyda, "could get married while Raz returned to his life in the human realm?"

"It was," Alard hesitated. "But now...I love him. I don't want to lose him."

"And the removal of the bond didn't also remove your feelings? That's interesting." Elan tapped a finger against his chin. "One would think that if someone wanted to intervene to end your marriage, they would have done so in a way to keep you from remembering it, or at least altered your feelings. The fact they didn't is very interesting, but then again, I've not dealt with memory-altering magic before."

"So, this might be something different from our kind of magic?" Meyda asked.

"Possibly. Let's look at this spell and see what we can figure out, hmm?"

Elan led them to his magic workstation. He whispered a cleansing spell, and all magical residue from his desk wiped away. Meyda gave him the walnut shell, and he unwrapped it, leaving both handkerchief and shell in front of him.

He grabbed a few liquid components from a nearby shelf and a clean glass tube. Elan measured them carefully into the container. "This should reveal to me which elements the spell consists of."

Elan dipped his finger into the glitter, then tapped it into the test tube, and put a cork over it. The glitter swirled, then melted into the chemicals, turning the contents in the tube violet. Elan hummed, uncorked the vial, and took a sniff of the mixture.

"It has been a very long time since I have seen this magic," Elan said after a moment. "I knew they still existed, but most of them live in the human realm, not here."

Alard stared at the violet liquid. "This is magic from a witch?" he guessed.

Elan chuckled. "No, my lord. We would know if a witch was in the realm. This is the magic of a fairy godmother."

Fi gasped, her wings fluttering her away from the magic. "They do still exist!"

"I thought they died out after the separation of the realms?" Meyda held her hand out for the test tube, which Elan gave her to examine.

"Yeah, they only exist as fairytales in the human realm," Alard pointed out.

"Then, obviously, the stories are wrong." Elan walked away from them toward a bookcase. He scanned the books, then pulled a large, dusty tome out and put it on a reading stand. "If there are still fairy godmothers hiding in the human realm, this will remind us of what they truly are."

Alard and Meyda moved to stand behind Elan, all of them reading the book. Fi hovered nervously nearby before flying up to the bookcases to read the spines until someone spoke.

The book spoke about a fairy made of all four elements, plus energy from the moon and sun. The fairy godmother could appear in any shape, any form, but most appeared human. They frequented the human lay lines, allowing them to access magic from both realms. A godmother was able to travel between the realms on their own accord, not needing a portal.

"It doesn't list their powers," Alard stated as the section ended.

"It doesn't need to," Elan said. "A fairy godmother grants wishes to better the life of the human they are assigned, as long as the human believes in magic and can still see them."

"Raz has both the ability and belief," Meyda stated. "But he wouldn't know godmothers existed. It would be a story to him, right, Alard?"

"Yes..." Alard stood up straighter. "Unless someone knew they existed and told him."

Fi held a book as she lowered herself back to the ground. "But why would Raz leave without saying goodbye?"

"I don't know," Alard said.

Meyda looked at the book Fi held. "What do you have there?"

Fi looked at the book in her hands like she had forgotten it was there, then held it out to Elan. It was clean, the pages still crisp, leather tight, not a speck of dust on the edges. "It said godmother on the cover. I thought it could help."

"I don't remember this book," Elan said. He touched the cover and closed his eyes, then gasped, almost dropping it.

"What happened?" Meyda asked as she and Alard moved closer to Elan. Alard took the book out of Elan's hands as Meyda put her hands on Elan's shoulders to steady him.

"It screamed when I tried to ask it where it came from." Elan stared at the book. "It screamed your name, Alard."

Alard looked at Elan, then held the book out in front of him. "Why me?"

Before Elan could answer, the book jumped from Alard's hands, and it opened in the air before him. Pages flipped to an image in the middle of the book. "Shit," Alard muttered, staring at the picture of Raz wrapped in the arms of a faceless fairy, the tears in Raz's eyes turning into blue and pink sparkles.

"That's...that's not him in the book, is it?" Alard touched the page, hoping to elicit the scream again, but the tome stayed silent.

"No, it's just an image. Fairy godmothers must document their magic so they can trace the effects later on," Elan explained.

Meyda moved to his side, then gasped. "He made a wish," she whispered.

"He's crying," Alard said, brushing his fingers along Raz's face.

Elan moved back to his workbench. "If this is the residue of a godmother's wish granting, I may be able to extract the essence of the wish and figure out what happened."

Alard nodded, letting Elan work while opening the book back into his arms. He flipped the pages back, trying to find evidence of his own of what had happened in the hallway. "Someone had to tell him this godmother existed," Alard repeated his statement from earlier. "Who told him?"

The book flipped back a page, and Alard saw an image of Raz looking over the courtyard, and a shadowed figure watching him from around the corner. "Who is that?" Meyda asked.

"I don't know, but we will figure that out after we find Raz," Alard growled.

"My lord, Your Highness, I'm ready," Elan called from his bench. Alard

shut the book, tucking it under his arm as he and Meyda walked back over
to Elan. The Sidhe had a bronze bowl in front of him, herbs already mixed
into it, candles hovering in a circle around the edges.

Alard, Meyda, and Fi stood beside Elan as he started chanting. He held
the walnut shell over the ingredients, spoke a few words, and then dumped
the glitter into the bowl. Violet smoke rose from the bowl, taking on the
shape of Raz's face, tears rolling down his cheeks.

"I wish to dissolve this bond between me and Alard. Please, take these
memories of him from me, and take me home so none of us have to suffer
anymore and for us both to find love and happiness, even if it isn't with each
other." *"Are you sure, darling?"*

"My heart's tearing apart with this decision. Just make it quick."

As the smoke faded away, Alard realized he was crying. The numbness in
his heart was back, trying to break him. Meyda pulled him against her side,
and Timmie hopped onto the top of his head, nuzzling Alard in his
own way.

"I'm sorry, my lord." Elan said solemnly.

"He wished me away," Alard whispered. "How could he...?"

"He wanted you to find love," Meyda told him. "You can hear it in his
voice that he didn't want to leave you."

Alard nodded. "But I had found love." He looked at Meyda. "I'm sorry,
Meyda..."

Meyda pulled Alard into her arms. "I would rather you have true love,
Alard, then face a lifetime without it to make our people happy." She
rubbed his back as Alard sobbed, the numbness turning to anguish.

Suddenly Alard pushed back, looking Meyda in the eye. "Did you mean
it, about you and Elan finding evidence of having a three-way marriage in
our realm?"

"Yes," Elan said, drawing their attention. "It is far back in our history,
mainly used for a king to have multiple wives so that he can bear multiple
children legitimately. It requires a few adjustments to the blessings and
procedure, and it has to all be done in the same ceremony, but yes, it is
possible."

Alard looked at Meyda, and she smiled. "If we can find him, and have
him remember his love for you, I am more than willing to marry you both,"

Meyda said. "I think together, the three of us are stronger together than just you and me. The kingdom will be better off for it."

Engulfing Meyda in a hug, he whispered his thanks into her ear. When they parted, he looked at all of them. "Looks like we're going to New York," Alard announced, hope reigniting in him.

He was going to get his husband back, and if the stars were in their favor, Alard and Raz would have their happy ending.

CHAPTER THIRTY-TWO

The plan took on multiple layers, everyone having their own parts to play. Alard sent Fi back to his castle with a list of items to get from his bedroom and desk: wallet, phone, clothing, and messenger bag. He had to describe them to her, knowing that Fi wouldn't recognize the human objects.

While she was gone, Elan, Meyda, and Alard worked on creating a spell that would put the entirety of the people in Alard's kingdom in stasis. It was a backup plan; time in the human realm passed slower, which meant Alard was going to be away for days. If Eldren went through on his threat of war, Elan would have the ability to stop it so no one would be hurt. They weren't sure how long it would last, but it was better than nothing.

Fi returned with the objects, and Alard left her with Elan as protection while he, Meyda, and Timmie flew to the Kingdom of Fire and Ice. It was nighttime when they arrived, and they made use of the long shadows in the obsidian castle walls.

"Where's the portal?" Alard whispered as Meyda guided him through the hallways.

"Servant's quarters," she replied, pushing them both against the wall as a pair of goblins walked past on patrol. "This way," she hissed, grabbing his hand and pulling Alard along. They ducked around two more corners before stooping low to crawl through a small archway.

"Where are we?" Alard asked as Meyda lifted her hand, letting fire extend from her fingers to give them light.

"Pantry," she replied as she walked past mounds of potatoes and onions. "The archway allows the gnomes to get in easily but keeps the goblins out of the food stores."

"That's efficient," he said, keeping close behind her.

They kept walking, Meyda's hand waving along the walls to inspect the reflective black glass. "I know...there it is." She stepped around a mossy area where mushrooms were growing and pressed on an indent in the wall. The glass shifted to the side, revealing a swirling vortex like the portal that had been in Alard's forest. It gave off a light of its own, allowing Meyda to extinguish her hand.

"Alright," Alard said, putting down his bag. He pulled out a set of clothing and held it out to her. "Put these on."

Meyda took the pile curiously. "What is this?"

"Human jeans and a t-shirt," he explained. "You can put it on over your corset and boots."

"I cannot simply wear my dress?"

"You need to blend in. Our human forms already look beautiful to their eyes, so we need to do whatever we can to not stand out." Alard closed his eyes and shifted back into his human guise. "See?"

Meyda wrinkled her nose at the fabric. "It feels rough," she complained, rubbing her hand along the jeans.

"Only on the outside. Please, trust me."

Sighing, Meyda made a motion for Alard to turn around. He did so, watching as best he could to make sure no one came around the corner. When he was allowed to turn back, Meyda was dressed in the human clothing, and her hands quickly braiding her hair up around her head. "This is weird," she stated.

"It's only until we find Raz, I promise." He grabbed his bag and slung it over his shoulder again. "Now, you need to get your skin color to match mine." Alard laid his arm against hers.

Meyda focused, trying to alter her appearance to match. "You're too light," she stated, unable to suppress the redness of her skin tone.

"Damnit. Maybe this isn't a good idea then."

"No, wait." Meyda closed her eyes again, and Alard watched as her skin, instead of trying to go pale white, faded into the ashy color that took on a burnt ground appearance. "Does this color exist in the human realm?"

"No, but if you darken it, it'll work." Alard watched as her appearance shifted to a brownish-black, and he stopped her. He grinned, seeing the shine of her skin from the vortex, and how the black skin created a striking contrast with her near colorless hair. "Beautiful," he said, smiling.

Meyda grinned. "Are we good now?"

"As we'll ever be."

"Then let's go." She turned to the drake on Alard's shoulder. "You can't come with us, Timmie. I need you to guard the portal and not allow anyone to close it until we get back." Timmie whined, pressing his head into Meyda's hand as she petted him. "I know, we'll be fine. Alard will protect me."

"And if you're good, we'll bring you back a present," Alard added. The drake grumbled but flew down to nest in Meyda's discarded dress.

Alard took Meyda's hand. "Through the looking glass we go," he stated, and together they jumped into the portal...

...and crashed into a janitor's cart in a tiny closet. Meyda yelped in surprise, and Alard cursed when his shin hit the corner of the mop bucket.

"What is that smell?" Meyda whined, pressing herself closer to Alard.

"Bleach," Alard told her, scrambling in the dark for a door handle. He saw Meyda start to lift her hand to give them light but grabbed it. "No, you could make something explode with the fire here. Also, no magic in the human realm, remember?"

"Right, sorry."

Alard reached into his bag and grabbed his cell phone. He turned on the flashlight and moved it along the walls until he found the door. He opened it and they stumbled out into a hallway of cream-colored tiles. Humans walked past them in either direction, most of them watching the phone screens and completely ignoring the appearance of two people from a broom closet.

All except one mother with her two toddlers. The kids pointed, and the mother shot them a disappointed look that made Alard blush as he kicked the door shut behind him. "Come on," he whispered to Meyda, taking her hand. "I need to find reception to make a phone call."

"Raz?" Meyda asked, her eyes taking in the windows of the stores they passed.

"No, James," he stated as they turned into the main terminal of the building. Both stopped, taking in the grandeur. The beautiful archways at the foot of stone columns reached far above them to a green ceiling. Tiny lights twinkled, laying out the constellations of the night sky for anyone to see. The words of hundreds of people talking, babies crying, and the rumble of trains echoed off the walls in a cornucopia of sound that washed over them.

"What is this place?" Meyda asked, her eyes trying to take it all in.

Alard lowered his gaze, noticing the black screens listing the names of towns, but when he saw the information rotunda in the center with a clock on top—two minutes past noon—he grinned. "We're in New York City. This must be Grand Central Station."

"It's amazing." Meyda grinned, squeezing Alard's hand. He was about to agree with her when a passing man in a business suit brushed past, knocking his shoulder into Alard's, causing Alard to stumble forward.

"Fucking tourists," the man muttered, never lifting his eyes from his phone.

"Are you okay?" Meyda asked, helping Alard regain his balance. "Should I bring him back here for his obvious disrespect against the crown? How do you punish the humans here?"

"No. No no no," Alard put his free hand on her arm. "We're normal people here, remember?"

She nodded. "I can see why no one likes humans."

"This is New York. The humans here are...special." Alard guided Meyda to one of the escalators. "Come on, let's go."

She gave a dubious look at the moving stairs. "How do I ride this?"

"Just step on." Alard pulled her along, and Meyda hopped onto the step behind Alard.

It took her a moment to center herself, then Meyda looked back at the main concourse and watched it get smaller as they rose. "This is much easier than flying."

"Oh, it gets better." They hopped off the top of the escalator and walked through the glass doors to the outside. The smell of hot dogs, car exhaust, and garbage assaulted them, and Meyda covered her nose.

"This is not better, Alard," she stated, shooting him a traitorous look.

"Sorry." Alard moved her away from the stink, finding a cleaner street corner before pulling out his phone. He had a signal, and it only took him a moment to dial James's number.

It took three rings before his best friend answered. "James Wilson, Attorney at Law. How can I help you?"

"James, it's Alard," he said, raising his voice over the sounds of traffic. "I'm so glad to hear your voice."

"Alard?" James's voice came back shocked. "Whose phone are you calling from? You're safe? Is Raz there?"

"It's Meyda's phone. Wait, how did you know Raz came through the portal? Were you there?! Are YOU okay?" Alard had known they were going to be at his place, but he had hoped they avoided the werewolves and explosion.

"Yeah. We came over after the courthouse and were attacked by Mr. Latex-Loving Lassie. Raz came in and like a true knight took the big, bad wolf down and untied Catherine and I but, Alard, we couldn't disable the bomb. We hid in your closet and survived the blast with just some scrapes and bruises. But the house has seen better. Oh, and the cops have some questions for you. Catherine and I got out of there before they showed up, but they came around asking about your whereabouts."

"Fuck," Alard growled. "I'll deal with the cops and werewolf clans later. I'm sorry you got caught up in all this. This is going too far."

"Hey Alard, it's okay. We're okay. We can do damage control on this later. But why are you back in the human realm without Raz?"

Alard quickly explained what happened with Raz and the fairy godmother. "I need your help finding him again," Alard concluded.

"I'm on it. Let me load up my laptop." Alard heard the door chime of James entering someplace, then the noise of the New Orleans streets faded to that of coffeehouse music. "I can see if the conference is still going on…"

"No, it ended that day," Alard told him, moving out of the way of a group of people walking towards him. He realized Meyda had moved to look at a table of wares that someone had set up on a folding table, and he went to stand beside her.

"Then he probably went home when he wished to go back."

"That's what I'm thinking. Home is Washington DC"

Alard kept feeding information, nodding to Meyda when she held up a crystal with the Empire State Building etched inside of it. Tucking the phone between his ear and shoulder, he grabbed money from his wallet to purchase it for her.

"Okay, I've got an address for his business," James said. "I'll text it to you. It's not a PO Box so it should be a real office instead of a home office."

"Wonderful." Meyda was moving on to another table and Alard followed. "Now I need to get there."

"There's an Amtrak Acela that goes from New York to DC. I think you can still catch the last one for today if you can get to Penn Station."

"Amtrak is a train, right?" Alard asked.

James laughed. "Yes, Alard, it's a train."

"Okay, we can do a train."

"Wait, we? Who's with you if it's not Raz?"

Alard watched Meyda hold a pair of earrings, hearing the lady explain about pierced ears. "Meyda."

"Alard, are you crazy?" James shouted into the phone.

"Right now, yes I am. Everything's okay though." Alard smiled as Meyda looked up, hearing James's voice through the phone. "All I have to do is go to Penn Station, hop on a train to DC, and then use my phone map to find his office."

"Yeah, that's it," James said. "And try not to lose Meyda in the process."

"I can do that." Alard thought for a moment, looking back at one of Grand Central Station's entrances. "Um, how do I get to Penn Station?"

James groaned. "You've never been to New York before, have you?"

"Nope." Alard waved for Meyda to join him since they needed to get moving. She put down the earrings and thanked the woman before rejoining him.

"Sweet baby Jesus," James sighed. "Go back into Grand Central and look for the Times Square connector..." Alard listened as James told him which subway numbers to look for and which direction to go. "And whatever you do, do not take your wallet out while in the subway trains. That's just asking for it to be stolen."

"Will do. Thanks, James."

"Keep me updated on what happens," James stated. "And I expect an invite to the wedding now."

"At this point, I think you've earned the best man position," Alard said with a laugh.

"Damn right." James laughed with him. "Good luck."

CHAPTER THIRTY-THREE

Except for the questionable smell and rude humans talking into their phones, Meyda liked this New York City. While Alard spoke on the phone, she took a moment to absorb the information that her senses gave her.

The first thing she noticed was the lack of earth. The ground was two different shades of gray, the darker having lines of yellow and white stripes. She figured the latter served as a road. Did the stripes show people which way the trail went? It seemed that each side of the double stripe separated those going left from right as the yellow carriages rolled past together like a caravan.

The spires of glass and steel reached up higher than even the oldest trees back home. If they weren't in a hurry to find Raz, Meyda would insist Alard take her to the top of one so she could see what this city looked like from above.

A gust of wind whipped around her, and she turned to face it, letting the breeze caress her cheeks. The air hit her like it did when she rode Timmie, and her mind drifted to the fire drake and how he would handle this realm.

Probably bite the ankles of all the humans that bumped into her and Alard.

She should bring him back a present. Something to show him these buildings that they could spend days weaving around in flight. That desire led her to the tables of trinkets, and to a hunk of glass with a building drawn inside of it. Alard gave her a green paper to trade for the glass, and when the nice trinket human gave her coins and papers back, she put them in her pocket.

"Okay, I know where we need to go," Alard stated as he slipped his phone away in his pocket.

"I thought we were going to Washington Dee See," Meyda said with careful pronunciation.

"We are. But first we need to find the subway leading to the train that will take us there."

"A train?" She asked. "Is that like a long caravan of wagons? And what is a subway?"

"A train is like a caravan, only the cars are metal and there is just one driver." Alard rubbed the back of his neck. "I've never seen a subway before. I think it's more like the cable cars I told you about, but underground."

"This is turning out to be a real adventure." Meyda grinned. "I'm glad you let me come."

Alard laughed. "Like I let you do anything. You would have come whether I asked you or not. I just accepted the inevitable instead of arguing."

"Yup, you're going to be the best husband ever."

They reentered Grand Central Station and returned to the large chamber with the glowing stars on the ceiling. How could these humans capture stars and bring them inside? She would have to ask Alard later to explain that magic.

Alard squeezed her hand, bringing Meyda's attention back to her best friend. "I think I found where the subway is." Together, they made their way across the star chamber and to a set of stairs. The walls had signs with colored circles and human letters or numbers in them.

"What are these?" she asked Alard, pointing at the sign.

"The names of the different subway trains," he replied. "We're looking for the 'S' train."

Meyda shook her head as they continued. "Humans are weird. They should be more creative when giving their items names."

Alard chuckled. They stepped beside a big machine with a laptop-like screen in it and pulled out his wallet. "Give me a moment. I need to get us tickets."

Once he secured tickets, Alard had Meyda go through the turnstile. He explained why they couldn't just jump over it, which seemed odd, but if the humans needed people to give them money to make the subway work, it was a worthy cause.

The city smell was worse down in the subway, and Meyda crouched down as she saw a large fieldmouse dragging an apple along the tunnel bottom. "Alard, look, they have mice here too!"

Alard looked and took a step back. "That's a rat, Meyda. Not nearly as nice as mice."

"Oh." She stood back up. "Poor creature. I guess it had to become mean to deal with the rude humans."

A horn sounded, and a light appeared down the dark tunnel moments before a large metal snake whooshed past them. A screeching noise was next as the snake slowed down until a pair of doors stopped in front of them. "This is a subway?" she asked Alard, who nodded in reply. "It is very odd."

"I know," Alard said as the doors opened. Humans started to exit the subway, and Alard pulled Meyda out of the way before she got trampled. When the car was empty, they boarded and found seats.

Across from them sat an old woman wearing a yellow plastic cloak with the hood drawn halfway down her face. A metal basket on wheels stood in front of her, filled with black plastic bags. Next to the woman was a man with skin as dark as dried lava, and his hair floating like a cloud around his head. A small child with the same skin sat close to the man, and Meyda assumed that they were father and son. The child waved shyly at her, and Meyda smiled, returning the gesture.

When the doors to the subway closed, there was a quick jerk that made Meyda fall into Alard a moment before the subway started to move. There was nothing to see out the windows, just dark walls and her reflection. She was about to ask Alard why there was no light when music started to play.

They both looked up to see five men in black outfits at the end of the subway room. They had some kind of string instrument that Meyda was unfamiliar with, and wore big, circular hats. The hat and their outfits had beautiful designs woven along the edges of the fabric. "Who are they?" she asked Alard.

"Musicians. A mariachi band, I think."

Meyda grinned. "They provide music on the subway. They must be very good to have a job serving the people like that."

As the band got closer, the musician in front was holding out a velvet-lined wooden box. Meyda watched the father give his son a green paper, and the boy put it into the box. Figuring that it was a way to thank the musicians for their music, she reached into her pocket and pulled out the papers and coins that she had gotten back from the trinket man and put it all in the box. "Your music is very beautiful," she told the man, which made him smile before moving on.

"That was my change, wasn't it?" Alard asked once the band had passed.

"The trinket man gave it to me. I wanted to thank the humans for sharing their gift of music with us." Meyda looked up at Alard. "Was that wrong?"

Alard shook his head, wrapping an arm around her shoulder and hugging her close. "No, not wrong at all. Quite the opposite."

Meyda grinned and leaned into Alard's shoulder. The human world was weird, but she was starting to like it.

———

They were able to catch the two o'clock train out of Penn Station to Washington DC, and Alard spent the next two hours entertaining Meyda by first telling her what everything was that passed by the window. Then, in Wilmington, a young woman sat in the seats across the aisle from them, a pet carrier placed on the ground under her feet.

Meyda had been curious and asked the woman about the creature she was carrying, and the woman—Sarah—reached into the soft case and pulled out a baby black kitten. The last hour of the train ride had Meyda sitting with Sarah, holding the kitten and dangling a tiny ribbon in its face to bat. Alard took pictures and video on Meyda's phone of her new animal friend for her to look back on later.

When they arrived at Union Station in DC, Meyda waved her new friend goodbye, as well as Sarah. It took Alard dragging her away to let poor Sarah continue her trip back to her dorm.

"Alard, before we go back, can I get a kitten of my own?" Meyda asked while Alard traced his finger along the wall map laying out the metro lines.

"We could, but your parents might not appreciate you having a creature from the human realm at your side," he replied absently, his mind focused on figuring out which line went to Dupont Circle. It was the closest stop that James could figure let off near Raz's company.

"They let me keep you around," Meyda said.

Alard blinked, his brain acknowledging the remark before he understood the joke she was making. He turned his head to the side, looking at her with narrowed eyes. "Funny."

"Plus, I think that the kitten would be a good companion for Timmie."

"Or lunch."

"Hey!" Meyda slapped Alard's arm. "Timmie wouldn't eat a helpless tiny kitten."

"First of all, Timmie almost ate me the first time we met him," Alard pointed out, looking back at the map, tracing the red metro line this time. "Second, he eats the rodents that get into both our castles. They are tiny and helpless at that size."

"And he keeps them from getting too big and becoming dangerous." Meyda defended her pet drake from Alard's allegations. "And maybe I should have let Timmie eat you. We wouldn't be in this mess now."

"Meyda." Alard sighed her name, not looking over his shoulder.

She looked at Alard, then rubbed her hand against his arm. "I didn't mean it like that."

"I know." He turned his head to give her a quick half-smile. "Let's focus on Raz first, and then we'll look into adopting a kitten. It can be my wedding present to you."

Meyda squealed, hugging Alard's arm tightly. "Best. Husband. Ever."

"Just remember that when you have two of us." He looked back at the map, finger continuing to move along the red line until Dupont Circle appeared. "There, found it. We need to get on the red line."

"Is this a train or subway?" Meyda asked as they started to look for the metro entrance.

"Another subway."

"Oh, maybe they will have music on their subway here too!" Meyda turned to walk with Alard, then saw a sign with a green logo and pointed. "Alard, it's that drink place you love so much! Can we get some before we go find Raz, please?"

It was like taking a field trip with a child, Alard realized as he let himself get dragged toward the familiar scents of coffee and pastries. Seeing that he hadn't slept in almost a day, however, getting a coffee was a good idea.

Meyda ended up not liking the bitter taste of the coffee, and Alard found himself trying to juggle two cups while standing in a crowded subway car during the evening commute. Meyda sat next to him, enjoying a strawberry banana smoothie instead.

In his mind, Alard was working on what he would say when he found Raz. In his wish, Raz asked to forget ever meeting Alard, so it was already going to be an awkward situation. The thing about magic, though, is that there is always a way to break it. Alard just had to figure out the right way to break past the godmother's magic to unlock the hidden memories.

Easy. Or so he told himself.

He had had Fi bring him the clothes from when Raz had picked Alard up at the nightclub. Alard hoped that it would help Raz's mind identify him subconsciously. He couldn't reproduce the settings, so it was all that he had.

But what do I say? Alard struggled with the words. He was great with them in court, or when he was fulfilling princely duties. Talking about his intimate feelings was new, and he was afraid that one wrong word would ruin any chance of getting Raz back.

They reached their destination while Alard was crafting his script. The royal pair squeezed out of the car and started the long escalator ride up to the surface. Meyda was comfortable getting on and off the moving stairs on her own now, so Alard worked on finishing at least one of the coffees on the slow climb.

The streets of DC were much different from the ones in Manhattan. It was more open, the buildings tall but nowhere near the size of the skyscrapers that made up the NYC skyline. Across from the subway entrance was a park, trees making up the circumference. Meyda grinned at Alard and took off running, barely avoiding getting hit by a taxi as she did so.

"Meyda, wait up!" Alard shouted, running after her.

He reached her in the center of the park as she stared up at the big fountain. Her fingers reached out to the small waterfall in front of her, and she closed her eyes while enjoying the sensation. Alard realized that they had not touched real earth since they had arrived in the human realm, and Meyda was probably feeling disconnected at this point from the elements.

"I'm sorry," he told her, sitting on the fountain's edge. "I should have taken you to water earlier to acquaint yourself here."

Meyda opened her eyes, working to keep them from glowing. He could see the pink flecks in the amber of her human guise iris's trying to shine through. "It's okay. I didn't realize that I needed it until I saw the fountain and the water beckoned me to join it."

"Yeah, I have it easier here since the wind is everywhere, and I can go to a park if I need a hit of earth connection." Alard leaned back and ran his fingers through the water gathered at the fountain's basin. "Just warn me before you go hunting for a fire. That element is dangerous here."

"Yes, my lord," she teased, then went back to conversing with the DC water supply while Alard pulled up a map of the area on his phone and plugged in the address James had found. The office was in a building on the corner of Connecticut Avenue NW and S Street. It was a few blocks north from where they were and located on the second floor above a steak house.

Alard knew he couldn't just walk in and expect to be seen. He didn't want to do this in the middle of Raz's job in case it went badly. It would make Raz's life harder trying to face his employees the next day. Maybe it was better to wait for Raz to leave his job, follow him to someplace with less people to observe them and talk then.

Feeling water hit his face, Alard shook himself out of his thoughts to look at Meyda. "What, Meyda?" She was staring off beyond him, her eyes locked on a specific target. Alard turned his head to see what she was gazing at, and his heart pounded.

Raz, wearing a well-cut business suit, was sitting on a bench about fifty feet from them. He was shaved, his hair cut short and styled as if he was sitting for a cover shot of GQ instead of an evening in the park.

Alard's mouth went dry, the words he wanted to say flying straight out of his head. Raz was gorgeous, and all Alard wanted to do in the moment was run to him, kiss him, and never let him go. Instead, he was stuck in place, staring, fear of rejection keeping him rooted to his fountain perch while Raz pulled a book from his briefcase and started reading.

"Go to him," Meyda hissed. She flicked the water from her hands and sat down beside Alard.

"I don't know what to say," Alard whispered. "What if I screw this up?"

"Staying here and staring like a creeper isn't going to end any better." She nudged his shoulder. "Just be yourself and be honest. You can be charming when you want to."

Alard took a deep breath. "I can do this," he said to himself as he stood up. He readjusted his clothing, making sure he wasn't wrinkled or hadn't somehow gotten coffee on his shirt, before crossing the distance between them.

"Raz?' Alard hesitated, six feet separating Alard from the one man he loved more than anything on Earth. He braced himself, refusing to let the curious stare of a stranger get to him. Alard knew what he was walking into, and he was going to fix it.

"Yes? Do I know you?" Raz put a finger in his book before lowering it to his lap.

Alard gulped. Nope, no backing down. "We met last week in New Orleans. The conference?"

"Ah," Raz chuckled, a smile coming to his lips and melting Alard's heart. "Sorry, my friends and I partied a bit more than we should've last week. Everything from last week is still a bit fuzzy."

"That's okay. I'm Alard. Fairchild. We met at the coffee café on Canal Street."

"The one with the instruments hanging from the ceiling?"

Alard smiled. "Yeah, that would be it."

"I stopped there most mornings before heading to the convention center. Cheaper than paying the price at the hotel." Raz leaned back into the bench. "I don't recall meeting you though."

How to approach this without making it about me, but something else Raz might remember on that day... "I was helping three homeless men with some legal paperwork. Jacob had just inherited his sister's estate, and we were going over the will."

Raz thought a moment, his eyes going distant. "I do remember seeing homeless people in the back while waiting for my order."

"They're hard to forget. People call them the Three Musketeers—"

"—of St. Charles," Raz finished, his smile returning. "Now that you mention them, it rings a bell. But it's strange; I still don't remember you being there."

Alard opened his mouth to try another pre-marriage memory but was cut off as someone approached from Alard's left. "I hope I'm not interrupting," a man asked, adjusting the backpack strap on his shoulder. Tall and wearing khakis and a sweatshirt for Georgetown University, the man looked every inch like a young professor. "I wasn't sure if I had enough time to change before we went to dinner."

"You look fine just the way you are," Raz stood, leaning in to kiss the man deeply. Alard felt the ground fall out from under him, but he managed to keep himself upright through sheer force of will. "Gregorio, this is Alard, someone I met at the convention last week. Alard, my boyfriend Gregorio."

"Pleasure to meet you," Gregorio said, holding out his hand while flashing a brilliant smile. Alard plastered a smile on his face and shook the man's hand back.

"Hey Alard," Meyda was at his side, wrapping her arms around Alard's free one. "We need to get going before we miss our train to the place with the thing you wanted to see." She gave his arm a gentle tug.

Alard turned to look at her. Meyda wore her own fake smile, nodding her head away from the other couple. "I guess we have to go. It was nice seeing you again." Alard hoped Raz didn't hear the hitch in his voice.

"Always." Raz waved goodbye as Meyda all but dragged Alard in the direction of the metro station. Alard grabbed the black gate at the edge of the park grounds, turning his head back to look at Raz one more time.

"You sure you don't remember him?" Alard heard Gregorio ask Raz, his back to where Alard and Meyda stood.

"Not him. The girl did seem familiar though." Raz shrugged, then took Gregorio's hand. "Come on, you're going to love this bistro up by my office."

Meyda reached up to turn Alard's face to look at her, her smile gone and sympathy in its place. "Come on, let's go."

Alard nodded, letting Meyda lead him to the down escalator and away from Dupont Circle. Away from the painful vision of the love of his life having moved on with another man. Away from the remnants of his heart lying shattered on the concrete walkway.

Chapter Thirty-Four

Meyda hadn't been sure how she would be able to help Alard on this trip, but something inside her had warned that it would be bad if she didn't come. So, she put on the ridiculous clothes Alard gave her, suffered through the horrible smells and harsh landscape, and ignored the creepy looks that the human men gave her, all to make sure Alard had someone at his side.

She had been sitting on the fountain's edge, her fingers still making waves as they wiggled in the water, watching Alard and Raz talk. Meyda didn't understand why her parents were so up in arms about the two men. Her father took it as a personal insult, which Meyda had rolled her eyes at because the only one who should be insulted was *her*, but one look at them in the library had eased any potential insult.

Yes, she still had to give Alard a hard time, but that was part of their friendship. She always gave him a hard time because he was an idiot who wore his heart on his sleeve and took everything that went wrong internally, finding a way to blame himself for the bad things that happened around them. She slapped the back of his head to stop him from thinking that way.

Meyda wasn't sure if a simple slap was going to fix this, though. It had been hours since Alard had spoken. He had just...shut down. Meyda, who had no idea what she was doing in the human realm, relied on her memory to get them back on the metro and to Union Station. She found a door to get outside—it was laid out almost the same way Grand Central Station had been—and then followed the call of water to guide her to a place they could rest and hide from the humans for a bit.

Now Alard lay on the ground (real earth!) under a tree, his eyes staring through the branches at the stars above. Meyda sat on the stone and brick edge around a pool of water, dipping her toes into it and resisting the urge to dive in and take a swim. She could; she had cast an invisibility spell around herself and Alard so no humans would bother them. However, just because she was invisible didn't mean that the water wouldn't cause ripples from her movement, and that couldn't be easily explained away.

Meyda didn't know how to help her best friend. The wish worked, and Raz had no memory of Alard. Raz had been placed on a path to find love and happiness, and Meyda would be happy for him if it wasn't at the expense of Alard's heart. When she asked what he was thinking while they waited for the metro to arrive, he just replied, "Gone" and hadn't spoken since.

Looks like her gut had been right, and Alard needed her.

"Are you done with your emotional spiraling yet?" Meyda called over, hoping...no, willing Alard to move or say something or anything but lay there like a breathing corpse. As predicted, she received no response.

"This isn't your fault," she said for the tenth or hundredth time. She lost count at this point. That time at least got a deep sigh from Alard, and he closed his eyes. It was something, at least.

"You can't just give up." Meyda hopped up and walked across the concrete walkway to join him on the ground. "We came a long way to find you a husband, Alard, and I, for one, will be very upset if we don't return with one. You don't want me to be upset, do you?"

"Meyda," he muttered.

"Yeah?"

"Not helping."

Meyda huffed and absently played with a few twigs in front of her. "To be fair, what you're doing right now? That's what's not helping. We knew what we were walking into coming here."

"I wasn't expecting him." Alard sighed, his fist clenching at his side.

"Gregorio. Fuck, he's beautiful. I can see why Raz would be attracted to him."

"Yes, because you're such an ugly piece of dragon dung," Meyda muttered, rolling her eyes. "Plus, I seem to recall you telling me that looks aren't everything when you had that crush on that crusty elf from the Rainbow Falls region."

"That was different," Alard pointed out. "It wasn't Raz."

"And the only reason they are together is the wish. I bet if you asked, Raz wouldn't even know how they met. And yeah, Raz's fairy godmother has impeccable taste, but she had to give Raz someone who had to go against the emotional void you were going to leave in him." She leaned over Alard, looking him in his eyes. "You're not an easy person to forget."

Alard gave her a weak smile, but it was a smile. Meyda called victory. She held out a hand, helping Alard sit up. "We're going against old magic, of course it's going to be difficult. It's going to hurt, but you need to decide now if Raz is worth going through what you just did again and again until we find a way to work."

"I don't know if I can."

Meyda huffed. "Alard, you've stood up to my father threatening to put your head on a pike and didn't waver."

"Yeah, I had my panic attack after I left the throne room, and Raz was there to help me through it." Alard pressed his palms against his eyes. "It just hurt, standing there and seeing no recognition in his eyes. None of the love he had for me."

Meyda put a hand on his shoulder. "I can't even imagine how it feels, but we're going to get him back." She squeezed his shoulder, then let it go to reach for his messenger bag. Meyda pulled out the godmother book Fi had found, flipping it open. "There has to be something in here that counteracts the wish."

Alard was quiet again, and Meyda watched as his shoulders stiffened, and his jaw clenched. Suddenly, Alard pushed himself fully to his feet, arms in fists as head turned up to the sky. "Fairy Godmother of Razi Miller, I am Prince Alard of the Kingdom of Earth and Sky. I demand you make your presence known to me, now."

"Whoa, you went full angry royal brat," Meyda said as she stood. Not that she blamed him. "Do you think you can summon her?"

"We can try." Alard looked at her, pure rage in his eyes.

I'll take that over nothing. Meyda hugged the book to her chest and stood at his side. "I am Princess Meyda of the Kingdom of Fire and Ice. Together we call on all four elements to bring you before us."

"Alright, alright, I heard you the first time." An older woman stepped out from behind a tree. She wore black leather pants and boots, a white blouse with rainbow suspenders, and her hair was spiked up in the air with one side colored pink, the other blue.

Alard gasped, and Meyda looked at him. "You know her?"

"I do." Alard took a step forward.

———

At first, Alard thought he was seeing things. Monique stood in front of him, hands on her hips and a friendly smile gracing her lips. He wanted to run and hug her in relief. He wanted to punch her in the face. Instead, he stopped his approach and glared.

"How could you do this to me?" Alard asked, his voice dropping low.

"I did nothing to you, my lord." Monique closed the distance, bowing to both the royals. "I only did as my godchild requested."

"We saw the wish," Meyda said. "You didn't even try to stop him."

"I did ask him if he was sure that he wanted this," Monique pointed out. "He had his mind set the moment he summoned me. There was nothing else I could do. I'm bound by my magic to fulfill the wishes of my godchildren, even if they are misguided."

Meyda bit her lip, then looked down at the book. "Who told Raz about godmothers? Both Alard and I thought they...you...no longer existed."

"It's true," Monique said. "There are very few of my kind left. Most of us work in children's hospitals, elf photographers for mall Santas, and with organizations like the Salvation Army. Anywhere we can be closer to children and hear their wishes."

"And yet you work in a vampire speakeasy," Alard drawled.

Meyda looked back and forth between them. "You've lost me."

"And you still haven't answered her question," Alard stated, crossing his arms across his chest.

Monique looked at Meyda. "You saw the wish, but you didn't see the entire story. Raz and I were not alone in that moment."

"Who was with you?" Meyda asked.

"Your mother, Your Highness."

Alard's eyes opened wide, looking at Meyda. Meyda shook her head. "No, my mother can be cold, but she wouldn't do something like that."

"She was trying to 'help' him with the situation." Monique shook her head. "But with the Queen there, I was unable to talk with Raz to convince him to not make the wish."

"What's done is done," Alard said. "And now you're going to tell us how to undo it."

Monique bowed her head. "I cannot do that, Alard, I'm sorry."

"Why the hell not?" Alard growled as he spoke.

"I, myself, am unable to break the wishes of my godchildren." Monique's eyes traveled to look at the book in Meyda's arms. "You, however, hold all the answers on how to break a magic spell."

"That's not cryptic at all." Alard forced himself to remain calm.

Meyda leaned against him for support. "But it can be broken?" she asked.

"Yes, just not by me." Monique gave Alard a soft smile. "Raz wished for both of you to find love, even if it wasn't with each other. But before that, I told him I would put him on a path to find true love."

"A path…" Meyda muttered, opening the book and flipping through pages.

"What are you looking for?" Alard asked.

"Shh," Monique said, her smile growing. "Let her concentrate. She was always better at magic than you."

Alard chuckled, but he couldn't disagree. He watched Meyda flip back and forth, her eyes focused, determined to find something.

"You made Raz use specific words when making his wish," Meyda said. "You made it so that only *Raz* would forget, not Alard. So that he wished for love *even if* it wasn't with Alard, not love *without* Alard."

"What are you talking about, Meyda?"

"I see it now!" Meyda closed the book, bouncing on her feet with renewed energy. "I see how to break the spell!"

"How?" Alard asked.

"When I watched you two in the library, I could just tell how much you loved each other," Meyda explained. "Then I read Raz's love line, and it showed me how much he would come to love you. That you were his true love."

"True love is one of the most powerful weapons any creature can yield," Monique stated. "That magic is older than mine. I must answer my godchild's wish, but I'm old enough to know how to work my way around my magic."

"You put the book in the library," Meyda said. "You wanted Alard to find his way back to his true love."

"And you had Raz return home where I could find him." Alard smiled, daring to hope that getting Raz back was still possible. "You gave him love and happiness with this Gregorio, though."

"I had to fulfill his wish for love and happiness.. There was always the chance that you wouldn't figure this out." Monique laughed. "Now, my lord, you know what you need to do." She looked at Meyda. "You know what needs to happen after you retrieve Raz, Your Highness."

Meyda nodded. "Elan is already working on it."

"Then I'll leave you to it." Monique wrapped Alard in a hug. "Just believe that it will work, and it will."

Alard hugged Monique back. "Tell Catherine and James everything is going to be okay."

"I will." Monique stepped back and bowed. "It has been a pleasure serving you, my lord, my highness," she said before disappearing in a cloud of blue and pink glitter.

Meyda grabbed her boots and started to pull them back on. "Plan B?"

"Plan B." Alard agreed, his wounded heart gathering the pieces up and sewing itself back together.

CHAPTER THIRTY-FIVE

Plan B started at the coffee shop between the Dupont Circle metro entrance and Raz's workplace. Alard felt it was poetic that he was going to capture Raz's heart again in the coffee shop. All he and Meyda had to do now was wait.

After leaving Monique, Alard took Meyda to get a change of clothing and a bathing suit, as well as clothes for him. He then checked them into a hotel back in Dupont Circle. Meyda went for a long swim in the pool while Alard called James and updated him on what was happening.

Alard also talked to Catherine, who was recovering from the werewolf bite. She had reached out to her contacts with the werewolf pack in the bayou but none of them knew about a plot to kidnap Alard. The Alpha sent her regards, apologized for not knowing they had omegas in their city, and sent reassurance that the one who had attacked Catherine, James, and Raz had died in the explosion at Alard's house. Catherine promised to rebuild the place once the poison was out of her system.

Meyda and Alard had gotten a few hours of sleep, then they had changed and gone to get coffee. Alard introduced Meyda to the YouTube app on her phone, and she was watching every kitten video she could find while sipping on another smoothie. Alard was on his third coffee and now unsure if his bouncing leg under the table was a result of the caffeine or his nerves.

"You're vibrating the table," Meyda said around her straw, looking at Alard overtop the phone.

"Sorry." He put his hands on his leg and held it in place.

"Remember, you need to believe that this will work." Meyda put the phone down and rubbed her eyes. "Confidence! It's your secret superpower."

"Superpowers don't work like that," Alard pointed out.

"But magic does." Meyda looked over at the entrance and sat up. "Alright, it's go time."

Alard turned and saw Raz and Gregorio get in line. Both looked tired and Gregorio looked like he was whisper-shouting at Raz. Raz shook his head, saying something back. Gregorio stood up stiffly, then turned and walked out while Raz leaned his head back and sighed.

"Trouble in paradise," Alard said, not so secretly pleased at the public fight.

"That just makes it easier for us." Meyda stood up. "You stay here, and I'll bring him over."

"Right." Alard stayed in his chair as Meyda moved to the pickup area and asked the barista for a cup of ice water. The barista handed it to Meyda just as Raz arrived.

I can do this. Alard took a deep breath, psyching himself up that Plan B was going to work. He had to believe that this was going to work. Believe in himself and his love for Raz. Focus on his love for Raz.

"Oh, hello again!" Meyda said, acting like she didn't know Raz from beyond the previous day. "Raz, wasn't it?"

"Yes, it was." Raz's lips turned up in a half smile. "I don't believe I got your name."

"Everyone calls me Meyda." She sipped on her water. "I couldn't help but notice that your boyfriend stormed off in a huff. Is everything okay?"

"No, not really." Raz rubbed his forehead. "I just didn't feel like it was working out. I don't know, after seeing you both yesterday, I felt like something in my life was missing."

"I'm sorry. Well, Alard and I are here having breakfast. You're welcome to join us."

"I shouldn't. I have to get to work."

Meyda pouted. "Five minutes? Please." She held out the "ease" long enough to bat her eyes. Alard stifled a laugh behind his hand. Meyda knew how to get what she wanted.

Raz laughed, a real smile now. "Ok, five minutes."

"Perfect." Raz's coffee order came up and once Raz had his sugar and creamer in, Meyda dragged him over to the table and sat him in the seat next to Alard. "Look who I found!" she told Alard as if this meeting wasn't planned.

"Oh, hey," Alard said, sipping his coffee to keep him from moving too fast.

Meyda sat back in her seat, the very picture of bubbly optimism. "Alard has yet to tell me about what he did in New Orleans. Maybe you could give me a taste of the city."

Raz rubbed the back of his neck. "Well, as I told Alard, everything from that week is a blur. So, I guess I partied a bit more than I should have."

"Well, it was a whirlwind of a week." Alard shifted closer. "And I mean, you step into Oz, and it feels like you've been whisked away to another world."

"The nightclub, right? Oh yeah, I remember that place," Raz laughed. "We walked in and there was this guy sitting right at the bar making out with two drag queens. That guy has game."

Of course, Raz would remember James. Alard needed to tell James about that later. "You seem to start remembering stuff when I bring it up," Alard stated, turning so that he was facing Raz.

Raz shrugged. "I guess I just need reminding."

"Then let's find those good memories before we go."

Alard moved quickly, cupping the back of Raz's head as he pressed his lips against Raz's. *Focus on my love for him. Believe this is going to work.*

Come back to me, Raz.

———

Raz was shocked at the sudden movement and following press of lips against his. He was about to push away and slap Alard when his vision went white.

Warmth spread from the kiss through Raz's body like a house on fire. He needed water...air...*more*.

He barely noticed his hand grabbing the front of Alard's shirt and pulling the man even closer. Raz pressed back hungrily, not realizing how starving he was for that warmth. He moaned against Alard's lips, tasting the coffee the other man had been drinking.

That was when the dam broke somewhere in his mind, and memories flooded back to the forefront: dancing in a New Orleans park, stealing glances over a pile of books, holding Alard while he suffered through a panic attack, Alard attacking Grah to save him...

Making love in his hotel room that first night, staring into Alard's eyes and knowing that this was more than a one-night stand. Wanting to lose himself completely in those eyes.

Laying in Alard's bed, staring at the sleeping man and brushing the hair from his forehead. Pressing a kiss to his shoulder and promising to love him forever.

Two hearts locked together for infinity.

Raz gasped and pulled back, panting as he fought to catch his breath. Chairs scraped along the ground, and he was certain Meyda and Alard were both looking at him, worried about how he would react.

Tears traced down his cheeks as Raz clutched his shirt near his heart. It hurt, pounding against his chest stronger than he had ever experienced. Almost as if in that moment, he returned from the dead.

"Raz?" Alard whispered, his hand sneaking forward to try and pull Raz's hand from his chest. The gentleness, the caution and fear, so familiar to his ears that Raz sobbed again. Another hand—Meyda's from the heat behind it—rubbed along his back as she hummed softly to calm him.

When his lungs caught up to breathing like a normal person, Raz lifted his head to stare at Alard. *His* Alard. Raz took in Alard's worried green eyes, the front teeth biting his lower lip, the bangs hanging over his face that no amount of pushing back could keep in place. He was beautiful. He was perfect, and Raz had let him go.

"I'm sorry," Raz whispered, fresh tears leaving his eyes to join the others soaking into his clothes. "I'm so sorry."

"Shh, it's okay," Alard replied, pulling Raz into his arms. "I'm here. I found you, and I'm never letting you go again." He kissed Raz again, then pressed his forehead against Raz's. "I should have told you sooner how much you mean to me. I can't imagine another sunrise, another breath, another heartbeat without you at my side. You're part of my soul, Raz, and I could never love another as much as I do you."

Their tears splashed together on their linked hands as Raz took a deep breath. "I didn't want to go, but it was the only way I thought we could solve the problem..."

"You were never the problem. You are a gift, one I plan to cherish for the rest of our lives, if you want that."

"I want it," Raz cried, pulling Alard closer for another kiss. "I love you, Alard. I don't want anyone else but you. I'm so sorry..."

"Shhh," Alard hushed him, hugging Raz tightly. "I know. And hey, you did solve our bond problem; you just didn't know that Meyda had a different solution." Alard stroked his fingers through Raz's hair. "And honestly, did you think I wouldn't come and find you?"

"He is stubborn like that," Meyda pointed out.

Raz chuckled, and he sat back up, rubbing his eyes with his sleeve. "I hoped, but when I saw you and Meyda in the courtyard..." he sighed. "I thought if you knew it was my choice, you'd choose your duty to the kingdom over me."

Alard cupped Raz's face with his hands. "I will never choose anyone or anything over you," Alard stated. "You are everything that I wished for in a partner, and more. I will go to war to keep you."

Raz smiled, then looked over at Meyda. "Are you're okay with that?"

"I was okay with it the moment I saw you two together." Meyda shrugged. "And if I'm supposed to marry to unite the kingdom, who cares if I get one husband or two out of it?" She grinned. "Plus, it'll be nice having someone else helping me keep Alard out of trouble."

"Wait, two husbands?" Raz blinked, looking between Alard and Meyda.

"Oh, let me tell you my evil plan." Meyda rubbed her hands gleefully. "Elan has been researching and found out that generations ago, kings could have multiple wives at the same time. He just had to marry them all together in a single ceremony."

"So, if the kings of old could do it, why not you?" Raz laughed. "That's very progressive for your people."

"They'll adjust," she said. "I mean, they've been adjusting for a while now as we head to unification. What's one more thing to get used to?"

"I'm down for it," Alard stated, taking Raz's hand. "After all, I come out on top getting both what is best for the people, and what is best for me." He glanced at Meyda. "No offense."

"None taken," Meyda help up her hands. "And now you will have someone to give you that level of intimacy you crave that I can't give."

"I think I'm up for the task," Raz said with a wink.

"Then it's settled." Alard looked back at Raz, then pushed his chair away and got down on one knee. "Razi Miller, will you marry us?"

Raz laughed, pulling Alard back up while standing himself. "Yes, I will." He pulled Alard close and was about to kiss him before leaning his head back. "Wait, do I need to kiss you both at the same time to make this work?"

Meyda wrinkled her nose. "This is not an official ceremony, so no, you don't," Alard laughed.

"You sure?"

"Eighty percent sure."

Raz smiled, running his hand along Alard's cheek. "Good enough for me," Raz whispered before leaning in to kiss Alard again, his soul rolling in the warmth of their love.

CHAPTER THIRTY-SIX

Alard always admired Meyda's sense of direction, and having it work in the human realm was doubly impressive. She was able to backtrack the three of them all the way to Penn Station all by herself, since Alard was distracted making sure he didn't lose Raz in the crowds.

Once they were in NYC, they grabbed a cab—not to Grand Central Station, but instead to the pet store. Alard leaned back against Raz as they watched Meyda sitting in a playroom with a dozen kittens. In the end, she chose a tiny Siamese who had not stopped purring since Meyda picked the fluffball up.

After getting two bags of supplies for the trip back to the fairy realm, the trio (plus kitten) returned to Grand Central Station and found their broom closet portal. Meyda entered first while Alard and Raz guarded outside.

"It's going to be a while before we can come back," Alard pointed out. "You need to grab anything?"

"All I need is you," Raz stated. He motioned to his briefcase. "I wrapped up my outstanding projects and put up an emergency out of office notice on my email, website, and voicemail with no return date. I have enough money in savings to pay my bills for a few months at least."

"Good." Alard nodded at the thoroughness of Raz's last-minute plans.

"And anyway, I had been thinking about relocating to New Orleans if it meant I could be closer to the portal."

Alard smiled back at Raz, then his phone timer beeped. "Okay, you go next."

"See you on the other side." Raz slipped into the closet while Alard reset his timer. Five minutes later, he checked to make sure no one was watching him, then joined them.

Alard stumbled out of the portal to the sound of explosions, shouting, and the two distinct hissing sounds of a kitten and a fire drake. Raz grabbed his arm, helping him regain his balance. "What's going on?" Alard asked.

"Don't know. Meyda went to look, but she thinks that your disappearing act might have started the war."

"Shit, Elan was supposed to keep this from happening," Alard muttered. He looked at Timmie and the carrying case with the kitten inside. "And them?"

"Timmie is jealous."

Another explosion made them both jump. Alard watched the obsidian ceiling start to crack. "We need to get out of here. Grab the kitten." Alard reached down and plucked Timmie off the floor and put the complaining drake inside of his shirt. "Stop your warbling," Alard said, grabbing the bags of supplies and his messenger bag that Meyda had left behind.

Alard led Raz through the pantry until they found the stairs leading up into the kitchen. It was empty; abandoned due to the explosions just outside the window, Alard guessed. They walked to the window, pressing against either side so the wall protected them from sight, and then peeked out.

The explosions were coming from the swampland that bordered the farmlands of the Kingdom of Fire and Ice. Alard recognized the soldiers' armors from their colors alone; the two kingdoms were indeed at war.

"Okay, this looks bad," Raz said. "But you and Meyda could just go out there and order them to stop."

"We can try, but technically, our fathers control the armies." Alard looked back into the kitchen. "Where is she?"

"Getting my armor," Meyda said, strolling into the kitchen. "Not everyone can grow theirs at a moment's notice."

"Do I get armor?" Raz asked.

"No, you stay here and protect the kitten," Meyda said, adjusting and handing Alard one of the sword belts she wore on her hips.

"Seriously?" Raz's eyebrow rose.

"Someone has to watch it," Meyda said.

"So leave Timmie!"

The drake rumbled against Alard's chest, and Alard yelped as lightning burned against his stomach. "That's a painful no," Alard relayed as he pulled the drake out of his shirt and placed him on the windowsill.

"Besides, he's our ride." Meyda looked at Timmie and nodded. The drake shrieked in anticipation, spreading his wings to fly out the window before embiggening himself. Meyda then pointed at Alard. "Put on your armor this time."

"Yes, Highness." Alard shifted to his fairy form and summoned his bark armor, locking the sword belt in place through the layers. He strode to Raz, pulling him close for a kiss. "Stay here. I just got you back, and I'll be damned to lose you again."

"You say the sweetest things," Raz grinned against Alard's lips. "Just don't fly into a tree or something this time."

Alard wrinkled his nose even as he felt like laughing. "I love you," he said, stepping onto the windowsill.

"I know." Raz winked, then reached down to gather all the bags and kitten case, then left to find a safe room to hide in. Alard took a deep breath, then accepted Meyda's hand to climb on Timmie's back.

It wasn't hard to get the armies' attentions: A giant orange fire drake hovering over their heads, roaring and shooting lightning from its mouth into the air, was bound to get noticed. Meyda stood up, holding the reins in one hand. "Soldiers, stop this battle now by order of your princess and prince!"

Timmie shot another lightning bolt across the sky just to make sure they understood how serious they were.

"Princess Meyda!" A captain of the guard, one from Meyda's kingdom, took off his helmet and then placed a hand over his heart. "You are alive."

"Of course I am," Meyda stated. "Why would you think otherwise?"

"You and Prince Alard disappeared. It was said you had both been kidnapped by the trolls and ogres," the captain stated.

Across the battlefield, one of Alard's captains unwove the branches that created his helmet. "Your father ordered us to seize the castle, my lord!" he told Alard. "As the highnesses parents have seized yours."

"We can't leave them alone for a day," Meyda muttered.

"Technically, it's been almost six now," Alard pointed out. "Time difference."

"Right." Meyda sat back down. "Well, it is obvious to you both that the rumors are not true. Now stand down, and all of you come into the castle to care for your wounded. You are both to become one army soon, so I expect you all to treat one another as brothers in arms."

"I agree with the Princess," Alard added. "Send birds to your majors with this news, and word that we will be returning to my kingdom in short order."

"Yes, my lord. Your Highness," the captains stated, bowing their heads.

Alard leaned forward to look at Meyda. "When we're married, you're running the military."

Meyda scoffed. "Like I was going to let you anyway."

They hovered over the soldiers as they put away their weapons and started for the castle. The injured were carried by soldiers on both sides, heading into the throne room where the medics were setting up a triage system.

Timmie sat down and let Alard and Meyda off to survey the medics' work. Satisfied that their orders were being followed, Alard touched Meyda's arm. "I'm going to find Raz," he stated, then turned and started for the kitchen.

One of the goblin royal guards stood outside the meditation room near the center of that floor in the castle. He bowed to Alard. "My lord, your consort is inside. I found him in the hallway with a hellion in a fabric bag and felt he would be safer there."

Alard smiled, nodding his head to the guard. "Thank you, Lieutenant."

Opening the door, Alard jerked to the side as a shaft of wood slashed down where his head had been moments ago. He looked up and saw Raz holding a bo staff, caught somewhere between fight ready and realizing who he had just swung at. "Alard! Sorry, I wasn't sure who was coming in."

"No, that's fine," Alard said. "Better to be safe than sorry."

Raz moved the staff to rest against the wall. "Are we good?"

"At least here, yes." Alard picked up the cat carrier and saw the kitten curled up in the back in the tiniest ball, hissing. "Poor kitten. It's been a crazy day for you, huh?"

"Not just it," Raz pointed out, running his hand through his hair. "I think I'm on my third adrenaline rush of the day."

Alard nodded in understanding. "We'll get some rest soon." Just not now, not while there's a bigger battle waiting for them in his kingdom.

"Where's Meyda?" Raz asked.

"Commanding the armies." He reached for his messenger bag. "Come on, let's take all this upstairs to Meyda's room, then we can go find her."

It didn't take long for them to go up two floors and walk into Meyda's suite of rooms. Knowing that the three of them were going to leave soon, Alard went into Meyda's guest room and started to set up the items for the kitten including a bowl of food and water, a litter box, and a bed with toys in it. Raz lay on the bed watching while trying to coax the tiny Siamese out of the carrier.

"Will it be safe here?" Raz asked.

"I'll leave a note on the door so the gnomes here know not to enter," Alard said as he found a shelf higher up to put the food bag. "There's no window here to worry about, and the gate for the fireplace is locked in position. Plus, Timmie doesn't go into this room, so his scent won't linger on things."

Raz finally got the kitten out, keeping the tiny fuzzball against his chest as he petted along its head. "Good."

"Let's go." Alard held his hand out for the kitten, then carefully lowered it into the pet bed. "Here's your food, water, and poop box. Your mommy will be back soon to cuddle you."

Raz held the door open as Alard walked out backwards, making sure the kitten stayed in the pet bed until they closed the door. Alard then walked to Meyda's window seat and pulled a piece of stationery from the portable wooden lap desk's side drawer. He wrote a warning to the servants about the kitten inside and to keep the door closed, then stuck it to the wall with a wet bit of clay.

They walked back through the halls to the throne room of Fire and Ice. The obsidian walls cast a red glow in the room as lava traveled through the rock like veins in a leaf. A moat of steaming water outlined the floor, its warmth coming from the stone wall beside it. The rest of the floor was a glass mosaic, hundreds of colors that shone up, the circular symbol of water dropping on a flame in dark, large shards to be noticed at the exact center of the room.

Medics were dipping fabric strips into the warm water moat so they could clean the dirt and blood from the wounded. Meyda walked through the room, kneeling to check on the clumps of soldiers. Alard nodded to his own soldiers that looked up at him before taking Raz's hand and joining Meyda in the center of the floor.

"We need to get to our parents," Alard stated. "Otherwise battles like this will continue to pop up everywhere."

Meyda sighed, looking at the controlled chaos of her throne room. "Agreed." She took Raz's free hand and squeezed. "Where's the kitten?"

"In the guest room of your suite," Raz told her. "Alard put all the supplies out so it should be okay for a while."

"Then we can go." Meyda summoned two captains to her side, one from each kingdom. "We are leaving for the Kingdom of Earth and Sky. You two are in charge. Keep this parlay going until we return with news. Have the kitchen make meals for your men and check the barracks for bedrolls so everyone can rest."

"Yes, highness," the captains said before they stepped aside to divvy up the duties between them. Meyda, Alard, and Raz watched them, making sure the captains worked peacefully with one another before they turned and strode out of the throne room to where Timmie waited.

As they flew across the kingdoms, Alard surveyed the damage to the swampland and adjoining forest. A swath of land had been cut through from the marching army, the ground burned and dead from the abuse. Every so often, they would see a larger clearing where battles had happened.

Alard closed his eyes at the sight of still bodies on these clearings. These deaths were his fault. If he hadn't...no, he couldn't let his mind go down that spiral right now. Later, when this conflict was over, he would find a way to make restitution to the families and clans who lost members. It was the least he could do.

Raz hugged him from behind, and Alard leaned into his embrace. Alard could only hope that when the people met and got to know Raz, they would understand why Alard had left to find him. At least, he hoped.

"Where should I land?" Meyda called back to Alard. "Courtyard or out front?"

They were circling his castle now. The goblin army for the Kingdom of Fire and Ice held the grounds. The marketplace just beyond the castle's drawbridge was on fire. In the training yard, Sirus and Melody paced with their aviation unit as black-armored archers stood spread out along the parapets, their bows drawn with arrows at the ready in case the griffins tried to take off.

They all looked up as Timmie's shadow cast over them. Meyda pulled the drake to hover and pointed at the archers. "You, archers, stand down! Release the griffins at once," she ordered, and the bowmen lowered their arrows and released the tension from their draws.

"Sirus! Melody!" Alard called down as the griffins started to take off. "The marketplace is on fire. Take your men to check on the villagers."

"What about your parents, my lord?" Sirus asked, coming up to fly next to them while Melody started giving directions to their battalion.

"We will handle them personally," Alard stated. "Report back to me on the damage and what supplies are needed from the castle to help."

"Yes, my lord." Sirus bowed his head, then swooped away from them to join Melody flying over the marketplace.

"The rest of you lay down your arms by the order of the Prince and Princess!" Alard shouted to his kinsmen. "This battle is over. Tend to your wounded and the villagers."

"Together," Meyda added.

They watched as the soldiers did as they were told. Soldiers from the Kingdom of Earth and Sky followed in the griffin's wake to the marketplace while the rest cared for their wounded comrades.

Inside the castle, though, the sounds of battle continued. Alard shook his head, then looked at Meyda. "I think we'll need a more dramatic entrance to get their attention," he told her. "Our parents seem to have forgotten our purpose to this realm."

"I'm pretty sure I know who's to blame." Meyda smirked, then leaned toward Timmie's ear. "Go in through the roof."

CHAPTER THIRTY-SEVEN

F i stood in front of the thrones with Elan, her hands and wings
bound. King Quin and Queen Norah were off to the side of the
throne room, their hands similarly bound, but they were under
guard while sitting on two chairs from the dining hall.

The once pretty grasses and flowers of the throne room were dead and
burned away. Scorch marks and crumbled stone decorated the floor,
tapestries struggled in vain to stay aloft even though they were shredded, and
the fountain was now a block of ice.

The room was unwelcoming and cold, and Fi blamed the woman sitting
in the queen's throne.

Queen Willa sat up straight, a twisted smile on her face as she stared
down the grand librarian. "Your attempt at that little stasis spell failed,
Librarian," she hissed at Elan. "Now tell me, where did the children go? You
were the last to see them, after all."

Elan didn't appear fazed by the glare. "I have already told you, they came
to the library to seek counsel, and I am not allowed to speak of what is said
in counsel. If I did, the trust that I have with creatures across the realm
would be destroyed, as will my appointment as a neutral party in the realm."

"Your duties come second to the demands of your rulers, Librarian!"

Eldren, pacing behind the thrones, moved to Willa's side and pointed a finger at Elan. Fire danced along the digit, threatening to shoot forth. "Now tell us what they are planning!"

The last words from Eldren were drowned out from the loud crack of lightning that attacked the roof of the throne room. The marble broke apart, smashing down into the frozen fountain and the dead remnants of the family crest. Elan grabbed Fi and ran to the side of the room where Quin and Norah had been pulled by their guards, the walkway above shielded them from the falling debris.

With a thunderous roar, Timmie landed in the center of the throne room. He lowered a wing and two people in armor slid off the drake's back and pulled their swords from their sheaths.

Fi caught a glimpse of Raz sliding up to take Timmie's reins, and relief filled her heart. "They found him!" she whisper-yelled at Elan. "Everything is going to be okay now!"

"We don't know that just yet," Elan said. "But it is up to the children now."

———

Goblins were an interesting bunch when it came to being soldiers, Alard noted. They took commands well, fought with every fiber of their being, and enjoyed their work. The one thing they lacked, though, was the ability to adapt when taken by surprise. Instead, they were reduced back to their lesser instincts, and attacked whomever they felt was a danger to them, even if it was an ally.

"Get ready to show off to your fiancé," Meyda teased Alard as they shifted into a back-to-back position while the startled goblins gave their war cry and surged forward.

"Hey, we're both your fiancés too," Alard pointed out as he deflected the blade of the first goblin to reach him.

"Yeah, but Raz already knows how awesome I am." She ducked the wild swing of a club before jamming the pummel of her sword into the stomach of her attacker, then kicked the goblin away from them.

Alard grunted, taking the impact of a club to his side while avoiding a pike to the head. He leaned back, forcing Meyda to bend over so neither of them was impaled. Standing back up, Alard blocked another attempt with the club, his sword slicing it in half, and followed up with a roundhouse kick to the goblin's face to knock him out.

"We're in agreement not to kill them, right?" Alard asked over his shoulder. He didn't want anyone else's death on his conscience.

Meyda jumped back, pressing up against him again. "I'd prefer not to. I mean, it isn't a great way to start off a marriage with team homicide."

Alard laughed. "I've got an idea then." He handed Meyda his sword, and his wings beat until he hovered up onto her shoulders. He closed his eyes, focusing on his magic. The air around them started to swirl, moving faster and faster until they stood in the center of a tornado filled with goblins.

Meyda grabbed onto his feet as Alard started to fly upwards, bringing the swirling guards with him. When they cleared the hole in the roof, Alard pushed the air magic away from him, sending the goblins toward the forest where they could land safely among the trees.

They landed back in the throne room, now empty except for the royal families, Fi, Elan, Raz, and Timmie. Meyda handed Alard back his sword, and they strode forward to where her parents stood on the throne dais.

"Alard!" Norah cried in joy, seeing her son still alive. Alard wanted to rush to her and cut her free, but for the moment, they were still in danger. He gave her a curt nod, then refocused his attention on Eldren while Meyda focused on Willa.

"Children, just where have you been?" Willa asked, calm and collected.

"Fixing your mistakes, Mother," Meyda stated, her voice all but growling as she spoke.

"Do not speak to your mother like that!" Eldren took a step towards Meyda, but Alard raised his sword and aimed the tip at the King.

"Your Highness, I would suggest you stay your tongue or else you will be complicit with your wife's actions," Alard said, sparing a glance of warning to Eldren before glaring back at Willa.

"And what, dear daughter, have I done in err?" Willa crossed her arms over her chest, ice daggers all but forming in her eyes.

"Manipulating Raz into summoning his fairy godmother to wish away his connection to Alard," Meyda stated, chin tilted up.

Willa scoffed. "I was helping the poor boy understand the mess he had created, since no one wished to be honest with him."

"I disagree."

Timmie lowered his wing again, revealing where he had been keeping Raz to protect him from the soldiers. Raz slid off the drake, patting Timmie's neck affectionately before striding forward. "I already understood the problems my presence and marriage were on the kingdom. Alard's father had laid it out for me, and I was in the throne room when you arrived and threatened war. No one has hidden the consequence of my continued attachment from me, which is why you knew I would be willing to find any solution to resolve them."

Willa gave a curt laugh. "And yet here you are, a human within our realm, believing for a moment you have any say in what happens in this kingdom."

"He will have a say," Meyda stated. "I asked him to marry me."

"You did what?" Eldren exploded but refrained from moving when Alard lifted the sword point a hair.

"Tell me you aren't serious?" Willa asked icily.

"Alard and I are very serious." Meyda motioned for Elan to join her. "Even before Raz made his wish, I had been researching on if a three-way marriage was possible. Elan found a precedent which shows it has been done before. Therefore, I have decided to take two husbands instead of one."

As Elan approached, Norah, Quin, and Fi followed on his heels. Meyda waved her hands, and their bonds shattered. Fi squealed and took off flying to Raz, wrapping him in a tight hug.

Alard felt his parents come to his side, just out of reach. "We also know you're responsible for Raz's kidnapping and the destruction of my home in New Orleans." Alard looked at Eldren. "The werewolves hired to bring me back before blowing the portal called me a highness. Everyone in our realm knows I am a lord, and your kingdom uses the highness title."

"The result of uneducated creatures left behind during the split," Eldren spat out.

"Then how did they know exactly where to take me in this realm?" Alard watched as Eldren tried to come up with a retort, but instead he looked at his wife. Sensing that Eldren was starting to see their side, Alard lowered his sword away from the king.

"Grah used that term too," Fi stated, her arms still wrapped around one of Raz's. "He told me that the letter he got about the search for breaking the marriage bond was being asked on behalf of the royal Highnesses."

Elan lowered his head. "I admit to sending that letter out but could not speak of it per my neutrality duty. But it was Queen Willa who penned that note and asked me to send it out discretely. She said she didn't want to endanger the Prince."

"But it was fine endangering his 'consort'," Raz spat the word out.

"And you almost got Alard killed!" Meyda shouted.

"None of you get to judge me!" Willa shouted, her voice echoing off the marble walls. "I have done everything for you, daughter, to make sure you inherited this kingdom as its rightful Queen. Who taught you combat? How to read and write? Pushed you to master your herb magic as well as inherit elemental powers?" She strode down the stairs and stood in front of Meyda, staring her daughter down.

"What I did was ensure that when this marriage came, you were prepared to rule, as I have, our kingdom." She looked at Alard next, scoffing. "And you, you are too soft to rule this realm. You may be fairy now, but you stink of human emotions and weakness. I knew the moment you left to learn about your human origins that our realm was teetering toward disaster."

"So that's it?" Raz asked. "All this because you couldn't stand the fact Alard used to be human? That I'm here at all."

"You are a creature not even worth my time," Willa snarled.

"Sorry, lady. From where I'm standing, you fit that description." Raz walked to Alard's side and took his hand.

Alard glared at the enraged queen. "You took away my true love, threatened both our lives, as well as those of my friends in the human realm, and staged a coup of my kingdom when mine and Meyda's backs were turned. A coup that cost lives from both kingdoms. My people, *your* people died because of this hatred you harbor." Alard squeezed Raz's hand tightly before turning to face Eldren. "I will only ask you once, Your Highness. Did you have any knowledge of your wife's misdeeds?"

Willa snapped her head to stare at her husband, who watched her for a moment, then looked at his daughter, before returning his attention to

Alard. "I knew of her hatred of humans. I don't harbor any love of them either, but I would never do anything to harm my daughter."

"You threatened to put my head on a pike!" Alard shouted. "I am your daughter's best friend and husband to be. How is that not harming her?"

Eldren sighed. "I cannot excuse my words beyond the fact that I am fast to anger. I would never have followed through on that."

Alard evaluated him, then nodded and looked back at Meyda. "I believe him," he stated.

"As do I," Meyda agreed, then returned her gaze to her mother. "But I cannot excuse your actions done against the three of us, Mother."

Willa's lips lifted in the hint of a snarl. "What will you do then, daughter? Lock your mother up in the dungeon to waste away while you allow this human trash to tell you how to rule?"

"Nothing of the sort." Meyda took a deep breath. Alard could tell that she was taking this hard from how stiff and still Meyda was. They had discussed what to do if Willa confessed, but Alard had left the decision of punishment up to Meyda.

Willa is Meyda's mother, after all. It wouldn't be right for Alard to decide.

"However, you are no longer welcome in the Kingdom of Earth and Sky," Meyda looked to Alard, who nodded in confirmation. He had her back on this. "Instead, you will return home to our kingdom immediately. Then, once I am crowned Queen of the Realm, you are banished to your home in the Lands of Ice."

"You're banishing me?" Willa asked, her arms dropping to her side.

Meyda nodded. "It's better than you deserve, but my heart isn't made of ice like yours."

"And me?" Eldren asked.

"You were only reacting to the fallout from Queen Willa's actions," Alard stated. "You may remain. In fact, we would be honored if you take charge of reparations for the damages from the armies' battles from the last few days."

"That I can do," Eldren bowed his head and brought a fist to his heart. "You have my sincere apologies, Prince Alard."

Meyda hadn't stopped staring at her mother during the exchange, waiting to continue once Alard was done. "You will remain in the south until such time that you truly understand what you have wrought across two realms. You will not get to celebrate our wedding, nor will you have any contact with our heirs until you have proven that all three of us can trust you again."

Alard exchanged a quick glance with Raz, confused. *Heirs?* That was something they needed to talk about later.

Willa looked from her daughter to Alard, then focused her glare on Raz. "Your presence will only continue to corrupt the souls of our people," she stated.

"You told me that the realms split because the rulers of old felt that the human desire for greed and power would destroy everything." Raz chuckled. "If that's true, you're looking pretty human yourself right about now."

Howling, Willa lunged from her spot at Raz, only to fall sideways as Fi flew in and landed a solid punch on the queen's jaw. Fi put herself between Raz and Willa, rubbing her hands together. "I've been waiting to do that," she told Raz, beaming.

Meyda walked over to join them. "I will always love you, Mother, but I am no longer scared of you. I hope you find wisdom and peace in your solitude." Meyda looked up at Timmie, the drake still standing in the center of the throne room. "Timmie, take my mother home."

The drake nodded and walked forward. Not allowing Willa the dignity of riding him, he bent his head down and picked her up by the back of her dress.

"Let go of me, you horrid beast!" Willa shouted as Timmie took to the air, flying out of the roof.

Alard watched Meyda a moment, her gaze never leaving the hole. He stepped forward, putting a hand on her shoulder. "You okay?" he asked.

"Not at all." Meyda turned to him, and Alard saw the tears running down her face. He sighed and pulled Meyda to him, holding her as she cried against his shoulder. A moment later, Raz joined them, keeping Meyda in the center of their embrace.

"We've got you, Meyda," Raz whispered, his hand rubbing along her arm to soothe her.

"We've got each other," Alard added, smiling at Raz over the top of Meyda's head. "Now and forever."

Meyda sniffled, looking up at the both of them. "Lucky me," she teased, and all three of them laughed.

Alard hugged Raz and Meyda tightly. Days ago, he had been worried that returning home was going to take him away from everything he cared about in his life. Instead, after a few twists and turns, Alard realized that he didn't want to be anywhere else but right here.

Chapter Thirty-Eight

" Are you a part of the wedding?"

Raz turned from his reflection, his hands still straightening his tie, golden-brown like the leaves of a cherry blossom in fall. Alard leaned against the doorframe, arms crossed, his white tunic only laced up halfway and untucked from his black leather pants.

"I better be," Raz answered, abandoning the mirror to join him. Alard reached up and adjusted Raz's tie before flipping the shirt collar down over it. "I hear one of the grooms is drop dead gorgeous."

"Is that so?" Alard's lips turned up in a lopsided grin.

Raz hummed in affirmation. "And the other one has this amazing ass..."

Alard laughed, pushing Raz away playfully. "Elan says everything is almost ready and we should head down."

"Mmm, do we have to?" Raz loops his fingers on Alard's beltloops and pulled him closer. "I mean, the ceremony isn't for at least another hour." He leaned forward, pressing his nose against Alard's ear. "And you just smell so divine."

"Oh no," Alard moaned as Raz kissed along his neck, then nipped at his earlobe. "We can't, not right now."

"Whose gonna know?" Raz purred. He pulled Alard's shirt down off his shoulders, then trailed a line of kisses over his shoulder and onto his chest. He felt Alard growing hard against his leg and teased him with a slow grind.

Alard whimpered. "They're all going to know."

"You go down there like this, and they'll definitely know where your mind is." Sliding a hand down Alard's hip, Raz cupped his bulge through those leather pants. "You leave nothing to the imagination, love."

"I'm trying to be a responsible adult here."

Raz chuckled. "It's our wedding day. Screw being responsible." Then, to make his point, he nibbled on Alard's nipple. The prince gasped, and his knees buckled, falling forward into Raz's arms.

"You're incorrigible," Alard said as Raz sat him down on the edge of the bed.

"And you're talking way too much." Raz denied Alard the ability to reply as he kissed the other man. Alard's hands snaked up to hold Raz's face, fingers slipping behind Raz's neck to keep their lips pressed together. Raz, meanwhile, made fast work of Alard's pant laces, pushing them down so they puddled at Alard's feet.

Next was Raz's tie, which he just loosened before unbuttoning his shirt and sliding it off. It wouldn't go well if he sweated through the fabric before the ceremony. He dropped his pants next, then pulled Alard's hips tight up against his.

"Fuck," Alard groaned, grinding his hips against Raz. "So good."

"That's the plan."

Raz flipped Alard around so that he was leaning over the bed's edge. Both their briefs were removed, and Raz began to grind his cock against Alard's ass. "Can you reach—"

"Already have it," Alard interrupted as he held up a tiny corked bottle.

Raz opened it and poured a small amount of lavender-scented oil into his hand. Since there was no lube in the castle, Raz grabbed the bottle off his nightstand before they left DC. It was the better alternative to what they had used last time.

He stroked his cock, getting it nice and slippery before running his fingers around Alard's hole, sliding one, then two fingers in for a quick stretch. Alard moaned at the intrusion, grinding against the bed in response.

"Almost there, love," Raz said, stroking his cock once more before pressing its head against Alard's entrance. It was a tight, delicious slide into him that left them both panting for more. Raz needed more, and so he didn't linger long before starting to slide out again.

This wasn't a slow, sweet lovemaking session. They had their wedding to get to. So Raz moved fast, pounding into Alard with everything he had. He watched Alard grip the sheets, trying to hold on as he writhed on the bed. Alard made small noises of pleasure with each thrust in and whined as Raz pulled back out. If they had the time, Raz would explore what other noises he could get his husband to make. But for now, they had to finish before they were discovered.

Raz reached around and began stroking Alard's cock in time to his thrusting. Alard pumped into his hand, and it wasn't long before the prince gave a strangled cry and came all over Raz's hand.

Almost there, Raz let go of Alard and grabbed his hips with both hands. He thrust harder, feeling Alard tighten as he rode out his orgasm. A moment later, Raz joined him, grunting as he came deep inside of his lover.

Exhausted, Raz collapsed on top of Alard, struggling to get his beathing back in order. Alard was panting as well, and without realizing it, they slowed their breathing down to match each other. Then they both chuckled, and Alard turned his head for a kiss.

A loud banging on the door surprised them both. Raz and Alard both tried to stand up, but with their briefs and pants around their legs, they both fell back onto the floor in a tangle of clothing and limbs.

"Yes?" Alard managed to call out, his voice a mixture of laughter and groaning.

"If you are both done," David's voice came through the wooden door, "you have thirty minutes before the ceremony starts."

"Thank you, David!" Raz said as Alard dissolved into giggles at his side.

After a minute, making sure the gnome was gone, Raz laughed and stretched out on the floor. "That was way too close. Do you think he heard?"

"Oh, I'm sure he heard," Alard said, rolling to his side and off of Raz. He stood up and held out a hand. "Come on, let's get ready for real now."

"I need another shower," Raz said as he stood. The sliminess on his crotch and hand were beginning to become sticky.

"Same," Alard agreed. "Good thing my shower is big enough for two."

Raz followed him but stopped to check his forearm. No bond tattoo was forming, so their pre-wedding tryst wouldn't be visible or upset the upcoming nuptials.

"Are you coming?" Alard called from the adjoining bathroom.

Raz laughed at the phrasing, then joined him. A quick shower and they would still have plenty of time to get ready again.

———

It wasn't a quick shower, but they still managed to get out and get dressed before the ceremony was due to start. The fact they came out to two new sets of clothes on the bed helped tremendously, and Alard would find a discreet way to thank David for that later.

"I'm ready when you are," Raz said.

"Almost there." Alard tied his sword to his hip, then grabbed his official sash with the family crest embroidered along it.

Raz shrugged his jacket on and buttoned it. He held out his arms. "So, does it look weird being all dressed up but without shoes?"

Alard looked Raz over, then grinned. "No one is going to be looking at your feet."

They walked hand in hand to the rebuilt throne room. Meyda, Alard, and Raz had decided to make Alard's kingdom their home. It was easier on Meyda, who still had a hard time being around memories of her mother.

Eldren invited Quin and Norah to join him after the marriage, insisting that he didn't want to be alone when Willa left. Divorce wasn't an option in the fairy realm, but if it was, Alard was sure he'd be filing one for Eldren.

As a gift for their marriage, Elan and Monique combined their magic to create a new portal between the fairy realm and New Orleans. Not only would it allow both Raz and Alard access to New Orleans, but they could continue their lives in both realms.

Instead of in the forest, they used the courtyard tree to act as one entrance. With Alard's Garden District home destroyed, Catherine had sold the lot on Alard's behalf. Now he and Raz owned a tiny apartment sharing the same courtyard as the vampire speakeasy, with a handmade raised flower garden surrounding the tiny fairy house of two helpful brownies. The portal was the door to the linen closet, which Elan joked about being a reminder of their grand adventure.

How Elan made the closet smell like a subway station, neither he nor
Raz understood. The Grand Librarian called it "new portal smell" and that
it would fade in time. Alard didn't trust the Sidhe's words at all.

Meyda agreed that Raz and Alard should keep their lives in the human
realm, as it was part of them both. She also pointed out that she could run
the kingdom better without their constant make-out sessions behind the
tapestries.

"We were just reliving the pre-marriage bliss," Alard had told her,
blushing.

Of course, Meyda would confer with them both on substantial
decisions, but the day-to-day affairs were hers to work. Alard assured her
that, like magic, Meyda was better at fairy politics than he was. This
agreement also gave Meyda more alone time with her books and pets, just as
she always wanted. Alard knew that she would barely miss them, and they
were both just a quick text message away.

Raz and Alard stepped into the throne room, and their eyes were drawn
to the decorations. New tapestries hung from the second-floor walkways,
alternating in colors from pink, green, to brown. They were blank,
enchanted to embroider the crest that would appear on their arms at the end
of the ceremony. Similar flags hung along the parapets outside where visitors
from across the realm waited to celebrate the marriage the moment the crest
appeared.

The roof was repaired, but a crystal skylight remained in the spot
Timmie had broken through. It was forged to create a rainbow of colors in
the facets as the sun shone down on the dais in the center.

The fountain, unable to be fixed, had been removed. Instead, a gazebo
was erected in its place, flowering vines climbing up the wooden frame.
Windchimes hung along each side, the wind blowing them now to create
music for the ceremony. Around the base, the brownies had diligently
worked to return the garden to its former glory for this day, now sporting
the colors of the future rulers.

The marble floor, along with the walkways, were now crowded with
guests. Servants and the military leadership from the united armies stood on
the balconies above, their lives now a sworn duty of protection to the trio.
Many of them had seen Meyda and Alard grow from babies to the adults
they were now.

On the floor around the gazebo, family and friends from both realms waited. James and Catherine stood arm in arm near Fi, who bounced with joy at being invited, and even more, as she watched Alard and Raz enter the room. Norah, Quin, and Eldren stood opposite them, all smiling as they watched their children with pride. Monique, her mohawk sporting the pink, green, and brown color scheme, had her arms clasped over her heart, and would never admit that she was already crying.

Timmie had made a nest in the vines, curled around his little sister, simply named Kitten for now. They both gave the pets a quick scritch before joining Meyda and Elan in the gazebo. Elan had a table behind him, the three crowns of their parents waiting with a trio of silver rings. The Grand Librarian had his formal robes of purple velvet on, the tails extending past the steps he stood on to reach the pulpit.

Meyda had opted for a white wedding dress, her pink flowers threaded through the veil that flowed down her back. Brown and green vines grew along her arms from shoulder to wrist, more pink flowers blooming along the way. Tiny crystals were sewn into her waistline to resemble a belt.

"Took you boys long enough," she chided as Raz and Alard approached. "I was wondering if I should just marry myself and get this over with."

"You look beautiful, Meyda," Raz said, having gotten used to her sense of humor now.

"As do you both." Meyda grinned at the boys, happiness evident in her eyes.

Everything was perfect, just how Alard knew it would be.

Elan raised his hand, and the wind stopped blowing, silencing the chimes. "Shall we proceed?" he asked.

Alard nodded, and the three of them moved to the kneeling cushions on the ground. Alard and Raz helped Meyda kneel first, then they joined her on the cushions on either side of her. They took each other's hands, three sides of a box with the pulpit making the fourth.

No offense to Elan, but Alard zoned out of the ceremony after the first five minutes. His head remained bowed, but his eyes looked across the way at Raz. His eyes were closed, focusing on every word coming from Elan's mouth. Then Alard noticed that Raz's lips were moving, mouthing Elan's words. Alard couldn't help the snort that came from his nose, which he faked a sneeze to try and cover.

Meyda and Elan were looking at him, both annoyed. "Sorry," he whispered to them both.

"Bless you," Raz said, smirking.

Alard really wanted them to get to the whole kissing part already.

Elan continued, and Alard schooled his features back into the serious lord and survived the rest of the speech and blessings intact. Elan climbed down from the pulpit and stood in the center of them, holding the three rings.

It was part of the ceremony that Raz had brought in, wanting that bit of his human traditions to blend in with theirs. They skipped personal vows, instead having Elan read a version of a group vow that came from the ceremonies of old, affirming their acceptance of each term. He then held the rings up, blessing them with the magics of life, and put one in each of their hands to slip on themselves.

Next came the crowning, as their marriage was also the union of the realm. Elan stood before each one, repeating the coronation pledge with each of them in turn. Elan placed Quin's crown on Alard's head, Norah's on Meyda, and Eldren's on Raz. It was Eldren's gift to the human, an apology for past behaviors and a symbol that he respected Raz for who he was, not what he was.

The ceremonies and pledges completed, Elan had them stand up and move closer to each other while returning to the pulpit. "Let it be known across the realm and beyond that, on this day, the four kingdoms are now once more united as one." Elan raised his hands over them, then nodded at the three.

Raz started, leaning in to kiss Meyda on the edge of her lip, respecting her request to them both for a quick and dry kiss, touching the least amount of her lips as possible. She turned to Alard, and he grinned. "Remember, no tongue," he warned Meyda, who slapped his arm in return before kissing the edge of his lips.

"I don't mind tongue," Raz teased, stepping closer to Alard.

"Good." Alard pulled Raz closer, kissing his husband properly. Raz melted in his arms, and Alard dipped him while getting a bit of his tongue to play along Raz's lips.

Alard helped Raz stand back up, and the three of them put their left arm into the center of their threesome, clasping each other's hand. Alard couldn't see the glow that the three of them created, but he felt the warmth washing over him before hearing the collective inhalation of breath from the parents.

The tattoo formed on all three of their arms and the tapestries. One heart, the color of bright moss that guided travelers to find their true north. The second heart appeared pink, the color of pure joy and happiness. The third heart was brown like the ground they stood upon, providing support to all living things.

After that, the infinity symbol returned, silver thread weaving itself between the three hearts, joining them together forever. A white glow hovered over it, forming words in the fairy language: *Beat not once for a moment of joy, but forever in a lifetime of love.*

Cheers from the people outside echoed through the halls of the castle as the tapestries finished their embroidery. Applause from their guests followed. Alard pulled Meyda and Raz both into a tight hug, holding everything he ever needed in the world right there in his arms. Alard smiled as tears stung his eyes. He couldn't be happier, or more grateful, than in this single moment.

He finally got his happy ending. No, a happy beginning, with much more to come.

———

Thank you for reading! Did you enjoy? Please add your review because nothing helps an author more and encourages readers to take a chance on a book than a review.

And don't miss more from B.A. Richards coming soon. Sign up for their newsletter at barichardsauthor.com

Until then, discover OF KINGDOMS AND CURSES, by City Owl Author, Amy Woodruff. Turn the page for a sneak peek!

You can also sign up for the City Owl Press newsletter to receive notice of all book releases!

Sneak Peek Of Kingdoms and Curses

By Amy Woodruff

Bridget Adams could separate her life into two distinct parts: Before and After. The simplicity suited her. There was only one problem...she couldn't remember the Before. The After she knew well. In the After, she was the ward to a Witch named Cora, head of the Virgo coven. Under Cora's care, Bridget studied herbs, practiced combat, and learned how to stay silent. In the After, she was one of the few humans living in the Kingdom of Vassuryn.

In the After, she was forced to bury dead bodies in the woods.

Looking down at a half-dug hole, Bridget leaned against her shovel and wiped sweat from her brow. There was no task she hated more. The first time Bridget had seen a Warlock die from magic use; she had actually volunteered for the job. Bile rose in the back of her throat at the memory. She thought she'd come up with a clever plan. The hasty idea had involved her dragging the Warlock to the woods around dusk, so that she could escape at nightfall. But Cora had known better. Within minutes, Bridget had been captured and returned to the coven. Her back still bore the scars of her punishment. Since then, Cora always sent a burly Warlock with her on errands. Once, when he was distracted, she tried to escape again. And again. She never got far.

"I'm not here to watch you sit around and daydream in the woods. Get back to work. I want to make a stop in Bryxton before it gets dark," Dante barked, a snarl on his puffy face. Behind her, he leaned against a tree and sipped from a small, silver flask. Under his breath, he muttered something about being done with kids. With thick arms and a sinister demeanor, Dante was Cora's main henchman. The only thing he liked more than torturing Bridget was ale.

Glaring, she heaved the shovel back into the stiff dirt. Even if she did get lucky one day and finally escape, she didn't know where to go. To the east, the Fae Kingdom of Elyria treated humans even worse than the covens. Although, as the ruling kingdom, Elyrians generally treated all the other species with contempt, according to Cora. To the south, Kastron's border was closed indefinitely to anyone with a coven mark. The Nymphs blamed the covens for their lack of independence. And the human realm was out of the question. The only gate back to Bridget's home was in Elyria, and Cora had made it clear it was impossible to access.

The gate haunted Bridget's dreams. Every night, new scenarios regarding her past plagued her mind. She longed to know about her old life, her *real* life, and how she traveled through the gate and ended up in Cora's care. Bridget's early memories of her seven months in Vassuryn were a blur of confusion, pain, and sorrow. Whenever she tried to remember those first days, her body physically rejected the memories. Vomit escaped her lips, or she passed out. In her possession, though, were two things Bridget believed were from the human realm, and she clung to them like a lifeline. A note and a necklace.

The necklace, an amethyst on a gold chain, never left her neck. Likewise, the note never left her pocket. Wiping her damp and dirty hands on her green top, Bridget pulled out the wrinkled paper. It was ripped down the middle and specks of blood colored the corner.

Your name is Bridget Adams. I'm sorry. He will...

Every day, Bridget cursed whoever tore the note and cut off the rest. It was pathetic. Her name was the only thing of the Before she knew. Sometimes, she would sit in the dark and repeat her name to herself, over and over, to make sure she didn't forget. And sometimes, she crumpled up the note and longed to throw it away because whoever had written it had clearly known what would happen to her when she crossed the gate. It was the same thing that happened to all humans when they crossed into Elyria.

They were cursed.

Bridget pushed her shovel into the dirt a little harder. Cursed. The word taunted her. Each human who crossed the gate was cursed to lose their memories. If she wanted to return to the human realm, it would happen to her again. Not that she cared. She would gladly give up every memory of

Vassuryn to go back, even if she had no idea what awaited her there. On her loneliest nights, she liked to believe her dreams were real memories. Some things seemed to repeat—golden brown eyes, neon clothes, dark braids, and buildings that touched the sky. The images were vivid in her dreams, but they faded into fuzz when she awoke. With one last flip of dirt, Bridget finished the hole.

Behind her, Dante grunted, "Finally. It's about time. Hurry up and get it buried so we can leave."

It. Bridget clenched her jaw. She couldn't stomach looking at the dead Witch as she dragged the body toward the deep crevice. If Bridget remembered correctly, her name was Beatrix. The Virgo coven constantly moved camp. Beatrix had been in charge of camouflaging their tents to blend into the forest. However, the large spell always tired her. That morning, Cora had asked Beatrix to perform the spell again, even though the coven hadn't gathered any new herbs, flowers, or dirt that week. With no enhancers and nothing to help channel her magic, it only took a few minutes for Beatrix to bleed from the eyes and fall lifelessly to the ground.

Bridget had seen at least ten Witches and Warlocks fall in the last two months. Each time, Cora repeated her favorite lesson: all magic comes at a price. And lately, the coven had been performing more magic than Bridget could ever remember.

With a sigh, Bridget leaned down and began to push the body into the hole. As she did, her necklace popped out of her shirt and caught hold of the buckle of Beatrix's muddied cloak. Before Bridget could unhook it, the body rolled into the grave, snapping off her necklace in the process. The back of her neck stung as she jumped forward to grab it, but it was too late. Bridget ground her teeth together when she spotted the necklace in the hole, a glimmer of purple and gold in the darkness. Beside her, Dante used the tip of his boot to kick a pile of loose dirt into the grave.

"Stop," Bridget screeched. She scrambled to her feet and pushed him in the chest. "My necklace fell off. It's still down there."

Without a word, Dante grabbed her by the collar and shoved her in the hole.

When Bridget slammed onto Beatrix's lifeless form, she let out a sharp gasp. Searing pain exploded across her back. Through her ringing ears, she heard Dante's faint chuckles. After she caught her breath, Bridget rolled over and grabbed her necklace. The clasp was broken, and she couldn't get it back on. Blinking away the water pooling in her eyes, she shoved the necklace into her pocket and hoped a shop in Bryxton could fix it.

As she grabbed onto a loose root to climb out, a sharp zing went through her temple. Bridget swiped her hand in the air but felt nothing around her. Shaking her head, she grabbed the root again. Without warning, blinding pain crashed through her mind. Screaming, she bent over and braced herself on her knees. The fire burning in her brain left her breathless. Then, for a split-second, she saw a roaring river. When she thought she could take no more, the feeling suddenly subsided. Bridget stayed hunched over, breathing hard as she tried to clear her blurred vision. Throat tightening, she watched drops of blood splatter the dirt in front of her. When she wiped her nose, red stained her black leather gloves.

"What the hell is wrong with you? Elyrian soldiers could be nearby. Are you trying to get us killed?" Dante bellowed.

"Me? You're the one who pushed me down here," Bridget accused. "I must have hit my head the wrong way."

She glanced around the hole in confusion. The excruciating pain had disappeared, but a poking ache wouldn't leave the back of her mind. Hesitantly, she reached for the loose root again and clasped it tightly. When nothing happened, she quickly pulled herself out of the open grave.

As fast as she could, she filled the grave with loose dirt. When she was done, Bridget left a stone marker before Dante forcibly steered her in the direction of Bryxton. On the way, she tried not to feel guilty about her thoughts every time Cora asked her to bury one of the Witches or Warlocks. Because it was not dealing with dead bodies that made her hate the task...it was the reminder the fallen coven members gave her. All magic had a cost. And to break her curse, the price was her life. Humans had unsuccessfully tried for centuries. Magic was ruthless and merciless, and her curse held no loopholes. So with each new grave, Bridget could only see one thing: she would never remember her past life again.

———

Don't stop now. Keep reading with your copy of OF KINGDOMS AND CURSES, by City Owl Author, Amy Woodruff.

And sign up for B.A. Richards' newsletter to get all the news, giveaways, excerpts, and more!

Don't miss more from B.A. Richards coming soon, and find out more at barichardsauthor.com

Until then, discover OF KINGDOMS AND CURSES, by City Owl Author, Amy Woodruff!

There's only one thing Bridget Adams wants: to get home.

After being trapped for seven months in the Kingdom of Elyria, where magic is ruthless, permanent, and always comes with a price, she's tired of dealing with curses, especially ones that take everything from her. In Elyria, all humans are cursed. Whenever one enters the magical realm, they lose their memories. Forever.

The only things Bridget knows about her past are the small tidbits Cora tells her, which isn't much. The leader of the nomadic Witch coven is merciless, and with Bridget essentially owned by Cora, she always keeps Bridget by her side. No matter how many times Bridget tries to escape her grasp, she always fails.

In the name of helping the coven, Cora places her in a tournament to compete to marry the Fae Prince, Cade. Believing her freedom is in sight, Bridget agrees to join and plans to sneak away before it starts. However, an unexpected binding contract restricts her to the palace grounds. Forced to participate, Bridget navigates the dangerous tasks of the tournament, until she accidentally stumbles upon the prince. Cade has secrets of his own, though, including ones that involve the human realm, and when he offers to help Bridget return there, she decides to trust him.

As they grow closer, it becomes clear things aren't as they appear. She discovers her presence in Elyria and the tournament is part of a greater plan, one that has deadly consequences. As secrets, history, and conspiracies unravel around her, Bridget begins to realize the greatest curse of all: love.

———

Please sign up for the City Owl Press newsletter for chances to win special subscriber-only contests and giveaways as well as receiving information on upcoming releases and special excerpts.

All reviews are **welcome** and **appreciated**. Please consider leaving one on your favorite social media and book buying sites.

Escape Your World. Get Lost in Ours! City Owl Press at www.cityowlpress.com.

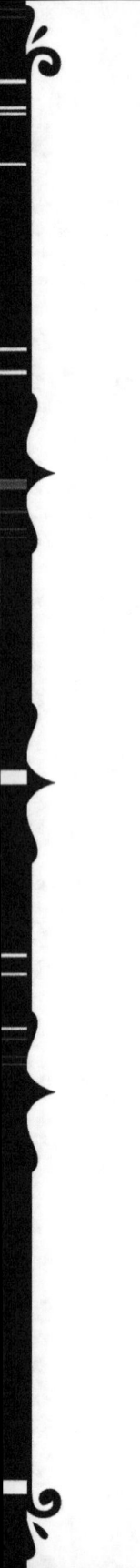

ACKNOWLEDGMENTS

This story was my MFA Thesis while obtaining my master's in creative writing at Western Colorado University. Therefore, it's only proper they get the first paragraph in this section. Thank you, Russell Davis, David Rothman, Fran Wilde, Kat Howard, Candace Nadon, Michaela Roessner, J.S. Mayank, Trai Cartwright, Rick Wilber, Andrew Sellon, Kevin J. Anderson, and Tyson Hausdoerffer, for all your guidance and support. This book wouldn't exist without you.

Thank you to my cohort, the Ethans cohort, and my screenwriting cohort for the encouragement, love, and swift kicks to keep me going. Bless you all for dealing with my crazy.

Thank you to my amazing writing mentors who got me to the point where I could write well enough to get into the writing program in the first place. Thank you, Michael Stackpole and Aaron Allston. I hope to keep making you proud, and I promise to not use my skills for evil. *Mostly.*

Thank you to the amazing team at City Owl Press. Jessica Shearer, thank you for taking a chance on me and this story, and all the hard work kicking this manuscript into shape. You've helped make one of my childhood wishes finally come. Thank you, Yelena Casale and Tina Moss, for bringing me into the City Owl family and being so enthusiastic about the future of my book. A big thank you to Jenny Slinger for not throwing the Chicago Manual of Style book at me while taking out hundreds of commas in this book. Finally, thank you Carrie Jones, for making sure I got all the other little pieces together to help bring this book into the world.

Thank you to my friends and family who supported me on this journey, especially to my partner, Bethany Kesler. Thank you for understanding when I needed to quit my job to go back to school, for those long nights reminding me I wasn't a fail boat, helping me recover from the deaths of both my parents while on this journey, listening to me plot out this book ad nauseum, and everything else you did behind my back to keep me alive and moving.

And finally, no thanks to my cats. You four are the worst distractions ever in my career. Stop sitting on my keyboard.

About the Author

B.A. Richards is a transmasc author who spends their time writing fictional romances that allude them in real life. Living in Lebanon, TN with their partner and a small pride of cats, their aim is to introduce readers to interesting characters and fantastical worlds they can get lost in when the real world sucks. When not writing, they can be found teaching others to write, reading the newest romantasy, or practicing their sword fighting in the backyard.

barichardsauthor.com

instagram.com/b.a.richards
bsky.app/profile/barichards.bsky.social
tiktok.com/@barichardsauthor

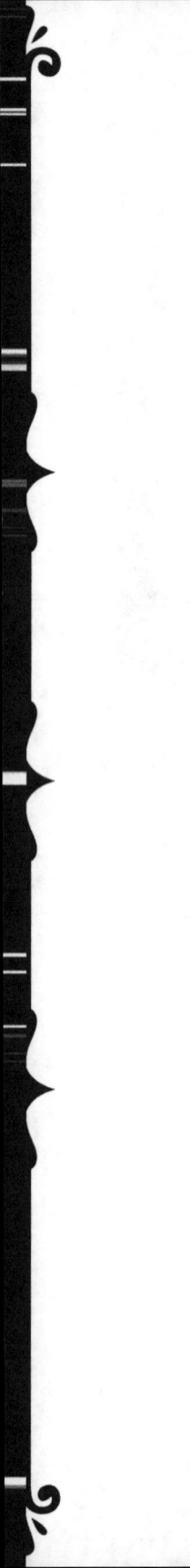

ABOUT THE PUBLISHER

City Owl Press is a cutting edge indie publishing company, bringing the world of romance and speculative fiction to discerning readers.

Escape Your World. Get Lost in Ours!

www.cityowlpress.com

facebook.com/CityOwlPress

x.com/cityowlpress

instagram.com/cityowlbooks

pinterest.com/cityowlpress

tiktok.com/@cityowlpress